'Thrilling . … t written by the
master h … on, and Percy
deli … formance'
New Yo…

'Verdict: a truly dark urban horror tale'
Sci-Fi Bulletin

'Written in vivid, often lyrical prose, but with exhilarating comic-book energy, *The Dark Net* is a megawatt defibrillator to the reader's heart. Quirky but very human characters confront an explosive emergence of the supernatural into our world, in this imaginative, spooky, swiftly paced tale threaded through with dark humour'
Dean Koontz

'An impressive, propulsive narrative velocity at work here'
Metro

'*The Dark Net* kicked my ass with its deft mash-up of both blackhat hacker culture and black magic. Percy reveals an upgraded, rebooted battle between good and evil – a fast, fantastic, throat-punch of a read'
Chuck Wendig, *New York Times* bestselling author of *Blackbirds* and *Zeroes*

'*The Dark Net* channels the spirit of your favourite sprawling and epic 1980's horror/thriller novels into a tightly paced, nasty, unrelenting twenty-first century nightmare. An addictive and frightening read'
Paul Tremblay, author of *A Head Full of Ghosts* and *Disappearance at Devil's Rock*

'Percy's narrative is as lean as a jaguar, and it sprints ahead with a clean, swift motion . . . Restrained yet lyrical, his prose raises his characters off the page, while making Portland more than a generic urban setting'
Locus

Also by Benjamin Percy

Thrill Me
The Dead Lands
Red Moon
The Wilding
Refresh, Refresh
The Language of the Elk

BENJAMIN PERCY

THE DARK NET

HODDER

First published in Great Britain in 2017 by Hodder & Stoughton
An Hachette UK company

This paperback edition published in 2018

1

A CIP catalogue record for this title is available from the British Library

Paperback ISBN 978 1 473 65223 1

Printed and bound in Great Britain by Clays Ltd, St Ives plc

Hodder & Stoughton policy is to use papers that are natural, renewable and recyclable products and made from wood grown in sustainable forests. The logging and manufacturing processes are expected to conform to the environmental regulations of the country of origin.

Hodder & Stoughton Ltd
Carmelite House
50 Victoria Embankment
London EC4Y 0DZ

www.hodder.co.uk

For Lisa

What if the breath that kindled those grim fires,
Awaked, should blow them into sevenfold rage,
And plunge us in the flames; or from above
Should intermitted vengeance arm again
His red right hand to plague us?

—John Milton, *Paradise Lost*

Cyberspace. A consensual hallucination experienced daily by billions of legitimate operators, in every nation . . . A graphic representation of data abstracted from the banks of every computer in the human system.

—William Gibson, *Neuromancer*

PROLOGUE

HANNAH WASN'T BORN BLIND, but sometimes it feels that way. She has retinitis pigmentosa, what she calls RP. Like, I'm so sick of this stupid RP. Which makes the disease sound like one of those jerks she goes to middle school with—the BGs and BJs and RJs—who talk too loudly and wear chunky basketball shoes and toss French fries dipped in mustard across the cafeteria and draw dicks on people's lockers with permanent marker.

She was diagnosed at five. She's twelve now. But she acts like she's forty. That's what everyone tells her. "An old soul," her mother says. "Stick in the mud," her aunt Lela says. If she had a smartphone, if she had boyfriends, if she hung out at Starbucks and Clackamas Center Mall, if she didn't rely on her mother's help to pick out her clothes, if she didn't prod the sidewalk with a stupid cane or wear stupid sunglasses to hide her stupid absent eyes, if she could see, maybe then she wouldn't be such a boring grump, maybe then she would act more like the rest of the giggling, perfume-bombed lunatics her age.

At first she couldn't see at night, crashing into walls on the way to the bathroom. Then her sight fogged over. Then her peripheral vision began to decrease, like two doors closing slowly, slowly, over several years, until there was only a line of vertical light with color-blurred shapes passing through it. If she held something directly in front of her face, she could get a pretty good sense of it, but one day, within the next five years or so, darkness will come. She'll live in a permanent night.

Hers was an accelerated case. And there was no cure. That was what the doctors said. So her mother prayed. And gave Hannah vitamins A and E. And restricted her intake of phytanic acids, so no dairy, no seafood. Hannah tried a dog, but she was allergic and got sick of cleaning up his crap. And she visited a school for the blind, but that felt like giving up, despite the crush of bodies at her middle school, the eyes she could feel crawling all over her while the occasional BG or BJ or RJ whispered a Helen Keller joke.

Then a doctor at OHSU approached her about an experimental trial. Would she be interested? She knew all about gene therapy and about the retinal transplants that had so far failed to develop synaptic connections with their hosts, but she didn't know about this, a prosthesis built by a Seattle-based tech company. It converted video images captured by a camera into electrical pulses that bypassed the diseased outer retina and poured into over one thousand electrodes on the inner retina. They called it Mirage.

"It's all very *Star Trek*," the doctor told her, when describing the device, not glasses so much as a silver shield that wrapped your eyes. She liked his Indian accent, the buoyancy of the vowels, making his words sound as if they were gently bouncing.

Her mother worried that people would stare, and Hannah said, "They already stare." At least they'd be studying her now with awe and curiosity rather than pity. "I'll be a cyborg, a Terminator!"

Her mother could never afford the surgery—the removal of the post subcapsular cataracts and spoke-wheel pattern of cysts, the insertion of the casing and array and antennae along the periphery of her sockets—which didn't matter: the tech company would pay for everything, so long as she agreed to serve as their lab rat and advertisement.

Now, three weeks after she went under the knife, it is time to take off the bandages. Now it is time to wire up the Mirage. To see. The doctor tells her it might take time for her brain to process this new sensory experience. "Think of it like this. What if I gave you a new set of lungs that allowed you to breathe underwater? The first time you jumped in the river and took a deep breath, your body would fight the feeling, thinking you were drowning. There will be a little bit of that at first. A little bit of drowning. But I believe it will pass quickly."

Hannah knows the sun is a yellow ball of fire—she can still see the smear of it—but the image has been replaced more by a feeling of warmth that tingles the hair on her arms and makes her turn her face toward the source. Yes, a pine tree has a reddish trunk and green needles and cuts away the sky when you stand beneath it, but for her the sensory analogue is the smell of resin and the feel of scabby bark plates beneath her palm and the sound of the hushing, prickling breeze when it rushes through the branches. The ability to see has become an abstraction, something she can only vaguely imagine, like time travel or teleportation.

She sits on an exam table with the doctor leaning in and her mother hovering nearby. He tries to make small talk—asking how's school, is she excited, will she do anything to celebrate—but she can barely manage a response, all of her attention on the tug of his hands, the wounded ache of her eyes.

"We don't go out to restaurants very much, but we're going to one tomorrow," her mother says. "Benedikt's. For lunch. To celebrate. With my sister. She writes for the paper. Maybe you've read her articles? She writes about other people's problems, but let me tell you, she has plenty of her own. Anyway, as long as Hannah is feeling up for it, that's what we're planning."

"That's nice," the doctor says. "Almost done." Then the last bit of bandage pulls away and he says, "There."

A part of Hannah feels lighter, more buoyant, now that she's unrestricted by all that gauze and tape, but another part of her feels more panicked than ever—as if, when he said, "There," a light switch should have turned on in her head. For now there is only darkness. Her brain churns. She can taste her breakfast in her throat.

He leans in and thumbs aside her lids and shines a light on the still-sore incisions and nudges the outlet. "Good, good. Okay. I think we're ready for Mirage."

Hannah has worn it before, more than a month ago. She ran her fingers along the shape of it then, the sleek silver shield that wrapped her eyes. But that was just playing pretend. This is real. The doctor fits it into place, tightening the band around the back of her head and neatening her hair. Two bulges, almost like the nubs of horns, swell next to each of her temples. These are the brains of the thing, a cluster of microprocessors. The right one carries the small power switch. The doctor asks if she'd like to do the honors.

She nods and blows out a steadying breath and snaps the switch.

"Well?" the doctor says.

"Hannah?" her mother says. "Did it work? Is it working?"

There is a game she sometimes plays. The wishing game. She'll say, "I'm looking forward to our trip to Costa Rica," or "I'm riding a horse across the Scottish Highlands," and then, as if a spell has been cast, an image will crystallize. She is on a white sand beach with coconuts thudding the sand and dolphins arcing from a lagoon. She is pounding across a bog, through swirling mists, while the horse kicks up divots of mud and bagpipes honk and wheeze. No matter how expensive or distant or impossible the dream, the wishing game makes anything possible.

"I can see," she says. She has said this many times before, has whispered it into her pillow and coat collar and closet, testing the words in quiet places to see if they spoil once released to the air. But this time it's true. She can see.

It is difficult for her to comprehend images, her frame of reference so far limited to her other senses. What she sees is like an echo. And inside the echo there is another voice. There is a blazing white above, and a muted white all around, through which things—people?—move. Her mother asks, "Can you see me? Hannah?"

She sees something, but is it her mother? It must be. But everything is mixed up. She can't forge colors with shapes or shapes with distance or distance with texture, every different input temporarily fizzling her brain, making her want to shout, "Does not compute, does not compute!" As if someone put a banana under her nose and a shark in front of her face and jazz in her ear and a broom in her hand and said, "What a beautiful sunset."

"I don't know," she says. "I can't tell what's real."

THE DARK NET

CHAPTER I

Lela stares at her reflection in the dead computer screen, a black cutout against the fluorescent blaze of the newsroom behind her. Her face appears an oval smear with hollows for eyes, a gash for a mouth, as if she were looking into some haunted mirror. She lifts the phone to her ear and dials the number for Alderman Robert Dahm. The ring purrs. Her pen hovers over a yellow legal tablet. There was a time when she found it impossible to concentrate at her desk, one of forty cubicles surrounded by glass-walled meeting rooms and editorial offices here at *The Oregonian,* where she has worked Metro the past five years. But she has learned to focus, to crush down her attention and blur into white noise the copy machine whirring, the printer and fax machine bleeping, the cell phones and landlines ringing, the televisions blaring, the voices calling all around her, just as she has learned to tolerate the smell of mildew that clings to the walls and the taste of the burned black coffee in the lounge.

She has never heard of the company Undertown, Inc. That's who City Hall says bought Rue Apartments, the four-story stone building in the Pearl District, long ago condemned and surrounded by chainlink. The Rue was one of her first big stories at the paper—back when she was freelancing—a feature about the ten-year anniversary of Jeremy Tusk's death. She's since become a staff writer at *The Oregonian,* and Tusk has become a celebrity serial killer. Plug his name into Google and a long list of hits will come up, including leaked crime scene photos and occultist conspiracy theories. There's a display dedicated to him at the Museum of Death in Los Angeles and at least two direct-to-video horror films have cited him as an inspiration.

Lela is thirty now, she was twenty-four then, when she toured through the weed-choked lot, the thirty-unit building with the broken windows and a gnarled tree growing on its roof. In her article she described its shadow-soaked hallways as *palpably dark*. She described Tusk's two-bedroom apartment, still cobwebbed with police tape, as *tomblike*. She quoted a detective as saying, "Up to me, we'd burn the place down, raise a barbed-wire fence, keep everyone the hell away. Cursed ground."

The alderman's secretary answers and patches her through. "Lela Falcon?" he says, and she says, "Yes," as though he's the one bothering her. His voice, a nasal whine, asks what he can do for her this afternoon.

"Why didn't you tell me about the Rue building?"

"The Rue—you mean that the property sold? Why does it matter?"

"Of course it matters. You know it matters."

"So you can write another story about that demon-worshipping psychopath cutting people up and making their skin into curtains? Maybe I don't want you dredging up all those bad memories. It's not good for the city."

"It is good. It *is* good. That's the story. A new chapter. Portland moves on."

"You write a story, you bring up all those nasty details, people get upset."

"No. Don't be stupid. You're wrong. It's the opposite spin. New building, new city, new era. Bluebirds and hopefulness and all that happy crappy bullshit."

His sigh makes a wind in her ear. They talk another five minutes. Due to a tax foreclosure, the property belongs to the city, and last she heard, they were going to convert the lot to green space, landscape it with trees and shrubs and grass and benches. Last she heard, from the alderman's own mouth, it was not "appropriate" to develop the lot for residential or economic purposes due to what had happened there.

Now the city of Portland has sold the lot to Undertown, Inc., for an undisclosed purchase price. A generous one, the alderman says, one they couldn't refuse in these lean times. "It will be a good boost. We need a good boost."

"And construction is already underway? I'm hearing about this how many weeks later? Who are these people? What are they going to do with the lot?"

Robert doesn't know. Something about the Internet. She asks him for contact information—she wants to reach out to Undertown—and he says she'll have to figure that out on her own. All this time her pen gashes paper, scratching out notes.

"You know, you should smile more," he says, and she says, "How do you know I'm not smiling?" and he says, "You never smile. It might help you—that's all I'm saying. Professionally. Personally. Try it sometime."

With her pen she stabs down a period that tears the page and says, "You're no help," and hangs up. She plugs the pen in her mouth and gnaws on it. The plastic is already scored from her teeth. Dozens of yellow legal tablets surround her, wrinkled and torn and coffee-stained and stitched with her handwriting, much of it a coded shorthand illegible to anyone but her. Their leaning piles are decorated with empty coffee cups and chip bags and crumpled blobs of cellophane dusted with muffin crumbs. She has tacked to the foam walls of the cubicle a photograph of her standing alone before Multnomah Falls and a film noir calendar with every square darkened with reminders about meetings and deadlines.

She is pale. So is everyone else in Portland, but she is particularly light-skinned and freckled, which makes the black bags beneath her eyes all the more obvious. Her gingery hair she keeps knotted into a braid that might be called churchy or grandmotherly but that she thinks of as classic. Men, usually men in bars who have drunk too much to know better, have called her face everything from elfin to pointy to fawnish. She didn't let any of them stick their tongues in her mouth, though they tried. She has lost track of her latest coffee—one of twenty she might drink in a day—and spits out the dregs of two cold cups before finding the one that goes down lukewarm.

She pushes out of her chair and leans over her cubicle and asks the Metro intern—an acne-scarred kid named Josh, a com-jo major at Portland State—to do some digging. "Undertown, Inc. Get me whatever you can on them."

"Ever heard of Google?" he says. His voice still has a crackly pubescence to it.

He knows she hates using computers. Everybody knows and nobody will shut up about it. They all think it's the most hilarious thing in world history. Calling her a Luddite. Asking her if she's updated her stone tablet with the latest software. "Do what you're told. That's what interns are supposed to do."

"Fine."

A minute later, he has the company website up on the monitor. "Under construction," it reads.

"Exactly," she says. "Under construction. Nothing else?"

"That's all. No phone. No email. I also searched the domain name —to see who's paying for the site—but whoever it is, they dropped the extra fee that buys anonymity."

"Why would they do that?" she says.

"Because they're shy?"

"You're no help either."

She calls City Hall and asks a favor of the clerk in Records. Promises to buy him lunch so long as he digs out the file on the Rue Apartments, gets her the contact info for the buyer, Undertown, Inc. She waits with the phone clamped against her shoulder until he rattles off an email and a number with an area code she doesn't recognize. "No billing address?" she says, and he says, "Nope. Paid for through an anonymous escrow account."

"What's with these fuckers?" she says, and he says, "Excuse me?"

"Nothing. Thanks," she yells to the phone when it's already halfway to the cradle. Then she pesters Josh to get her intel on the email —Undertown@hushmail.com—and phone number. He takes a look at the slip of paper and says he can't.

"Can't? Can't? What's with this *can't*?"

"Hushmail is an encrypted service, and if you're serious about privacy, you're probably using TOR, a network within a network that bounces all traffic through multiple servers making it impossible to figure out who you are, where you're from."

"Wait—what? English please."

He says, "Cavewoman translation: it's secret email."

"Why would you want secret email?"

"Because you've got secrets?"

"Okay," she says. "Then look up the phone."

"I can't."

"Again," she says, "this *can't*. I don't like it."

He taps the area code, 473. "It's fake. The one most scammers use. That's not a real place. It's the area code to nowhere. Probably a Blackphone. Or else they're using encryption software."

"How do you know all this crap?"

He throws up his arms and lets them fall. "I don't know. I'm friends with nerds. I wasn't born during the Civil War. Et cetera."

"Who are these nerd friends?"

"Okay, friend. Singular. A hacker buddy of mine. He's deep into this kind of stuff."

She tells Josh he can go, but not far. She might need him. She lets her hand sit a moment on the phone before lifting the receiver, checking the dial tone, dialing.

The first time someone answers, there is no *Hello,* no *How can I help you?* "To whom am I speaking?" That's what the man on the other end of the line says. He speaks in a baritone broken by an accent that makes his mouth sound full of glass. Eastern European, she guesses, but what does she know? She's a reporter. She's an expert on nothing because she knows a little of everything.

She is rarely at a loss for words. But something about the voice—its deep, almost otherworldly register—unsettles her. She clicks her pen a few times before telling him her name, her position, asking if he might be willing to spend a few minutes talking to her about Undertown for an article she's writing about the Pearl District, the urban renaissance in Portland.

There is a gust of breath. Then a click followed by a dial tone that fills her ear like a siren.

She hangs up the phone and tries again. The ringing goes on for two minutes and never changes over to voicemail. She tries again, and again, and again, until her ear grows hot with the phone mashed against it.

From a good height, she drops the phone into the cradle. The clattery *dong* of it makes a few people pop up in the cubicles around her. She gives them the finger, and they drop down again. She clicks her pen a few more times, then tucks it in her pocket, grabs her purse, drains her coffee, and starts for the door.

The cubicles are arranged like a gray-combed hive, and she navigates their alleys. Computer screens flash in her passing. She spots one of the Arts reporters contorting her body into a yoga stretch, a Sports columnist watching two televisions at once. Many of the desks are unoccupied, empty except for a balled-up sheet of paper, a broken keyboard. Every year they lose more ads, more subscribers, and every year their staff shrinks, so that one person scrambles to cover the work of six.

Out of the corner of her eye, she spots him. Brandon, her editor. Everyone else wears jeans and fleece, but he slinks into the office every day in an Oxford pinstripe with a tie noosed around his neck. "Where you going? Lela?"

"Out."

She races along a long line of file cabinets. One of the Sports clerks turns the corner. He carries a tall pile of Hot Lips Pizza boxes. She flattens against the cabinets and dodges past him and through a warm cloud of pepperoni.

Brandon gets slowed down by the clerk, but catches up before she reaches the hallway, the bank of elevators. "What are you chasing?"

"A story."

"This for tomorrow?"

"Definitely not, but it might be hot."

"What's it about?"

"Can't tell. Too early. Bad luck to share."

"I still need copy for Sunday."

"The fall farmers' market and the Willamette 10K. You'll get it."

"I better."

He will, but barely. She's behind on everything—she's always behind, always chasing a deadline that is instantly replaced by another—and soon enough she's going to lose more time to family. Tomorrow she's scheduled to have a celebratory lunch with her niece, Hannah, who is getting fitted today for a retinal prosthetic. Lela hopes it works. For her niece, of course, but also for herself, for the story.

She could pitch it any number of ways—human interest if she pushes the personal, Metro if she pushes innovation at OHSU, Science if she pushes the biotech boom. No matter which direction, the story has legs, front-page potential, the kind of feature that could get picked up for syndication.

Her sister, Cheryl, is always giving her a hard time about this kind of thinking. "Can't you ever have a thought that's unpublished?" she says. "Don't you ever feel like a vulture?" No. Yes. Maybe. Whatever. Her sister will never understand. They aren't hard-wired the same. That's what it means to be a writer: everything is material. You are never not paying attention. There is nothing that is not worth learning and processing into a story. And if somebody feels used, gets their feelings hurt, too fucking bad. That's the business.

At the elevators she punches the DOWN button and watches the numbers—red and dotted, like needled skin—click their way up to the fourth floor. Brandon is winded from chasing her and breathes forcefully through his nose. She refuses to look at him, though he stands so close she can smell him, his standard odor of Barbasol and chai tea. She hates his face, the weak chin, the eyebrows constantly knotting over his nose, his forehead rising high into a receding hairline—and she hates his edits, the way he double-checks her sources and trims away all her good, meaty descriptions. The elevator dings and the doors open, and she walks through them and hits simultaneously the LOBBY and CLOSE DOOR buttons.

"What about a follow on the OES choir? Their experience singing at Carnegie Hall with all those other private high schools?"

"That doesn't deserve a follow."

The doors start to close, and he puts out a hand to stop them. "I'm getting pressure from above. The reader survey says people want more stories that make them feel good."

"I didn't get into this business to make drooling idiots feel good."

"Then maybe you should get out, Lela. Apply for a staff position at a magazine."

She pushes the button again. "Not until I accomplish my goal of frustrating you into a heart attack."

The doors start to close, and Brandon puts out a hand to stop them again. "Oh, and the Halloween parade. You're on that?"

She raises a hand in a swatting gesture. "On it. I guess."

"And the storm—do you know about the storm that's headed our—"

His words are clipped by the closing doors. The elevator sinks.

✣

She drives a beater Volvo station wagon that used to belong to her parents. She never locks the door. The radio was stolen years ago, a black rectangle with wires dangling from it. Now there is nothing to steal but gum wrappers and coffee cups. She ripped out the backseat to make room for her dog, a German shepherd named Hemingway, and the car is shagged over with his hair. It takes a few cranks to turn the engine over. She hears her phone buzzing in her purse and doesn't bother answering it, knowing it is likely Brandon pestering her further. She doesn't own a smartphone. She owns what her friends call a Flintstone phone, whatever the rep at Paradise Wireless offered her for free five years ago. It looks a little like a scarred bullet. The numbers are worn off the keypad. When she is having a conversation, other voices ghost in and out, due to some echoey distortion or a faulty antenna that pirates other calls.

She does not text. She does not Facebook or Twitter or Instagram or any of that other digital nonsense, the many online whirlpools that seem to encourage boasting and bitching. She doesn't care about your crazy cat, your ugly baby, your Cancún vacation, your Ethiopian meal, your political outrage and micro-complaints and competitive victimhood. She doesn't want social media eroding her privacy or advertisers assaulting her with customized commercials. There's too much noise and too little solitude in the world. Everybody should shut the fuck up and get back to work.

The Oregonian assigned her an email address, but she hates to use it, prefers to call or write letters. She likes things that are tactile.

That might be one of the reasons she became a reporter: the memory of her father reading the newspaper at the kitchen table every morning until his coffee went cold and his finger pads blackened with ink. Last Christmas her sister, Cheryl, bought her an e-reader, and Lela held it with the tips of her fingers like something found moldering in the back of the fridge. She returned it and used the money at REI on a Gerber belt knife, a fleece headband, a pair of SmartWools.

Now she drives to the Pearl District, the semi-industrial area that has been, over the past fifteen years, slowly redeveloped. There are homeless men slumped on benches and pushing grocery carts, muttering to themselves. There are shelters and psychic readers and soup kitchens and tattoo parlors. But alongside the cracked windows and boarded-up doorways, there are lofts and theaters, Peruvian restaurants and French bakeries, bars and coffee shops, so many coffee shops, as if the city were under some narcoleptic spell. Old buildings of marble, cream brick, red brick are interrupted by new buildings of glass that jut up sharply. Bronze water fountains—called Benson Bubblers—burble on almost every street corner, making it sound as if it were raining even when it is not.

A man stands on a milk crate. He raises his arms to the sky and talks about damnation, hellish torment, the doom of the world. This is Lump. So named because of the warts that cover every inch of him. Even his tongue—she has noticed—carries a gray jewel of flesh at the tip. He wears layers of black, sweatshirts and jeans and jackets that have been scissored and torn and resewn in such a way that they appear like one ragged complicated cloak. The crows keep him company. One perches on his shoulder now—two others rest on a nearby sill. She once saw him on a park bench surrounded by twenty or more. They are his eyes, he says. Like spores he hurls to the wind to know the news of the city. She has used Lump as a source more than once. The street sometimes knows things before the rest of us.

The sidewalks are wet, the same dark gray as the buildings and the clouds above, the gray of Portland, its defining color. The sun tries to bully through but can't manage more than a white splotch. This is early afternoon, and with the noon rush over, only a few people scatter the streets. A woman in low-slung jeans and knee-high leather boots walks a tiny dog. Two androgynous hipsters—one with blue hair, the other cardinal red, both of them skinny-jeaned and nose-ringed—lean into each other for a kiss. She spots a homeless teen—you can always recognize them, no matter their clothes, by their soiled backpacks—and a man in a black fleece talking excitedly into his Bluetooth headset. A bus knocks through puddles. Pigeons explode from a maple stripped of leaves. She heads to the north end of the Pearl between the Fremont Bridge and the Broadway Bridge, and finds a parking spot a block away from the Rue. Before she gets out of the Volvo, she pulls out a bottle of Adderall and strangles off the cap. She shakes out one pill. Then, after a moment's pause, another. She drops them into the cup holder and crushes them with the butt of the bottle. She digs around on the floor for an empty fountain drink. She slides the straw from it. Bites it in half. Then uses it to snort the pills. Her eyes water and she sneezes. It would be easier to swallow them for sure, but she likes the brain-burning jolt she gets from sniffing them. She kicks open the door, checks her reflection in the side mirror, and wipes her nose before setting off. She drags her purse with her. It is fat-bottomed, made from canvas, the size of a small suitcase. She jokes that she could pull a lamp from it, a pogo stick, five dwarves, and a trampoline, like some demented Mary Poppins. Due to the shouldered weight of it, she has a habit of leaning to the left. She burrows through it now to make sure she has what she needs: pen, notebook, camera.

She can hear a MAX train rattling down a nearby street, and she can smell the mossy funk of the Willamette River, and she can see up ahead the cavernous space where the Rue once stood. She slows her pace. She wears a pair of hard-soled Keens, and they clop the pavement and make her realize how quiet the street is. In the times she visited this place before, she noticed the same, the quiet, as if some mourning shawl surrounded the block. But now it is a construction zone and ought to be filled with the steady *tock* of hammers, the *boom* of dropped pallets, the growl of backhoes and bulldozers.

A crow caws. She looks up to see five of them watching her, roosting on telephone wires, appearing against the gray sky like notes on an old piece of sheet music. She gives them a wave and wonders if they'll pass the message along to Lump.

Now she stands before a temporary wall—made from tall sheets of plywood—that surrounds the acre lot. There is a Dumpster, two pickups, and a trailer. When she cocks an ear, faintly she hears what at first sounds like whispering. Or feathery breathing. She listens another moment and the sound clarifies into digging. The *shush* and *clink* of shovels, the heavy *plop* of dirt filling wheelbarrows.

When she wrote the article about the Rue—about its famous tenant, Jeremy Tusk—she rounded up some of the old neighbors, the ones who were willing to talk. They said they noticed the sounds long before they noticed the smell. The sounds of what turned out to be saws drawn along bones, cleavers severing joints. Some guessed Jeremy a hobbyist, a woodworker toying with some project. When the police kicked down his door, they found four plastic storage bins full of hydrofluoric acid with as many bodies bathing in them, dissolving slowly. More were stored in the fridge and freezer. Ten skulls grinned on the bookshelves. And a lampshade glowed on a side table and a jacket hung in the closet and curtains hung from the windows—all stitched from tanned flesh. There were designs chalked and painted on the floors and walls and ceiling. Black and red candles burned down to nubs. Gemstones, eggs, antlers, daggers. A crow mask and a deer mask and a wolf mask sitting on a shelf. He ritualized murder, communed with a darker frequency.

Lela walks the length of the barricade, past rain-smeared posters and black-and-white tangles of graffiti. Someone has spray-painted what looks like a hand, a red right hand, with fangs coming out of the palm, across the door. A padlock hangs loose on the latch. She slides the tooth of it out. She creaks open the door—with the same slowness and care that she opened the fridge in Jeremy's apartment so long ago. It was still there, as though waiting for someone to plug it in, fill it with a gallon of milk, a bag of red apples. The interior released a smell so profoundly rotten, she felt fouled for days for having drawn it into her body.

Inside the construction site, she discovers a roughly hewn crater, several stories deep. The walls of it are cut flat and striped with concrete and stone and gravel and clay that looks like the firm red muscle of a heart. At the bottom of the pit, grayed by shadow, a dozen men lean on shovels or kneel with trowels and whisks. They are digging, unearthing, working around mounds of varying heights. An archaeological dig. This happens often. Construction begins and one of the workers discovers a shattered pot or seed cache or an atlatl dart, and a team of UO scholars drives up from Eugene to excavate.

Every mound glints with whites and yellows and browns, as if shellacked. It is then she recognizes the bones. They poke from the dirt, tangles of them, puzzles of ribs and femurs and skulls. She is looking at a graveyard, and she is looking at it now through the eye of her camera. She has drawn it from her purse, and she has thumbed the cap and twisted the focus without even thinking. It is ingrained in her, a part of her muscle memory, her constant need to document what she finds compelling.

Though it's dark at the bottom of the pit, she turns off the flash. She doesn't want to be noticed. Not yet. The camera clicks as she takes shot after shot, but none of the men turn toward her, focused on their task.

One of them—small, appearing almost like a child except for his old man's face—wanders among the burial mounds. He looks so delicate and different from the other blockish men. She guesses him their supervisor. He is as bald as an infant, and what little hair he has springs in downy tufts around his ears. He says something—in a language she does not recognize, his words sharp with consonants—to one of the workers. Something reproachful that makes him hand over his trowel and step away from the mound.

The small man leans in and blows away a puff of dust. Then, with surgical precision, he removes what appears to be a skull, maybe human, though it seems too long. Some dirt falls from its hollows when he holds it up for everyone to see. Then he carries it to a table made from a sheet of plywood laid over sawhorses. Here it joins an arrangement of bones.

She has visited two archaeological sites for stories. A weeklong OMSI camp, themed around Lewis and Clark, that dug into a section of Fort Clatsop. And a summer class with UO that excavated a Paiute village in Christmas Valley. In both instances, the sites were gridded with string. The archaeologists were exacting about measurements, the precise location of every obsidian flake and broken bone and fibrous sandal found within the grid. She was expecting Indiana Jones, but it felt more like the slow disarrangement of a 3D jigsaw puzzle.

That isn't the case here. No grid. No map. No sifting screens. Not even a ponytailed grad student in cargo shorts drinking from a Nalgene bottle covered with National Park stickers. Here instead is trouble—of this she feels certain.

Whoever Undertown is—whatever they're building—they don't want their project shut down by this discovery. So they must have erected high walls around the site in order to take care of it secretly. Actual walls that matched the privacy of their digital walls.

She snaps several more photos, wishing she brought the long lens, wishing she could get closer. There is an underground exit at the corner of the pit. A black hollow framed by a brick doorway. Maybe an entrance to the tunnel system that runs beneath Portland. She doesn't notice it until someone—a black-bearded man—steps from it and calls to the others. They pause in their work and he waves to them, and one by one they set down their tools and follow.

A staggered ramp runs from the top of the construction site to the bottom. Lela tromps down it without hesitation. She tries to keep her footsteps quiet, but the ramp is loose on its scaffolding and the boards boom below her. At the bottom of the site, the air is cooler. There is a musty, almost sulfuric taste to it. The noise of the world falls away completely except for a muffled growl of a jet somewhere overhead.

She goes first to the table. It is clotted with dirt and busy with yellow-brown bones. She snaps a photo and reaches for the skull. Its deformity is clear now—too long and thin, almost snouted—what she imagines a baboon or warthog might look like beneath the skin. The teeth are as long as her fingers. Lines run across the bone, sometimes straight, sometimes curled, sometimes arranged into what appear to be pentagonal patterns. It reminds her of the beetle-bitten wood found on a tree when you peel the bark damply from it.

She hears the small man before she sees him. "No," he says in a high, raspy voice. "No trespass!" His face is tight with anger. He stands in the doorway to the tunnel, the shadows thickly surrounding him. She is already backing away, already retreating up the ramp when he calls over his shoulder. She doesn't recognize the language he speaks—could it be Latin, like something out of a Roman Catholic service?—but the meaning is clear as the other men kick their way up the stone stairs.

She's talked and fought herself out of plenty of dangerous situations. She's been threatened with a knife, a gun. She's been undercover in a heroin den—a graffitied room with two soiled mattresses and a lava lamp—when an addict started feeling her up and paused his hand at the battery pack for her hidden camera. When he asked what it was, she said, "An insulin pump. I have diabetes," and then offered to tie off his arm while he shot up.

Sometimes you talk and sometimes you fight and sometimes you run. She runs now, pounding up the ramp. It elbows, ten feet off the ground, onto its second level. Here she skids to a stop.

Down below, the small man is speaking rapid-fire in another language, making his hand into a blade and cutting the air in her direction. The men pour out of the tunnel and head toward her, some of them gripping trowels in their hands as though they were knives.

She doesn't realize until now that she still holds the skull in her hand. She sets it down on the platform. Then twists off an anchoring clamp and hefts the bottom ramp. It scrapes half off the scaffolding. She kicks it—once, twice—and it loses its purchase and falls to the ground with a *whoomp* of displaced air that sends a cloud of grit into the approaching men.

She scoops up the skull, her finger hooking an eye socket, and considers hurling it down as well. Anything to stop their progress. She pauses her hand. She has photos, but the skull is hard evidence. Something tangible to share with police, professors. She shoves it into her purse and sprints the rest of the way up. The camera thuds against her chest. Her eyes water from wind or nerves, blurring her vision of the workers fumbling with the fallen ramp and the black-bearded man clanking up an extension ladder toward her.

CHAPTER 2

CHESTON'S APARTMENT—on Lovejoy, at the edge of the Pearl—looks out on other apartments, other offices, all of them walled with windows. He lives on the top floor, the tenth of his building. He owns a telescope, a Celestron Astromaster on a tripod, and when he isn't working, he's watching.

He's watching a woman now. She skids around a corner and hammers along the sidewalk at a full sprint. A ginger-colored braid swings wildly with every step. She clutches an enormous canvas purse. A block away, she rips open the door to her car, an ancient Volvo jeweled with guano, and vanishes inside. A few seconds later the station wagon grinds into gear and lurches into the street and cuts off a delivery truck that lays on its horn. She speeds away, trailing a cloud of black exhaust.

Cheston whirls the telescope back to the corner where she first appeared. One man—soon joined by three others—stands there, breathing heavily. The telescope brings them close enough to see the whites of their eyes. They watch her car retreat and then say something to one another before returning back the way they came.

It is only 4:00, but this is October and the dark is coming. Cheston prefers the dark. That's one of the reasons he loves Portland, where it rains 170 days a year and where it is gray-skied more often than that. Sunlight burns his eyes, forks a migraine up his forehead. Sometimes he keeps a forty-watt lamp burning in the corner, but otherwise his office is lit by the underwater glow of his computers. He wears sunglasses when hunched over his desk, staring at the bank of screens.

He keeps it dark, too, so that people can't see him. But he can see them. Through his telescope. Mostly people sit. They sit and eat their Chipotle burritos. They sit and read their celebrity gossip magazines. They sit and stream shows on Netflix. They sit and check to see if anybody liked their shit on Facebook. But every now and then, something terrible or wonderful happens. He has seen people arguing —couples slamming doors, gesturing wildly, hurling books at each other—and he has seen people making up—in bed, on the couch, at the table, one time pressed up against the window and smearing their bodies pinkly through the fog of their sex.

They all have their secrets, and that is what he is hunting for, secrets. His telescope scans the buildings—honeycombed with light—hovering in one place, swinging to the next, all of their apartments the same even as the bodies inside them swirl and change shape. Spying gives him such satisfaction, makes him feel powerful, knowing the things he shouldn't know, the things people prefer to keep hidden. The way the wife eats a grape that has fallen to the floor, the way the husband picks his nose vigorously and browses porn websites and sometimes puts a knife to his wrist and bows his head for a good long minute before sliding it back into the block. They lure him. How can he not watch?

He feels a similar energy when at his desk. He rents out seven blade servers for other users to host their sites. He is a landlord of sorts. He owns digital real estate. He loans it to others to use as they will. The servers are arranged on a metal chassis next to his desk and wired into several network routers to shuttle the data around and plug into the net. Their lights blink. Their components tick and pop. Their fans and heatsinks hum and stir the air with warmth he tries to battle back with air conditioning he keeps year-round at a cool sixty degrees. He bleeds electricity. He imagines his apartment as a gaping drain with white energy swirling constantly down it, which is why he loves this two-bedroom unit so much, since utilities are included in the rent.

Most of his payments come from Undertown, Inc., and they pay in bitcoins. Over a year ago, an instant message appeared from a user named Cloven, requesting a private chat. He accepted—not knowing what to expect, maybe some file requests, maybe some dirty talk—and when asked if he might be interested in working for Undertown, he accepted that too. He was a sophomore at Reed College then, on academic probation, not showering, not shaving, not really sleeping, all of his time spent coding and popping Adderall and eating Oreos and drinking those big plastic bullets of 5-Hour Energy. He had stopped going to classes after testifying before the faculty senate about distributing pirated movies and music through the college Ethernet. He figured it was only a matter of time before they kicked him out.

They never got the chance. He dropped out to run his own business, a legitimate business, the kind that affords him the best kicks, the best equipment, the best apartment, all the Thai takeout in the world. Like his neighbors, he has his secrets. Two of his servers operate as respectable hosts, legitimizing him in the eyes of his ISP for the high-volume traffic. The other five belong to the Dark Net. He has a bribed contact at CenturyLink who regularly and silently expunges those logs.

Undertown is pleased with his services so far. Cloven calls sometimes—always on the Blackphone, always through Skype and always via a TOR network to avoid a trace—his voice deep and rasping and mysteriously accented. Somehow it hurts to listen to, as if it is penetrating him. Cheston has been promised more work, more responsibility. What this might entail, he cannot imagine, but he has told Cloven he's ready for whatever, whenever. Zero Day is a term Cloven has mentioned more than once. They are preparing for Zero Day, which is assumedly some kind of launch. Cheston doesn't ask. It's better, he's found, to simply do as he's told.

Thousands of lives stream through his blade servers, and he feels charged by them, as if his mind is a circuit board and his veins cables that course with electricity and information. On any of his three monitors, as their host, he sometimes likes to look. He knows he shouldn't—he knows he might feel safer, nobler otherwise—but he cannot resist. He keeps his desks arranged in an L shape, with three HD LCD monitors atop them. His is a homebrewed workstation, an amalgamation of parts mostly bought off Newegg and running on Linux. AMD 4.0 GHz eight-core processors on a gigabyte motherboard with 32GB RAM and an EVGA GeForce graphics card supporting the monitors. The cases are windowed, decked out with blue LED lights. In the other room, his bedroom, he has a netbook from

ZaReason and a Nexus 9 rooted Android tablet stuffed with all sorts of hacking apps. He uses them the way a watchman might in a casino or prison, to study through a fisheye lens what sort of trouble people might be getting into on his property. There he sees things most cannot imagine.

It is only 4:30 and already the streets look like shadowed canyons. The streetlamps buzz to life and throw pools of light. Apartments glow. He tucks his hair behind his ears—its color orange, parted down the middle—and leans into his telescope, scanning one of his favorite addresses: across the road, third floor, corner apartment, a young woman. Her name is Carrie Wunderlich. He knows this because he has followed her, studied her, for months now. On Mondays, Wednesdays, and Fridays, at 7 a.m., she spins at the Y. She showers and dresses and leaves with her hair still wet, on her way to Hotspur Chiropractic Health, where she works as a receptionist and massage therapist. When she goes out for lunch, at least once a week, she orders soup and salad. She shops at the co-op. He has stood so close to her, he has smelled her perfume, a puff of spiced apricot. At home she wears yoga pants and a too-big OSU sweatshirt. Every night she drinks one glass of white Zinfandel, poured from a box in the fridge, and plops on the couch to watch reality television. Above her gas fireplace hangs an oversize print of Van Gogh's *Sunflowers,* and that's a little how he thinks of her, as his slim-stalked yellow sunflower bobbing across the way.

She has come home today with a man. The same man who picked her up last Saturday and drove away in a silver Jetta. Cheston keeps watching as if something will happen, but nothing happens. They sit there, on opposite ends of the sofa, drinking her pink wine, moving their mouths in conversation.

Lightning leaps from a cloud. Thunder mutters. Rain spots and then drums the window, smearing the image of them. They approach the window to watch the storm, and the man puts his arm around her waist and draws her close. Cheston strangles the telescope. The image of them trembles.

When lightning strikes again, it is closer, and then closer still. Thunder shakes the window. He pulls away from the telescope in time to see the outage before it arrives. Off in the distance the buildings go black, block by block, black black black, rolling toward him, a landslide of darkness.

He feels a sudden emptiness when the blackout strikes his building. The air conditioner sighs off. The room instantly warms. His computers and servers continue to glow, now powered by backup batteries that can only last so long. Undertown demands uninterrupted service, and for now, they have it.

He leans into the telescope again. The building across the street is unlit and gives nothing back. He doesn't like to think about what might be happening over there, what secrets he might miss out on. He closes his eyes and counts to a hundred. The computer and server fans moan. Sweat beads on his forehead.

He opens his eyes and still the city remains dark, as if a black blanket were tossed over it, and he counts to one hundred again. Lightning webs the sky, strobing his view of downtown. It makes sparkling nests on the roofs of the two highest buildings, Wells Fargo and Big Pink, the U.S. Bancorp Tower. The thunder is continuous now, a muttering and booming, like some furious conversation heard through a wall.

Lightning strikes the Broadway Bridge and outlines it blue. And then, as if some spark has taken hold and flared into fire, the city erupts with light. The grid-work pattern of the streets illuminates like circuit boards. The air conditioner sputters to life again, and he sighs his relief along with it.

Then the power returns all over the city. A spike. The lights in the buildings all around him flicker and blaze hot. A few apartments flame out, go dark. A streetlamp explodes with a sparking rain.

He can hear the surge muscling its way through his system. There is a flare. One of the servers spits and flashes and smokes, and when he goes to investigate it a moment later, he discovers the drive destroyed.

✣

The Internet is his home. Some people might call it a fantasy world, because it is not something you can smell or taste or run through your fingers like black sand, but it is every bit as real as anything we experience. He can vividly remember nightmares he had as a child —a shadow man who stood in the corner of his bedroom, a gathering of thin bears that surrounded a picnic—far more vividly than the lunch he ate yesterday. They're as real as anything. The Internet is as real as anything. If, in his mind, he has spent hours with a woman —cupped her breast, tasted her spit, snapped the lace band of her panties, both their bodies shuddering with pleasure—and the hours add up to days and then weeks, how is that not real? If he feels something, if his mind is cavernous and pliant enough to be stimulated so?

The Internet has trapdoors and invisible wires. It has secret passages, secret paths and secret codes, secret languages. It has vaults and cellars and attics full of darkness no spotlight can cut through. You can travel through time, you can travel through walls. With a trembling of your fingers, you can make things appear and disappear. You can hurt people. You can help people. You can buy people. The Internet is a landfill and a treasure trove. Every object and every person and every place and every thought, *every* secret exists there. Every appetite can be satisfied there. Unlike a body, unlike the world, the Internet is limitless.

It is where he belongs. Not here, on the streets, in the rain, splashing through puddles and dashing from awning to awning, heading to the tech store a mile away. His hair plasters his scalp and water runs down his collar. He gathers up the hood of his jacket. Across the street, a lamp throws a funnel of rain-swept light. In it stands a figure. A man. The one who sometimes preaches on street corners—Cheston believes—the one lumped with warts. He wears what looks like several black trash bags, torn through to accommodate his arms and legs, one of them hooding his head. His shape is made more uncertain by the wind that rips against his body and makes the bags flutter. Cheston cannot see a face, but he can feel eyes, and they are tracking him.

He hurries on. He shivers and jams his hands deep in his pockets and every few steps glances back the way he came. His hood eats up so much of his vision, giving him only a periscope to see through rounded by darkness. The first three times he turns, the bag man remains beneath the streetlamp, but when Cheston spins around again, he is gone. Cheston pulls off his sunglasses to see better, bites down on the stem of them.

He hurries faster still. Not only for the bag man and the dark and the rain, but for Undertown. This is Friday evening, when people return home from a long week at work and loosen their ties and their belts. They have an appetite. They want to indulge. Traffic on his servers multiplies. He has never met any of his employers, but Cloven's voice frightens him. It sounds like it is coming from the bottom of a well. And his employer has been clear on this one matter: the servers should never fail. He must keep the caverns open. If something goes wrong, Cheston will be held responsible.

It is only a block now to the tech store, GEEK. The letters on the sign glow red in the night, the four windows a blazing white beneath them. He hates fluorescent light. Its color the color of hospitals and police stations. It makes his eyes flutter. Brings on a headache. But this evening he feels nothing but relief when he pushes through the door.

A chime fills the store and slowly bottoms out. The color white is everywhere. White light, white drop ceiling, white tile floor, white metal shelving. It penetrates him. He hurries on his sunglasses and they instantly fog over. He pulls them off again to smear clean. He squints at the counter, abandoned, and then down the aisles, empty as well. He calls out, "Hello?" He pulls back his hood. Rain drips off him and patters the entry rug. The counter next to the register is dirty with Mountain Dew bottles and fast-food wrappers, a nest of wires, a motherboard. Cheston holds his hand over a soldering iron that still gives off heat. Through the center of the store reach six long aisles. At the back, three tables display desktops and laptops and printers. Cheston walks the width of the room, glancing down the aisles, each of them a corridor of ink cartridges and controllers and processors and video cards, spools of cords, blister packs of flash drives.

In the last of them stands Derek, who owns the shop and lives in the basement below. He is short, the size of a twelve-year-old, though he might be forty. Doc Martens, the style with the bulky heel, cheat him a few inches. He always wears a short-sleeved polo tucked into pleated khakis with a braided leather belt. His forearms, which are exceptionally hairy, he keeps crossed across his chest. His face is clean-shaven but rashed along the neck. His hair is parted tidily down the middle with the sideburns trimmed weirdly high. "Greetings," he says.

"What are you doing?"

He wears a smartphone in a harness on his belt. A white cord reaches across his chest and splits into his ears. He tugs on it and the earbuds pop out, and he wraps them around his knuckles and tucks them in his pocket. "What's that?"

"I said what are you doing?"

Derek does not blink when he says, "Listening to some kickass music. Then I got interrupted. By you." He clomps past Cheston and stations himself behind the counter. Here he keeps a stepping stool that he climbs onto, and now they are nearly the same height. "You got water all over the floor."

"Bad storm."

"Good storm. Good for me. Storms always do damage. And I'm going to be doing a lot of business tomorrow. A *lot*. I assume that has something to do with why you're here?"

"Blew out a blade drive."

An eyebrow arches. "Did you?"

"I did."

Derek keeps the drivers locked up in a glass case behind the counter. He does not look at them but nods his head in their direction.

"I'd appreciate it if we could do this quickly." Cheston rolls back his sleeve to reveal the pale flesh of his forearm, interrupted by a black patterned square, a QR code that contains his credit card information.

Derek looks at the tattoo and hoists his upper lip. "Really?"

"Do we have to go through this every time?"

"I just think it's messed up. Commercializing your body like that. Soul selling even. Gross. Really gross."

"It's the way of the future. Ten years, we'll all be inked up."

"So predicts the great Nostradumbass."

"How much?"

Derek slowly withdraws the scanning gun from its cradle, fires the red line of it across the counter, up the round swell of Cheston's belly, pausing at his heart. "You know that's an interesting question. Because you're not a standard sort of customer, are you? You've got a lot at stake, don't you? With your little business." He turns the gun one way, then the other. "Hmm. How much *should* you pay?"

"There are plenty of stores. I don't have to come to this one."

"But I know *things* about you." Derek's lips tremble a little. "Isn't that worth something?"

"You're not the only one who knows *things*."

"What do you know, Cheston?"

"You think I don't know who my guests are? I know who I'm hosting. I know what you're up to. I could rat on you just as well as you could rat on me." There is a long silence between them. The wind gusts outside and Cheston says, "Have you ever heard of the Panopticon?"

"No, Cheston, I have not heard of the *Panopticon*."

"It's a building with a circular structure. It could be a school or a hospital or a prison. A philosopher named Jeremy Bentham designed it. There's a watchman stationed in its center. From his inspection house, he can see into all the rooms, or cells, but no one can tell whether or not the watchman is actually watching. They must assume he is." Cheston slides his sunglasses to the end of his nose and studies Derek over the top of them. "Assume he is. Assume *I* am watching."

✣

A few minutes later, with a receipt crunched in his pocket and a plastic bag swinging from his hand, he pushes through the door, into the street, where the night hisses with rain. There is a hard division between the harsh white light of the store and the penetrating black of the street.

Sometimes, at the end of the day, after so many hours of staring at computers, his eyes will not focus. The world lags and warps and fuzzes over. So he cannot be sure whether it is a trick of the night or the fault of his vision, but he thinks he sees something. What, he cannot say. Maybe a pale dog or maybe a headlight flashing off a puddle. But he feels observed, hunted. It feels like there is an unseen presence haunting this night.

He blinks hard. Then runs and walks and runs again the next three blocks. With the air so full of water, breathing feels like drowning. He thinks he hears a clicking, like claws on concrete. Every few steps, he checks over his shoulder, making his vision whirl and his balance unsteady. The occasional car cuts the darkness, its engine coughing, its tires swishing. Otherwise, he is alone, the only people he sees safely ensconced in the bright orange squares of lamplight that pattern the buildings around him. They float above the danger and doubt he feels.

He passes an alley, a wedge of shadow. Every nerve in his body tells him to give it wide berth. He angles toward the curb, slips into the street. The water there is calf-deep. His shoe fills with it and threatens to tear away. He curses and lurches back onto the sidewalk just in time to see the man emerge from the alley. The man he saw earlier. The bag man. Lump.

Lump staggers, his face cloaked by the plastic torn around his face like a poncho. They move past each other, close enough to grab. The man's face swings toward him at the last second, damp and warted, so that it appears tadpoles surge beneath his skin. "You don't have to go to hell," he says. "You can be saved. It's not too late." Only then does Cheston notice the crow on the man's shoulder. It opens its beak and rasps at him.

Cheston sprints the rest of the way home, his legs trembling and his throat feeling burned out by the time he arrives. He pauses a moment at the entry to stare across the street. At her apartment. His sunflower. The window remains dark, though the rest of the building blazes with light. Maybe she left or maybe she's in there. With that man. Cheston bares his teeth and keys the lobby door. He nods at the doorman at his desk. The elevator closes around him like a steel coffin that feels like it is being lowered instead of raised—and he does not feel safe until inside his apartment. The buzz of his computers, like angry wasps, calms him. He rips the blade drive from its packaging. Wires it in and powers it up. It blips and chugs to life.

He blows out a sigh, what feels like his first breath since leaving the apartment. He checks his phone—to see how long he has been gone, how long the driver has been down, hoping no more than thirty minutes. He checks his Blackphone and on the Skype app he sees five missed calls and just as many messages. They are all from Cloven. And all of them say the same thing: "What have you done, Cheston?"

His vision shifts again, as if traveling him away. He takes off his sunglasses, knuckles his eyes, puts them back on. He plops into his desk chair. His computers are asleep, and his eyes collide with his reflection in the dark screen and look away. He twitches. He cannot sit still—standing up, sitting down, swiveling in his chair one way, then the other—trying to take in the whole room at once, his body guarding against something. He shakes the mouse. The screens brighten and make his eyes feel full of ashes. He fits on his sunglasses again. He unzips and thrashes out of his jacket and tosses it on the floor.

His fingers spider above the keyboard and then stutter out a note. "So so so totally sorry," he writes. "Huge-ass storm came through. One of the drivers fried. RAN to store to get another. Literally dying right now from lack of breath. LOL. Everything restored. Again, apologies."

The response comes immediately. "We are nearly at Zero Day," Cloven writes. "And we lost 20 percent of our capacity for forty minutes."

He understands the subtext. He is supposed to quantify time and space, the incalculable amount of commerce and exchange that could not take place during a peak time. It wasn't just citizen traffic; Undertown was engaged in something that had been interrupted. Cheston can only write back, "I'm sorry. I mean, my bad, but there was nothing I could do."

He can't tell whether it is sweat or rainwater oozing down his face. He hits refresh, refresh, refresh until the next message appears—a long minute later.

"We are willing to forgive you. So long as you are willing to do as we request. We mentioned before that your role within the company might change, that your responsibilities would greaten."

There is a glass eye at the top of each of the monitors, a webcam, and he notices then their green lights throbbing to life.

"Yes," he writes. "Of course."

"Open this, then."

The email comes with an attachment. He clicks on it without hesitation and the computers all begin to chitter at once. A red code scrolls across the screens, filling his sunglasses with its script like blood-laced vessels.

CHAPTER 3

MIKE JUNIPER HAS KNOWN about the storm for days, and now it is finally here. He has three different apps on his phone—Weather Bug, Weather Underground, AccuWeather—and he thumbs through them a few times daily. In the morning, after he fetches the newspaper and pulls off the plastic bag and scans the headlines, he always licks a thumb and flips to the last page to study the five-day forecast. His eyes often cut to the window, where sunlight burns or where clouds cluster. It doesn't make much sense, he knows, paying so much attention to something completely out of his control. But it makes him feel more connected to and protective of his clients, who suffer the elements in alleys and doorways.

That's what he calls them, his clients, which they appreciate. "You work for us? That the idea?" they say, and he says, "Exactly." He works for them. Feeding them meals. Offering them beds. Giving them soap and toothpaste and deodorant, underwear and socks, whatever castaway gloves and rain jackets and shoes get dropped off in cardboard boxes and plastic garbage sacks.

Juniper runs The Weary Traveler, one of several shelters in downtown Portland. He has forty beds, five showers, a kitchen, and a lounge where people can read the paper, watch TV, play cards or board games. The building, which huddles between two high-rises, is square and hatted by a sprung red roof, like some failed cousin of a Pizza Hut. Above the reception desk hangs a large cross that looks like a sword and gives off a pale blue light. The walls are blushed with mold and the linoleum is cracked and the ceiling is stained yellow from the cigarettes people used to be able to smoke here, but it's a welcome refuge to many. Some sleep here for one night and others for thirty, after which time he's obligated to review their case and extend or deny their stay. He has trouble saying no. Some of his clients have been with him for years.

Juniper himself has been here for twenty. Nobody asks him what he did previously, as people mind their business in a place like this. And nobody has recognized him and he doubts they ever will. The name he's changed and the beard he's grown and the muscle he's gained from weightlifting make that nearly impossible. He's only in his mid-forties, but his previous life feels like something that happened a century ago. His forehead juts, a thick shelf that throws a shadow over his eyes. His hair is curly black. His hands are enormous, his mouth small. He wears jeans and flannel, thermal longsleeves.

He helps out the occasional teenager. There are many in Portland, but they try to keep away from the shelters because the admins are obligated to report underagers to social services. And he caters to the occasional family. Just yesterday, for instance. A hollow-eyed mother whose baby had worn the same diaper for three days straight. Whenever the boy needed a change, she'd simply scrape out the waste. She wasn't on drugs, though some of them are, and she wasn't mentally ill, though some of them are. She was out of work and on her own and didn't want to ask for help until she had no choice. That's what Juniper's here for—to help, to make a difference, as a kind of compensation or atonement. These people have hit rock bottom and someone needs to hoist them out, and he's happy to be the one to do it.

Most of Juniper's clients are middle-aged men. One of his regulars sits in the lounge area now, a room crammed with mismatched couches and recliners and tables, a potted fern, a game cabinet, a coffee station.

Mitch Gunderson used to work as a horse vet until he took a hoof to the head that dented his skull and damaged his short-term memory. He still favors Wranglers and flannels. He's presently stirring creamer into his fifth cup of coffee.

"What do you think, Mitch?" Juniper says. "Gonna be a bad one?"

Mitch stops his spoon, looks to the window, says, "Wouldn't mind a big storm. I've always been a fan of enormous weather." Then returns to his absent stirring.

Sure enough, the pressure shifts, the temperature drops. Juniper keeps a thermometer—round-faced with a faded picture of a crow on it—screwed next to one of the windows. He can see the hand on it slide back a good fifteen degrees, like a clock losing time. "Oh boy," he says. "Here it comes."

A gust sends a fistful of leaves skittering across the windows. The door breathes open slightly and the wind gasps inside. A streetlamp burns outside, and by its light they can see the maples bending with the wind. Lightning begins to zap and string the night, and they can see now the shape of the thing, one of those frontal thunderstorms shaped like a monstrous anvil. The gray, lightning-laced shelf of it moves toward them, eating up the sky. The moon has risen, a white rind that the clouds soon eclipse.

Today has been slow. A few of his regulars have checked in and are showering or resting upstairs, but he expects the storm to bring more his way. Mitch stands by the window and sips from his coffee and says, again, "I've always been a fan of enormous weather." He's tall and lean with big ears made more prominent by his baldness. He still carries the dent of the horse hoof at the temple, and his eyes have a faraway focus to them. He lets out a long appreciative whistle. "That's a storm all right." He glances at his wristwatch, which stopped ticking years ago. "I suppose I should head on home, but if I do, that means I have to spend time with my wife." He takes a loud sip of coffee and runs a tongue across his lips for the taste. "So I'll just stay here. I'll just ride her out."

Mitch's wife abandoned him after the accident. They had never had children, and she didn't want one now. That's what Mitch had become, essentially, an absent-minded child. He hasn't seen his wife in two years, but he talks about her as though she's waiting, impatient for him to get home and fix a gutter, mow the lawn.

"That's what we'll do," Juniper says. "Ride her out. Together."

"Yep."

"Let's see what the box has to say about all this." Juniper picks up the remote and powers up the TV hanging from the wall, flipping through the stations until he settles on KGW, the local NBC affiliate. A reporter—a woman in a blue-and-gray North Face jacket—stands in the rain next to a tree that snapped in half and crunched through a minivan. Glass and leaves litter the street. She signs off, reporting live from Tigard, and the camera cuts to Matt Zafino, in a charcoal suit, standing before a radar map. He uses his hands to pantomime the swirling force of the storm. He talks about changing pressure systems, dew points, supercells.

"We're in for it," Juniper says.

That's when the rain arrives. It doesn't begin gradually—it comes all at once—as if someone slashed the belly of the sky, lashing the windows, pounding the roof, filling the shelter with a roar they can feel. They can barely hear each other, but that doesn't stop Mitch from muttering the occasional "Boy" and "Damn" and "Would you look at that." A steady stream pours off the roof, like a silvery beaded curtain that obscures the view and distorts and refracts the headlights of the pickup that approaches the building.

"Who's that?" Mitch says.

"That's Sammy's truck."

"Sammy," Mitch says. "Who's that?"

Mitch knows him, even if he can't remember. Sammy is a regular. Most nights he sleeps in his truck, a rusted-out Ford with no muffler and spent shocks. He siphons fuel out of luxury cars with a garden hose, so his breath often smells like gasoline. He collects scrap metal around the city and visits the shelter for meals and clothes and showers.

The truck careens toward them, approaching so quickly that Mitch flinches, as though the grille might crash through the window. Then the pickup comes to a rocking halt, parked diagonally across two spots, its nose right up against the entrance. The engine clanks and squeals and dies. The driver's door kicks open, and Sammy jumps out and hunches down and splashes his way through a puddle.

"Christ, is this guy drunk?" Mitch says.

Sammy pushes his way inside and pauses on the bristle mat. His sweatshirt is soaked through, clinging to him. Water puddles the floor where he stands. His eyes are already big, but they appear now to bulge from their sockets.

"Are you drunk, buddy?" Mitch says.

"What's the matter?" Juniper says. "Sammy?"

Sammy opens and closes his mouth several times before saying, "I . . . I hit something."

"Hit something?" Juniper says.

"A horse?" Mitch says. "Did you hit a horse? I once treated a horse that got hit by a semi. Never thought she would make it, but by god, she pulled through."

"What'd you hit, Sammy?"

Mitch finishes his coffee and sets it down with a hard clink. "Let me fetch my med kit and we'll see about that horse."

Sammy shakes his head hard enough for the water to spin off him. Then he wipes his face, dries his palm on his sweatshirt. He glances back at his pickup, and though it already looks like something salvaged from a junkyard, Juniper homes in on the dented bumper, the broken grille.

"Not a person?" Juniper says.

Sammy is still looking at his pickup. "No. Not a person. I'm not sure what I hit." The thunder snarls. "But it's in the back of my truck. I put it there, in the back of my truck."

✣

Juniper and Mitch follow Sammy outside to the back end of the truck. The rain stings and the puddles soak their shoes and the wind shoves them off-balance. Sammy drops the tailgate. A smell hits them. A sulfuric urine. Juniper snaps on a key chain penlight to cut through the darkness.

"See." Sammy motions at the thing. "Told you."

For a moment no one speaks. Then Mitch says, "What in the hell is that?"

"You're the veterinarian," Sammy says, his voice desperate. "Was hoping you could tell me."

"How'd you know I was a veterinarian?" Mitch says.

It looks like a dog. Only hairless. And pale. And huge, bigger than a mastiff. The tongue, which hangs from its open mouth, is tar black. Beyond the animal lies a tangle of copper wire, three hubcaps, and some sheet metal.

Juniper says, "How'd you get that thing up in here by yourself?"

"Wasn't easy."

When Juniper says, "Help me get it inside," the other two men swing their faces to study him. He knows his fear shows in his expression, clench-jawed enough to crack a tooth.

"Inside? Inside the shelter?"

"Why would you want this thing inside?"

Anything Juniper says, they'll ask more questions, so he says nothing. He leans forward, the tailgate biting his belly, and grabs the animal by the ankle. Cold, clammy, the muscle rolling around beneath the skin, the sensation like handling an uncooked turkey. He leans back, and the leg unfolds, and he leans back farther, and the body drags a few inches. "Help me out, would you?"

Mitch takes the front two legs, Juniper the back, and when they heft the dog off the tailgate, they can't manage the sudden weight and it thuds to the ground. Maybe one hundred fifty pounds, maybe more.

"Can I help?" Sammy says.

"You just get the door." Juniper readjusts his grip and so does Mitch, and they hoist the dog up. Its head lolls as they stutter-step toward the shelter with the rain battering them.

Sammy holds the door, the wind gusting, bullying a mist inside. They scrape their shoes on the mat, but not enough, the floor still slick when they negotiate the dog past reception and into the lounge. "Where do you want it?" Mitch says through gritted teeth, and Juniper says, "Up on the coffee table."

Sammy squats and hooks a hand under the dog's belly, hoisting it up. A checkerboard knocks to the floor, the pieces clinking and rolling under the couches and chairs. The dog is too big, its long legs spidering over the edge of the table, but with some nudging, it balances there. All their eyes are fixed on the animal. The dog's snout is wrinkled, a nest for needled teeth. Its skin is bald except for a white bristling along the hump of its back.

"I suppose we ought to call somebody?" Sammy says.

Mitch lays a hand tentatively along the animal's ribs, which press through its pale skin, as if to ascertain no breath stirs inside it. Then he smells his palm and wrinkles his nose.

Sammy says, "Maybe we should call the police department?"

"I'm a veterinarian, and I've never seen an animal like this one."

"Maybe some local breeder is up to something funny?"

"I've never seen an animal like this. Not like this. Not that I've seen."

"What do you think, Mike?" Sammy only now notices that his friend has left them, gone to stand by the window, where he stares out at the rain, the streaming designs it makes on the glass.

Juniper takes his time responding. "Help me carry it to the walk-in freezer, and I'll take care of it from there." His voice matches the strained feeling inside him.

"The freezer?"

"What in the hell do you want to put it in the freezer for?"

He can see their reflections in the glass, the questioning glance they share with each other. He faces them, forces a smile. "The thing's dead, right? So there's no rush. I don't want anyone driving over here in this weather, and I don't want the thing stinking up the lounge either. First thing tomorrow, I'll make some calls. You leave it to me."

CHAPTER 4

Sometimes Lela feels like her life is a race that she will never win because it will never end. As soon as she fulfills one deadline, another three appear. There's no time to reflect, to feel any sense of accomplishment. She never looks back. Everything angles forward. She lives in the future tense.

It's not as bad as it sounds. No reflection means no regret. She lives without regret. How many people does she know—too many—who spend their days unloading their worries on social media or to their therapist, because they keep churning through their mistakes. I shouldn't have challenged my boss during the meeting, shouldn't have slept with that guy I met at the bar, shouldn't have given away my vinyl collection, shouldn't have ignored my mother when she kept calling out of loneliness. She doesn't need any lead-weighted anxiety to distract her, burden her, when she lives life at a sprint. The past is past. All that matters is how right now will lead to soon enough.

Work dominates. Work makes her happy. Her sister doesn't believe this. Her sister often says things like, "When someone's on their deathbed, they don't say, 'I wish I had worked more.' They don't reflect fondly upon all the time they spent at their desk. They remember birthday parties and camping trips and church suppers, time spent with family, friends."

Lela doesn't bother arguing with her. Her sister lives on another planet where logic doesn't apply and Jesus hands out candy canes and rides around on a hovercraft made of white clouds. But if she did respond, she would bring up their father, an architect who spent his career blueprinting and supervising the construction of office buildings and restaurants and churches and houses all over the metro. Whenever they were driving, Dad never took a direct route, always going out of his way to visit a building of his, and when they passed it, he would slow and point and say, "I made that." That's the kind of satisfaction she feels every time she picks up a paper and sees her byline. "I made that." As much as she hates fiddling around with computers, she knows that online archives have given her words even greater permanence. They'll outlive her. That's her idea of the afterlife, immortality. She prays at an altar built from twenty-six letters.

Because of this she neglects most everything else. Sometimes forgetting to shower, brush her teeth, eat. Never remembering birthdays or anniversaries. A man she recently dated called her self-absorbed, but that was absurd, since she spent no time acknowledging herself, all of her time chasing down the stories of others. She was absorbed, that's all, lost in the adrenaline-spiked labyrinth of headlines.

She feels bad for her niece, Hannah, who has grown up in a house full of crosses. As if the girl didn't have enough to feel lousy about—nearly blind and barely a teenager—her mother's idea of a fun birthday party is a piano recital followed by a Bible reading followed by off-brand Fudgsicles. It's amazing Hannah hasn't turned out to be a total freak. Instead the girl is the definition of poise and cool, never complaining, always ready to fire off something witty or interesting. About her mother she says, "I tried paying attention to you, but then I fell asleep for a thousand years." About an NPR report she says, "Successful sanctions should involve depriving people of cat videos." About a political debate she says, "I hope this guy wins a Grammy for best broken record." The kid cracks her up with her smartassness and startles Lela with her maturity. Sometimes she feels like they should swap roles, so that Hannah might be her cool aunt. Maybe Lela should spend less time at the keyboard, if only to spend more time with her.

Lela just got off the phone. A yellow legal tablet sits beside her, its pages ink-scratched with notes. First she talked to the race coordinator for the Willamette 10K. Then she set up an interview and photographer for tomorrow morning, when at the farmers' market she'll meet with a local artist who sells birdhouses made from crap she pulls out of Dumpsters. Lela will follow through on both stories—she always does—but god, they're so boring and pedestrian compared to the one she's stumbled upon. The Rue. Undertown. The construction site. The deformed skull. The men who pursued her. There's something here—some wonderful trouble—that thins the line between reporter and detective. That's her favorite kind of story, the kind that makes her feel like she's not simply educating or entertaining, but inciting change and potentially thrilling an audience. When you know someone's pissed about what you're writing—when you know you're potentially in danger—that's when you know you're doing your job.

Rain drums the hood of her Volvo. The skull sits on the dash. The designs on it draw her attention, and not for the first time she wonders what they mean. The recesses of the eyes and nose remain pocketed with shadows, no matter how frequent or bright the lightning. She has sprayed her hands twice with sanitizer, but they still feel filmed from her handling of the skull, somehow infected. So she wraps her spring roll in a napkin before dipping it into a plastic cup of peanut sauce. A take-out container of pad thai steams on the seat beside her.

She is parked two blocks from the Rue. She wants to return to the site—to investigate the tunnel, to go beneath. The storm must have sent everyone home, but then again, the crew might be working through the night to clear away any evidence. They probably think she's reported them. She ought to report them. She will report them. But not yet. Because once the police get involved, she will be interrogated and stuck at the station for hours she doesn't have. And, let's be honest, she hates working with others. In fact, she'd rather shove a screwdriver in her eye than work with others. This way, she hands over the answers to the PD at the same time she hands over the story to the paper, rather than waiting for some overworked, cigarette-stinking detective in an unmarked Dodge Shadow to slowly, stupidly work his case. It belongs to her. She's subordinate to no one.

She hasn't seen anything, no movement other than a rain-soaked concert announcement torn by the wind from the plywood barrier. And then a dog—that's what she thought it was anyway, though it appeared too big, too pale—trotting across the street in the near distance. She promised herself half an hour, so she'll wait another five minutes before pulling on a rain jacket and creeping close.

Then a police car careens around the corner and sends up a wave of water. No siren but its cherries are flashing. They color the rain and the puddles and the windows all around. It blasts past the Rue and stops at a building down the block. She sits up in her seat and wipes the condensation off the windshield. "What's this?" she says.

She can barely make out the two officers hurrying their way inside. They're soon joined by another squad car, and then another, and then another, all with their racks throwing light, spinning the street with color.

She spends so much time alone, with only her dog to keep her company, that she's gotten in the habit of talking to herself. "More trouble," she says. Because in journalism, only trouble is interesting.

✣

Her name was Carrie Wunderlich. She worked as a receptionist and massage therapist at a chiropractor. No way she could afford a place in the Pearl on that salary, so she must be a rich kid leeching off her parents. The cops know that and not much else. Pretty, nice, mostly kept to herself. That's what her neighbor said, the one who called 911 in a panic, freaked by the screaming heard through the wall. "The kind of screaming you hear in a horror movie," he says, "when someone's being torn to pieces by a monster."

An accurate description of what they find inside the one-bedroom apartment. The door is splintered in its hinges. The lights are on. The blood hasn't yet dried, still glistening, obscenely red. The forensics team wears booties over their shoes and the carpet sucks and gurgles beneath them. Their camera flashes match the lightning outside. The couch cushions are shredded from errant knife slashes, the foam soaked through. At first they aren't sure whether they are dealing with one body or two or three. Then someone starts counting limbs. Then someone finds the head of the boyfriend—that's what they're calling him anyway—in the fridge.

They can't understand how this much carnage amounted in so little time. And the security cameras tell them nothing, the system overloaded by the power surge, but soon they contact other businesses in the area and ask them to review their tapes. The storm had chased everyone inside, so it's no trouble spotting the heavyset figure who marched down the sidewalk, not hurried, but driven, staring straight ahead, oblivious to the rain. He had longish, almost orange hair parted in the middle. He wore sunglasses. No rain jacket. His white polo was splattered with blood so that it appeared almost tie-dyed. The only trouble is, they can't get a clear shot of his face, every image blurred, as though he were half-erased.

Flies buzz the air. Dozens of black fat-bodied flies. Too many for this season, too many for a modern apartment with its windows fastened shut. The flies taste the gore and batter themselves against the windows and orbit the lights. The detectives swat at them and breathe through their mouths and say, "Where in the hell did they come from?"

Everyone stares at the framed print hanging over the gas fireplace. Van Gogh's *Sunflowers.* Stamped in the center of it, the bloody print of a hand—a red right hand—with thick and thin lines oozing from its bottom.

Lela doesn't see any of this, not firsthand, but a patrol officer fills her in after she slips him a twenty and she eavesdrops on the tenants clustered nervously in the foyer. The red right hand is what bothers her most of all, though at first she isn't sure why. The red right hand, the red right hand, like some face in a movie she recognizes but can't place, making her chew on her pen and wonder, *Where else have I seen you before?*

Her pen cracks beneath her teeth. And just like that, she's broken through and found the memory she's looking for. When she visited Tusk's apartment, so many years ago, to write the retrospective on Portland's most notorious serial killer, the walls and ceiling and even the floors were busy with designs, some chalked and some painted. Many were of a red right hand.

The same red right hand—she now recalls—that marked the plywood wall surrounding the construction site. She hadn't paid much attention to it at the time, but it's clung to her like the afterimage of a slap.

Then she spots someone outside. Across the street. Watching.

Lump, the street preacher. He's cloaked with garbage bags, so that he appears like part of the night, but she's certain it's him. The rain has paused, but lightning still webs the sky. He's pacing and the storm's strobe-light effect makes him appear to leap from one part of the sidewalk to another.

She knows how people treat Lump. As if he weren't there. She's seen them—in Pioneer Courthouse Square and along the Willamette River—staring at their phones or turning their heads away as if they'd prefer to forget his existence altogether. But he was there. Watching the city. Watching them all. He roams Portland day and night and knows it better than any beat cop or security camera.

She pushes through the entry, into the cool night, arrowing toward him. At that moment a crow flutters down from some high sill of the building and lands on his shoulder. She can hear it *kak-kak-kak*ing from across the street. He pets its feathers and whispers to it.

"Hey!" she says, and starts across the road. "Lump! Can I buy you a coffee? Can we talk?" She sees him there one moment, frozen in a blue blast of lightning, but when darkness comes again, he has rushed into the shadows, merging with the night.

CHAPTER 5

TWENTY YEARS AT The Weary Traveler have taught Mike Juniper patience. He has encouraged people to take their meds, to sit down with counselors, to change and wash their clothes, to submit to delousing. He has talked a woman out of stabbing her ex-boyfriend with a pair of garden shears, and he has talked a man out of leaping off a ledge. Juniper's voice is calm, his words slowly uttered, as gentle and convincing as his hands, which take his clients by the elbow, the shoulder, leading them in what he hopes is the right direction.

But tonight his patience is thin. Old men tend to take their time—reading the newspaper, puttering along country highways, gathering change from their pocket at the cash register—but Sammy and Mitch are more than old. On any evening, he'd need to encourage them upstairs, to brush their teeth and find their bunks and call it quits, but tonight they're confused and they're scared and they're not able to walk more than a few steps before turning back the way they came. They keep asking questions. What hideous breed of dog was that thing? Shouldn't they call the cops or animal control? Why deposit the dog in the freezer among the pork chops and chicken breasts and ice cream?

That's what they're calling it. A dog. But Juniper knows better. It's not a dog. It's a hound.

He hurries them along as best he can, monitoring them in the bathroom, trying to shush them in the halls, promising to talk again first thing in the morning. And then, at last, he is alone. People think he's crazy to run The Weary Traveler without a twenty-four-hour staff. He hires out janitorial and he brings in cooks and counselors during the day, but otherwise he's on his own. He has to be—for moments like this.

He clenches his jaw until his teeth ache. Paces an uncertain circle in the lounge. Off one of the tables he picks up a chess piece—a black knight—and fidgets with it absently, twirling it, tossing it up and down to catch, squeezing it so tightly it bites his palm.

Inside the shelter everything is dark except for the glow of the cross hanging above the reception desk. Outside the rain slows to a drizzle and then surges again. Lightning strikes nearby and for an instant the night vanishes, replaced by a blue-white ghostland diamonded with a million raindrops that appear frozen in the air.

The security, lighting, and temperature at The Weary Traveler are controlled by a software system linked to Juniper's smartphone and the tablet mounted near the entry. At nine o'clock the front door locks, the bolt sliding into place with a *shunk* he can hear from the lounge. This is followed by a whirring gust as the heater ramps up, nudging the temperature to seventy degrees.

The window darkens with the shape of a hooded figure walking past. He turns into the alcove out front and tests the door with a hard rattle. At first Juniper believes this to be one more client—someone hoping to escape the storm—but then the crow squawks and clacks the glass impatiently with its beak.

Juniper goes to the door and taps the tablet mounted there. The screen lights up and he punches in his security code and opens the Nest app and overrides the locks. Lump slumps inside. Water glistens and dribbles from the folds of his makeshift poncho, a collection of many torn garbage bags. A black cowl of plastic surrounds his face, but he pulls it back now. His face appears like something that grew out of a rotten log. Gray and bumpy, almost fungal. But Juniper doesn't turn away.

Instead he leans in. And listens to what Lump has to tell him. While he speaks, the crow takes a short flight around the room before returning to its master. It fluffs its feathers, casting off the raindrops that jewel them.

"You're sure?" Juniper says. "A red right hand?"

Lump nods and draws up his hood. "I thought you should know," he says before ripping open the door and heading once more into the night. "Demons walk among us."

✣

Then the power goes out for the second time that night. The lightning recedes at the same time the lights sputter off, on, ebbing to a brownish dusk, then full dark. The ceiling fan in the lounge slows its rotation. The light of the blue cross fades. The heater gives a dying gasp. The whole building seems to momentarily shrink.

He waits for everything to buzz back to life, and when that doesn't happen, he snaps on a Maglite fetched from the reception desk. He has a generator out back, but that can wait. He shouldn't put this off any longer. He goes first to the kitchen, past the big-basined sink, the industrial-sized oven, to the open stretch of counter where he keeps the knives. They dangle from a magnetized strip screwed into the wall. He pulls down the biggest one, a butcher knife, with a *snick*. Iron or silver would be better, but steel will have to do.

His fingers gnarl around it. His hands are big, meaty, but blood can slip the strongest grip. He opens the supply cabinet and balances the Maglite on a shelf and pulls down a roll of duct tape and picks at it, peeling away a strip to stick to the knife's hilt. He then wraps his hand several times over, until it is silver-mittened. He bites the tape, tears it off the roll, pats it in place. The blade points at the floor, his arm a scythe. He gashes the air experimentally. Good enough.

Without the heater whirring and the fridge droning, everything seems terribly quiet. Except for the throb and lap of the rain. The dark is broken by the occasional lightning flash, and the silence punctuated by the mutter of thunder. His shoes, still wet from his time outside, squeak as he makes his way toward the walk-in freezer at the far end of the kitchen.

He reaches for the handle, then stops his hand. He leans his head against the door, mashing his cheek up against the stainless steel. It's cold, echoey, like an arctic seashell. Maybe he hears something, or maybe not. The night plays tricks on your senses. He changes his grip on the Maglite, so that it will double as a club, then takes a deep breath.

The Maglite concentrates into an orange eye when he reaches again for the handle—and then he springs the latch and pulls back the door, and the light opens up into a yellow funnel that illuminates the floor of the freezer.

Empty. Except for a tub of ice cream fallen off a shelf. The warm air crashes up against the cold and steam swirls, obscuring the dark even further. He steps forward, raising the hand that grips the knife. In the back corner, beyond a crate, two eyes catch the light and spark like candle flames.

He might cry out, but the sound is lost against the snarl of the hound. The steam whirls when it leaps, its body missiling through the air. It knocks its paws into his chest. He falls flat on his back, unaware of any distance traveled. One instant his breastbone is battered, the next moment his back slams the floor. The Maglite goes clattering off, wheeling the air with shadows.

He holds up his free hand just in time to brace its neck. He cannot see much of anything. Just flashes of teeth, tongue, eyes, paws. In its breath he smells death. The hot, paralyzing reek of carrion. Its jaws clack together, gnashing the air, then close around his arm, shaking it, piercing and tearing the flesh.

Lightning might as well have struck him. The interface between his brain and his body feels sputtery as though his nerves have grown frayed. The past few seconds he has been demanding his right arm into action—to slash, damn it, *stab*—but only now does it respond, arcing through the air, plunging into the hound's neck, and then again, clacking against its ribs, and then again again again, until at last the thing goes still. It collapses its weight onto him, soaking him with blood he knows runs black.

He rolls the hound off. The knife scrapes the floor when he gets on his hands and knees. He tries to settle his pulse. He reaches for the counter. He pulls himself into a crouch. Then a standing position.

The pain hasn't arrived yet, but he knows his arm is in bad shape, in need of stitches, maybe even a cast. He retrieves the Maglite. He runs some cold water over the wound while he chews away the tape binding his hand and frees the knife. Then he burrows around for the vodka he keeps at the rear of the spice cabinet. He splashes the wound before wrapping it in a flour-sack cloth and then with a quarter roll of cellophane.

"Hello?"

He goes still. It must be one of his clients, maybe drawn downstairs by the disturbance. Again—from the hallway, closer now—"Hello?" This time he registers the voice as a woman's. Plenty of women stay regularly at the shelter—Meg, Hettie, Jan, among others—but none tonight.

That's when he remembers the front door. When he overrode the locks and allowed Lump inside, he never reset security. His eyes jog between the dead hound, bleeding out a black puddle, and the door that leads to the hallway.

"Just a minute," he says, trying to keep his voice calm. "Just stay where you are, please. I'll be right there."

Whoever she is, she doesn't listen. She steps into the kitchen just as he swings the Maglite. The yellow beam cuts the dark and strikes her face, and she holds up a hand and squints her eyes. "Are you here for a bed? I normally don't check anyone in after nine." He keeps the light steadily trained on her as he approaches, trying to blind her, blocking her view of the hound with his body.

She retreats into the hallway—trying to evade the light or keep some distance between them—and only then does he drop the shine from her face. She blinks, hard, as though she has sand in her eyes. "I'm not looking for a bed."

"Clothes? Food? A shower? What?" His voice comes out more severely than he intended.

"Information," she says.

It's only then that he really sees her. Auburn hair pulled back in a braid. Mossy-green eyes. Nose dusted with freckles. A North Face shell and Keen hiking shoes. A giant canvas purse that bulges at her side. She looks like she should be leading nature walks at Multnomah Falls, not pushing her way into a shelter late at night. "No one came when I knocked."

"But you decided you were welcome anyway?"

She shrugs. No apology.

"It's fine. You startled me—that's all." He starts toward the lounge and hopes she'll follow.

She does. Her voice trails close behind him. "I'm pretty sure that's a health code violation."

He turns on her and she nearly runs into him. How much did she see? And what kind of excuse can there possibly be for a hairless hound—the size of a pony—stabbed to death on a kitchen floor?

She trades her purse from one shoulder to the other. "Your arm. It looks like it got carved up for a snack." Her eyes stare directly into his. She leans in and he can't help but feel shoved around by her intensity. "What happened?"

"Oh, this." He raises his arm, and it hangs in the air between them. "It's nothing." The blood has spotted through the makeshift tourniquet. It throbs in time with his pulse.

"But what happened?"

He starts once more for the lounge. It's easier to lie with his back to her. "There are no pets allowed here, but sometimes someone will try to sneak one in. A dog took a bite out of me. I'm glad no one else got hurt."

"Where's the dog?"

"I'm sorry?"

"You said you got bit by a dog—and that wound is fresh—so where's the dog?"

His eyes jog back toward the kitchen, and he motions to one of the chairs before plopping onto the couch. The springs shriek beneath his weight. He balances the Maglite on an end table as if it were a lamp. "I'm sorry—who are you? What are you doing here?"

She doesn't take a seat but stands over him. She clutches the purse as though worried he might snatch it. "We've met before," she says. "I interviewed you two years ago. An article about how the recession surged the homeless population."

It takes him a moment. The darkness of the room—the pain in his arm—the questions whirling through his head. She's a reporter. A reporter at *The Oregonian*. She stopped by unannounced and got annoyed when he wouldn't pose for a photo. When she asked him, "Why not? Everybody likes to get their picture in the paper," he had to lie to her then, too. The truth is, he couldn't risk being recognized, no matter how many years had passed.

"Right," he says. "You. That explains it."

"Explains what?"

"The way you barge in here and assault me with all these questions."

She doesn't flinch. If anything a smile bends the corners of her mouth.

She's silent. She's trying to get him to say something. Another reporter trick. Hit your subject with a thousand questions or shut up and make them uncomfortable enough to answer. "Are you here for another story?" he says. "What do you want from me?"

She says she's looking for someone. A homeless man. The street preacher most everyone refers to as Lump. She thinks he might know something about a story she's chasing. She wants to ask him a few questions. "I tried following him earlier. I was in my car; he was on foot. Lost him down an alley." She drove around another fifteen minutes before spotting something in her rearview—a black figure darting away from the shelter. "Was it him? Was he here? What did you talk about?"

Juniper wishes he could turn his back to her again. Her eyes feel like they're inside him. "Haven't seen him," he says.

"Did he tell you about the murder?"

Now he leans forward. "You think Lump killed someone?"

"No. I don't think Lump killed anyone. But I think he might have some information. And he was certainly in a rush to share it with you."

"You're wrong. He wasn't here." Juniper checks his arm again—the pain now jolting, electrical. "Afraid I can't help you."

She nods longer than she needs to. "I see," she says.

"You see what?"

"I see." She reaches down and picks up a black feather from the floor. She strokes the length of it. "When I say the following, does it trigger anything for you? The Rue building, Jeremy Tusk, Carrie

Wunderlich. Anything? Even the slightest connection or recollection?"

She'll know he's lying, but he might as well keep it up. "No. Nothing."

Her unblinking stare continues. Accompanied by another one of those deliberate silences meant to make him uncomfortable. It's working. But he holds her eyes and doesn't say anything more.

She snatches the Maglite off the table and runs. For the kitchen. Her shoes clopping the linoleum. The beam rising and falling with every arm swing. He's too slow to catch her, though he tries. When he catches up to her in the kitchen, she has the light trained on the hound. Or what used to be the hound, now a black pile of ash.

CHAPTER 6

ASK SOMEONE IN PORTLAND where the Hadal District is, they'll look at you funny, say they don't know. Every city has a place like this. A place unmapped. A place the GPS goes dark. A place people don't go, except by accident, and then they'll drive fast to escape it.

On the east side of the Willamette River, among the graffiti-riddled warehouses and bridge stanchions, there are unlit streets that sparkle with broken glass, that flutter and scuttle with sun-blanched newspapers and plastic bags like desiccated jellyfish. There are rusted-out shopping carts, boarded-up windows, and the occasional figure cutting in and out of the shadows.

Puddles reach across the roads, retreating slowly into drains clogged with trash. Juniper splashes through one now. He wears a black ball cap and a black shell with the collar turned up. He's a big enough man that when he walks the streets, no one bothers him, though he hears voices in doorways whispering, sees the silver flash of a knife blade. The power zaps back on across Portland—and the sudden glow is like the blue hint of dawn—but all the streetlamps in the Hadal remain black, knocked out by bullets or bricks.

He turns down an alley so dark the shadows feel palpable, like something cool that licks and caresses. A pile of garbage bags oozes something foul. A rat scuttles away from his tromping approach. A distant yowling makes him go still—listening—until he is satisfied it is a dog he hears, not a hound.

He turns the corner and finds what he's looking for. In between a moneylender and a pawnshop sits a squat brick building with moss springing from the mortar joints. BLOOD BANK, the sign reads in red lettering. "O Negative, Be Positive," "U Give Blood, We Give $."

You let them prick you with a needle and fill a pint bag, you get fifty bucks. Officially, you can't do it unless you test clean, unless you're eighteen, unless you show your license, your social security card, your proof of address. Unofficially, as long as your blood isn't diseased, you're welcome. This isn't exactly the Red Cross.

A woman walks out the door. The side of her head is buzzed and tattoos reach down her legs in the design of fishnet stockings. Her arm is bandaged at the elbow. She goes to the bodega on the corner. It sells everything from ice cream to coffee to booze, pretzels, candy, bananas, decorative bongs, Lotto scratch tickets, T-shirts silk-screened with wolves and marijuana leaves. The shelves behind the register are stacked with cigarettes as brightly and neatly arranged as crayons. Juniper knows how it works. You knock on the counter—two slow raps followed by a fast one—and the clerk will know what you're there for. Skulls. He'll push you an Altoids tin crammed with little white pills blackened at their center. They're supposed to make every nerve in your body feel like it's having a mellow orgasm that lasts twenty-four hours.

The bodega and Blood Bank are owned by the same person. That's who Juniper is here to see. He pushes into the brightly lit space. The walls are decorated with graffiti art that shows monsters eating each other. The waiting area is empty except for an old man snoring in a corner chair. A flat-screen TV mounted on the wall plays music videos with the sound off. A clerk stands behind the counter, smiling vaguely. He is as hairless as a mannequin. No eyebrows even. His cheeks are pierced on either side so that you can see his molars. A sketchbook lies open before him, and he has scrawled in it, with a black pen, a portrait of himself. "Have you given to us before, or are you a first-time donor? Can I get you a form?"

"I need to talk to Sarin."

The man's teeth are too long and black-rooted. "I'm afraid I don't know who you mean."

Juniper knows how he looks. Old and oversize and squarely dressed, so that people guess him a preacher or a cop. In a way he supposes he's both. "I'm not police, if that's what you're wondering."

The receptionist cocks his head. Juniper thinks he sees a flutter of movement in the corner of his eye, like a worm peeking out and then retreating. "Then, what are you?"

Juniper almost says, *Friend, I'm a friend,* but catches himself. He isn't sure what to call Sarin. "We go way back."

"If I knew a woman by the name of Sarin, I would not presume her to be here, in a place like this, on a night like this."

Two doors frame either side of the desk. The left hallway leads to a large room in which a nurse moves on slippered feet from padded table to padded table, tapping veins, checking bags, asking donors to squeeze a racquetball to get the blood flowing and telling them they're welcome to treat themselves to the complimentary apple juice and cookies. The right hallway leads to the refrigerators stacked with blood bags, an accountant's office with a walk-in safe, and finally, at the end of the hall, a black door. Both entries are controlled by wireless locks and keyless remotes.

"It's urgent."

"She's not here."

"Yes, she is. I need to talk to her. It's an emergency."

The holes in the receptionist's cheeks bunch up, each one toothy, his grin a grin of many mouths. "Don't you think you're a little out of your element?"

"I'm only telling you as a courtesy. You can ignore me or you can warn her. Either way, I'm going through that door."

The man's hands are pale, the fingers like knitting needles, and they slip off the counter, reaching somewhere below, likely to a mounted spring holster.

Juniper throws his body across the desk—quick for a big man—and with both hands he takes hold of the receptionist by the head. He then slams his face down onto the sketchpad—once, twice, three times—until he goes limp and slumps to the floor. A splat of blood brightens the nose of his self-portrait. "Sorry," Juniper says. "No time to argue."

The old man in the corner keeps snoring. Juniper leans over the desk and spots the remote switches. He flips them both, and the doors give a metallic shout as they come unlocked. He yanks the right one open and heads down the hallway to its end.

Here a black door awaits. The knob of it is a brass knob shaped like a skull. He hesitates only a second before twisting it.

✣

She sits in the center of the room. The adjustable chair—like something out of a dentist's office—is upholstered in cracked black leather that matches the color of her tank top and pants and motorcycle boots. At first glance, she appears fifty, maybe sixty—her skin creased and beginning to droop, her hair white except for a stripe of black that runs back from her temple—but she is older by decades. Her voice is rough and deep-throated, the sound smoke should make rising from a chimney. "What's it been? A year?"

"Something like that."

"I lose track of time."

"Good to see you."

"I'd offer to give you a hug, but I'm caught up in something." She lifts her arms to indicate the IV lines, all bright with blood, at least ten of them. The pint bags dangle from hooks overhead, arranged in the shape of a chandelier, feeding into her wrists, her elbows, her neck, her back. That's why she looks sixty instead of ninety or a hundred or a hundred and ten, whatever her actual age is. The constant transfusions keep her young. She says it's not because she's afraid of dying. It's that she's sick to death of it. She likes this life, she says. She doesn't want another one. And she's had many.

"Something's happened," he says. "I need your help."

"Been a while since something happened. Is it wrong for me to feel excited?"

There comes a noise from the hallway, a stumbling and gasping, and a moment later the receptionist staggers into the room. He holds a Glock out before him. "I'm sorry," he says. "I'm so sorry. I tried to stop him." He sniffs his bloodied nose.

"It's all right," Sarin says, and her eyes settle on Juniper. "The big man and I go way back."

CHAPTER 7

JUNIPER IS AN UGLY MAN—he knows this—with the close-together eyes and craggy brow and weak chin that bring to mind a 50,000-year-old cave dweller. But as a child, in Texas, before his features hardened and thickened, there was something impish about his appearance that might have contributed to his fame.

Heavenly Visitor. That was the name of the book, based on his experiences, published when he was six. He was swimming in a lake, wearing his snorkel and fins, pushing through a thick section of lily pads with the hope of scaring up turtles, when a canoe struck the back of his head and knocked him out. No one realized what had happened for several minutes, his body face-down and floating among the plants. By the time they pulled him out, he had no pulse and his body had purpled along the edges. His father pumped his chest and blew breath back into his lungs—until at last he rolled over and gurgled up a puddle of lake water.

He died. For over ten minutes. And then he came back. That's what they told him when he woke several hours later at St. Hannah's, in the children's ward, in a hospital bed hooked up to an IV. They said he was a miracle. They said he was God's precious little angel. And he believed it. Because of the light. It hadn't been the kind that waited at the end of the tunnel. It had surrounded him, poured through him, a sun-currented ocean. It felt like the beginning of good, as when his mother started his bath or opened the oven to pull out cookies or punched the power on the television to tune in to his favorite program.

He had always been an incorrigible liar. He saw a lion in the woods. He found a twenty-dollar bill on the sidewalk, no, not in his mother's purse. He didn't know who punctured the couch cushion either. A black-haired bully named Marco punched him in the nose, and just because the principal claimed no one named Marco went to his school didn't mean it wasn't true.

So when his parents seemed keenly interested in this light—calling it the light of heaven—he kept going. He gave them what they wanted to hear. Yes, that's right, he had hovered over the lake and watched his father pump his chest, and then—uh-huh, definitely—there had been angels, one who appeared beside him and took his hand and told him not to be afraid.

He goes by Mike these days, but back then he was Timmy. Timmy Milton. And Timmy Milton's words came tentatively at first. The concussion made his head hurt and his lungs felt bruised, but the way his parents and the nurses gathered around his hospital bed roused him. They pressed him gently, but he could tell how excited they were, their eyes brightening, their breath held.

Every Sunday they attended the massive Cornerstone church complex off the freeway, and he now shared the same version of heaven the Cornerstone minister had shared in his sermons, along with a few improvements. Heaven was everything they hoped for, a city in the clouds where a warm breeze blew, and he had never felt so safe and happy in all his life. Mr. Meow was there. So was Pop-Pop—but he wasn't old and crooked in his wheelchair anymore. He was strong and wearing a white uniform with stripes on it. When his parents exclaimed, "His naval uniform, it must be true, how would Timmy know that otherwise!" Juniper did not remind them of the black-and-white photo albums his father kept in his office closet. And then he mentioned the baby and they went quiet. "Was it a baby girl?" his mother asked, and he said yes because he could tell by her tone that he ought to. She seemed happy, Juniper said, but he never learned her name—and his mother began to cry and said, "That's because we never had the chance to give her one."

They cried and hugged him and called him a dear, dear, special, God-blessed boy.

The Cornerstone minister declared little Timmy a miracle, a messenger of God, and by the time he left the hospital, a crowd of reporters from the local and national news had gathered. There was no going back on it now. None of it was true—nothing except for the light, a sense of goodness and energy that lingered with him—but the more Juniper told the story, the more true it seemed. Everyone *wanted* it to be true, and he didn't want to disappoint them.

They asked him about the angels, and he said they looked like beautiful people, except when they were moving, and then they looked like flashes of light. They asked him about Jesus, and he told them about the bearded man on the white horse that made no noise when it galloped. Jesus smiled down at Juniper in a way that made him feel fizzy, like when you sip a soda, and told him he had to go back home to see his parents, who loved him very much, and do a job. A very important job.

"What's that? What job did Jesus Christ tell you to do?"

"Tell everyone about heaven," he said. "Share the good news."

The interviews led to the book, *Heavenly Visitor,* penned by his parents. And the book led to the national lecture circuit. He had an agent and manager and lawyer who referred to him sometimes as a brand. His mother homeschooled him as they traveled from parish to parish, sometimes with six hundred people or more in the audience. He learned how to attach his own lapel mic and apply his own foundation before he stepped out under the bright lights. He learned not just to tell his story, but to sermonize. He let people touch him, and he would touch them back, cupping a cheek, and they would close their eyes and smile as if the Holy Spirit coursed through him.

And maybe it wasn't the Holy Spirit, but something lingered in him, as if he were a man struck by lightning who retained some spark in his fingertips. He saw things sometimes. A gray shawl shimmering around an old woman in a wheelchair—and an orange glow crackling around a baby at the baptismal font. Shadows would gather where none should be. A whisper or a scream would turn his head and reveal nothing. He sometimes dreamed things before they happened. He worried more than once that he might be crazy, but when every day you're told you're special, a messenger of light, it's a challenge not to believe it.

This continued until he was twenty. His family then lived in a gated community in Burbank. They had a pool and hot tub, granite and stainless steel everything, stucco walls and a Mexican tile roof, topiaries in the front yard, a casita in the back, Cadillacs in the garage.

Then something happened. He began to notice a face in the crowd. The same face. Whether Juniper was in Tucson or Buffalo or Oklahoma City. Man or woman, Juniper could not tell, in a dress or in a suit, the fabric always funereal. He, she, *it* had night-black hair that reached past the shoulders. And eyes of the same color, glistening like hundred-year-old eggs. Its face was long and pale and bony and bent to one side. The thing. That was how he began to think of it. He asked others about it—his manager, the stage crew, pastors—but no one seemed to know what he was talking about. "Where?" they would say, and Juniper would no longer be able to locate the pale, bent face.

One time, when everyone brought their hands together to pray, the thing lifted its cupped hands and a big black fly fluttered free of them and circled the stage and finally alighted on Juniper's sleeve, and he crushed it and the black guts burned his wrist and stained the shirt so that he had to throw it away in a hotel garbage can.

And then he woke one night, in a Best Western in Tacoma, to a shadow darker than the rest. The thing stood at the foot of his bed. A streetlight burned through the shades and lit its bent face. Beside it crouched a hound. It yawned widely and slurped its muzzle with a black tongue. Juniper heard a humming, and it took him a moment to recognize the black flies, their bodies battering the walls and ceiling.

Juniper felt as well as heard its words, like a cold wind that carried twigs and gravel in its currents. "Normally I don't pay any attention to the pulpit." There was such depth to the voice, a throbbing bass that went beyond maleness and into the elemental. "But you make so much noise, little Timmy. You have so much reach, so much impact, that you're difficult to ignore. You burn with too much light."

Juniper tried to retreat, crabbing back against the headboard. He almost cried out for help, but his throat felt strangled of air, thick with a brinish liquid that he knew was lake water. He gagged and coughed up onto the pillow a splatter of duckweed, a black water beetle that scrabbled off under the covers.

"You should have died, little Timmy. You should have stayed wherever it is you went."

Juniper almost said he came back for a reason—he had a purpose, a job to do here on earth—but the thing seemed to anticipate this and made a dismissive motion with its long hand and said, "You're furthering the cause of the light. It's a twisted, fib-soaked, money-grubbing version of it, but still. The time has come for silence." The thing cocked its head in debate. "But I think I'll make you suffer first. Then you can share some of the pain and hopelessness with all those who are so eager to listen to you."

The hound whined and the thing petted it.

Finally Juniper found his voice. "Who are you?"

A siren called in the distance, maybe an ambulance or maybe a police car, and the thing turned its head curiously toward the window before speaking. "In your sermons—which I must say are quite good, you're an excellent performer—you're always talking about the light. You can probably guess what that makes me . . ."

"The dark?" It felt at once silly and terrifying to say.

The thing shrugged. "Part of it at least. One shadow of many. There is no singular Dark. Just as there is no Vulture. There is much, there are many, always circling, feeding on carrion." When the thing moved toward him, reaching for him, the tendons of its arms creaked like old ropes.

✣

He believed it a dream when he woke in the morning to his phone ringing. A terrible dream. He took the call—fielding an invitation to a weeklong residency at a Houston megachurch—and put it on speaker and stumbled to the bathroom to lift the seat and drop his boxers. The piss came in a white stream that soon went orange and pungent before sputtering to a stop. "Can't you talk them up a bit?" he asked his agent. "Their coffers are deep, and I bet we could get another ten thou without too much trouble."

An unbearable pressure followed, and he gritted his teeth and tried to empty himself further. He dropped to the floor. A sudden sweat made his skin slick. He noticed then the flies crawling across the ceiling and the bruise on his belly in the shape of a long-fingered hand. He tried to massage the pain, to rough away whatever blockage stopped him up, but that only made it worse. There was a feeling like a pulse, but out of rhythm with his heart. And then something gave, and when he pissed, he pissed blood. From the other room came his agent's voice: "Tim? Tim, are you okay?"

He wasn't. The MRI revealed the tumor. It looked like a giant piece of chewed-up gum stuck among his organs. They cut out what they could, but the cancer had metastasized, spread throughout his body. He could choose chemo and radiation, or he could choose nothing. He chose nothing after hearing his odds of survival. He'd take quality of life over quantity. A few good months. That's what he had to look forward to. He still didn't know if the thing in the hotel room was real, if it had done this to him, or if he had once more built a fantasy to make sense of his nearness to death.

He told his parents about the cancer and they hugged him and wept with him, but it wasn't thirty minutes later that they brought up his estate, and signing it over to them. And then they proposed a platform for his death. *Letters to Heaven*—that's what they'd call it. There would be a book, maybe a television special. They'd announce it on the *Hour of Power* at the Crystal Cathedral. For a fee, Juniper would deliver messages directly to loved ones, or Jesus, or even God directly. What did he think? "We can make your death great," his father said.

He could barely muster the request to be alone. He felt suddenly vacant, as if everything that had once filled his life had spiraled down a drain. He stopped preaching. He refused to attend Sunday service. He unplugged every phone in his house. He stopped checking his email and wouldn't answer the door.

He closed down his investment accounts, ignoring the penalties and fees. It didn't feel like his money. It felt stolen. Maybe he had done some good—giving people hope—but it was hope founded on a lie. He started writing checks. And every check he wrote—to charities, to libraries, to YMCAs and domestic abuse shelters and literacy programs, none to churches—made him feel unburdened, truer.

His last three hundred thousand he cashed out. He planned to drive up the coast and hand out stacks of bills at diners, rest stops, beaches, Walmart parking lots. He liked the idea of making a palpable difference. Here you go, he'd say, buy yourself a meal, buy some diapers for your kid, put it toward rent, whatever. He just wanted to walk away from the transaction knowing he had earned nothing but a smile in return. That felt like a more honest currency of light than any he had dealt before.

He bought a used Buick and grew out his beard. He toyed with different names when checking in at dive motels, and finally settled on one. Mike for his middle name and Juniper for the trees that blurred past his window as he drove north. Some of them were thousands of years old, he knew, and they appeared unkillable but tormented by their long life, twisted and gray.

To avoid an investigation, he left a suicide note that said they would never find the body. There was a brief media frenzy, but he was by all accounts dead when a few weeks later he walked along the Willamette River in Portland, feeding seagulls torn-up pieces of bread and handing out hundred-dollar bills to the bench-sleepers and trash-can-pillagers. "You look like you could use a little help," he would say, and more than one person said in response, "So do you, buddy."

There was blood in his cough and his urine. Every few steps, he had to pause and close his eyes to make the world stop quavering. His skin was bruised and sunken in some places, red and swollen in others. He felt like he was growing inside, shrinking outside.

He wasn't walking anywhere in particular, just following a trail of litter and syringes and shopping carts stacked high with cans. He spotted a group of teens wearing ratty hoodies and stained jeans. They catcalled, practiced skateboard tricks, handed out the *Street Roots* newspaper, bummed for change.

Juniper dropped a hundred-dollar bill in a ball cap, stuffed another in an outstretched hand, and it didn't take long for the teens to close around him, everyone snatching the bills he offered and saying, "Thanks!" and "God bless!" and "You're a good man." He didn't smile. He let them take it all, every last bill, hurling the last of it in the air as though it was confetti. He said, "That's it, that's all I've got on me!" and sank to the ground and remained there long after they departed and the sun began to sink and the shadows thickened. He didn't feel any sort of peace, only a crushing exhaustion, like the weight of night.

He vaguely heard the boots clomping toward him and vaguely felt the toe nudge his shoulder. His eyes were crusted over, and it took some effort to open them. A face swung into view—a woman with white hair and a black stripe running through it. Black jeans, motorcycle boots. Sarin, though he didn't know her name then. She smoked a cigarette, and when she spoke, it ashed on him. "You're the one giving away money?"

"I was."

"I all of a sudden get twenty, thirty customers—throwing down hundreds, asking me for hits—so I naturally get curious." She paced a circle around him, studying him from different angles. "You're one of those saintly do-gooders, then? Give away all your money before you croak?"

He tried to speak, but his lungs felt deflated, and he coughed and turned on his side. He was on a ledge before a black metal fence that overlooked the wide gray stripe of the Willamette.

She got in the way of the view, crouching before him. She looked old enough to be his mother, but acted twice as vital as he was. The tip of the cigarette burned bright when she sucked on it. "You're on the spectrum, I see," she said.

"I'm what?"

"You're like me. You've got a little light in you."

He didn't know how to respond to this. His life felt so utterly absent of light that he had stopped believing in any of it.

"Somebody put a mark on you," she said, her words made of smoke. "What did you do to piss them off? Or were they just in a bad mood? Whoever they were, they obviously wanted you to suffer." She dropped the spent cigarette—nothing but filter—and crushed out the ember. "Fucking demons."

Juniper had put the man—the black thing in the hotel room—out of his mind. He was nothing more than a nightmare. Or a hallucination from the cancer fingering into his brain. But her words recalled the vision of him now. His voice like many deep whispers sewn together. His tendons creaking when he moved like the floorboards of a rotten house.

"Jesus. I can smell it on you even. You stink, you know. Like sulfur." She laid her hand across his cheek, then ran it down his neck, his chest, flattening her palm over his heart. "Lucky for you I've always been a sucker for charity cases."

The warmth of her hand changed over to a searing heat, focused through her fingers.

When he said, "What are you—?" she said, "Shh."

There was a throbbing sensation. At first it felt like a second heartbeat. Then it grew more intense, like a mouth sucking greedily. The edges of his vision blackened and fluttered, as if a bird were perched on his head and beating its wings. Gravity seemed to shift, the world flipped over, as if she were carrying his weight, everything balanced, centered around that hand of hers.

And then she was pulling something away from him, something that didn't want to leave. It looked like a kind of octopus, but black with too many tendrils dangling from it, many still clinging to him until she yanked it fully away. She lobbed it then—through the air, off the ledge. Together they watched it tumble through the air before splattering against some rocks and oozing into the river. A few seconds later, several fish went belly-up and pinwheeled away in the current.

"All right," she said, and wiped her hand off on her thigh. "There's my good deed for the year. You owe me some whiskey, I'd say. A swimming pool full of it."

She left him there, at the edge of the river. Eventually he rose to his knees and wept, a position of prayer, but he did not thank God. He thanked her, whoever she was, whatever she was. He thanked the light.

He had been given another chance, and this time he wasn't going to waste it on himself. Stashed in the trunk of the Buick, he still had a duffel bag of cash, more than a hundred large—and he pumped it all into opening The Weary Traveler. He would earn his oxygen by helping others.

Over the next year, he asked around about the woman. No one seemed to know who she was. He thought he would never see her again, but then one day, there she was, pushing her way inside the shelter, a lit cigarette pinched between her lips. "There you are," she said, and blew smoke and walked through the cloud of it. Her eyes tracked his body, which had filled out again, slabbed with muscle and sheathed with a healthy layer of fat. "You look good. Healthy anyway. Kind of like a grizzly bear in jeans."

"I keep thinking I dreamed you, but here you are."

"Here I am." Her lipstick was a purplish shade of red that clung to her cigarette. "How about that whiskey you owe me?"

That was her standard. She would appear unannounced—sitting on a stoop or leaning against the hood of his car—and ask for something. The favors started small. Pick up a shipment at the docks in Seattle. Stash these duffel bags in your basement, she would say, and don't even think about opening them. "I know I'm not a saint," she said, "but I'm no devil either." The drugs she sold—the pills called Skulls—they were 100 percent organic, non-addictive, A-grade happiness. Some blend of dopamine, adrenaline, and raw sugar, or so she claimed. "I'm not only helping myself, making some bank—I'm improving the lives of the miserable, bringing a little sunshine to a cloudy city." The same applied to her Blood Bank. Not only did the transfusions benefit her—helping her outlive her expiration date by several decades—but she was paying people who needed cash for a renewable resource. "They sit down for a few minutes, and when they stand up, they're fifty bucks richer and a pint lighter. I basically run a charity."

There were questions he was afraid to ask her. About what had happened to him, and about what she was asking him to do, but he preferred this new role of his. Unthinking. Purely helpful. In his old life, he was supposed to have all the answers everyone sought. Now he didn't have any. And he was happily vacant. It was easier not to think. It was easier to be a servant. Hand somebody a plate of hot food, offer up a fresh pair of socks, a fluffed pillow upon which to rest their head. Sarin was trouble—of this he was certain—but he owed her, and she wouldn't let him forget it.

Then something happened. Sarin asked him to drive her to a meeting at a warehouse. "Don't say anything, even if asked directly. Just stand behind me and look tough. Oh, and if the need should arise, don't be afraid to use this." She dropped a pistol in his lap, and he nearly drove off the road in surprise.

He said he wasn't sure this was a good idea, and she said, "You don't want to protect me? Don't you think you owe me that much? I think you do. I know you do."

"I've never held a gun in my life."

"Thought you were from Texas?" she said. "There's no safety, so all you have to do is pull the trigger. Easy."

The warehouse was empty except for a folding table and two chairs. A small Asian man occupied one of them. He wore a black suit with a red tie. His hands were folded neatly on the table. To either side of him stood two men. Their jackets bulged suspiciously along the left sides. Beside them a hound panted. The floor was concrete and oil-stained. Pigeons cooed in the rafters, and shit and feathers and bits of nesting straw dirtied the floor. Rusted iron ribs held up the roof, and sunlight speckled in from the holes in the sheet metal, and shadows gathered thickly in the corners.

"We're the good guys. Just remember that," she whispered to Juniper as they crossed the twenty yards of floor to the table. Their footsteps filled the space with thudding echoes. The men were heavily tattooed. They all carried the same design on their skin—suction-cupped tentacles, curling from their shirtsleeves and collars and hairlines—which came into focus as Juniper drew near. He had shoved the pistol into his waistband beneath his fleece. The grip bit into his hip, but he resisted the urge to readjust it.

The man at the table did not stand but smiled and addressed Sarin. He spoke another language, one that Sarin shared, and when his eyes flitted to Juniper, it was clear he wanted an introduction but got none.

Sarin knocked a cigarette from a pack and sparked it with her Zippo. "Where's Babs?"

Babs, Juniper would later learn, ran an underground club called The Oubliette. He also dealt and pimped on the side. Sarin controlled the east side of the river, and he controlled downtown. He was the one who arranged the sit-down.

At that moment there came the whirring of a tiny motor. Everyone turned toward the sound. Out of the shadows rolled a three-wheeled scooter with a grocery basket between the handlebars. Seated on it was a man—though his considerable size made his gender at first uncertain—wearing sunglasses and dangly earrings and gold chain necklaces and bangled bracelets and sparkling rings and a purple velour jumpsuit. His head was shaved, and the skin of it was as black and polished as obsidian. He was smiling but didn't say anything until his scooter squeaked to a stop a few feet away.

"Welcome, everyone," he said, his voice high and fragile. "I'm glad we could all come together for a friendly chat." He lowered his sunglasses to eyeball Juniper. "And who, pray tell, is this big old piece of meat?"

Sarin said, "We look after each other."

"Do you now?" Babs said, and then slid his sunglasses back into place. "I bet you do."

"Can we get on with this?" Sarin said.

Babs asked her to please sit—"Stay awhile, girl"—and she did, and they all went back and forth, sometimes in English, sometimes in what Juniper guessed to be Japanese, their words growing more severe and sometimes punctuated by long, uncompromising silences. The word *Yakuza* came up more than once. It was a turf war—that became clear. These men wanted to expand their operation to the West Coast and wished to headquarter on the east side of Portland. At one point Juniper caught the hound studying him with its lip curled and a thick line of drool oozing from between its teeth. He quickly looked away. He didn't know that they were sometimes called Grims or Barguests or Shucks. He didn't know they were the companions of the dark, the guardians of the gates of hell. He only knew that the mere sight of them made him feel like he was swallowing a blade.

"Somebody's got to give." Babs's bracelets clinked when he motioned from one side of the table to the other. "Either y'all offer more money or y'all negotiate more real estate, or our asses are going to be sitting here the next hundred years."

Sarin ashed a cigarette. "Why should I give up anything? I was here first. Fuck that. Not for the price point they're offering."

The man in the suit said nothing in response to this, only smoothed his tie and crossed his arms.

Sarin tossed away her cigarette and stood and said, "Come on. We're leaving." With one hand she led Juniper by the elbow, and with the other she reached into his fleece and ripped out the pistol.

He didn't realize the bullets were blasting from the muzzle until after the shots pounded his ears and the bodies of the men and the hound slumped to the floor.

Babs remained on his scooter, shaking his head. Gun smoke drifted in the air between them. He wiped away some blood that had splattered his hand. "Well, I guess you told them."

Juniper didn't realize he had been holding his breath. "Jesus H. Christ," he said with a gasp, and Sarin said, "He's got nothing to do with it."

"Why," Juniper said. "Why did you do that?"

Blood pooled around the bodies, and merged, like the shadows that spread at dusk. Sarin avoided the blood when approaching them, kicking them each softly. When one moaned, she fired another round into his head.

She flipped the pistol and handed it to Juniper butt-first. "I don't like it when people tell me what to do."

Babs backed up his scooter, shifted gears, and rolled away from them. "Good night, folks," he said over his shoulder. "Pleasure as always. If it's any consolation, I would have done the same."

Juniper's ears whined in the aftermath of the gunfire. So he wasn't sure he could trust his hearing. What sounded like a fire slowly catching or insects chewing their way through something. It came off the bodies, and he noticed then their skin was darkening, cracking, and from those cracks leaked a gray dust. In no more than a minute, they were gone. Nothing remained but the scorched outline of where they once lay.

"What are you people?"

Sarin smiled and pinched another cigarette out of a pack and popped it between her lips and spoke around it when she said, "I already told you. We're the good guys."

CHAPTER 8

EVERYONE HAS A PLACE—a listening place, Lela calls it—where they feel most connected and thoughtful, almost transcendent. For some people, it's an alpine lake ringed by pines. For others, it's a gray stone church with light streaming through the stained glass. For Lela, it was here among the stacks of books and maze of shelves at Powell's.

The store took up a whole city block. Its books and its layout were not neatly arranged, but pleasantly cluttered, matching her mind. She always knew where she was, but she wasn't sure how, since the building encouraged misdirection. The lighting was sometimes dim and sometimes bright, and the shelves were mismatched, and the split-level floor plan narrowed and widened and shot up or down into staircases surprisingly.

Sometimes, when she was looking for inspiration—an angle on a story, a shot of lyricism to the jugular, or just space to think—she'd come here. The smell of ink and paper made her mind buzz, and the mild funk of mold caused her nose to run. She would buy a short cup of coffee and wander, pulling books off the shelves, seeing what leaped out at her.

Tonight she comes with a clear purpose. She needs help. This happens every now and then. She stumbles upon some mystery—usually troublesome—that bothers her mind. She knows it's important even if she doesn't know why. She makes inquiries, and someone says or does something that makes it clear she's moving in the right direction. She discovers a clue, what she calls a happy accident, and then moves with a more dogged intentionality toward an answer, seeking out those who can help her get there more quickly.

That's how she feels now. She has her mystery. She's found her right direction. She's got a handful of happy accidents. But she has no narrative, no frame that holds it all together. That's where Daniel comes in. She bothers him for answers with the regularity that others consult Google. He's better than Google. And fuzzier.

She enters the bookstore at ten to eleven. Over the loudspeakers she hears the announcement warning shoppers Powell's will soon close and they ought to take their selections to the register now. Her feet squelch and rain drips off her as she works her way through and around and up and then up again to the rare books section, the crown of the building. Powell's was once the site of a used car dealership and the architecture is rather industrial, but the Rare Book Room feels like something out of an English library, decorated with antique furniture and tidily organized and dark-wooded and glowing with lamplight. Here she finds Daniel.

He's an owlish man with a head that is bald except for a half-circle of gray puffy hair. He wears sweaters and slacks year-round. Rather than bifocals, he perches one set of glasses on his head and another on his nose, trading them out. He calls them his cheaters, and he keeps extras all around because he constantly misplaces them. His voice always comes across as uncertain, stammering, rising in pitch as if every sentence ended in a question mark. On occasion he slips into a British accent, though he is originally from Corvallis.

His desk is an antique, like all of the furniture in the room, and she catches him standing up from his chair and pulling on his jacket. "Not so fast," she says, and he says, "Oh!" and fumbles the correct set of glasses into place, so that he might see her.

"Oh," he says again. "Lela?"

"I need your help."

"But it's late? It's time to close?" He pulls out a golden pocket watch and unlatches its cover. "Isn't it?"

"I wouldn't ask if it wasn't important."

"Of course you wouldn't." He winds the watch and tucks it away. "Would you?"

Again, the voice sounds over the loudspeakers—announcing that the store has closed, that all customers must depart immediately—

and Daniel winces as if he's been caught doing something indecent. Then he sighs and begins to peel off his jacket. "Well, if it's important, I suppose we'd better sit down for a chat?"

She reaches into her purse and withdraws the skull and sets it delicately on the desk before him. "Tell me about these symbols."

✣

An hour later, the store is dark and she sits alone in an oasis of light thrown from a lamp with a stained-glass shade. A pile of books sits before her on the desk. Daniel fetched them for her—most from the Purple Room, where they keep the occult books—and set them in a neat stack that she immediately disarranged.

"This'll be great," she said. "You're the best." She convinced Daniel to leave her here—it's not the first time—so long as she promised not to cause, as he put it, "any disorder that I shall come to regret, yes?"

She promised.

She takes notes in a yellow legal tablet. First replicating the designs on the skull and indicating the different vectors they come from—snout, left and right cheekbone, forehead, cranium. There are circles and crescents and triangles and stars and what looks like a whirlpool design.

Then she works her way through the books. She studies hieroglyphs and understands how symbols are sometimes meant to chronicle history. And she looks up hobo ciphers scratched on fence posts and sidewalks, and she studies wartime correspondence sent across enemy lines, and learns about symbology as a secret language. Here are tattoos meant to impart power and wisdom, and runes meant to doom a person to death or disease. If you scratch down a certain pentagonal design on paper—and if you send it to a person by mail, or sneak it under their pillow, or rip it up and put it in their food—then they will supposedly perish within a week.

Most of the books are old—brittle and yellowed with red mites chasing away from the light when she turns a page—but some are ancient. These he pulled from climate-controlled glass cases. The one she cracks open now has a mottled leather cover with what looks like a warped face cast onto it. There is no title. It is handwritten in slanted black letters with sharp corners.

She has trouble with this book. The language is not always English, and even when it appears to be, the letters bend occasionally into shapes she cannot translate. There is no table of contents, no index, no chapters, no clear design—just a bramble of ink and illustrations. But she encounters two words over and over again. *Door.* And *open.* And she begins to understand that these signs and symbols, many of which appear replicated on her skull, are meant to beckon or allow entry, like keys. Her skull is a key. Could that be right? An honest-to-goodness skeleton key? But to what?

She reads a word aloud, "Demonis," that opens into a yawn. By this time it is nearly two in the morning. The rain takes on a lulling timbre, a thrum that would be nice to fall asleep to. Her eyelids slip lower. She slaps her cheeks softly, pinches her thigh, stands up to stretch and swing out a few jumping jacks. She needs to use the bathroom and splash some water on her face.

A gray glow seeps in through the windows and burns hellishly from the exit signs, but otherwise the store is dark. She fetches a lipstick-sized flashlight from her purse. It doesn't give off a lot of light, but enough.

In the bathroom she locks herself in the stall. For a long time after she's done, she rests her face in her hands and listens. One of the sinks drips, a counterpoint to the rain drumming outside. But beneath that she thinks she catches something. A *click-click-click*ing. A sound she recognizes distantly. The sound her dog, Hemingway, makes when he roams the wood floors of her apartment. The sound of claws.

Maybe it was a register clinking to life. A pipe settling. A mouse scurrying in the walls. She flushes and slides the lock and washes her hands and splashes her face and dabs it dry with a paper towel. And listens. Nothing but the rain.

The door to the bathroom snicks closed behind her. When she

climbs the stairs and reaches the landing and moves toward the Rare Book Room, she sees, at the far end of an aisle, that one of the windows carries the shrinking steam of something's breath.

At least she thinks so. What else could it be? A vent's gust. She swings the flashlight left, right.

She isn't far from the Rare Book Room. The desk is an island of light. She knows she shouldn't look at it directly, for fear she'll ruin whatever night vision she's established. But her notes are there, her purse is there, the skull is there. She has kept it close since she stole it from the construction site—has guarded it as though someone might snatch it away any instant—and now it feels irrevocably distant. She can't not check to see if it remains.

She braves a quick glance—yes, there it is, beside the pile of books—and then starts toward it, edging along the wall. She sweeps the flashlight back and forth. Gilded lettering and brass lamp stands flash back at her. Probably she is imagining things, but she can't help but feel that skin-tightening certainty that she is not alone. This is confirmed a second later by the thud of a book knocked off a shelf in the near distance followed by the *click-click-click* of something scurrying away.

She quits with the caution and sprints for the desk. She shoves her hand inside her purse and half expects her knife to be gone, replaced by something fanged or clammy. Then her palm rounds the grip. She yanks it out and thumbs the blade and holds its point before her. Her arm shakes. The blade quivers with light. "Who's there?" She doesn't like how her words come across as a shriek.

She gets behind the desk, as a defense, and in doing so knocks her hip against the landline phone. It gives a quick chirp as the receiver pops from the cradle. She considers calling the police, but it would be minutes before they arrived, and then she would have to explain why she was hiding out in a closed store and what she was doing with human remains in her possession. She takes a deep breath and tries to convince herself the noise came from a rat—there are plenty of those infesting downtown—or a cat, like the ones roaming the feminist bookstore on the east side.

But the skull won't allow her to calm down. This skeleton key. It pulls at her. As if it contains some haunted gravity. As if it would draw the very shadows out of the night like crows dragged into a funnel cloud. The skull makes her feel as though she ought to be afraid. It's right to be afraid.

A minute passes, maybe two, before she shoves the notebook, pen, and skull into her purse and then shoulders the strap. She wills herself to move, but it's difficult to come unfooted. To travel from light into dark.

She heads for the staircase, where she has just two flights of stairs to chase down. Her footsteps echo through the store and make it sound like she's chasing herself, so she pauses every few steps to address the silence. The farther she goes, the more relief she feels, so that by the time she hits the lower level, the Orange Room, she's convinced of her foolishness.

That's when she notices again the sound of claws clicking. Fast and constant. Like marbles dropped down a stairwell. The emptiness of the building manipulates the noise so that she can't be certain whether it comes from above or below or before her. Then it is gone.

She trades her knife to the other hand and wipes her palm dry on her shirt. She cocks her head, listens. She tries not to feel, not to taste, not to see or smell, tries to make every nerve in her body twist into a receiver so that she might hear better.

There. Beneath the rain, she again catches the *click-click-click* of something pacing the Orange Room. It is already down here. Or it was always down here. Or there is more than one.

She waits. Her eyes ache from looking so hard, tracking through the tables and shelves and carts and pillars and potted plants. There is the dark and the rain falling through the dark, so that it appears the night is moving, is alive. Everything is a threat. She does not run, but moves in short, quick-footed steps to reduce the noise of her passage. And then, from around the corner of an aisle, it appears. The hound.

Dog doesn't feel like the right word. It's as large as a man on all fours and hairless except for some white bristle along its back. *Hound*. That's the only description that fits. It gives a huff and starts toward her in a loping, sidelong way. The distance closes between them quickly, twenty yards, fifteen. She can't help but scream—and the hound drops down and springs into a leap. She stops mid-stride, pivots sideways, and swings her body behind a bookshelf.

She hears it clack its teeth. She hears the air *swoosh,* displaced by its body. She hears it hit the floor and fall on its side with a grunt. Then she hears it scrabble upright and start toward her again. She runs. She can't see clearly—her flashlight wobbling and the shadows pressing in—but she runs as fast as she can, hoping she doesn't catch her toe on a raised tile, slip on a fallen novel. And she can't help but look back.

In doing so she nearly swings her flashlight into the fanged mouth of the thing. Maybe it's a trick of the light, but she swears its tongue is black. In the split second it takes her to process this, she veers into the bookshelf—hard—knocking her shoulder into one of the dividers.

She hears something splinter—hopefully the wood—and her body spins painfully around before hitting the floor. She loses her grip on the knife and flashlight but holds the purse tight. The hound tries to slow, but can't keep its footing on the tile. Again it slides past her, rolling over, righting itself with a snort.

She stands, and they face each other, both panting. A thick rope of yellow drool descends from its chops. The hound is too close. She can't outrun it. So she changes her strategy. The bookshelf beside her is ten feet tall. She springs into motion and ladders her way up. One of the shelves snaps beneath her weight, and the books rain down on the hound, already below her. It doesn't bark, but it whines in a way that sounds like metal sharpened on stone. She drags her body on top of the shelf, and rather than pause, she leaps for the next aisle.

When she pushes off, the bookshelf wobbles and groans. She hits the floor in time to see it slowly tip away from her. For a moment it appears as though it might fall back into place, but she gives it a shove and it loses its battle against gravity. With a great *clack,* it strikes the bookshelf beside it, which then tips into the bookshelf beside it, and then the next, and the next, dominoing onward, hundreds of books flitting their pages before thundering to the floor.

She doesn't wait around to see if the hound survived. Before the last shelf has fallen, she is already bounding up the steps that lead to the exit on Eleventh. She hunts for the lock before realizing the door is open, gasping in and out with the wind. Something crunches underfoot. What turns out to be a pair of reading glasses. Daniel's? Was he attacked when he left her earlier that evening?

She doesn't have time to think, but she can't help but feel a needle-prick of dread. She hopes he isn't hurt, hopes he merely dropped his glasses, hopes he left the door unlocked because he was absent-minded and not dead. Because of her. This won't be the last time she worries she's brought harm to those close to her.

She races into the night, pounding forward, almost to her Volvo, the only car on the street. She fumbles in her purse for her keys, drops them in a puddle, and only when she crouches down to snatch them does she notice her tires. Flat. Slashed.

She regularly walks between Powell's and *The Oregonian* offices. Tonight she runs. The sidewalks are gummed with leaves, and the gutters are creeked, and the streets puddled from the rain. She keeps swiping her face, everything blurred, from the downpour or her tears, she isn't sure.

She is getting close—another block, hang a right, she'll be there—close enough that her run slows to a stumbling walk. She breathes in ragged gasps. Her heart jitters in her chest. Her eyes pulse. She grips the purse with both hands as if it's somehow holding her up.

Then her breath catches, though she needs the oxygen so badly. Because another hound is bounding toward her. It is one block ahead and on the opposite side of the street. This one is shorter than the other, with black spines of fur prickling its back. It does not howl or bark or snarl. There is no sound outside the splash of its paws.

Until the bus blasts its horn. The scroll of its electronic sign reads OUT OF SERVICE. The driver crushes the horn with his hand and opens his mouth into a black O of surprise. The hound tries to change direction, jackknifing in the middle of the street, but the bus catches it.

Its body strikes the grille with a wet thud. The brakes scream. The hound rolls under, thumped once, twice, by the wheels. The bus skids to a stop and leaves behind a black smear of what could be burned rubber but looks like blood. The hound won't follow her any farther, though it wants to; its back legs remain still, while its front paws continue to twitch and claw the air.

A final burst of speed takes her around the block—to the marbled lower level of her office building. She shoves open the glass doors and enters the brightly lit foyer, where her heart jitters and the rainwater drips off her and she gulps for breath so that she might answer the security guard who stands from his desk and keeps asking, "What's wrong, what's wrong, what's wrong?"

CHAPTER 9

SARIN SAYS THEY shouldn't jump to any conclusions. Sure, it looks bad—a grotesque murder, the mark of a red right hand, a location proximate to the Rue. But maybe it's a coincidence. Or maybe it's a copycat.

She's speaking to Juniper but talking to herself. She's worried, he can tell. Her usual smirk has bent into a frown. She can't decide whether to stand or sit. She smokes her way through three cigarettes in five minutes, dragging on them so hard, he can hear the tobacco sizzle. Normally, after a blood infusion, she gives off a ruddy glow, appears somehow fuller than before. Her face is caked with makeup, but the foundation seems to crack now, along her forehead, the sides of her mouth, as if she is aging before his eyes. She has unhooked from the donor bags, and her body is stamped with Band-Aids that she scratches at absently.

"But let's say it *is* him," Juniper says. "Let's say it is Jeremy Tusk. Do we wait for the fight to come to us?"

She waves away his words as though they were smoke. "Tried that last time. Almost got me killed."

"So what, then? Tell me what to do."

She uses one cigarette to light another. "Did you come armed?"

He's come a long way since that moment in the warehouse so many years ago. He holds open his jacket and shows her the shoulder holster that carries a Beretta Storm Compact and two clips. His utility belt is weighed down with a flare, a flask of holy water, and custom-made, iron-coated handcuffs. Then he hoists his pant leg, revealing the ankle-sheathed KA-BAR serrated knife.

"There's my Boy Scout," she says. "Let's go."

"Where?"

"Where else?" The cherry burns bright and the smoke tusks from her nostrils. "When you're hunting for demons, you go down."

✣

Good doesn't always look like how you imagine it. Sometimes it cusses and wears a leather jacket and motorcycle boots and chain-smokes. Sometimes it deals a little on the side. Sometimes it kills.

This isn't Tusk's first life. And it isn't Sarin's either. She keeps coming back, over the years, the centuries, like a trick candle flaring back to life. She isn't sure what to call herself. Custodian or guardian or soldier. "I guess I'm like a bad cop. And a bad cop's better than no cop, right?" She likes to think of herself as anti-heroic, but Juniper knows better. She fights the dark. She takes an interest in the larger metro, but she can only claim the east side of Portland as her territory. There is a balance to the world—of light and dark, right and wrong, good and evil, yin and yang, up and down, spicy and sweet, Sonny and Cher, however you want to think about it. And she operates by a more simplified, elemental version of any religious doctrine: "Any time things get too dark, the world goes blind." This she says with a spark of her Zippo.

There are others like her, Juniper included. Everybody's met a few of them. Those who claim to hear voices or see things no one else can, who follow hunches and suffer from vivid dreams. They'll burn sage and talk about your aura and claim a ghost visited them during the night. Whatever you want to call them—touched, sensitive, prescient, special—they are tapped into a higher frequency than the rest of the population. Dogs have a sense of smell ten thousand times more powerful than a human's. Some insects can sense radiation, and some birds can see temperature. The rare person is similarly heightened. Usually their awareness develops with the onset of puberty, as if some new antennae grew along with their body hair. The severe cases tend to claim a territory and occasionally fight to maintain their control of it.

"The best way to think of it," Sarin once told him, "is like a spectrum. I'm high on it, you're low on it, but we're both *on it*. And when you're on it, you make a choice as to which side you're going to soldier for."

The men Sarin killed that day in the warehouse, they didn't just want the east side for drugs. They wanted it for the dark. There was a time when Juniper would have rolled his eyes at this, but he was willing to believe anything at that point. Getting a black, squiggling ball of cancer ripped out of your chest and seeing three people crumble to ash will do that to you.

He is enlisted in Sarin's fight. He owes her. Downtown Portland isn't her turf. It belongs to Babs. Here Juniper keeps a low profile as Sarin's eyes and ears on this west side of the river. He has his own life—his own quieter way of fighting the dark, devoting himself to the shelter—but his work there occasionally entangles with his obligations to Sarin. Such as the time when the Portland homeless began to disappear. Because Jeremy Tusk was killing them.

Back then Tusk taught as a lecturer at Portland State, the same place he had earned his PhD in philosophy, but he was terminated midway through that spring semester when he stopped showing up for class. He had presented at several conferences on Carl Jung, and his dissertation concerned occultist pathology. It was never clear whether Tusk chose his apartment at the Rue or the Rue chose him. His research consumed him, and he maxed out his credit cards buying rare books, some inked in blood and bound in human flesh. These were his tutorials as he performed rituals—with red candles and black eggs and moonstones and goat's blood—one of which called from the other side a dark force that would empower him. It worked, but not in the way he expected. A demon inhabited him. His body became its puppet. And it was hungry. Feeding on the homeless and prostitutes, the disenfranchised, the invisibles, those who would not be missed.

Except by Juniper and Sarin. This was their vocation—the poor, the weak, the sick—and when several of Juniper's clients vanished, he started asking questions. First to the police, who said, "Maybe they went to California. Shouldn't you be happy? Isn't that your goal? Reduce the needy?" Juniper then turned to the streets, offering cigarettes, beer, egg sandwiches for information. There were rumors of a shadow man. Someone who came out at night to hunt. Every shelter was full every evening, and those who were turned away might not make it to morning. That's what his clients said. And this shadow man left his mark—a red right hand—on sidewalks, buildings, windows all throughout Portland, claiming it, like a dog pissing on posts.

So Juniper patrolled the streets, checking in on encampments in Forest Park, beneath the Burnside Bridge, the abandoned Victorian on Sauvie Island, offering up snacks and toilet kits, the occasional six-pack of beer, asking if anybody had seen anything. While Sarin spent those same nights curled up in alleys, doorways, pretending herself to be a victim. Waiting.

And then Tusk came. She was curled up on a bench in a tree-studded park walled in by high-rises. It was 3 a.m. The city was dark except for the intermittent streetlamp, and silent except for a low-grade hum rising off the semis on the freeway. He walked past her several times, circling experimentally, before pausing a few feet away.

She watched him through her eyelashes, feigning sleep. He wore loose-fitting khakis and a billowing dress shirt that could not hide how dumpy he was. In his hand he gripped a sawed-off baseball bat as long as a forearm. He hadn't cut his hair in a long time and kept the greasy strands of it parted in the middle and tucked behind his ears. She knew him by the shadow he cast. It did not match his body. The head like a Halloween gourd—the back hunched—the arms long and hooked, and the fingers the same.

She was tucked into a sleeping bag the color of a dried-up tongue. One of her arms reached inside it, where she kept a long blade made of silver. Tusk breathed through his mouth. Took a step closer. She thought she might smell him. An oniony sweat.

"You," he finally said. "You're the one who thinks this city is yours."

The sleeping bag was unzipped, and she threw it off easily to slash at him as he lunged for her. He shrieked—like some nightmare bird—and retreated a few steps. One of his fingers dangled by a stubborn ligament, and the open knuckle pumped blood. He smiled through the pain. "I can't wait to take a bite out of you."

"Come and get it," she said.

His voice did not match his body, too low and guttural and big-tongued, a beast's. "I'm not alone you know. I've been busy. Gathering shadows."

At that moment every streetlamp in a block radius fizzed out, and the shadows came alive. One raced past in the shape of a bear, huffing and grunting and making a wind that made her eyes water. What looked like a tall man with a buffalo head stepped out from behind a nearby tree. The others were not so distinct, just blurred figures that scurried and oozed and gibbered and moaned. Something slithered through the grass. Something rattled a sewer grate. A carnival of shadows.

Tusk was not a man, not anymore. He was a vessel. Something had inhabited him. Something old and powerful and sulfuric. All this time he had been murdering for pleasure but with purpose. He murdered in the name of darkness, and darkness answered. The Rue was a place of summoning, a night-black doorway with a knife as its key and Jeremy Tusk—or whatever his true name was—its gatekeeper.

Sarin should not have come alone, but remained in place until what looked like a two-headed buzzard swung out of the sky and raked at her forehead with its shadow claws. She screamed and the night screamed back. All at once the shadows came for her—knotting around her like a slow cyclone—and she could not run fast enough, slash hard enough, scream loud enough.

Tusk circled behind her, close enough so that she could hear his haggard breathing. She turned but not soon enough. He swung an arm and clubbed the back of her head. The world went black, then came back into haywire color briefly before unconsciousness rushed in for good and she fell flat to the ground.

His car was parked nearby—an old Lincoln as long and formal as a hearse—and he hefted her and dumped her in the trunk. There he bound her wrists and ankles, taped her mouth, before driving away.

Thirty minutes later she woke inside his apartment at the Rue. Her mind felt as tenuous and wounded as a leaf eaten down to the veins by insects. She forced herself to concentrate. Her vision wobbled into focus and the first thing she saw was the great red eye sketched inside a triangle on the wall. Palm prints surrounded it, a five-pointed constellation made of red right hands. Beneath it was a shaker desk that had been converted to an altar crowded with candles black and red. Their flickering light made the eye appear to move, to focus in on her, and she knew it might as well be so. Among the candles were figures built from sticks and bones and hair and ligaments, some in triangular and trapezoidal designs, others tied together in way that appeared almost buggy.

The room was otherwise empty except for black flies dirtying the air and the runic symbols chalked across the hardwood floor. She could hear him coming—the footsteps shaking the very air, as if there were many bodies smashed down and contained within his—and she pretended sleep.

He wore a black silk robe, unbelted and flapping around him like wings. He was otherwise naked. Beneath his considerable belly, a worm of a penis curled. He carried in one hand a long black dagger and in the other a can of Sprite. He sipped from it.

He could scissor off her toes, saw open her belly, hammer her teeth from her mouth, and she could feel the pain, the same as anyone. Just as she could die, the same as anyone. But she was more than a standard sacrifice. To kill someone like Sarin meant a black feast, a midnight Sabbath, a sundering of the balance in favor of the dark.

Some demons made people sick, and some demons made people go mad. Some made forests drop their needles and birds fall dead from the sky. A demon might guide your hand to a rifle's stock or to a thigh beneath a table or to a rope that will wrap around your neck and tighten when you fling your body from a balcony. You have seen the work they have done. A graveyard is defiled. A man brings a pistol to work; a boy brings a pistol to school. A semi lurches across the meridian to strike a school bus. These are singular episodes, containable maladies.

But every once in a while, one of the old ones will come. A Destroyer. And when the old ones come, the darkness organizes, becomes a widespread contagion. In Germany, where train cars crammed with Jews thundered toward smokestacks belching ash. In Rwanda, where machetes flashed in the night. Even now, in Juárez, where people are kidnapped and their headless bodies stacked up outside shopping malls; and in Iraq and in Syria, where men wrap themselves in shawls like shadows that can survive even the desert's sun and record videos of heads hacked from shoulders.

Tusk was inhabited by one of the old ones. Tusk had become the puppet of a Destroyer, and he was assembling a court of shadows. And if Sarin died by his hand, he would grow more foul and potent, capable of cracking open a doorway at the Rue that would spill shadows freely from it.

A fly landed on her eye, and she blinked it away. She waited until Tusk passed by and attended his altar, scratching a Lucifer match and lighting a black candle and muttering something under his breath. It was then she attacked.

Her ankles and wrists remained bound, but this did not stop her. She rose from the floor as quietly as she could manage. And then shoved forward. She battered her head into the small of his back. This knocked him into the desk. Immediately she dropped to a crouch. His body reeled back. When it did, she was beneath him, tipping his body at the knees. He bleated like a goat when he fell. The floor silenced him. The dagger clattered away. The Sprite pooled and fizzed.

She aimed first for his groin, and then for his larynx, ulcerating every nerve and paralyzing his breath. This stole her a good ten seconds, during which time she secured the dagger and freed her ankles and then her wrists. He was coming at her now, scrambling up from the floor, a head taller, a hundred pounds heavier, and she held out the dagger just in time for him to accept it. The point jammed into the recess of his belly button, the target that presented itself to her first.

She yanked upward, unzippering him, and he staggered back with his eyes wide and his hand on the hilt that now rose from his sternum. This did not stop him from speaking some incantation, even with blood bubbling from his lips, and she fled that place—the flies battering her—and ran through the shadow-tangled night and did not pause until she was pounding at the front door of The Weary

Traveler, where Juniper took her inside and into his arms. She could not stop crying for a long time, and when she did, she could only say, "He's gone. Thank god it's over."

✣

Except it wasn't. He's back. Tusk—or whatever his true name is, the name of the old one who inhabited him—has returned. Juniper feels it and Sarin does too. This is why they walk side by side through the nighttime streets of Portland, hooded, their boots clomping through puddles, their hands free at their sides, ready to reach for a weapon.

Tunnels run beneath the city—the Portland Underground, they're called—a maze of them that connect the Willamette docks to the basements of many waterfront hotels and bars, long ago used for shipping deliveries to avoid street traffic, now a crumbling curiosity. Walking tours visit some of them. Others are occupied by the homeless. Others few know about.

Like this one, in the Pearl District, where Sarin leads him. They enter an alley heaped with garbage bags. A figure waits for them here, next to a Dumpster, beneath a fire escape. Lump. One of his crows squawks a greeting. He stands beside a grate, steel, the size of a door. He is also on the spectrum—somewhere closer to Sarin—able to translate and manipulate the shadowy patterns of the world. "You're sure?" Sarin says, and Lump nods and kneels and yanks the grate. It croaks and flakes rust. A metal staircase leads down.

Juniper doesn't like to think about his previous life. But sometimes a memory will sneak up on him—him sitting by bedsides or preaching before packed auditoriums, promising miracles, describing a candy-coated heaven—and the sensation is equivalent to biting into tinfoil. A sickening surprise. But some of the old words still ring true. Like this verse from Mark: "In My name they will cast out demons; they will speak with new tongues; they will pick up serpents with their hands; and if they drink any deadly poison, it will not hurt them; they will lay hands on the sick, and they will recover."

Instead of uttering words from behind a pulpit, he is slinging from the streets a gun, a knife, his fists. This feels like a far more honest and effective way of living up to the same message—defending the light—which he supposes makes him a kind of ass-kicking version of the Great Commission.

Lump wishes them good luck and Godspeed, and closes the grate behind them before hurrying off on some other business. The air below the streets is cold and thick and mildewy. The walls are brick-lined, and between the bricks moisture weeps. Juniper and Sarin walk for a hundred yards. They don't lower their hoods, keeping their faces obscured. He can hear music pulsing, like the blood beat of the earth. From the ceiling dangle red glass Christmas lights, like fiery roots, faintly illuminating the passageway. The music grows louder, a pulsing electronica. They take one turn, then another, before the tunnel straightens out and thirty yards ahead they can see it.

The club is called The Oubliette, the letters etched into the stone archway that is its entrance. Inside, strobe lights flash, silhouetting the figure who stands in the doorway. A bouncer, bigger than Juniper, with tattoos of eyes over his eyelids so that it appears he is always watching. A line of thirty or so people waits to get in, all of them shaved and tatted and dyed and make-upped and pierced in a way that would seem strange anywhere other than Portland.

The bouncer presents a tarot deck. He selects a card and holds up its back side to a kid with an orange Mohawk and quarter-sized tribal plugs in his ears. "The Magician," the kid says, and the bouncer flips the card over to reveal the same before waving him through.

Some of the people in line complain when Juniper and Sarin cut past them—saying, "Wait the fuck up" and "Yo, check yourself"—but they don't pause until they arrive at the bouncer, and he holds up a hand to block him. "There's a line."

"We got business," Sarin says.

The bouncer's eyes slide to Juniper. "You don't look like you're here to party."

"Like she said. Business."

"What's this business bullshit? Business with who?"

"Babs."

"Babs is busy." He squints, trying to discern their faces below their hoods. "He's in a meeting. Said not to be bothered."

Sarin is fast, the lie spoken so quickly that for a moment Juniper believes it. "That's why we're here," she says. "For the meeting. We're late. Don't make us any later."

The bouncer scrunches his eyebrows, which pulls the star-point of the pentagram down his forehead like a drawn blade. "I wasn't told shit about—"

He doesn't get a chance to finish, because Sarin has slammed a Taser into his neck. Instantly he drops to the floor. His body spasms. Juniper turns to the crowd of people waiting to get in. "Come on," he says. "Free beer. Free beer, everyone!"

They hesitate only a second before charging inside, bullying their way toward the bar, and then Sarin and Juniper step over the bouncer and through the doorway and enter a ballroom-sized space with stone pillars interrupting it. At the far end of it, atop a short stage, a DJ with oversize headphones and a forked goatee works the turntables. Maybe a hundred bodies writhe to the music, cast in the silvery strobe light in various poses, their hands running along their bodies one moment, thrown to the air in celebration the next. Glow sticks smear the air neon green, pink, orange. At one point the music cuts off in a pause—and everyone goes still, frozen like an otherworldly garden of statues—and then a whistle blasts and the heavy bass returns, and everyone explodes into motion again.

The bar is long and scarred, with backlit shelves that make the bottles glow like potions, and a mirror mossed over with age. The centerpiece is a tank full of whiskey with a body floating in it. The Drowned, the signature drink, costs five bucks a shot and supposedly brings health and happiness and luck. Two bartenders try to deal with the sudden crush of bodies reaching across the counter, snatching whatever is in reach. "Free drinks," the voices call. "It's all free."

Sarin points to a door beside the bar. It has been glopped over with red paint so that it appears made of muscle. They start across the dance floor, shouldering people aside, most of them too caught up in the pulsing music to notice. Six cages dangle throughout the room, and in them men and women dance, dressed in black or red leather if they are dressed at all. Juniper spots a woman who appears to have a tail and a man with his naked body painted black and white to resemble a skeleton. He isn't sure of the gender of the person who has mere slits for eyes, nose, and mouth.

More and more bodies shove up against the bar, all of them crying for free drinks, free drinks. One of the bartenders smashes a bottle over a head. The other shoves and punches and screams over the music, "Back off! I said back the hell off!" Somebody hurls a pint glass and it shatters the giant tank, and a flood of whiskey pours out, carrying the drowned man with it, his body flopping to the floor.

Sarin and Juniper pass by unmolested. Juniper expects the door to be locked, but the knob twists easily. He probably just imagines it as hot in his hand, as though the room on the other side were on fire. Flies buzz along the door, dozens of them, appearing like nail heads in the wood. He nods at Sarin. Only then do they pull down their hoods and draw their pistols and rush inside.

CHAPTER 10

WHEN LELA WAKES, it takes her a panicked moment to remember where she is. She throws out an arm and knocks over a mop and searchingly flutters a ream of paper. She stands and bonks her head on a shelf that clatters staples, pencils, paper clips to the floor. Then she sees the line of light at the bottom of the door. The supply closet at *The Oregonian*. The staff keeps a cot in here to sneak in power naps. She spent the night on it. Her neck cramps from a pinched nerve. Her clothes remain damp. She stinks like mildew and BO.

She nearly trips over her purse and then checks it in a panic to make certain the skull is still there. She isn't sure what time it is when she steps from the closet, but the newsroom is bustling and the windows burn with sunlight. She rubs her eyes with the heel of her hand and yawns so widely her jaw clicks. The Books editor glances at her and shakes his head and snorts out a laugh. "Looking good, Falcon."

"What time is it?"

"Eight something."

"Shit." The Willamette 10K, which she's supposed to cover, has already started. But—no reason to panic—she should be able to make it to the finish line to interview the winner and round up some ambient details before heading over to the farmers' market.

There are obviously other things crowding her mind. Far more pressing than any empty-calorie civic-pride 500-worder. But she has never missed a deadline, and she doesn't plan to this morning, no matter the circumstances. She shoves a stick of gum in her mouth and rakes her fingers through her hair and starts for the elevators before changing her mind and ducking down a stairwell to avoid passing by her editor's office.

Her wild memory of yesterday—the Rue, the skull, the murder, the hounds—might mean she's gone nuts. She's perfectly willing to entertain that possibility. Bad food, lack of sleep, too much coffee laced with too much Adderall, whatever—she could very possibly be an unreliable source, seeing things and making connections that aren't there. Or . . . ? She's dealing with what can only be described as extranormal, supernatural, the kind of weirdness that might appear in the novels she doesn't normally read. She isn't sure which possibility frightens her more. But she can handle them both. She just needs time to think, to process.

In the lobby, the security guard tells her to hold up. He has a star on his shoulder and a baton on his belt, and his name tag reads STEVE. Some cream cheese whitens the edge of his mustache, and he holds a paper cup of Peet's coffee that steams through the vent. He doesn't seem to know what to say to her. Last night, she now recalls, he asked if she was all right and put a hand on her shoulder, and she knocked it away and said to mind his own business.

"Some guy," he says. "Some guy, last night, he tried to get in here. Said he was looking for you. Said the two of you had an appointment. Thought about calling your desk, but it was late and he wasn't on the guest sheet and I didn't like the looks of him, so I said you weren't here. Said you'd gone. He asked where to and I said home, I suppose. Hope that's all right? Hope I didn't mess up anything for you?"

"What did he look like?"

Steve crags up his face. "Like, weird. Creepy. Young and old at the same time. Not sure that makes any sense. His body could have been a kid's, but his face looked like a little old man's. Know what I mean? He sounded funny too. Foreign or something. Like he was chewing on metal. Hope I did all right, sending him away."

"You did." She eyes up the coffee. "Can I have the rest of that?"

"This?" He examines the cup as though surprised to find it in his hand. "Um."

She says thanks and grabs it from him. Some coffee sloshes her wrist, but she barely notices the sting. She's already out the door, knocking back the cup and digging out her cell. The phone is nearly drained, but she uses it to call Powell's and asks for a transfer to the rare books section. The ringing goes on too long. The taste of coffee goes acidic in her mouth. She remembers the glasses on the ground. Daniel's. She did this to him. This is her fault. Then, at last, he picks up, and she lets out a shout of relief.

"Lela?" he says. "Lela, is that you?" His voice is shrill and broken by a stammer. What in God's name happened, he wants to know, and is she all right?

She assures him she is, and tells him she's sorry, and hopes that she hasn't caused too much trouble. She was attacked last night. She'll fill him in later. "Things aren't safe right now," she says. "If anybody comes around, asking about me, play dumb. You've never heard of me. You never saw that skull. You have no idea what they're talking about."

"Oh dear," he says. "This is all terribly upsetting."

She tells him she has to go, but she'll be in touch. She has some follow-up questions.

He lowers his voice. "About the skull?"

"About the skull."

For the next two hours, this Saturday morning, she does her job. She shakes hands and asks questions and scratches down notes and hammers out copy and meets her deadline, but she feels barely present for any of it, as though she's hovering over herself.

Her Volvo has been towed, no surprise, so she takes the bus. She's so preoccupied that she misses her stop and has to walk ten blocks to her apartment, the second floor of an old Arts and Crafts home. Once there she fails to recognize that her living room is not as she left it. Granted, she doesn't clean very often, so it is difficult to see the mess overlying the mess. The walls are bare, but the floor is full. Small islands of T-shirts and pants and half-balled socks are staggered down the hallway, through the bedroom. Dishes and take-out containers stack up in the kitchen and collect clouds of fruit flies. Every corner is a leaning tower of newspapers and magazines. The couch is a coffee-stained nest of blankets. That's her standard. But every drawer and cupboard door is now open, the contents disgorged.

She should run back the way she came. She should call the police.

But she doesn't. The needling panic that bothers her now has nothing to do with her own well-being. It's her dog that matters. Hemingway. That stupid German shepherd with the black mask and bad breath and one floppy ear, the one who sheds fur like porcupine quills, the one who nudges her awake with his cold nose, the one who chews up the furniture and drinks out of the toilet and normally yelps and scrambles toward the door whenever she comes home. That one. Her only companion.

She drops her purse. She lost her knife in Powell's, so she pulls out her pepper spray, pops the safety cap. The apartment is small, only four hundred square feet, but she can't see all of it from here. The entryway opens into the living room, which runs into the kitchen and dinette. A short hallway leads to the bedroom and bathroom. She tries to make no noise, but that's nearly impossible, given the old hardwood floors that groan with every step. That's the only sound, aside from the swish and hum of traffic passing outside.

The rear entrance has an oversize doggie door that leads to a rotten patio that drops into a staircase that leads to the fenced backyard. That way Hemingway can do his business whenever he pleases. She's gone too often to walk him with any regularity. The doggie door—she can see now—has been ripped away, and the wood around it appears chewed.

"Hemingway?" she says softly, and hears a whine come from the bathroom. When she opens the door, she finds the inside of it crosshatched with his claw marks. He rushes her and smashes his head into her groin, her stomach, her hip, desperate for contact, comfort. She tucks away the pepper spray and holds his head in both her hands. One of his teeth appears broken from where he must have attacked the doorknob. He licks her with his warm rough tongue, and she scratches him over with her fingernails until he yips and flinches. Her hand comes away bloody. He's been cut. Or bitten. It's difficult to tell. But he's missing a patch of white-gray fur along his shoulder, a crater deep enough to reveal candy-slick muscle.

"Oh, my poor boy, my beautiful boy." She talks to him the way she can't seem to talk to anyone else, with gushing vulnerability. A few months ago, she dated a guy who claimed she never wanted to talk.

"You're a writer," he said. "How do you have so few words?" She tried to explain. Speaking was careless and fleeting in its effect. Writing was deliberate, permanent, more meaningful. But he left her anyway. Said dating her was like dating an autistic.

Hemingway licks her cheek, and she buries her face in his fur and breathes in his skunky odor and says, "I love you, I love you, I love you, you stupid dog."

✣

Half an hour later, after she cleans the wound with water and smears it with ointment, she clips on the leash and leads Hemingway to the bus stop. She doesn't feel safe at home. She wants to be surrounded by people. She stares at the back of her hand—where she has written BR12 with a Sharpie—and wonders briefly what it refers to, but then the bus pulls up with a shriek of brakes and a cloud of exhaust, and she forgets all about it.

At *The Oregonian,* she scans her ID, but the security guard—not Steve, another guy she doesn't know so well—holds up his hand. "No dogs allowed."

She tells him, with a straight face, that Hemingway is a service animal, and he says, "Where's his little vest, then? Service animals are always wearing those little vests."

"It's dirty."

"It's dirty?"

"Yes. I'm having it cleaned. In the washing machine."

"Why you need a service animal all of a sudden? I've never seen you with one before."

"I've been diagnosed with epilepsy, if you must know," she says, and he shakes his head and says, "All right, all right, have it your way," and waves her through to the elevators.

It's Saturday afternoon and the office is now mostly empty, so she sneaks Hemingway through the cubicles and under her desk without any trouble. She tells him to be a good boy and tosses him a treat from her purse, and he slurps it up and crunches it damply.

Only now does she feel safe enough to think. The person who

broke into her apartment was clearly looking for something specific; it has to be the skull.

After she ran from the construction site, after she climbed into the Volvo and sped away, she could see the men in her rearview mirror. They obviously spotted her plates, figured out who she was, where she lived and worked. They could have brought charges against her for what she did—trespassing, looting—but they didn't. Which confirms they're up to something illegal. She doesn't know how to puzzle together the murder and the hounds. But the slashed tires and the break-in and the late-night query as to her whereabouts all point to the fact that she's up to her neck in some dangerously deep shit.

She pulls the camera out of her satchel and stands and peers into the next cubicle. Josh, the intern, types at a keyboard and wears a set of earbuds that connect to a smartphone. "Hey," she says, and he doesn't hear her, so she says, "Hey!" again, louder this time, and when he still doesn't hear her, she throws a pencil at him.

"What?" he says, too loud, with the earbuds still in.

She motions at him to shut off whatever he's listening to, and when he does, she says, "What are you doing?"

"Copyedits and fact-checking on your pieces and a few others. Then I've got to log an interview. So don't ask me to do anything."

"Is Brandon here?"

"I haven't seen him for an hour or so."

"I need help with my camera."

"You really are pathetic, you know. My grandmother understands technology better than you, and she still has an AOL address."

"What's wrong with AOL?"

"Forget it."

"Get over here."

He sighs and saves his document and wanders over to her cubicle entrance. He's been wearing the same pair of pleated khakis all week, and they're stained along the pocket with ink, the knee with mustard. His cheeks are so flushed with acne that he appears permanently embarrassed. "What?"

She tells him she wants him to bring the photo up on the screen, so that they can zoom in and out, study the details.

He tells her to get up and she does and he sits down and then startles at the sight of the dog between his legs. "What the hell? Are you allowed to bring that thing in here?"

"Don't worry. He won't bite unless I tell him to."

Josh gives Hemingway a tentative scratch behind the ears—"Hey, buddy"—before knocking the mouse around and lighting up the monitor screen. Their computers are all hopelessly outdated, slow to load, regularly freezing up, not that she really cares. Hers whirs and ticks and groans now, and Josh says, "You can't leave this many windows open. You're asking for a crash."

As he closes out the browser—and the thirty-some websites tabbed there—her inbox comes into view. Josh comments on the ten thousand unread messages listed there, and she says, "If I actually read and answered all those things, I'd be a professional emailer."

"Your address must have gotten shared among some spambots," he says, and scrolls through the inbox, pointing out the number of messages flowing in since last night, hundreds, all of them with attachments. He lingers a moment, as if tempted by their solicitations. Every attachment is indicated by the symbol of a black paper clip, stacked up on the screen like tarry hoof prints. The computer makes a strained, choked noise, and he breaks from his spell. "Don't open any of this stuff, okay? It'll just infect your computer."

"The camera."

"Yeah, yeah, yeah." He plugs in the camera, and the computer takes a long minute to recognize it. He clicks on the external drive and opens up the storage. "There's like fifty million pictures on this thing that you have obviously never backed up. How far back does this go? Birth? Is your mother's ultrasound of you in here?"

"Open the most recent," she says. "Not today, not the stuff from the farmers' market or the race, but yesterday."

He scrolls through and spots the date stamp on the photos taken at the Rue. He clicks on the first of them—and the image takes over the screen. The carved-out square, maybe thirty feet deep, of the construction site. Busy with workers who shovel and trowel and whisk away the dirt.

"Zoom in on one of those graves," she tells him, and he magnifies by 200 percent, then 250 percent when she asks for more. He readjusts the frame so that the mound is centered. It takes a few seconds for the pixels to clarify. The screen is riddled with bones. Bones that do and do not appear human. Here are the long arms and legs of a man, but the fingers appear too long and the giant skull appears pointed, elongated, like that of a mastiff or cow.

She asks him to go to another mound, and he does. The skull is all teeth. And its vertebrae appear to extend into a tail. She notices markings along them. Runes and ciphers akin to those found on the skull in her purse.

Josh's voice is barely a whisper when he says, "Dude . . . what is this?"

"I don't really know."

She tells him to pull up the next photo. This one focuses on a construction worker. Black-bearded. Minutes later he would be the one to chase up the ladder while she took the ramp. She remembers his face then—on its way toward rage—but here he appears smudged, indistinct, greased over with charcoal. The other photos are similar. Every faced fogged. She asks Josh to clean up their faces if he can.

He can't. "Must be something off with the focus." Yet everything else remains clear. He calls up the final photo. Of the small man. His face, too, is nothing but a fleshy smear.

Lela leans against the desk and gnaws at her thumbnail, peeling away a sliver, sucking on it. Her mind retreats to the Rue, the way it felt shadowed even in sun. The bodies found in the apartment there—sawed-up in the fridge, treated into lampshades and curtains, dissolving in buckets of lye—and now more bodies buried beneath. How could one place nest so much darkness?

Josh gives up on the computer and leans back in the chair to study her. "My dad said that anyone who writes on the back of their hand is a moron."

"Huh?" She holds up her hand, the edge of her thumbnail peeled away to reveal the angry red beneath. Her knuckles are always inked with reminders. But today there is only the one, BR12, whatever that referred to. "Oh yeah. I am my own notebook and calendar." And that's when she remembers. BR12. Benedikt's Restaurant, twelve o'clock. Her sister and her niece. She was supposed to meet them there to celebrate Hannah's eye surgery. The Mirage prosthetic that would supposedly restore her sight. She checks the clock—late by hours. "Shit."

"What?"

"Nothing." Every family has a terrorist—her sister, Cheryl, says—an emotional terrorist. And Lela is it. Lela ruins everything, drains and upsets everyone with her pessimism and selfishness, the whole world revolving around her job. Maybe her sister's right, Lela thinks at moments like this, moments when she's clearly screwed up, but it's always been easy for her to move on, shrug off, forget, concentrate on the future, and forget about the past.

She's already there—already looking ahead—saying to Josh, "That interview you have to transcribe? Forget it. I need you on this." She taps the screen so hard that the monitor wobbles. "I asked you earlier to do some digging on the company that bought the Rue property. Undertown. What do you have on them for me?"

"Brandon told me not to—"

"Forget Brandon. He's a shit-for-brains clown. I want Undertown. Everything you can find on Undertown. Dig deep on the Rue. Look at the site before it was the Rue. That address. And the surrounding blocks in the Pearl District. I know college students are lazy and like to do all of their research on Google. Forget that. Get your ass out of the chair and check the physical archives at the library, historical society, City Hall. Dig through the stacks, crank some microfilm."

"What am I looking for? Do you think something happened there?"

"I have no idea. I'm following an itch. You feel an itch, you scratch till it bleeds. Understand, intern? This is me mentoring your ass."

"I guess."

She collects her purse, snaps her fingers for Hemingway to follow, and with the dog at her side, starts down the aisle of cubicles.

"Where are you going?" Josh calls after her.

"To apologize."

CHAPTER II

HANNAH LOVES THE HEAVY spiced sausages, the tangy shredded bundles of sauerkraut. Reuben rolls, pork shanks, baked onion soup, liver dumpling soup, potato dumplings. The German restaurant, Benedikt's, has always been her favorite. It is a white-walled, dark-roofed, heavy-timbered building located at the edge of Forest Park. She and her mother come here on special occasions—birthdays, holidays—and today is a special occasion. The Mirage works. She can see.

But today is special for another reason as well, though they do not realize it before pulling into the parking lot and finding it nearly full. An Oktoberfest banner hangs across the entry. Outside, on the patio, a huddle of men and women raise their steins in a toast and laugh too loud. "Maybe we should come back another time," Hannah says, and her mother says, "We will do no such thing. This is your day."

Clouds scud across the sky, and the sun winks in and out of sight. The air still smells damp and minerally from last night's storm, like a stone pulled from a river. The wind hushes and pushes the trees around. Tall firs rise around the restaurant and make it appear like a squat mushroom growing out of their roots.

Normally her mother leads her everywhere, taking her by the hand, maybe directing her by some pressure at the small of her back. On their way across the parking lot, they reach for each other out of habit, and then Hannah pulls away. "I'm okay."

Her mother's hand hangs between them before falling to her side. "Of course you are."

Hannah appreciates her mother. She does. But her eagerness to help feels like a kind of smothering. That might have something to do with why her mother never goes on more than one or two dates with a man. The intensity and weird doggish neediness of her affection.

They walk slowly, through the broad double doors, through the stone entry, to the hostess station, behind which stands a blond woman in a dark green dirndl. She asks, with a mouth full of too-white teeth, if they'd like a table for two.

"For three actually. Maybe she's already here? Lela Falcon? Red-haired? Thirtyish?"

"I don't think so, no. But I'll send her your way when she arrives." The hostess's eyes linger for a moment on Hannah, the Mirage, before tucking three leather menus into her armpit. She asks them to please follow her, and they do, through the crush of tables. Hannah lifts her feet high to avoid tripping on something she can't see. She holds out her hands to brush the gauntlet of wooden chairs and bent backs. She avoids the big blur of the restaurant and concentrates all of her attention on the head of the hostess, bright gold, like a sun rolling away from her. She can sense her mother behind her, her hands no doubt outstretched, ready to catch Hannah if she falls. At last they find themselves safely tucked into a booth.

It's easier to see when rooted in place, a stable view. Hannah concentrates first on her silverware, unrolling it from the linen napkin, setting it neatly on the table. Then she takes in the restaurant. Her mother has described the interior dozens of times. The crossbows that hang from the walls. The murals of mustached, leather-vested men raising foam-topped pints or hunting in dark forests. The deer mounts and decorative steins. The stained-glass windows that color the restaurant gold and red and blue. Sometimes, like today, a band will play polkas on a short stage in the corner. Her mother is not a drinker, but when they come to Benedikt's, she usually permits herself one beer, a Hefeweizen served in a tall glass stein with an orange slice floating below the foam. Hannah likes to run her fingers across the glass, smear the cold moisture off it, and smell deeply of the yeasty drink.

Smells, tastes, touches, sounds—until now that is how she has known Benedikt's, the sight of it a ghostly smear. Until now she never believed it to be such a truly dark space. The blackly polished wainscoting. The scarred timbers that rafter the ceiling and column the dining area. She feels like a hand has closed around her with only a little light peeking through the fingers.

"How are you doing? Are you doing all right?"

"I'm fine."

"You don't look fine."

"It's just—some things don't look like I expect them to. I'm having a little trouble processing." Like her mother, who looks older than she should, her hair threaded gray and her eyes hollowed and her chin doubled. Hannah knows the past few years have been hard on them both, but it's one thing to hear stress in her mother's voice, another to see it clearly in her face.

A figure appears beside the table, a man who asks, "How are you ladies doing today?" Her mother smiles sadly at Hannah, then looks up at the waiter—and screams.

He does not have the face of a man but a gray-skinned warthog, a fat snout spiked with whiskers and jammed with crooked teeth. A bright red hood surrounds his head and spills down his shoulders.

Her scream is not deep-lunged, but loud enough that several people swivel to stare at them. And then she laughs with both hands pressed between her breasts. "Oh," she says. "Oh my. You scared me."

It is a mask, a wooden mask. Beyond the hollowed eyes, a smaller, brighter set of eyes watch them. "Sorry." His voice muffled.

"It's not Fasching Day," her mother says. "Why on earth are you wearing that?"

"I know." He shrugs, a rise and fall of the red hood. "The owner thought it would be fun. It's Oktoberfest, you know. He bought the masks in Germany."

It is then that they notice, all around the restaurant, sneaking between tables, carrying trays weighed down by foaming beers and steaming platters, nodding and scribbling down orders, other waiters, all of them wearing masks. One wears a bear mask and one wears a badger mask. One wears a rabbit mask and another a wolf.

"Hey," the warthog asks, "are those Google Glass?" He points his pen at the Mirage. "I've read about those."

Hannah responds before her mother decides whether to be offended or not. "It's called Mirage. I'm blind. It helps me see."

"Oh," he says. "Really? Wow, that's so cool. And kind of awkward on my part. Sorry."

"It's okay." And it is. Intrigue is far better than the pity she earns when tapping around with a cane.

"So the glasses," the warthog says. "How exactly do they—?"

Her mother interrupts him. "Can I get a Hefeweizen? And water."

"You bet," the warthog says. "And for the young lady?"

"Coke, please."

He departs and Hannah says, "We should have asked for another water. For Aunt Lela."

Her mother says, "Hmmm," and fusses with her napkin.

"What? You don't think she's coming?"

"We'll see. She doesn't have the best track record."

Hannah looks toward the entry, hoping to catch Lela wandering in that very moment. With every shift of her head, it takes her brain a moment to get into conversation with the Mirage, to compute how close and far away everything is, how the colors and contours jumble together into objects she can identify. A table, a chair, a plate, a beer stein. Perspective challenges her more than anything, the depth and distance of things. The dining room slowly solidifies. Hands lift forks; mouths mash food and expel laughter and conversation. She looks for Lela, but then again, how will she know her? She is a grassy smell, a hard hug, a voice that speaks machine-gun fast, a presence that comforts her and relates to her so much better than her mother. Hannah would rather spend time with her than just about anyone, yet she doesn't even know her face.

Her eyes settle on the man with the wolf mask. When she spotted him earlier, she assumed he was a waiter, but now she isn't so certain. He hasn't moved. He stands by the bar. Facing them. Watching them? It's impossible to tell, but she's bothered by his stillness.

There is something different about him, something Hannah didn't process before. Not just his body, which is blockish, and not just the mask, coarse hair tufting from its top, a long snout needled with teeth, but . . . a darkness. As if he is enveloped in shadow, surrounded by a black shawl. Hannah holds her breath, scoots back in the booth.

"What's the matter?"

"Nothing. I just don't like that one."

"Which one?"

"The wolf one."

"Where?"

She points. And he sees her pointing. His head cocks as he studies her curiously. The dark shawl seems to flare red at the edges. Only then does he move, nudging between two tables, departing the dining area, heading for the door.

"Huh," her mother says. "Well, he's gone now."

Hannah tries to focus on something else, the menu. She splits it open. She can't shut her eyes, can't stop seeing, unless she powers off the device. She's tempted to now, but it was more than what she saw —it was what she *felt* when she looked at the wolf. Cold, and vulnerable, as if a knife were pressed to her neck.

"Hannah?" her mother says.

"It's nothing. I'm just getting used to seeing, I guess." It was just a man. A man in a mask. Dressed up like all the rest of them. Nothing to worry about.

The waiter returns with their drinks. "Any interest in some appetizers? Or are we holding out until the other guest arrives?"

"I think we can order," her mother says.

To be blind is to be habitual. To set the water glass in a precise location, meal after meal, so that when she reaches for it, her fingers don't fumble it to the floor. To try on clothes for her mother or her aunt, to learn which tops go with which pants or skirts, to hang them in the closet at four-inch intervals so that she can count the hangers right to left and find what she's looking for without delay. There is always something springing out of the dark otherwise, surprising, injuring, humiliating her. If a drawer is left open, it will bruise her hip. If a chair isn't pushed under the table completely, its leg will catch her foot and she'll tumble. If the knives aren't placed down in the dishwasher, she'll stab her hand when she empties it.

A place for everything and everything in its place, her mother often says. Routines define Hannah, and they've come to define her mother as well. Her mother guessed Lela would somehow screw up this celebration. That the prediction has come true grimly satisfies her somehow. Hannah hates this. Hates the depressingly rutted patterns of their life. So when the waiter turns to her and she orders the Wiener schnitzel instead of her standard bockwurst, when her mother stares at her a moment in surprise and says, "Are you sure?" she says, with biting certainty, "Yes."

✣

An hour later, when the waiter brings them their dessert, an apple strudel and Bavarian cream, he tells them about the goat heads. Carved wooden goat heads hidden in the forest behind the restaurant. If you find one, you win a prize. "Free meals, free river cruises, free movie passes, free tickets to go see the Trailblazers. All sorts of things."

Hannah finishes the strudel before she tells her mother she wants to do it.

"Are you sure?" her mother says, in the same unsettled voice as before, as if she hardly recognizes her own daughter.

"I'm sure."

"I'll come with you," her mother says. "We'll do it together."

"No." Hannah wipes her mouth and drops her napkin on her plate. "I want to go alone."

It feels right and wrong to say. The kind of scary she can deal with. Her mother opens her mouth to protest, then pinches her lips together and sighs through her nose and nods. "If it will make you happy."

✣

Hannah makes her way outside, where the clouds have thickened along with the shadows among the trees. The music from the band and the laughter from the beer garden fade as she whispers through the grass and then crunches through the pine needles, entering the forest. She touches trees as she passes them, palming the rough bark, and she wobbles her feet over roots and rocks. She kneels now and then to part the branches of a bush, to comb aside fern fronds. She covers ten feet of ground, then twenty, not rushing.

She feels it before she sees it, the goat head, tucked into a decayed stump. She peels back a damp clump of moss to reveal the sculpture, the size of a pool ball and made from dark polished wood, horned with slanted eyes and sharp teeth.

Her smile fails when she hears footsteps behind her. "I told you I was fine," she says. "I don't need your help. See?"

She holds up the goat head to the figure, and only then does he come into focus. The man from the restaurant. The one dressed as a wolf. He stands in a clump of sword ferns. The black aura surrounds him as though he carries the night like a shawl.

"Your aunt is Lela Falcon?" His voice is accented. His eyes are lost to the shadows inside the mask. The teeth of the snout seem to grin.

"How do you know that? Who are you?"

He says nothing, and she drops the goat head with a thud as the wolf starts toward her.

CHAPTER 12

THE WEARY TRAVELER has a basement. Concrete floor, whitewashed walls stained green and black with mold. A few bare light bulbs. At the bottom of the staircase lean two scabby bicycles Mike Juniper loans out to his clients. The furnace squats in one corner. Next to it are bins packed with Christmas and Easter decorations. The far side of the room—farthest from the staircase—Juniper uses as a makeshift gym with a bench press and dumbbells, a pull-up bar bolted to the studs of the open ceiling.

Here, against the wall, hangs a life-size crucifix that Juniper bought at a church garage sale. Jesus's body is sunken-bellied and crowned with thorns, roughly carved from the same wood as the cross. It is hideous. Meant to disgust and terrify. Which is why he put it here. To keep people away.

Juniper stands before it now with a Coke can and a plate stacked with sandwiches, grapes, a chocolate bar. He reaches out and the nail that pierces Christ's right hand depresses with a click. The wall gives way, swinging back—to reveal a stone passage. It curls downward, twenty steps altogether, lit by a bare bulb that fights the dark. The staircase ends at a locked iron door. Next to it a tablet is anchored. The passcode—1318—the chapter and verse in the book of Revelation where the number of the beast is mentioned. The screen becomes a pulsing red, like a heartbeat, as it awaits the next key.

The same sort of system that controls so many phones controls the shelter. The lighting, the heating and cooling, the smoke alarms and locks and general security, are all tied in to a controlling intelligence. Its voice is a mellow baritone. "Hello, Mike Juniper."

"Hello, Shelter."

The voice recognition activates and the tablet screen goes green.

A deadbolt *shucks* from its sleeve. He pushes through the unlocked door.

Beyond it, the room. Stone-walled, cement-floored, windowless. Speakers nested in every corner. Cupboards and tables and pegboards busy with curious tools. The air thick with the stink of mildew and bready gas. The door auto-locks behind him.

Sarin paid for the security system and this subbasement, what she likes to call The Dungeon. She waits for him here and snatches away the plate he offers. She can't seem to crack the Coke quickly enough to guzzle. She rips open the candy bar. "All this excitement," she says, around a bite. "I've worked up an appetite." Her voice is boastful, but he can see the strain in her face, the black circles beneath her eyes offsetting the paleness of her skin. Her blood sugar is low. Normally she needs a transfusion every few hours to feel like herself, but they've been busy. A fly lands on her sandwich and she shoos it away, and it joins the dozens of others dirtying the air. They come from *him*.

He sits in a massive chair made from ash and situated in the center of the floor. He is manacled in place at the wrists and ankles. The wood is old, scarred. His hair is long and orange, and sweaty strands of it cling to his cheeks. One of his eyes is bruised and swollen. His shoulder is gun shot, a weeping red mound purpled along the edges. He smells faintly of sulfur. He is shirtless, revealing his hairless sack of a belly and the pale breasts that rest atop it. His pants are damp from where he pissed himself. His wallet revealed his name was Cheston—and a quick Internet search uncovered his web-hosting service as well an old article in Reed College's newspaper about the Disciplinary Committee hearing that concerned his involvement in a music and video piracy network. But none of that matters because he is no longer the same person.

✣

Late last night, in the tunnels below Portland, at The Oubliette, behind the bar, they pushed through the red door and discovered they were too late. For Babs. The owner of the club was already dead.

His office was brick-floored. Roots and coax cables and Christmas lights threaded from the ceiling. Modems and routers and hard drives blinked with blue and green light. One wall was lined with file cabinets. The other with screens that streamed footage of the prostitutes he employed. Every john was unknowingly recorded by a hidden camera, the video stored here for later blackmail and extortion.

Manila envelopes and brown shipping boxes were stacked everywhere. Babs dealt some on the streets, but these days he got almost all his play online, shipping Molly and H and oxy off in boxes of jelly beans to mask the smell. All paid for with bitcoins on the Dark Net. He told Sarin repeatedly that the Internet was the future—for life, for commerce, for entertainment, for crime and for justice, for the balance—and she always shrugged and said, "Old dog, new tricks."

"You're going to get left behind, girl," he said. "You're going to be extinct before you know it."

But now he was the one on the floor, dead, the blood still pumping out of him, steaming in the chill air. He wore a neon-yellow tracksuit. The jacket had slid up to reveal the swollen brown wedge of his belly. Cheston hunched over him. One of his hands clenched the remains of Babs's torn-out throat.

Juniper closed the door, muffling the noise of the bar behind them.

Cheston's eyes jogged between them and settled on Sarin. "You." He stood and wiped his hand on his polo shirt with a red smear. "I remember you."

She answered with a gunshot.

✣

Now, in the basement of the shelter, Sarin focuses on her sandwich, tucking a lettuce leaf into her mouth mid-chew, following this up with a handful of grapes, washing it all down with a fizzy gulp of soda.

Cheston says nothing, but his breathing is like its own conversation, ragged and guttural, like a bear after a hard run.

Juniper walks over to a workbench stacked with hammers and saws and pliers. He selects a ten-foot length of chain that he loops around his knuckles. He does not carry the rest, but drags it across the floor with a clank and rattle. "Tell us your name."

"Cheston."

"Cheston is the body. Tell us the name beneath the name."

"Guess."

"Baal."

"No."

"Eligos."

"No."

"Astaroth."

"Guess, guess, guess, and keep guessing. Guess until your throat is sore. The Zero Day will come before then."

"Zero Day? What the hell is Zero Day?"

No response.

"Why did you kill Babs?"

"Because that fat bitch was in my way."

"In your way how? Why are you here?"

When Cheston doesn't respond, Juniper says again, "Why are you here?"

"I go where I want."

Sarin speaks up now, wiping her mouth with the back of her hand. "Not here. Not in my city."

"Your city?" Cheston laughs and the laugh becomes a cough. He hacks up a few flies. They ooze down his chest, sleeved in a yellowish drool that they crawl from. They tremble their wings dry before taking flight, joining the others that hover in the air like a black net. "*Your* city. If it ever was yours, it won't be much longer."

"Because of Zero Day? What will happen then? Why are you here, what do you want?"

"Everything wants the same thing. To feast. To fuck." Cheston's eyes are bloodshot and dilated, ringed red and bullet-hole black. He is smiling, but not for long. "To grow."

Juniper withdraws from his breast pocket two foam earplugs. He tucks them into place and makes sure Sarin has done the same. He sees Cheston's mouth move with the words: "Wait. Don't do—"

Then Juniper gathers the chain and pivots quickly, hoisting it and lashing out an arm so that the metal untangles—striking Cheston's shoulder, then wrapping around the chair's back, before swinging around the other side to bite his chest. It's more than the pain of impact. It's the iron. The iron burns.

Cheston throws back his head and screams. Even with the earplugs in, it is a disturbingly harsh sound, like someone blowing through a gashed tuba. The chain falls away, and his skin blisters and weeps where the links touched his skin.

"Why are you here?" Juniper asks again, and when he receives no answer, he gathers the chain and circles Cheston, draping it over his shoulders, mashing it into his face, cramming it down his pants. The screams are so powerful he can feel them, like a terrible wind, and dust falls from the ceiling and the lights ebb and a hairline crack creeps along the concrete floor.

Sarin continues to eat through all of this. She shakes the Coke can empty and cleans the plate of every crumb with a licked thumb.

Juniper removes the chain, letting it puddle on the floor before the chair, and then plucks out the earplugs. He knows pain will never be enough, not for the answers he seeks, but pain readies the way for emotional frailty. He will begin with an appeal to vanity. "You're weak. It was easy to find you and it's easy to hurt you. Of course you're not Baal. Of course you're not Astaroth. You're a name no one knows. You're an errand boy, aren't you? What are you here for, slave?"

He mewls. Tears of blood run down his cheeks. "You're not a good man. You're a sadist. You enjoy hurting me, I know it."

"You're not the only one, are you?" Juniper says. "You're not special enough to be the only one. You're just the stupidest, the sloppiest. The one who got caught. Are there more? Tell me. Or I'll work you over with the chain again."

"There are more, there are more." His voice gurgles, his lips sputter. "There will be many more to come. A whole fucking battalion." His words give way to a coughing fit that makes him retch another pond of flies.

"Legion," Juniper says. "You're supposed to say *legion*. Didn't you ever read the Bible?" He slaps the man's belly, takes hold of the fat there, gives it a hard yank. "Are you sure they're not stashed inside of you? This battalion? Because it looks like you've got a lot of storage space." His belly button is as big as a mouth, and Juniper shoves a few fingers in it. "No? Not in there? Then where are they? Where'd you come from? Where are your buddies coming from?" He starts to lean all his weight onto the belly, up to his forearm in slippery fat.

His answer comes as a pained shriek. "From the Dark Net!"

Juniper leans back, gives the belly a gentle pat. "There we go. See how easy this can be. Now explain what you mean by the Dark Net."

Sarin says, "That's where Babs was doing business."

"Is that why you killed Babs?" Juniper says. "Because of some shit going down on the Dark Net?"

"He already has the tunnels wired. The Oubliette is located beneath a Paradise data center. We wanted to work with him—we promised he would be rewarded for helping us—but he refused." He smiles weakly. "Told us to go to hell."

Juniper walks away and plunges his hands in a barrel, now half-empty and speckled with dead flies. He rubs his palms together, scrubs between the knuckles. He's not sure any amount of soap would help him feel clean. His reflection ripples on the surface of the water. "Why do you need the tunnels wired? Why the data center?"

"To open the door." His voice wheezes and cracks around the edges, so that it sounds like other voices folded into it. "To ready the way."

CHAPTER 13

AT BENEDIKT'S, CHERYL WAITS as long as she can—finishing her coffee, listening to the polka band, paying the bill—but still her daughter doesn't return from the woods out back. She hates to be such a worrier. Hannah once told her it was a chronic condition. "When we go to the beach, you warn me about sharks and sneaker waves. When we put up the Christmas tree, you double-check for bugs and fuss over the stand because you're sure it will tip over. Doesn't matter what the situation is, you imagine the worst-case scenario." Hannah's right. It's the way Cheryl's hard-wired. It's the reason she's been on a steady diet of Zoloft the past few years. Ever since Hannah's eyes started to fail, both their ways of seeing changed, though they know a different kind of darkness.

Cheryl forces herself to walk, not run, after twenty minutes have passed, to the restaurant's entrance. The hostess thanks her for coming and Cheryl says, "My pleasure!" with too much enthusiasm. The music and the laughter from the beer garden fade as she crosses the parking lot, passes the Dumpsters, and enters the tall stand of firs. The air instantly cools and thickens with blue shade.

She almost calls out for Hannah, then doesn't. There's no need to worry. That's what Hannah would tell her. I'm fine, *Mom*. Quit hovering, *Mom*. Stop making such a fuss, *Mom*. Give me space, *Mom*. But it's hard. Even now. Her daughter might not be blind, but she's certainly disoriented. What if she tripped and hurt herself? What if she—

No, she's fine. She's playing a game in the woods. That's all. And good for her, pushing boundaries. The guts her girl has. The grit. It should make Cheryl proud. It does make her proud. She'll say as much when she finds her daughter—and then, when Hannah shrugs off the attention, Cheryl will ask if she's found any of the hidden goat heads and whether she wants to go home.

But that's not what happens. Cheryl rounds a blackberry thicket to find a man in a wolf mask bent over her daughter. It is an image out of a fairy tale: the shadowy woods, the gray-muzzled wolf kneeling over the girl, appearing to feed. And so it takes a moment for the reality to sink in, for her to cry out, "What are you doing?"—her voice not a scream, but almost there. "What's happened?"

The man whirls around, still in a crouch, and for a moment it appears he might lunge. It's the man. The one Hannah said she didn't like in the restaurant. He stands, his body thickly set, and lifts the mask to reveal the face of a man with a beard so black it appears like iron shavings. "You are the sister," he says.

"I'm her mother. Get away from her!"

But he doesn't. Instead he seizes Hannah by the arm and drags her from the ground, her legs limp beneath her. "Both of you will come with me." His teeth are long and yellow, visible when he speaks in flashes beneath his beard.

Lela has always accused her of being weak, a bore. But right now, with her daughter in danger, Cheryl feels like she could hurl a car, kick over a tree. She jams her hand in her purse until she finds what she's looking for: the pepper spray Lela gave her. She flips the cap, thumbs the button, extends her arm—and lets loose a poisonous stream.

It splatters his face—his eyes and mouth—sheeting his skin and clouding the air all around. He lets go of Hannah and drops to the forest floor and shoves his fists into his eyes. His body convulses with pain.

Hannah lies on her side, the ferns mashed and spiked all around her in a green splash. Bits of moss and dirt stick to her clothes when Cheryl goes to her and hoists her into a seated position. "Come on, sweetie. Come on. Can you stand for me? Can you do that, love?"

Her daughter doesn't say anything at first. Only nods. Cheryl can see her own frightened expression reflected in the visor of the Mirage.

The man continues to writhe when Cheryl helps her daughter

stand and leads her out of the woods and into the parking lot. She knows she should go into the restaurant, ask for help, call the police, get words on paper. But something tells her to flee and she panics—and now here they are, a mile away, locked in traffic, edging forward a few feet at a time. Her nose runs and her eyes weep, maybe from the pepper spray, maybe from fear.

NPR plays on the radio, some news about millions of passwords hacked from a large corporation. She snaps it off and wipes her eyes. "What happened, Hannah?"

"I don't know."

"How can you not know?"

"I don't know." Her daughter wipes some of the dirt off her jeans and tentatively touches the Mirage. "I don't trust my eyes. I don't understand what I see."

"What do you *think* you saw?" She curls her grip around the steering wheel so tightly the rubber squeaks. "Hannah? You can tell me anything. You know that, don't you? Did that man do something to you? Thank god I came when I did. I feel sick. I feel sick all over just thinking about it. What did he do to you? You can tell me. It's okay. You didn't do anything wrong. Was he one of those perverts?"

"No."

"He wasn't about to . . ."

"No. He was talking about Lela. He wanted to know where she was, when we had last seen her."

"Lela? *Lela*. What do you mean, Lela?" Cheryl can't process this and swings her head back and forth, trying to split her attention between the road and her daughter and nearly rear-ends the semi in front of them. She stomps on the brake and the car rocks, and Cheryl throws out an arm to catch Hannah. It's instinctive. She does it all the time. And Hannah can't stand it. Says that if she wants to keep her safe, she should keep both hands on the wheel.

"I'm sorry," Cheryl says. "I'm just so scared. I'm just so glad you're all right. But what's this about Lela? Is that what he meant when he called me *the sister?*" Her tone shifts from scared and uncertain to accusatory. "This is her fault, then. She never thinks about anyone but herself. And now she's made yet another bad decision—pissing off the wrong people—and it's affecting us all. I could kill her. I really could."

Her daughter is quiet a long time before she says, "I'm seeing things I shouldn't see. I don't know if they're real or not. They look real."

"What?" It takes Cheryl a moment to follow. She's too focused on Lela, her stupid, reckless, selfish asshole of a sister. "What are you talking about? What did you see?"

Hannah's hands twist in her lap as if she's worrying an invisible rosary. "When I looked at the man, I saw something. It was like a shawl. Like a black shawl. And when he came near me, when the shawl touched me, I felt sick." She wraps her arms around her stomach and leans forward. "I still feel sick."

✣

God is punishing Cheryl. She knows she shouldn't feel this way, but she can't help it. She didn't grow up in a religious family, but when their parents slammed head-on into a logging truck coming over the Santiam Pass, she found God at the same time Lela rejected Him. She was twenty at the time, her sister sixteen. They lived with an aunt and then with each other until Lela graduated high school. There must have been a time—when they were younger, just girls playing dress-up and house—that they got along, but she can't recall it.

And then she got together with Joe, and they found themselves drawn to a church, though the congregation met in a vacant store in a strip mall. Cheryl wouldn't recognize it as a cult until years later, when the headlines in the newspapers referred to it as such.

They were called the Light of the World, and her ex-husband, Joe, soon became one of the deacons. Theirs was one of many congregations nationwide, all under the leadership of a woman named Katherine Prophet, to whom they tithed 50 percent of their income. Prophet would travel from congregation to congregation, giving sermons and leading workshops. She wore silken robes, striped purple like the evening sky, and carried a staff and wore an oily arnica-based perfume.

The Light of the World had its own bible—printed up at Kinko's—that read like a combination of Catholic mysticism and new age spirituality. In the final year of the church, Prophet's sermons became more and more apocalyptic, and everyone was directed to sell their possessions and travel to Wyoming, to an elaborate cave system where they would weather the end of days. There were air filters piped in and thousands of gallons of water and lockers full of dried goods and an armory of assault rifles and ammunition. Cheryl remembers the shoes especially. Getting to pick out twenty pairs of shoes for Hannah, in ascending size, that would supposedly last her through the years. She isn't sure how many people crushed into the cave altogether, maybe five hundred, but after a few weeks, the apocalypse failed to arrive and everyone wandered away, and soon Prophet was facing charges of gunrunning and money laundering and embezzlement.

The months that followed were difficult for Cheryl, mostly a blur. She can remember a lot of crying and yelling. Joe headed to Alaska, looking for work at a cannery, and never came home. She moved in with Lela for a few months, and when her sister called her an empty-headed dumbass who preferred fantasy over reality because it inflated her sense of worth, Cheryl slapped her and said, "Don't you dare talk about me like that. Don't you dare." She went back to school and became a case manager at a social services agency on the east side, walking distance from her home. This felt like a kind of penance, helping the beaten wives and neglected children, the strung-out, the diseased, the disabled, the poor and helpless. She had become her own church, a congregation of one.

These days, God is no longer present in Cheryl's life. Except when she is at her highest and lowest—moments like this one—and suffers from paroxysms of faith. As she drives her daughter home, she whispers, "St. Michael, St. Michael, let blue flames surround me," one of the prayers of her old church meant to stave off evil. "St. Michael, St. Michael, let blue flames surround me."

✣

They live in a rented bungalow off Hawthorne, and on its front stoop they find a bouquet of balloons—left by a neighbor, along with a card congratulating Hannah on her newfound vision. "We're so happy for you," the script inside reads. "What a miracle and what a gift." Cheryl felt the same until now, as her daughter speaks of auras.

There is a black balloon tied among the dozen. It looks wrong, the opposite of festive, but Cheryl barely registers its presence as she collects them from the stoop and hurries inside to set them on the kitchen table.

Hannah is already in the bathroom, the door half-closed. She has complained of feeling ill the whole ride home, and now Cheryl can hear her heaving, again and again, until it sounds as though she might turn inside out. She knocks tentatively and her daughter says, "Get this thing off me," and so she helps remove the Mirage and wash Hannah's face and brush her teeth before ushering her to bed, pale-skinned and shivering.

Cheryl tries to stop herself from praying, but she can't. She falls to the hardwood floor with a bang of her knees and knits together her fingers and asks for God to give her guidance and watch after her dear, dear daughter. Then she trembles her way through twenty or so Our Fathers and feels a little calmer. The singsong orderliness of the words always does that to her.

She tries calling her sister, but it goes straight to voicemail, and she tries leaving a message, but the storage is full. She tries to tidy up the house and she tries to watch TV and she tries to read the newspaper—hunting for her sister's byline, where she'll maybe find some clue as to what's going on—but nothing works. Her attention keeps looping back to the wolf in the woods hunched over her daughter as though to feast.

Then Hannah screams and Cheryl hurries to her room and snaps on the light and discovers the black balloon. It has somehow separated from the others and bumbled down the hall, where it now hovers at the foot of her daughter's bed.

Hannah sits upright. She is no longer screaming, but it looks as though she is, her mouth a hole and her body shuddering. Her eyes are open and staring so fixedly at the balloon that Cheryl could swear she sees even without the Mirage.

Hannah does not respond when Cheryl calls her name, not until she grabs her daughter by the shoulders and gives her a little shake. "Mom?" she says, lost in her own private darkness, and they embrace.

It is only then that Cheryl notices the abrasions. On Hannah's neck, her cheek, her wrist and forearm. What look like bite marks. Cheryl asks her what happened.

Her voice is so brittle when she says, "They came for me in my dreams. They came for me."

"Who?"

"Them. The shadows."

Cheryl pulls up Hannah's shirt to discover her belly, too, is reddened with bites—and across her back run five bloody lines, like the slash of a long-nailed hand.

✣

The doorbell chimes—a long, drawn-out, two-toned note. This is immediately followed by a hurried knocking.

Cheryl checks the window before unlocking the door, letting her sister inside. Lela barges in, because that's the way she enters any room, aggressively kinetic. Her face is flushed and she seems even more keyed up than usual. "So sorry! I'm so sorry. I totally forgot and I'm a terrible person who should be stabbed with hot pokers for the rest of eternity. But something is going on. Something weird. Something scary. Something I don't totally understand and—"

"I'm glad you're okay," Cheryl says. Yes, she's so annoyed with her sister right now. But Cheryl loves her, and right now she can't do anything but drag her worried sister into a hug.

Lela usually goes board-stiff at any contact, but this time she allows the hug and blasts out a sigh. "Thanks, sis. I really feel like a piece of shit."

Hemingway is with her—ears perked, eyes bright—and the German shepherd gives Cheryl an inquisitive sniff before clacking across the hardwood and heading to the bathroom and slurping loudly from the toilet.

The front door remains open, and Cheryl sees no sign of the Volvo out front. "Where's your car?"

"Long story." Lela's purse is always stuffed, but today it looks like she's smuggling a bowling ball in it. She sets it down on the counter with a clunk. Then she turns around and closes the door and twists the deadbolt and leans against the frame as though to brace it. "Okay. I have so much to tell you, but first I want you to tell me about Hannah. You see what I'm doing? Trying to be better? Thinking about others? That's what's happening right now. So tell me—it worked? The Mirage actually worked? Is she stoked? Are you stoked? I am. I want to see this thing. It's sounds so sci-fi. Where is she? I want to see her. Are you okay? Are you still pissed at me? I apologized, you know."

Cheryl realizes that her arms are crossed, her back is slouched, as if she's been gut-punched. "Hannah's on the couch."

"What's the matter?" Lela says. "Is something the matter?"

But Cheryl only motions her forward, out of the entryway, into the living room, where Hannah is curled up beneath a Navajo-patterned blanket. The TV is off. A table lamp throws an orb of light. The dog has found her and nudges her arm with his wet muzzle, begging for love. She gives him a scratch behind the ears and says, "Good boy."

"Hey, kid," Lela says, and kneels by Hannah and combs her hair back from her forehead. "So sorry I missed lunch. What's wrong? You get in a fight?"

"No."

"You sick?"

"A little."

"But I came here to party."

Hannah gives her a smile. Her eyes are open but faraway.

"Where's the thing? The Mirage? I've got to see it."

Hannah doesn't respond except to scrunch shut her eyes—and Lela looks at her and then at Cheryl with questioning concern.

"Whatever trouble you've gotten yourself into," Cheryl says, "we're all being punished for it now."

CHAPTER 14

LELA AND HER SISTER fight often about God. Lela will accuse her sister of magical thinking and lay out her own atheistic principles as flatly as possible. Such as when she told Cheryl this story about a guy named Bob. Bob's wife goes to pick the kids up at school. It's sleeting. It's 4 p.m., then it's 5 p.m., then it's 6 p.m. Bob starts to worry but wonders if maybe his wife told him about some errand or playdate and he simply forgot. He calls her cell, no answer. Then immediately he gets a call back. "I was getting worried," he says, but it's not his wife on the other end of the line. It's a man. An EMT, it turns out. His wife is dead. His son is dead. His daughter is in serious condition. Bob drives like hell to the hospital, and the car skids out on the ice, pinwheels into oncoming traffic, gets crushed. Bob dies. Then, a few days later, so does his daughter.

That's an article Lela had to write last February. There was no moral, she told Cheryl. There was no right or wrong. Just randomness. The cold fucking indifference of the world. You write for a newspaper long enough, this becomes paralyzingly clear. Your parents drive their minivan into a logging truck when you're sixteen, this becomes paralyzingly clear. The universe has been around for a long time before us—and it will go on without us. We're the merest speck in the unfathomable reach of its timeline and geography.

Lela has devoted her life to facts, truth. Not telling people the stories they want to hear but the stories they need to hear. But now she doesn't have a reasonable explanation for what's going on. And she doesn't want to excite her sister's praise Jesus sensibility. So she offers up the quick version. "I'm investigating some illegal activity connected to real estate development in the Pearl District." That's what she says. "The bad guys are pissed."

They're in Cheryl's room, talking in hushed voices, not wanting to upset Hannah any further. The wallpaper is floral-patterned. Precious Moments ceramic figurines line the bureau. The alarm clock is islanded by a white doily centered on her nightstand. The carpet is striped from its daily vacuuming and the bed is neatly made with a country quilt and throw pillows stitched with nauseating affirmations like *I Believe in Myself* and *Live, Love, Laugh!*

Lela resists the urge to mess the place up. And she resists, too, the want to discount everything that Cheryl then tells her. Maybe the red marks on Hannah's body came from the man in the woods and Cheryl simply didn't see them before? And maybe she misheard him? Maybe he wasn't actually using them to get at Lela? Maybe the shadow glitch on the Mirage is a beta problem, no different than a CD skipping or a DVD occasionally banding the screen with black lines? Is there an explanation here that isn't Ouija? Maybe.

Or maybe, probably not. Lela doesn't say a word. The truth is, the more she hears, the greater her fear and guilt and doubt. She doubts everything she has ever believed. Rather than admit this, she says, "I need to make some calls."

"Who are you calling?" Cheryl says, squeezing her hands as though trying to strangle the last bit of water from a dishrag. "The police?"

"Not yet." She almost apologizes for getting her sister into this mess, but holds back. "Can you put something together for dinner? I haven't eaten all day, and I think my head's not on straight because of it."

Cheryl opens the bedroom door and lets out a yelp. The black balloon floats into the room, dangling a silver ribbon like a jellyfish's poisoned tendril. Lela snatches it from the air and squeezes it in her hands and pierces it with her fingernails until it pops into flaccid shreds. The air expelled smells ammoniac and makes her gag.

"Look at us," Cheryl says. "Jumping at shadows."

Cheryl closes the door behind her, leaving Lela alone. Lela plugs in her phone and waits two minutes before punching the power button. It sings to life. Immediately it registers twenty messages, which she ignores, along with the warning that her storage is full. She dials Josh's number, and a few seconds later her ear fills with the pubescent crackling of his voice: "Hey."

He followed up, as she requested, and has some intel. "I don't really know where to start, so I guess I'll just list off stuff I wrote down." The Rue, for one. The address has a long history of ugliness. "I read your articles. The ones about Jeremy Tusk. Pretty good stuff. Kind of scared the shit out of me. Do you know that the Museum of Death—this place in LA—has a whole exhibit on Tusk? They have a bloodstained T-shirt and a few messed-up drawings he did and a diary he kept and even one of his skin-shade lamps."

In the diary, Tusk talked about why he did what he did. Because the shadows told him to. That's what he said. The shadows visited at night, sometimes in the shape of a giant bat that clung to the corner of the ceiling or a hunchbacked rat that roosted in his closet, and said they would hurt Tusk if he didn't do as he was told. They knew about him from his scholarly articles and conference lectures, from the books he had harvested, from the ceremonies he had performed in the name of research. "They are hungry for flesh and thirsty for blood, and I am like their fork and their mouth, their instrument of consumption," Tusk wrote.

But thirty years earlier—Josh is kind of surprised Lela never dug this up herself, it would have made for an eerie embellishment—in one of the Rue's second-floor apartments, a husband killed his wife and then himself. And then ten years before that, the maintenance man hung himself in the furnace room. And thirteen years before that, a fire gutted the building and killed three families. And two years before that, a girl disappeared from her bedroom at night, never to be seen again. And then, in 1912, during the construction of the building, three laborers died when a steel beam collapsed. "I mean, I'm sure every old building has its share of bad luck, but this place seems kind of crammed with nightmares."

"How far back did you go?" she says. "Anything before the building went up?"

"I was getting there. I'm kind of doing this telescoping thing, see. So I checked with the historical society and also consulted the library and City Hall archives. I didn't realize how shitty the Pearl used to be. Like, it's all foo-foo now. Galleries and lofts and bistros and whatnot. It used to be nothing but rail yards and warehouses and shacks for blue-collar immigrants. The Rue went up in 1912. For a while it was used by rail workers and the factory workers hired on at the Weinhard Brewery and area warehouses, then it was briefly a brothel, then it was just a shitty apartment building."

"What about before 1912?"

"I can't be sure about an exact address, so we're talking about a more generalized area now. But in the mid-1800s, ten lumbermen were found in their camp. Dead. Naked. Some of them were hanging from trees, strung up by their guts. Others were laid out in the mud, their limbs cut off and mixed up, sewn into the wrong places on the wrong bodies."

She doesn't realize she has her eyes closed until she tries to scratch down a note. "Anything else?"

"I got a few fires and a smallpox outbreak but can't be certain of the exact location. And then, on a whim, I checked out some Multnomah legends. There were a few that stood out. All of them about the Shadow People. Like, the Shadow People took bites out of the sun until there was no more light and a long winter came. Or the Shadow People would sometimes sneak inside of an elk or a wolf or a bear or a person and pretend to be them, use their skin like a costume to do messed-up stuff like eat babies or burn a village or shove somebody off a cliff. There were five Shadow People—it was like its own insurgent tribe—and they supposedly haunted an area off the Willamette where nobody fished, nobody hunted, because they didn't want to get gobbled up by shadow mouths or raped by shadow dicks or whatever. But then I guess a bunch of warriors from all the local tribes got pissed and gathered together at a meeting in the Gorge and said they weren't going to put up with this shit anymore. It was like an Indian UN meeting or something. And they banded together and finally took the Shadow People out in this shock-and-awe campaign during which the moon eclipsed and the Willamette ran red. Then they buried them, and even though they performed a cleansing ceremony, nothing grew over the burial site for many moons or some shit."

"Jesus." Her mind quickly links the five Shadow People to the five exhumed skeletons. That would make the skull in the other room a link to a time when darkness roamed freely. She shakes her head to clear away the thought, dismiss the connection. She is looking for a logical explanation for all of this, not more superstition. "Do you happen to know why five is always such an important number?"

"Five fingers to control a hand. Five senses to know the world. Five wounds to kill Christ. If you're talking about a pentagram, the top point can indicate the spirit lording over the four elements of matter. Or, if you flip it over, the two points at the top and the one at the bottom are supposed to look like a horned goat with a beard."

"I wasn't sure about you at first, intern, but you're pretty okay."

"Thanks. That's the nicest thing you've ever said to me."

"Don't get used to it," she says. "I have a policy of giving out no more than one compliment per decade."

"Oh, here's one last nugget. The guy who built the building. Samuel Fromm. He was a known associate of Aleister Crowley."

Night has fallen. Lela goes to the bedroom window and pulls aside the shade and stares out into the dark nothing of the backyard. "Why do I know that name?"

"The wickedest man in the world? Occultist? Practitioner of black magick? Come on, Lela. You really need to spend more time on Wikipedia."

The bedroom door shudders in its frame and she opens it, and Hemingway pushes inside and nudges her with his cold wet nose and whines.

"All signs point to creepy. What about Undertown?"

"They seemed legit at first."

"At first?" she says.

"Yeah, at first. They're like a junior version of MongoDB. Obviously you don't know what that is. They're one of the biggest names in Internet databases. Storage centers for all web content and the junk people send and receive online. Undertown is a start-up competitor. They're also in the business of tracking and ad serving."

"But?"

"But I found a few sketchy news items recently. Out of Europe and on Al Jazeera. Database sharing of personal information. Undertown was housing data for some hospitals and insurance companies, and then allowing others to access the information for a fee. I didn't have time to translate most of what I found, but it looks like they've got a lot of real estate on the Dark Net."

"What's the Dark Net?"

He tells her about the Deep Net, which is hundreds of times the size of the surface Internet, all the information that is unlisted, unsearchable, much of it legit, academic and government and military databases. The Dark Net is like the basement of the Deep Net. Mail-order drugs, weapons trafficking, human smuggling, terrorist communications, spy communications, insider trading, intellectual property theft, death porn, and kiddie porn. "Anything nasty or forbidden. Anything people don't want other people knowing about. It's the red-light district, it's the torture chamber, it's digital hell."

Hemingway sniffs her butt and worms between her legs, and she shoos him away. "Do you need some sort of secret invitation or something? How do you get on to this thing?"

"It's easy actually. You just—"

"You mean, you've been there? I thought you said it was only for underworld weirdos."

"You have to wonder about somebody's motives for being there, but there's a contingent of normals too. Lots of journalists actually. Anyone looking for dirt but especially overseas correspondents. Bloggers too. People who worry about censorship. People who worry that if their location or identity gets leaked, they might end up killed or tortured or imprisoned. And then there are the nerds. Bitcoin traders and gamers and such. That's why I go on there. For the free songs and movies."

"Free as in you steal them?"

His voice cracks when he says, "I'm a poor college student working as an unpaid intern. I get a hall pass."

"Go on."

He explains that normally, when you're accessing a website, you're trafficked through multiple routers to get to a server. But the path is traceable. On the Dark Net, those routers would be masked and the URLs wouldn't even be traceroute-able. "You're no one." The standard browser and network is available through TOR, and the websites are seemingly random strings of symbols capped by .onion. "Like kyxt5ww37e9ryb.onion or 7zh42mtc4n2n2.onion. It's not like shopping on Amazon or browsing *Huffington Post*. Most of the websites look garage-made. Message boards and indexes, junk heaps of posts, links, files. Stolen PayPal accounts for sale, fake IDs for sale, movies for sale, people for sale. It's hard to say how many people are down there. Some say four hundred thousand, some say a million. You're off the grid—in an unfiltered, unmoderated, many-layered netherworld—and because of this you're nearly impossible to police. It's a maze of anonymity. And probably the majority of stuff going on down there is put-you-in-prison-for-a-long-time illegal."

Hemingway whines again, this time swiveling his head toward the hallway.

"Hold on a sec," she says.

But Josh doesn't seem to hear her. "You might want to be careful if you're looking for dirt on these guys. This could be some serious—"

She pulls the phone away from her ear, and his voice trails off to a garble. She hears something then. Not in the kitchen, where her sister putters around, but from deep in the house, what could be a footstep thudding or a cupboard door closing or a book toppling over on a shelf.

She rests the phone against her breast. Hemingway now creeps toward the hallway, his tail tucked and his body arrow-straight. The dog's hackles rise and a guttural rumble issues from his chest.

CHAPTER 15

LELA DOES NOT SILENCE Hemingway, and does not call out for her sister, but tiptoes down the hall. At the threshold of Hannah's bedroom, she pauses, not wanting to step inside and flip on the light, not wanting to look. If she doesn't look, she can go on pretending that this night will be different from the last. She can remember all those other occasions when she investigated a noise and it turned out to be nothing.

She nudges the light switch. And sees the man, black-bearded and block-bodied, from the construction site. And from the woods behind Benedikt's, according to her sister's story. He is hunched over, with one leg planted on the floor and one arm steadying the tableside lamp he must have knocked into—while the other half of his body remains outside, lost to darkness.

Once he sees her, he pulls himself fully into the bedroom and stands upright. He is the same height as she, but far broader, with a short muscular neck that upswells from his shoulders. His beard grows too far up his cheeks, the black hairs like so many bristling fly legs.

For a finger snap, she knows nothing, just the vacancy of panic. Then Hemingway's growl rolls into a snarl that crashes apart into spittle-flecked barking. Beside the dog, she feels a little stronger. Her hand goes to the first thing within reach. A book. *Through the Looking-Glass,* the Braille edition. She hurls it. It opens up midair with a flutter before the man knocks it aside. She grabs another book, then another, pitching them overhand—and the man slashes his arms in defense. When there are no more books, she throws knickknacks, a glass bauble, a yellow agate, a clock that splits his eyebrow. He curses her in a rough-edged language she does not recognize and then stomps around the canopy bed and crosses the ten feet of space that separates them.

"What's going on?" she can hear her sister shouting from the kitchen. "Lela? What's wrong?"

Hemingway lunges in between the two, his tail rigid and his ears flattened and his snout peeled to show his teeth. The man rears back. His boot strikes the dog's breast with such force that Hemingway lifts several feet in the air before collapsing on his side, yelping and scrambling helplessly.

There is a small pink recliner with the shape of her niece worn into it. Lela darts behind it, gripping its back as if it were a weapon. The man edges one way and she another, so that they are circling the chair slowly, close enough to see the pores on his nose but not close enough for him to grab her. He tries. And then seizes the chair instead and flips it over.

She backs away as he continues his approach, matching him step for step. He seems in no hurry now, intentionally lingering, as if this were some terrible foreplay.

"Lela?" Her sister's voice is closer now, coming down the hallway.

"Stay back! Call 911. Now."

Lela debates racing for the kitchen to yank a knife from the block, but she doesn't think she'll make it. And that would bring the man closer to where Hannah rests in the living room. She retreats three fast steps, and in doing so her buckle chimes. She bought it at a flea market, an oversize brass rectangle that carries the shape of an elk anchored to a leather belt with a basketweave pattern. She twists off the buckle, slides the belt from the waist loops, wraps the leather around her knuckles once.

"Where is the skull?" he says, and she says, "Fuck you."

His hands are open, and his arms spread to either side of his belly, ready to catch her if she runs, but not ready to stop the buckle when she snaps her arm, whips him across the face with it. He cries out and brings a hand to where his mustache split, revealing broken teeth and the red gleam of gum beneath. She does not wait, lashing him again and again, across the shoulder, the skull.

He goes low and barrels toward her and jams a shoulder into her stomach and smashes her into the wall. She feels the plaster crack and the breath *whoosh* from her lungs, making her go limp enough that he can argue her body into a hold that bends both arms painfully behind her back.

But Hemingway has recovered enough to attack again. The man cries out—his hot breath in her ear—and she looks down to see the dog's jaws clamp down on his calf and shake hard enough to rip the fabric and the skin beneath.

The man releases her. He punches the dog in the snout, wrenches an ear. She stumbles away and retches from the bruised pain in her abdomen. Just as the man balls his fist and readies another blow to the dog, she swings the belt at such an angle it loops his neck—and she stations herself behind him and twists the supple leather so that it cannot be easily unbound. She leans back, putting all her weight into the knee that prods his spine. He claws at his neck and at her, trying to find his breath. They fall back onto the bed and the frame cracks and he makes swampy choking sounds.

He gets a grip on her hair and snatches out a handful, but she does not loosen her grip, not until Hemingway limps toward them. For a moment she fears her own dog—the wrinkled snout, the ire boiling in his gut making him unrecognizable—and then the fear gives way to relief when the jaws snap at the man's groin, then his belly. He tries to kick Hemingway away, but there is no stopping the dog. It has succumbed to something base and frightful, the back-of-the-brain response Lela can very much relate to now.

There is a squelching sound as the dog snatches and tears and burrows his triangular face into the man. His body no longer writhes. One of his hands dangles at his side. She tells Hemingway to stop, but the dog won't. She struggles to stand.

The man's body flops away from her and thumps the floor and still the dog growls, bites, claws. She says it again—"Stop, stop!"—and only then does Hemingway pull back, his face a red mask. The dog licks its chops and pants and waves its tail hesitantly at her.

"Oh no," her sister says. She stands in the doorway with a hand over her heart. "Oh Jesus."

Lela spots some movement out of the corner of her eye. Outside the window, another figure stands, this one smaller, appearing like a child, round-headed but with an old man's face. He wears a black turtleneck. He opens his mouth to reveal his tiny pebbly teeth—and then hisses at her before darting off into the night. She can hear his footsteps slithering across the grass and then pattering along the sidewalk until they are no longer discernible in the nighttime groan of the city, and only then does she relax and pull Hemingway into a whimpering hug.

Both their hearts are sprinting. She pets him and cries silently, and it takes a moment, through the smeared lens of tears, to understand what is happening. Her hands—as she roughs her fingers across Hemingway, scratching her thanks—should come away damp and tacky with blood. Instead she feels like she's combing clots of dried mud from him. She wipes off her tears. Hemingway studies her with a cocked head. His snout, once red, is now gray, as if pasted with ash.

"Did you call the police?" she says to Cheryl.

"The line," her sister says, her voice cracking. "The line was cut. Do you want me to use yours? Your cell?"

Then they observe something Lela likens to time-lapse photography. The black-bearded man is no longer young but old. A slow exhalation comes from him, and with this he appears to deflate and wither, a kind of hurried dry rot setting in. There is a sound like thousands of termites chewing their way through rotten wood when his skin grays and tightens and cracks and crumbles, everything sloughing away, so that his teeth and then his bones rise out of the mess, until they too yellow and fissure and crumble to a chalky residue, and then there is only a smear of ashen waste in the shape of the man who once filled these vacant clothes.

"No," Lela says. "Don't call."

Her sister whimpers and covers her mouth, and the dog goes over to sniff the remains. Lela closes her eyes and opens them, and the scene remains the same. Just like that, as if a switch has turned, her entire belief system changes. She's always said—show me proof, where's the evidence—and now here it is. Maybe the feeling won't last. Maybe this night will fade like the bad dream it seems. But right now, she believes. The New Testament, the Qur'an, the Tipitaka, the

Book of Mormon, the Śruti and the Talmud and the Tao Te Ching. All of it. Everything is true. Anything is possible.

Right now there are thousands of transmissions streaming through everyone. Emails, phone calls, text messages, Wi-Fi and radio and television signals. Right now there are billions of particles of dark matter swirling through this very room, millions of bacteria creeping across her hand, and she can't see any of it. Right now there are thousands of smells that her dog perceives and she does not. Is it that much of a reach to believe that other forces might surround her? Not anymore. Not after what she has witnessed.

This isn't about chasing a story anymore. The story has found her. She is living the story. She is the story. Letters on a page don't matter. Deadlines mean nothing. For the first time in a long time, she feels a singularity of focus. She isn't researching old files and she isn't dreaming up future headlines. She is firmly lodged in the blurred-edge present, where she is being hunted and her sister and niece are in danger because of it.

Hannah is calling for her mother, but her mother isn't answering. Cheryl's eyes are closed and her fingers are sewn together as she mutters a prayer. "St. Michael, St. Michael, let blue flames surround me. St. Michael, St. Michael, let blue flames surround me."

Lela stands and grabs her sister by the shoulders and squeezes her fingernails into the flesh, and Cheryl's prayer trails off as a stare seals between them. "Your daughter needs you. And I need you. Okay?"

Cheryl doesn't complain or scold, doesn't make any bullying demands. Instead she looks at Lela needily and wilts before her as if she were the big sister. "What are we going to do?"

"Get your shit under control. Pack a bag for you and Hannah."

"Where are we going? The police?"

"I think we need a different kind of help."

By the time Lela washes Hemingway's face off with a wet washcloth, her sister and niece are ready. She shoulders her purse, weighted with the skull. "Give me the keys," she says, and snaps her fingers.

Cheryl says, "I can drive," and Lela says, "You drive like an old lady."

"Well, you drive like a crazy person."

"A night like this, the crazy people are in charge."

Cheryl looks like she might fight her, but Hannah utters a sick whimper and she attends to her instead. Lela snatches the keys, swings open the door, and says, "Let's go."

Cheryl doesn't have a garage, her Chevy Malibu parked in a weed-choked spit of gravel alongside the house. Lela hurries there. Hemingway limps beside her. She looks up and down the block, where the night swells around the pools of streetlamps, before hoisting Hemingway into the passenger seat and cranking the key. "Come on," she yells at her sister.

But Cheryl lingers in the yard, hovering near Hannah, who looks as pale as a mushroom. One of Hannah's knees buckles. She wobbles in place. Then leans forward and pukes between her feet. It takes a minute for her to get it all out, and then her mother ushers her into the backseat and belts her in and says, "It's like she's got some darkness in her."

Lela shifts into reverse and stomps on the accelerator. The driveway's entry is so steep that the rear carriage strikes the street with a screech. "Sorry," she says, and then drives randomly for a few blocks, left, left, right, left, left, right, keeping her eyes on her rearview mirror, making sure they aren't followed.

CHAPTER 16

THROWING UP HELPS. It helped earlier too. Hannah knows the feeling won't last, but for the moment her balance feels more stable and she can think her way through the pain rather than being owned by it. Her head pulses. Her bones might be rotten chalk, and her muscles might be wet clay. The bite marks and scratch marks burn. If she were a color, she would be some shade of yellow veined with green, the color of infection.

Her mother dabs at her cheek with her sleeve and says, "It's going to be all right," and her aunt Lela crushes the gas and cranks the wheel one way, then another, making Hannah lean so hard at one intersection that her head hits the window.

"Lela!" her mother says. "Please. You're going to get us killed."

"That's exactly what I'm trying to avoid."

"Slow down. For Hannah's sake."

Their speed ebbs slightly, but their direction keeps changing and the engine still whines like a strained lawnmower. Hannah feels another twinge of nausea and thinks it might help if she could see. Mazing through darkness bewilders and dizzies her. Her hands find her backpack, the zipper, the Mirage. Cool and slippery in her hands. "Can you help me?" she says to her mother, who seems relieved by the question. A simple task, a way to serve.

"Of course," her mother says, "but are you sure you want to wear it?"

"I don't want to be in the dark right now."

Her mother fits the visor into place and lifts the hair behind her ear and tucks the plug into the lightning port there. Then Hannah takes a deep breath and presses the power button on the stem. It takes a minute, but gradually her mind makes sense of the sensory data flooding through it. It's like growing a new hand, she supposes, and trying to figure out how to peel an orange, sign your name.

In the front seat sits a woman. Her aunt. Lela. That is Lela. She strangles the wheel with her hands while they fall down what looks like a lighted tunnel, a nighttime street. Lela's eyes jog between the road and the rearview. She's watching Hannah. Their speed decreases further, and the car slides briefly into the other lane before she corrects their course. "Wow," Lela says. "Cool. They're like Jetsons' sunglasses." She's trying to make her voice sound happy, joking, Hannah can tell, and she's mostly succeeding. "Can you see me?"

Hannah studies her aunt for a long moment. "I can see you."

"Well?" Lela says. "Come on—what do you think? Is this how you imagined your crazy aunt Lela? How do I look?" She twists her head around and gives her a quick, goofy expression before returning her eyes to the road.

Hannah can't help but smile. "You look . . . like one of my favorite people."

Over the next few minutes, her mother prays and her aunt babbles. She talks about all the movies they're going to watch—"Hearing *Star Wars* isn't exactly the same as seeing it"—and all the sports they're going to play—"I can throw you a baseball and not knock your teeth out"—and all the volcanic sunsets they're going to enjoy.

But Hannah only half hears her aunt's voice. In part because the sickness is rising in her again, making her nerves feel haywire, her skin cold, her stomach sloshy and acidic. And in part because she's distracted by the nighttime city. The marquee of the Laurelhurst Theater, which flares upward like an electric peacock feather. The yellow squares that stack into the windows of a high-rise apartment. The neon smears of a bar, pizza parlor, Chinese takeout. The clusters of crowds, the streams of bicyclists, so many bicyclists, their wheels spinning with reflectors and their handlebar lights flashing a warning. It's kaleidoscopic.

And then they start over the Burnside Bridge, and the downtown rises before them, pillars and tiers of light that range the sky and slur their reflection across the river. Above the city, clouds gather and sop up the yellow-green glow. But something cuts through them. Something darker than anything else in the night. Hannah leans so close to the window, her breath fogs it. "What's that?" she says.

Her mother keeps praying, but her aunt ceases her idle chatter and says, "What? What do you see?"

Hannah tries to describe it. Up the river, north of downtown, in the Pearl District, something binds the earth and sky, a thick black pillar. Like an unlit skyscraper. Or a massive spotlight, except one that specially casts darkness.

Lela leans over the wheel and squints. "I don't see anything."

"It's like before," Hannah says. "Like in the woods," and only then does her mother stop praying.

✣

Ten minutes later, they find a parking spot and walk two blocks. Or maybe *walk* is the wrong word. Hannah stumbles, resting often against garbage cans, light poles, her mother. The night air feels good at first, but then it begins to seep into her and she shivers. Her mother takes off her cardigan and wraps it around Hannah like a bandage. They stop before a building tucked between buildings. Its sign reads: THE WEARY TRAVELER, ALL ARE WELCOME.

Through the glass Hannah can see a lit cross hanging above the reception desk. She's still making sense of colors, but she pegs the glow of the cross as somewhere between ice blue and dying lilac. The lights inside are dim otherwise. Lela tries the door and finds it locked. She raps her knuckles on the glass. Waits a few seconds. Then starts pounding with the meat of her fist.

"What are we doing here?" Cheryl says, and Lela says, "Just trust me, okay?"

A minute later the door opens and a man stands in the crack of it, studying them. His forehead juts out and throws a shadow over his eyes. His shoulders are so muscular they seem to round out of his neck. One of his arms is mummied in bandages. He looks like a caveman in flannel and denim. But his voice is gentle. "What do you want now?" he says to Lela.

"Shelter. Like the sign says."

He touches his bandaged arm then, as if reminded of the pain. "Whatever article you're working on, I'm not interested in helping."

"I'm not here for an article. I'm here for help."

"I'm sorry," he says, and starts to close the door.

Hannah feels heavier by the second. Like a darkness is pooling inside her, weighing her down. Something gives. Her ankles, then her knees, her hips, a slow and total collapse. Her mother tries to catch her, but Hannah slips through her scrabbling hands and slumps to a rest on the concrete stoop.

Their voices sound farther away than their faces. They kneel beside her and touch her face and pet her hair and ask her if she's all right. She tries to say, "Clearly," but can't find the breath.

She is vaguely aware of cool air on her belly. Her aunt has lifted her shirt. She is showing the man something. The bite marks. The scratch marks. The hot streaks that offset her otherwise marble-cool skin. "You see this?" she says, yelling now. "We need your help. You need another reason? Because if you need one, I could tell you the story about the guy who broke into her house and crumbled into a pile of ash that looked *a lot* like the one on your kitchen floor."

Only then does the man nod. His body is so big that it seems to take him a long time to lean down, to scoop Hannah up in his arms. She has never felt so small.

✣

Inside, he cradles her with one arm and uses the other to swipe a tablet that hangs near the door. He engages a security code. Locks slam into place. An alarm chirps once to confirm the seal. In this building, with this man, for the first time since the restaurant, she feels safe. He smells like leather and straw. "This way," he says, and leads them down a hallway and into the dining room that runs up against the kitchen. He sets Hannah on one of the tables, and she nearly blacks out from exhaustion.

She isn't sure how long she lies there. Voices fade and bodies slide in and out of view. Sometimes she is awake and sometimes asleep. Every part of her aches. Even the tips of her fingers. It is a poisoned feeling, a rotten feeling, as if her skin sleeved over a black and gelatinous core.

She hears something. A busy sound. The air wing-beaten with whispers. They're talking about her, she realizes. The voices overlap, like wind currents wrestling for control of the air, shrill and deep, calm and questioning.

It's then that a face swings into view. A woman. Not her mother and not her aunt. Silver-haired except for a long black stripe running back from her temple. She's a tired kind of pretty. Her skin drooping and puffing off her face. Her breath smells like menthol cigarettes when she says, "She's got a hitchhiker."

"What are you talking about?" Her mother's voice. Sounding far away, underwater. "What do you mean by hitchhiker?"

The woman doesn't answer, so the big man does. "Somebody's put a mark on her. Something's taken an interest in her," he says. "Jumped on her back, so to speak."

Hannah's mother always said you can tell a woman's true age by looking at her neck. This woman's is long and wrinkled and wired with ligaments that rise from the sharp anchor of her collarbone. Her leather jacket hides how thin she is. She wears something else. A redness that surrounds her. Like a fiery cloak. Edged with yellow and black. It ripples from her body and gives off heat when she leans in.

"You see me, don't you?" she says. "You see me as I am?"

When Hannah doesn't respond, the woman says, "You're like me, aren't you?"

Hannah tries to flinch away, to say, "No!" but the woman takes hold of her face and says, "Don't be stupid. I'm trying to help." Then their mouths come together in what might look like a kiss, but is more a joining of breath.

Hannah sees then. In a rush, she sees everything about this woman. The experience is like falling through a vast house tipped on its side, doorway after doorway, room after room, window after window, crowded with so many views of a life.

The feeling goes beyond her mind and tracks through her whole nervous system. Hannah sees a dark-wooded courtroom full of men with powdered faces and white wigs. They hear arguments that a young woman has blighted crops and spread disease and committed lewd acts. She is stripped and a birthmark along her thigh declared the mark of the devil, and she is named a witch and sentenced to death, and she resists the guards, and they knock her over the head and carry her dumbstruck to the holy river where she will be drowned and purified surrounded by a cheering rabble. She is tied to a kind of seesaw that plunges her below the surface, and she holds her breath and slices through her trusses with a blade she kept hidden in her mouth, and she swims downstream to escape, and when minutes later the seesaw rises from the river dripping and empty of its victim, the rabble goes silent with terror.

Hannah sees a long line of men, bearded and filthy and jeweled with sores and rib-slatted from starvation, stripping off their clothes and folding them into piles and proceeding into the showers at Dachau. The guard tells them to hurry—*Beeile dich!*—and then clangs the door closed behind them. He grins through the small glass window, which splatters red with his blood a second later. The lock turns and the door swings open, and the woman steps through holding a pistol. She uses the same words as the guard—*Beeile dich, Na los*—but with a different sort of smile on her face. Now is their chance, she tells them. The guards are dead and the fence is down, and they must run and they do, and the sky above the camp is gray-ceilinged from the smoke that rises from the furnaces that would have been fed their bodies.

Hannah sees mountains. The moon hangs overhead, silvering the patches of snow and the surrounding peaks. A long line of luxury cars is parked along a winding, pine-bordered road that leads to a chateau. The windows shimmer with the uncertain lights of candles. Inside, some people wander around in robes, all of them wearing masks. Bird masks and goat masks and wolf masks and devil masks with twisted horns rising out of them. Someone slits the neck of a lamb and with its blood paints a giant cipher on the marble floor. Everyone gathers around it and begins to chant so that their voices become one voice heard even through the windows. Outside, the woman glugs and spritzes gasoline. Then she steps back and sparks a match and tosses it, and the flame catches midair. Just like that, the chateau is surrounded by a roiling blue skirt that brightens orange as the flames take to the wood. Glass shatters. Metal warps. At first the people remain inside, shrinking away from the fire, and then they scramble out the front door, out the windows, and when they do, they die. Gunfire sounds all around the house as the woman circles it. Bodies drop, one after the other, a pile of them by the front door. Some make it out of the house, but their robes catch fire and make them easy to find in the dark. Her breath smokes and the gun smokes and the house smokes. She waits until the roof collapses, until the glowing frame is visible, and even then a torch-lit body comes screeching from inside, and the woman fells it with a single shot to the head.

The woman—Sarin, that is her name—has lived many lives. She dies and then she comes back, dies and then comes back, always fighting for the light, like a sun wresting away the night morning after morning.

The images continue to unscroll, and Hannah feels visually gorged, as she sometimes does with the Mirage, unable to close her eyes, to stop the influx. Her mother always says she is growing up too fast, but now she is growing *in* too fast, her mind filling with memories and understanding that are not her own.

And then Sarin sucks in one last bit of breath before falling back. Coughing and gagging. Her skin is now gray and deeply creased, the wrinkles on her face multiplying by the second so that she seems in danger of crumbling to pieces.

The man tries to help Sarin, but she swings an arm, motions him away. She gags then. Vomits a black splattering mess. She has consumed and expelled the hitchhiker inside of Hannah. The puddle of it writhes with movement. Flies and moths and beetles and other unrecognizables with long legs and longer stingers crawl from the bile and test their wings and buzz away.

✣

Hannah has never been so hungry. A plate of pancakes sits before her. She uses a knife to smear a hunk of butter across them. Then pours syrup until only the plate's outer rim remains white. The smell is more than a smell. It's a feeling, the sweet steam rising off them.

She stabs her way through three cakes, saws off a triangle, brings it to her mouth. The cakes are so dank with syrup, they dissolve in her mouth. She relishes the sweet burst of maple mellowed by the wheaty wholesomeness—and then pulls back the fork, the tines sliding between her lips.

It isn't long before the plate is empty. She asks for more. More pancakes. Then four eggs, over hard, crisped brown around the edges. A little salsa on the side. Five sausages, one that she shares with Hemingway. Toast smeared with butter and grape jelly. A banana. A small cup of yogurt sprinkled with granola and frozen blueberries. Two tall glasses of whole milk and a short glass of orange juice.

She eats quickly and without interruption. There is no noise except a happy grunt, a thirsty gulp, and the occasional knife-shriek across her plate. When she finishes, she leans back and rubs her bloated stomach. The fullness applies to her mind as well, confusedly jammed with information she has not yet processed.

Only then does she take in the three adults and one floppy-eared German shepherd watching her. Her mother stands with her hands pooched deep in her cardigan pockets. The man—Juniper, that's his name—has his arms crossed and his legs spread shoulder-width. And her aunt Lela sits at the other end of the table, stooped over with her hands tented together. "How do you feel?" she says.

Never better. Cleansed. Enriched. Maybe she should feel crazy—given what has happened to her—the kind of crazy that makes you crawl into the corner of a padded room and bash your temple with your palm and hum nonsense songs. Maybe that feeling is there, but it's buried deep, like a pain scrubbed away by a numbing shot that calms and warms her into a state of narcosis.

"Should I make more?" Juniper says. "Or are you done?"

"I'm done now. I'm good."

Juniper stands and lumbers toward her and pulls out the nearest chair. He studies her curiously for a moment, then puts out a hand. It's three times the size of hers, cracked and callused. The skin of his forearm sleeved in bandages. Hannah looks to her mother, who nods, and then she allows him to take her hand. His grip closes around hers. "That was close. You got here just in time."

"Where's the woman who helped me? Sarin?"

"She had to go. Removing that hitchhiker took a lot out of her."

"It made her sick instead of me?"

"Yes." He appears uncertain how to respond. "But she'll be fine, I hope. She'll be back. She wants to talk to you more."

"Why?"

"Because she thinks you're special."

"Is that what she meant? When she said, *you're like me*?"

He nods.

"Is she your mom?"

"No."

"Your sister? Wife?"

"Not my sister and not my wife, no."

"I guess she seemed too old to be any of those things."

His laugh sounds like a bark. "She wouldn't love to hear that, but yes, you're right. She's very, very old. Not her body so much as what's in it." He pats her hand, rubs the knuckle ridge. "Mother, sister, wife. She's none of those things, but in a way I suppose she's become all of those things. I don't know what the right word is. Friend, colleague?"

Hannah licks the syrup off her lips. "Does she think I'm special because I see dark things?"

His eyebrows are thick black bands that raise now. "Your mother told me about what happened. In the woods."

"It's because of my glasses. The Mirage."

He still has hold of her hand, a warm rough pocket. "Says who?"

"What do you mean?"

"Who says it's your glasses? Your eyes are just your eyes. Some people can see better up close or far away or at night, but your eyes are just a biological apparatus, nothing special. We're talking about a different kind of seeing here. The aperture is inside you. Do you know what that word means? Aperture?"

"Like in a camera?"

He nods. "Like in a camera." He holds up a glass between them so that his face appears warped and magnified before setting it back down. "And sometimes it's not until puberty when those who are tuned in—extrasensory, touched, on the spectrum, whatever you want to call it—start to encounter the world differently. Just about everyone guesses that there's more to our lives than sight, sound, smell, taste, touch."

"Do you mean like Joan of Arc hearing the voice of God?"

His big shoulders rise and fall in a shrug. "Everybody's got a different way of explaining it."

"Are you—what did you call it—on the spectrum?"

"Yes," he says. "The outer edge of it. Or the lower rung of it."

"What does that mean?"

"You know those cell towers you see on the hillsides?"

"Yes."

"Sarin's like that. And maybe you're like that. Whereas I've got more in common with a bent antenna on an old truck."

"What if I never wore the Mirage?"

"I suspect you'd find other ways to see, sense darkness all the same." He digs his mobile out of his pocket and holds it up. "Lots of people have the same device, but would you believe they all weigh a different amount? Depending on how many emails or songs or photos or books might be on them. Digital information has mass, because everything has a charge. Everything is energy. Everything is a balance of positive and negative. And I can't sense the difference between my phone and another, but the most sensitive scale might be able to. There are all sorts of things out there that I can't sense, that most can't sense. But you're different. More than different. Yes, you're high on the spectrum, but you're somehow upgraded by the Mirage, and that makes you extraordinary, the next level of spiritual warfare. And that's a good thing. That's a very good thing."

"But I can tell from your voice it's also a bad thing."

"You could say that." His forehead creases with worry. "Earlier, at the restaurant, when the man came for you? I think he just wanted you as bait. A way of getting to Lela. But I think you surprised him. He must have sensed you were a threat to put a hitchhiker on you. If you're a threat, you're a target."

"They want to kill me."

"Or worse."

"What's worse than killing?"

"Believe me. There's worse."

"Am I old too? Inside, I mean."

"That I don't know."

"Aunt Lela is always saying so. She calls me an old fuddy-duddy sometimes, but other times she calls me an old soul."

Juniper looks at Lela, who gives him a pinched smile. "Maybe that's so. I couldn't tell you. All I know is, you're part of the light, which means you're part of this fight."

"So what am I supposed to do?" Hannah says.

He leans back in his chair and settles his hands over his knees and cranes his neck toward her mother and aunt. "In the long run, I don't know. But tonight, you're stuck with me."

CHAPTER 17

HANNAH IS TUCKED into bed and Cheryl wishes she could join her daughter there, but she can't seem to settle down. She is a parade of nervous tics, jittering her leg, chewing the inside of her cheek, squeezing the bridge of her nose, picking at her fingernails. She paces Juniper's office while he sits at his desk, his eyes small but watchful beneath the ledge of his forehead. She knots and unknots the belt of her cardigan, pushes her hair out of her face. She doesn't speak for a long time—and when she does, her voice comes in a skittish rush, saying the same things repeatedly with different words: "I don't understand" and "Why would God let this happen to us?"

Juniper lets her speak without interruption until now. "There's no such thing as God."

This quiets and stills her, and she stares with a gaping mouth. "How can you say that? After what's happened tonight?"

"I've gone through the Christian thresher. I know all the Sunday school songs." Earlier he filled a glass, all the way to the lip, with Scotch and ice. He's drained it now, but fishes out a cube to suck. "It's comforting, I know. The idea that Space Dad is watching out for us. And if you appeal to him earnestly enough, he'll parachute down and grant you wishes. But I'm sorry to say that's not the way it works." He looks a little sad, and she thinks he must be drunk.

Of course, this isn't the first time she's heard such a claim. She's thought it herself, especially in the years since her church, the Light of the World, dissolved into an FBI investigation and tabloid news story. But at a time like this, the possibility of a godless world makes her feel as though the floor beneath her has suddenly revealed itself to be a rope strung hundreds of feet in the air. She can't abide that kind of vulnerability. "Don't say that," she says, and goes to a bookshelf, pulls a leather-bound Bible off the shelf, hurls it at him. "You're just going to make things worse!"

The book opens up in the air, its pages fluttering violently. He holds up an arm to try to catch it, but it falls open-faced on the floor. "Maybe we should talk again in the morning," he says.

"God is going to take care of me and my daughter!" Her volume doesn't make it sound any truer, but she feels like she needs to make the appeal regardless.

His voice is gentler when he speaks again. "I'm not trying to be an asshole, okay? There's hope. There's plenty of hope. Believe, but believe differently." He takes more ice into his mouth and crunches it down. "Believe in light."

"What the hell is that supposed to mean?"

"It means there's plenty of good in the world to offset all the ugliness. But you can't just sit back and expect someone to take care of you. You've got to fight for it."

But that's exactly why she stuck with the cult even when it asked her to hand over all her money and wear a tinfoil pyramid on her head and hide in a cave system. That's why she kept saying she was married a year after her husband took off for Alaska. She wants someone to look after her, damn it. She hates the whimpering defeat in her voice when she says, "You're going to help us?"

"Of course." His face softens. "But you're part of this struggle too. Believe in the light, but don't forget to believe in yourself." He swishes his glass of half-melted ice, then crushes a yawn with his fist. "It's late."

She can't sleep. Not after what's happened. Not while her sister is gone. A few hours ago Lela went off on some errand she wouldn't disclose, saying only that she had questions that needed answering. But she'd be back, she promised, before dawn. When Cheryl said, "I'll wait up for you," Lela said, "Don't do that." But she will. She doesn't dare fall sleep, as though shutting her eyes will snuff her sister out.

"If you're going to bed, can I use your computer?" she says to Juniper. She has appointments stacked up all next week at the social services agency where she works. Those cases will now have to be relegated to someone else, because there's no way in hell she's leaving her daughter's side after what's happened.

"You should sleep. I'll let you use my laptop in the morning."

She snatches his glass and tips it back, the cubes knocking against her teeth, the meltwater at once chilling her mouth and burning it with the residue of whisky. "I'm sorry I threw the Bible at you." She picks it up off the floor and neatens its pages and slides it back on the shelf. "Please, can I use your computer?"

"Fine, fine, fine." He rubs his eyes tiredly and splits open his laptop and logs his password and stands from his chair and motions to it. "I'm going to go pass out now." He pauses in the doorway. "There's a pretty hefty firewall on there, so your browsing might be limited."

"I just need to email."

"Should be fine, then. But if it isn't, don't wake me up."

He leaves her there—closing the door behind him—and she is overcome by loneliness. A part of her is maddened by him, and another part of her wants to follow him into bed. It's been years since she had sex, and she doesn't particularly miss it—it always felt compulsory and unclean to her. But on this, the most fucked-up day of her life, she can't help but ache for the comfort of having someone beside her, a warm body that feels like a pillow and defense. She wants him, she wants God, she wants her sister. Someone, *any*one, to offset the emptiness inside her.

She opens up the browser and logs in to her email and sees the twenty or so new messages in her inbox. Some from clients, some from friends, others spam. She fires off several missives to clients and her fellow case managers, informing them she'll be out of the office this coming week due to an unexpected illness in the family. She thanks them for understanding and apologizes for the trouble and reminds them that someone will have to make the home visit to Donna, one of her elderly shut-ins. She writes "Sorry" five times. She knows she says the word too often, but in this case it feels warranted.

The clock reads 3:00 a.m. She's in a daze at this point, only half-awake, her peripheral vision fogged up and her balance wobbly. So she isn't thinking clearly when the laptop chimes and another email pops into view. She doesn't recognize the sender—Cloven@hushmail.com—but she opens it anyway because of the subject line, YOUR SISTER'S FAULT. There is nothing in the body of the message except an attachment, a .wmv file that loads into a media player.

At first she doesn't understand what she sees—the picture appears smeared with black grit—but then something comes into focus. A sign. The Weary Traveler. The shelter they're staying at now. The lamp beside the door glows orange. A few moths flit beside it, battering the glass. A hand emerges then, a hand that belongs to whoever controls the camera, black-gloved. It reaches into the open-bottomed square of glass and twists the bulb until it darkens. The hand drops to the doorknob. A gentle twist. Locked. The camera continues around the side of the building, down an alley, until it comes to a lighted window. In the dining room, Hannah lies on a table. The group of them huddle around her. The woman, Sarin, leans in as if to give mouth-to-mouth. Hannah's body tenses and Cheryl screams and reaches for her, while Juniper holds her back. Here the video goes dark. She checks the feed and sees that it hasn't paused but ended.

She doesn't realize that she opened more than a video when she clicked on the attachment. Within the program another was hidden. An .exe application. The computer hums as the Trojan sets to work, disengaging the firewall and eating its way through the hard drive. It does not limit itself to these files, but streams through the Ethernet cable that plugs into the walls and in a manner of seconds overrides the larger system. The mainframe forfeits control.

Before she has finished the video—its time signature thirty seconds—the security system disengages. Next to the front entry, the red light on the alarm blinks, blinks, blinks, and then goes dark. A moment later the locks disengage, all over the building, their combined *shuck* sounding like a giant pistol hammer cocked. This includes the lower levels, the space beneath the basement that houses Cheston.

That's when the computer screen goes dark, as if snuffed by a hard wind. "What the . . ." she says, and strikes the keyboard repeatedly.

A script appears, lit red, running swiftly from the top to the bottom of the screen and scrolling down. She leans in to try to make sense of it. Her body stiffens and her mouth slackens and her eyes reflect the code as if it is her own blood circuitry.

What happens next is out of her control. She is separate from herself. She belongs to the worm that possesses her and now the shelter. She does not know that she opens the desk drawer and wraps her fingers around a long-bladed letter opener shaped like a serpent. She does not know that she rises from the chair and walks slowly from the office and into Juniper's chambers. She does not know that she stands over him in the dark. She does not know that he murmurs awake and reaches for her as if expecting a naked body. She does not know that she knifes him again and again and again until he goes still. She does not know that she descends one set of stairs, and then another, and then another, beyond the basement, to the room below. She does not know that she frees the man named Cheston from his constraints or that he pets her hair and nibbles her ear and says, "Thank you," before snapping her neck.

CHAPTER 18

When Lela called Daniel, he said, "I tried to leave you three voicemails to see how you were doing, but your phone is full," and she said, "It's been full for years. I can't figure out how to delete them," and he sputtered out an "Oh," and a "dear," and an "I see," before saying that he had some answers and she ought to meet him in the Rare Book Room at Powell's tomorrow morning, first thing.

"Tonight," she said.

"Tonight?" A huffing pause. "You can't be—but I'm already home. I'm in my pajamas, if you must know."

"I thought you slept in a jacket and tie."

"What? Why would I do that? I don't under—"

"Forget it. Tonight, Daniel. It's got to be tonight. I wouldn't ask if it wasn't important."

Again, a stammering response, but eventually he agreed to meet her at the northwest entrance in an hour's time, and from there he led her upstairs to his desk, around which they stand now in a pond of light thrown by his green-shaded lamp. He cracks open an oversize book and licks his fingers and turns pages delicately and says beneath his breath, "Now where was it?"

Her eyes scan the room. Book spines glimmer; the wood blushes. The air is spiced with the smell of old paper, a cross of grass and vanilla. Daniel might have a reader's slouch and moley eyes and a frumpy suit that can't hide the pooch of his belly, but nonetheless she feels comforted beside him. Nearby, Hemingway is curled up in a horseshoe shape, one ear perked, but his eyes closed, snoring softly. The place is the same, the hour is the same, the arrangement of books and the skull on the desk is the same—but right now the danger feels very far away and the bookstore sheltered and cozy once more. Her family is safe. Sarin and Juniper have agreed to help them.

And she appears to be closing in on answers. There are a thousand reasons she should lock herself in a closet and wait for dawn, but for the moment, in her mind, she's winning.

"Who buys from you, Daniel?"

He looks up from the book and readjusts the glasses sliding down his nose and says, "Oh, I generally deal with three different types of customers. Those who walk in and buy on a whim. Those who are decorators looking for something old to class up a living room, and they're the absolute worst, I must say. And then there are the studious, serious buyers. They're not collectors so much as they are antiquarian scholars. They come from all over. China, Germany, Brazil, England, New York, and right here in Portland."

But in the case of every buyer, Daniel says, they decide to bring a book home because, whether they understand it or not, these titles hold stores of power between their covers. That's what he believes. He really does. Books are like batteries, he says. And you grow a little stronger by reading them, surrounding yourself with them.

"Such is the case with this title," he says, and closes it and pats the cover fondly. The leather appears branded more than stamped with the title and author, *Lock and Key* by Joseph Hilfin. "It doesn't look like much at first. I would classify it as in very good condition, given its age of some two hundred years, with the rubbing and chipping and staining along the cover, the minor tears and cracks in the pages." He runs a finger along the spine and says the hinges are tight with no separation from the binding. He describes foxing—the acidification of paper dating back to the nineteenth century that results in rust-like spotting—and the laid-in pages that are loose, complementary to the central text but not directly part of it, typically a map or ancillary material.

"This is interesting, isn't it?" He flips to the front matter and shows off the torn bookplate there. Only half of it remains—discolored and faded—but she can make out enough. The border is a seething tangle of serpents fanging each other. And the name of the owner, in red script, is cut off. "Crowley" is all it says, a name she recognizes somehow. From her earlier conversation with Josh on the phone. "Crowley." She says it aloud as if that will help spur the memory.

"Indeed," Daniel says. "And though I can't prove it as such, I find it very likely it belonged to none other than one Aleister Crowley, who during his time owned one of the world's largest collections of occult writings. As an interesting side note, a man named Jimmy Page later purchased Crowley's home and library and presently owns an occult bookshop in London."

"Think I've heard of him," Lela says absently, and pulls her notebook from her purse.

"Mr. Page? He belonged to a rock-and-roll band named Led Zeppelin that was apparently quite popular in the 1970s."

"Thanks, Daniel. I got it. Okay—Crowley, Crowley, Crowley." She flips through the notebook's pages until she finds what she's looking for. Crowley, the self-proclaimed wickedest man in the world. A practitioner of black magick, Tantra, Satanism. Samuel Fromm, the man who built the Rue, was a known associate of his. "What else can you tell me about him?"

Daniel says, "Crowley was interested in creating what is called a moonchild. A scarlet child. A child seeded and possessed by an ethereal being. A fetal avatar that would carry a superbeing into our world. Demonized. Possessed. This is accomplished by a series of magical and sexual rituals that call forth darkness. Oh, and another side note. The moonchild was the subject and title of a novel Crowley wrote in which a group of magicians attempts to impregnate a girl whose offspring will change the course of human history. Anyhow, I sold a pristine copy of it not long ago, and the buyer told me an anecdote about L. Ron Hubbard, the founder of Scientology, and Jack Parsons, one of the founders of the Jet Propulsion Laboratory in Pasadena. Apparently they were in touch with Crowley and attempting black magick rituals in order to birth their own moonchild, what they hoped would be the Antichrist."

"What does this have to do with the skull?"

It sits in the center of the desk, facing them, watching them, and they are both lost for a moment in its gaze. Ciphers etch every inch of it. The warped, elongated shape makes it appear like some shadow of a man bent by the low angle of the sun.

Daniel clears his throat and turns the book's thick pages. They don't flip crisply but roll like fabric. She can't read any of it—the text is in Latin—but she recognizes some of the drawings and feels repulsed by some of the illustrations, a man with a snake growing out of his groin, a woman with the head of a goat. A black beetle scuttles out of a fold and scurries across the desk and vanishes beneath the skull, and Daniel pauses only to say, "Oh my," before continuing.

"Have you ever had a key made?" he says. "Have you ever seen a locksmith work on a car or a front door and try to get the cut exactly right? The teeth must be just so. Just so. Or the grooves won't line up with the pins in the tumbler lock.

"This book is a kind of study guide in supernatural locksmithing. It teaches you how to open different kinds of doors for different kinds of darkness. Some allow people to go there, and others allow demons to come here. There are outright summons. Impregnations akin to the moonchild ceremonies. Solstice performances meant to channel power through sacrificial appeasement. And on and on. There are many different locks, many different keys. And these ciphers," he says, "the ciphers on the page and the ciphers on the skull are like the cut of a key."

"A key to what?"

He points a finger at the barbed heading at the top of a page. "A black site. Also known as a dusk or night chapel. A place of worship. Where unholiness gathers. And—with some encouragement—bleeds into this world." He stares at her for a long few seconds and then shows off his pipe-yellowed teeth in a grin. "It's rather splendid to think about, isn't it? Especially at this haunted time of year?"

"The Rue." She remembers what Hannah saw when they crossed the Burnside Bridge. A pillar of darkness rising out of the Pearl District. "The Rue is the black site."

"In this case I prefer the term 'night chapel.' Here's why: the skull." Lela told him there were five graves, arranged in a kind of circle, at the construction site. "This," he says, "seems to indicate the pentagram, a holy number and sigil to any dark parishioner. Some see it as a representation of the five wounds of Jesus Christ or the binding of the five elements. Or infinity."

She holds up her right hand, remembering the bloodied handprint that was Tusk's signature. "Five fingers."

"What's that?" Daniel says, and she doesn't answer, lost in thought. "Regardless, if the skull was one of five, then it seems to me it was ritualized and must be some kind of relic." He talks about how, over five hundred years ago, St. Peter's Basilica was built in the Vatican. There are marble towers staggered throughout the interior that were constructed to entomb the skull of a saint, the lance that pierced Jesus's side, and the cloth that cleaned his dead face. The Vatican did this because it understood the importance of relics. Go into any European church and you'll find more of the same—relics—typically constructed into the altar. A piece of an exhumed saint's body, maybe a hand or an ear, or a splash of a saint's blood. Sometimes priests will even wear the relics, such as a finger bone braided into a necklace or hat. "This isn't unique to Christianity. Just as hell isn't limited to Christianity. Virtually every religion has some iteration of the same thing, as though trying to get at the same truth that escapes them all. Relics are understood to channel and harness power. For good. And for evil." Daniel removes a handkerchief from his pocket, and though the store is cool, he wipes the sweat beading on his forehead.

She picks up the skull and holds it before her face. She can't fight the feeling that it's going to open its jaws and bite her. She remembers the story Josh told her over the phone, the one about the Shadow People that haunted the Northwest before the local tribes banded together to extinguish them and reclaim their territory. This skull was one of the husks they left behind.

"If they were exhuming the skeletons," Daniel says, "then I think it's fair to say they wanted to use them."

"For what?"

"That's what I was trying to tell you before. In the book here, *Lock and Key*. The designs on this skull match the designs in this chapter."

"What's the chapter called?"

"The layman's translation?" He tips his head and his glasses catch the orange light of the lamp. "Gates of Hell."

✣

The sky is a predawn pink. Lela does not walk directly to The Weary Traveler, but zigzags her way through downtown, checking over her shoulder every block, hurrying past alleyways.

She finds the rear entrance to The Weary Traveler unlocked. Inside several men busy themselves in the kitchen and dining room, helping themselves to whatever is in the fridge and cupboards. One is drinking directly from a milk jug, and another is trying to clean up the spilled grounds and murky puddles surrounding the coffeemaker. A few sit at the tables, pouring cereal, spreading jelly on toast, arguing over the crossword puzzle in the paper. The counter is a mess of bran flakes and broken eggs. Something on the burner smokes.

"What are you doing?" She yanks the pan of blackened bacon and snaps off the heating element.

"Making breakfast of course," says the man with the milk jug. He's older, lean, and tan with a dent in his forehead. He wears a white undershirt, fleece pants. His feet are bare and veined and slap the floor when he walks toward her. "Care for a glass?" He holds out the jug. "It's whole. The way milk ought to be."

"Where's Mike Juniper?" she says.

"Who's that again?" he says.

"Juniper. He runs the shelter."

The old man knits his eyebrows together, and then his face softens as the question escapes him. He seems to see her for the first time and once more holds out the jug. "Care for a glass? It's whole. The way milk ought to be."

She pushes past him and scoops a few spilled coffee beans off the counter and pops them into her mouth and chews them down for the bitter punch. She starts down the hallway. She can hear the television blaring in the lounge, and on the couch she finds a man in a hoodie, clicking through the channels. When she asks him if he's seen Juniper, he shrugs and returns his attention to the screen.

She heads to the entryway next and immediately notices the tablet hanging beside the door. It streams with what looks like a red rain, some ever-expanding code. Her brain is foggy from a severe lack of sleep and caffeine, but this is enough to jack her attention. Everything in the shelter is controlled by a central interface—that's what Juniper told her—the locks, alarm system, climate control.

Now her hair prickles and her flesh tightens, her senses going from bleary to acute. There is something tannic in the air. And though the light is dim, it is enough for her to see. Lela drops to her knees with a choked cry. She puts her hands to her mouth.

Above the reception desk hangs her sister, Cheryl, in a state of crucifixion, her head lolled to one side and her hands and feet nailed to the cross. Blue light surrounds her and blood mucks the wall below her. It spills to the floor and runs below the desk and floods forward like the entryway's red runner.

And finger-painted on either side of the crucifix, in big oozy letters, reads the following message: WE HAVE THE GIRL. BRING US THE RELIC.

Lela does not know about the worm that took hold of her sister last night, that still possesses the shelter, nor does she realize that Cheston has escaped from below or that Juniper lies upstairs on a blood-soaked mattress, his breath as shallow as his pulse. These discoveries will come later. For now she rushes through the building, calling out, "Hannah! Hannah!" to empty room after empty room, knowing her niece is gone but needing to confirm for herself the terrible knowledge that she has failed her family, that this is all her fault.

CHAPTER 19

THIS MIGHT BE the third time Juniper has come back from the dead, but he's hardly used to it. His mattress is soaked with blood. His body has holes ripped in it. He keeps trying to open his eyes, even as sleep grabs him, drags him down into its brain-crushing depths. *Tired* isn't the right word. *Spent, emptied, husked,* they're not adequate either. *Grave.* That's how he feels. Very grave indeed.

Something rouses him. A voice calling his name. He only wants to sleep, but his eyes creak open and through the scrim of his eyelashes he sees her. Her face hanging over his. Sarin. Her face creased with age and worry. A gray light filters through the blinds. The clock on the wall ticks its way toward 8 a.m. When he says her name, his voice comes out a croak that gives way to a cough. His chest rattles and he hacks something up that he promptly swallows down. All of this happens in the space of a few seconds, but miles and hours might as well separate them, since he feels as though he is living in some muted, slowed-down version of the world.

"You're going to be okay," Sarin says. "Everything's going to be okay."

Juniper doesn't believe her. Stab wounds aren't something she can simply rip out of him. His eyelids want to close, and he can't fight them any longer—and when he opens them again, the clock has swirled its way to nearly noon. At first he believes he is in a hospital and then realizes Sarin has transformed his bedroom into a kind of triage unit. All the lights are on, the room painfully lit with ghost-white fluorescence. And blood bags dangle over him like a bunch of balloons, their lines siphoning into his neck and elbows and thighs. He feels a tingly honeyish warm—from the blood rush or from some morphine prick.

He tries to sit up, and cannot, a half dozen different parts of him threatening to tear. His vision goes momentarily pointillist with the pain, as if trillions of atoms separate by an inch before crashing back together. He fumbles the lip of the sheet back to reveal the iodine smears and black stitches that make the puffy, red wounds look like eyes closed in suffering.

Sarin comes in through the door to stand beside his bed. "Everyone thought you were ugly before. Look at you now."

Even smiling hurts. "I'm Frankenstein's creature."

He wants to ask who did this, what happened, but his mind remains muddied up with the nightmare he just woke from. When Juniper died the first time, everyone wanted to know where he went, what he saw. He saw something then. An ocean of light. This time he saw its opposite. It came to him more vividly than any dream. The only word that feels right is prophecy. He experienced Portland as it would be.

Buildings burned and smoke dirtied the air. From different corners of the city came gunshots and screams and broken glass. A bus sped along and crashed through—one after the other—the cars abandoned in the streets, until one of its tires blew and it listed into the corner of an office building that cleaved the grille like a hatchet. In this apartment a wife knifed the cock off her husband, and the husband sheared the nose and nipples off her, and in this condo a boy jammed a pair of scissors through the neck of his father, and in this office the boss pulled the registered .357 from his safe and one by one executed the men in suits who hid beneath the desks in their darkened offices. A pregnant woman hung from a telephone pole, her skin purpled and swollen. Bodies hung everywhere—from balconies, from trees, from street signs—like the ornaments of some terrible holiday. And bodies lay everywhere, on the sidewalks and in streets and parks, more of them every minute as they fall from sniper fire or plummet from open windows, their arms and legs and necks twisted at unnatural angles, like the broken dolls of an angry child. Dogs and cats and crows and even a drift of long-snouted hogs fed on them. A gas line erupted and buckled the pavement, and from below came gouts of fire that made the air ripple.

And in the center of the city, in the Pearl District, where the Rue once stood, there rose a black tower. It pulsed and twisted, like a hungry root that reached thousands of feet and flowered in the sky, spreading into a pewter-colored lightning-lit mass of clouds a hundred miles wide. Every now and then something would crawl from it or fly from it or unpeel from it or ooze from it—and take to the city, looking for something to hunt down, play with, rape, tease, feast on.

This—Juniper knows, though he wishes he didn't—*this* is what was coming. This is what they were fighting. This is what he tells Sarin when she sits at the edge of his bed and touches her hand to his cheek. The woman—the reporter, Lela—enters the room with her arms crossed and her dog panting at her side. His words are clumsy and slow from the morphine. His eyes keep wandering from her face to the Halloween decoration he taped last week to his window, a grinning devil. His tongue feels as dry as skin and his words come out in a garble, but Sarin nods in understanding.

"We're not going to let that happen," Sarin says.

Lela doesn't strike him as the crying type, but she's crying now. Her cheeks are streaked and her face blushed. At first he's brain-addled enough to believe she feels for him, and he almost tells her, "Don't worry. I'll be fine." Then he realizes something. The absence of something. The missing among them. Lela's sister. And her niece. Cheryl and Hannah. They were here last night. They were here when this happened.

Sarin explains. Cheston is gone. Cheryl is dead. Hannah is missing. And a virus has compromised the system.

A line of packaged syringes and bottle of morphine sit on his night table. She rips the plastic off one, needles the bottle, sucks in a fat thirty milligrams. "This is the part where you try to get out of bed and play hero. But that ain't happening. Not today."

He wishes he could argue with her, but he feels—with all of these blood lines feeding into him—as helpless as a tangled marionette. He doesn't fight her when she stabs the syringe into his thigh, thumbs it empty. "Then what?" he says.

"You're going to rest. I'm going to take care of it." She shares a look with Lela. "We're going to take care of it."

"What are you going to do?" The morphine hits him hard. His

eyelids feel suddenly burdened with concrete. He closes them, just for a second. All pain vanishes. His bed softens, as downy as a cloud; he is floating.

Sarin's throaty voice speaks to him through the dark. "Stop them. Save the girl."

Juniper cannot open his eyes. He teeters at the edge of an unconscious void and doesn't realize that Sarin has already left him, that he speaks to an empty room when he says, "Or die trying?"

CHAPTER 20

THE TWO WOMEN spend the morning helping each other. Clearing out the shelter and locking its doors. Nursing Juniper. Pulling down Cheryl from the cross and bathing her body and toweling it off and combing her hair and wrapping her in a sheet that molds to the shape of her face.

They carry the shrouded body to the basement, and then through the hidden doorway and down the winding stairs—to the room. The room with the hinged chair with adjustable straps on it. With the cabinets and the tool bench and the floor dotted with dead flies.

Beside the body, Lela kneels. She doesn't know how to pray, but she does her best to pantomime it, for her sister's sake, braiding together her fingers and scrunching her eyes so tightly a few tears roll out of them. That is all the emotion she allows. She is obviously hard-shelled. She feels but she keeps it deep inside.

"What am I supposed to tell people?" she says, and Sarin says, "You tell them the truth. That she's gone missing."

There is an incinerator here, and they feed the body into it. After Sarin clamps the door in place and cranks the dial and the flames *whoosh* and a crackling sounds, she puts a hand on Lela's shoulder and says, "You understand why we have to do it this way, don't you?"

Lela says, "No one would understand."

"I'm afraid most people live in a different reality."

Lela listens to the ashes swirling and moaning through the vent pipes. Waves of heat pour off the incinerator. "That's where I was living until yesterday." Her affect is flat, her eyes bruised with fatigue and sadness, and she keeps her hands balled into fists, as though trying to contain herself, keep anything else from slipping away.

Sarin shrugs off her leather jacket. She looks unarmored without it. Bony, a bit hunched. Old. She walks to a line of cabinets and opens one up and pulls from it a Kevlar vest that she slips into with some difficulty. Then she digs out two pancake holsters that she fits around her shoulders and a third to tighten around her waist. Into each of these she tucks a 9mm. The jacket bulges over the top. She flips her hair out of the collar. The ammunition—all silver-topped cartridges with crosses cut into them to do more damage—she shoves into her pockets and into the duffel bag she pulls down and unzips. Then she turns to study Lela and asks the young woman to give her a sit rep.

Lela knuckles away a stray tear. "What?"

"Tell me what you know. I'll tell you what I know."

"I honestly don't know what I know. Except that I'm really fucking scared."

"Do your best."

They talked about some of this last night—when hovering over Hannah—but Lela gives her the whole story now. About Undertown, about the Rue, about the skull and the small man, about the murder and the red right hand, about the hounds, about Hannah and the woods and the wolf mask and the bite marks and the man who crumbled to ash. About the book, *Lock and Key,* and what she learned from it.

While listening to all of this, Sarin finishes a cigarette and starts on a second. "So where's the relic? Where's the skull?"

Lela glances at her canvas purse. She set it in the corner, and there it bulges like some sated belly.

"Bring it here."

Lela takes her time. Walking to the purse and kneeling beside it. Tucking her hair behind her ears. Clearing her throat. Pulling the skull out and holding it away from her body. Even when she carries it to Sarin, she doesn't hand it over. "You can't just give it to them."

"Who said that was my plan?"

"You can't break it either," Lela says. "I tried."

Lela tells her about what happened last night at Powell's. Daniel yelled at her—told her to stop, wait—when she snatched the skull off the desk and headed for the staircase. The railing bit her belly when she leaned over it and hurled the skull down. She expected a satisfying shatter, like a dropped plate, but instead the skull merely *tock*ed the concrete landing and thunked down the stairs and rolled to a stop. She chased after it, chucked it against a wall, slammed a door on it, no luck. She pulled down a fire extinguisher and hammered at the skull until the metal dented and cracked and spewed white foam. There was no use. The bones were somehow shielded, more than petrified.

Sarin reaches for the skull, and for a moment both their hands are on it. She tugs and Lela holds fast. It's only when Sarin says, "Enough force, you can break anything," that Lela lets go.

"I don't see how there's any way out of this," Lela says.

"I hear you." Sarin sets the skull on the duffel bag. "Lose-lose situation, right? They want the skull, but we can't give them the skull, no matter if they're holding the girl hostage." On a whetstone she sharpens the blade of a knife with a *snick-snick-snick*. "But don't worry. There's always a way out. And it helps that they're out of time."

"What do you mean?"

"Tonight's Halloween. Fall climax. Rituals are essential to these people. No question in my mind, that's when they're going to do what they're going to do."

"Shit," Lela says. "When churchyards yawn and hell itself breathes out."

"Zero Day."

"What?"

"I don't know. It was something we heard before. About Zero Day. That Zero Day was coming. I think it's come. I think it's now."

Lela says, "What's our next move?"

"They've been chasing us. Now it's time to chase them." She tucks the knife into an ankle scabbard and tells Lela she's headed to the Rue. "Below. That's where we'll find your niece."

"What are they going to do to her?"

"They're going to kill her of course." Sarin expands upon what Lela already knows, telling her the Rue is a black site, a night chapel, spoiled land, a kind of charging station for evil. "They're all over the place. The Paris catacombs, Guantánamo Bay, Lake Powell, the Bellagio, the House on the Rock, the Golden Gate Bridge." There are

purples and the shadows spread. Every mother tells her frightened child that a room is the same whether the lights are on or off. Nothing has changed but the ability to see. But that mother is lying. Everyone knows that bad things come in the dark. And now the dark is here.

And the dark has Hannah. She and Sarin are part of the same tribe, made of the same stuff. Doomed DNA. One foot in this world, one foot in the other. Saving her feels like saving some version of herself, giving Sarin permission to finally rest. The last few years, she has felt so tired. There is only so much pleasure you can mine from the world before you lose your capacity for awe. There are only so many fights you can take on before you lose your will to make a fist. Earlier, when she pricked Juniper with a syringe—doped him with morphine that melted the strain from his body and ironed the creases in his face—she felt a momentary jealousy. He had been excused from the pained tension of living. She's ready for that. She coughs. Sometimes so hard and so long that she has to pause and rest an arm against Lump. People would be wise to avoid the blackness she spits on the sidewalk.

They walk through the purpling twilight, nobody giving them a second look—they fit in with all the other costumed characters—until they pass an alley. A voice calls out from the shadows. "Who the hell do you think you are?"

Sarin skids to a stop and reaches a hand inside her jacket, closing it around the grip of a pistol. And then a man emerges from the shadows. Mid-twenties, a failure of a mustache clinging to his upper lip. He wears tight jeans, a white T-shirt upon which he has Magic-Markered HI, MY NAME IS SATAN. "Who the hell are you?" He puffs a cigarette. "Oh, wait—I got it." He points to Lump. "Monster." And then to Sarin. "Monster hunter." The kid takes a final drag that burns the cigarette down to its filter before tossing it on the sidewalk and heading back to the bar.

Only then does Sarin release her grip on the gun. She crushes the spent cigarette butt before continuing on her way, her heel smearing ash and kicking up sparks as she travels deeper into the Pearl.

CHAPTER 21

HANNAH DOESN'T RECOGNIZE FIRE. She knows the smell of its smoke, but not the way it moves. The ever-changing color and dimensions confuse her. It is a bird's wing. It is a silk scarf. It is sunlit water. In fact, it is a candle. A black candle a few feet from her. She tries to concentrate on its flame—focus all her attention on the way it pushes back the darkness—because that's the only thing that keeps her from screaming.

She doesn't know where she is—Babs's office at The Oubliette—but she knows it lies belowground. The air has the taste of earthworms, and she can sense the enclosing weight of the dirt above and below and all around her, as if she were trapped in a tomb. There are roots threading from the ceiling, but so are there coax cables and Christmas lights. One wall is lined with filing cabinets, and the other is stacked with television screens fuzzed over with static. There are USB hubs, power strips, cooling fans. Tangles of cables and cords. Laptops streaming with what looks like a red rain.

She doesn't know what happened to her mother, but she knows the man who took her had blood on his hands. And she doesn't know what will happen to her, but she knows it can't be good. Her cheeks are trailed with salt from all her crying.

A cool breeze bothers the air and the candle-flame snaps and bends. There are many candles set throughout the space—some on the floor and some on a desk and some on the filing cabinets. They illuminate the bricked chamber, maybe twenty feet tall and thirty feet wide, with several pillars interrupting it and two dark doorways channeling from it.

She lies in the center of this space. She stares at the candle, so she does not have to see what surrounds her. The massive pentagram chalked on the floor. The strange bones—some of them still clotted with dirt—arranged neatly at each tip of the five-pointed design. The bones are riven with ciphers, and the rib cages have obsidian blades run through them, and the skulls have black candles fitted onto their domes, and the wax dribbles and melts down their sides like flesh taking form. They came from the graves beneath the Rue, and they appear at first like the skeletons of men, but the skulls are warped strangely, one with nubs on the forehead, another with a shovel of a jawbone, another with eye sockets so big you could fit a fist through them.

One skull is missing. The one that would occupy the point of the pentagram directly above her own head.

The cold of the stone floor seeps into her back. Her wrists and ankles are bound, but even if they weren't, she wouldn't move. She is surrounded. How many are men and how many women, she doesn't know. They wear black robes and masks. Wolf masks and bird masks and bear masks and deer masks with antlers branching out the top. All except one. He is dressed in red and shuttles among them and speaks sometimes in English and sometimes in what she recognizes from school as Latin. She knows his voice. Last night, at the shelter, when she slept, he is the one who seized her, pulled a bag over her head, dragged her into the night.

In the place of a mask, he wears something like the Mirage. What appears to be a virtual reality helmet. A fat visor covers his eyes. Metal mandibles curve down the sides of his face. A red light pulses at the temple. Wires dangle from the helmet like dreadlocks. Some snake into the ceiling and others connect to his gloves. These are made of metal and circuits and kinked with wires and backed by swipe screens, and they make his hands appear five times their size. When he taps and slides a finger across the back of them, the screens along the wall sputter and move from static to halogen-bright to midnight-black.

Then there are the hounds. Two of them. Hairless and pale, black-gummed and needle-toothed. Their eyes are the bluish white of a hard-boiled egg, the eyes of the blind, but she knows they see. They pace the floor, winding among the masked figures. When they lick their chops, their saliva snaps like the electricity flowing into the room.

Yes, it's easier not to look. It is better to study the flame instead. If she looks at the flame, she doesn't have to see the darkness. The darkness that oozes off them—the same as the man in the woods behind Benedikt's. A shawl. An aura. Whatever you want to call it. A pollutant that infects the air around them. The flame. She needs to look at the flame. The flame happily blinds her.

What else can she do? Nothing. Here is the thing she hates most about being a kid: you don't have any agency. Everybody tells you what to do, and you do it *or else*. Her current condition is an exaggerated version of this, infantile in her total helplessness as she lies in wait for this room full of masked strangers to do with her as they wish.

The red priest carries a chalice. He offers a sip to each in attendance, an unholy communion. They raise their masks to taste. Every now and then, she catches a word she knows. *Cloven* and *leviathan* and *abyss* and *doorway* and *Zero Day* and *hail*. That is what they say before each of them drink: *Hail*.

From the desk the red priest selects a metal disc, a miniature gong, and approaches Hannah. He does not intrude upon the pentagram, but circles its perimeter, pausing at each corner to strike the gong. The sound—like the howl of a metal-throated wolf—lingers in the air. He waits until it stills to strike again. The hounds follow him, listening keenly. When the gong sounds for the fifth time, he reverses his cycle around the pentagram and removes from each skeleton the obsidian dagger or spearhead that pierces it, tossing them aside with a clatter. The cords trail behind him wherever he goes. Everything feels mismatched, too old, too new, a rupturing of worlds.

The red priest tips his gaze to study her. His face is barely seen beneath the visor, but he appears young to Hannah, with long orange hair curling out from the helmet. She sees bruises and scabs, too, as if his body were spoiled. "This is your aunt's fault, you know. That nosy cunt is the reason you're here."

"I'm sorry. Please." Hannah doesn't want to ask—not knowing

seems somehow better—but she can't help herself. "What are you going to do to me?"

"That depends on whether you tell us where to find the skull."

"I told you. I don't know where it is. I don't know anything."

A fly crawls from his nose and another few from his mouth when he opens it now. "So you say." He taps one of the command screens on his gloves, and the televisions zap again, revealing an Internet browser, TOR. His fingers *tock-tock-tock,* typing out domain names, negotiating pop-ups, entering commands and encrypted logins and passwords. The wall of televisions changes rapidly. Some of the screens flash the same browser image; others stream with red code, everything shuffling quickly, like a hurried Rubik's Cube, until all at once a vast picture takes form. A single image pieced together by the many screens. A red triangle. With an eye inside of it. Maybe it is the candlelight or maybe it is the shuddering screens—bothered by bursts of pixels—but the eye appears to gaze around the room, to find her there in the pentagram.

Then the red priest kneels beside her. His gloves sizzle with electricity. He runs one of them along her face, beyond her ear, and there fingers the lightning port. A joint axis permits another input. He reaches behind his own head—and jerks his hand, as though plucking a hair—unplugging one of the cables. This he fits scrapingly into her. "You think this place is scary," he says. "Just wait."

She remembers what Juniper said before. About how there are worse things than death. Hannah says, "Help me. Please help me. Please, please, please." She speaks quickly, in tune to the rhythm of her pulse, swinging her head around, taking in the masks leaning toward her, not really believing that any one of them will help her, but stupidly hoping a kind face hides among them. "I don't know where the skull is. I swear I don't know."

"Let's make certain."

Something happens then. When the red priest forces the cable into the port. Her whole body goes rigid. She sees too much, feels too much. This world and the other one streaming beneath. Double vision. It is as though a garden has suddenly pushed from a graveyard and unfurled all of its black petals. Or a secret library has knocked all of its books off its shelves at once to pages bearing the most gruesome illustrations and incantations. She has accessed the Internet—the Dark Net—and the eye on the screen is somehow peering inside her now, searching its way through every inch of her, looking for the skull.

Every day, these past few years, she wished to see. Now she wishes she could go blind again, go back to the way things were. There is so much about the world better kept in the dark. If she could scream, she would, but her nerves feel out of her control. Her back arches. She nearly bites off her tongue. She can't tell whether she is hallucinating or not, but high above her she spots a black shape—a crow—its wings beating the air as it circles the chamber and then vanishes through an open door.

And then she hears a voice yell, "Stop!"

The red priest yanks the cord out of her. She feels relieved, yes, but poisoned, mind-raped. She chokes back bile and tries to settle her breathing. To be free of that cable is to be free of a noose. The room reels and then settles, and only then does she see the woman, Sarin.

Everyone stares at her. Her arms are outstretched, and she holds the skull in one hand and a live grenade in the other. Her leather jacket, where it flaps open, reveals a vest of dynamite, red and ribbed like the roof of a mouth.

A man—a small man, no bigger than Hannah, with a shriveled face—approaches her. He speaks in a language Hannah cannot understand, and Sarin responds in kind. Then she spits. The small man looks as though he might lunge for her, but the red priest steadies him with a hand to the shoulder. "You've come," he says. "We hoped you would."

"Untie the girl."

"And then you'll give us the skull?"

"Not until I know she's safe."

"Of course."

The red priest makes a chopping motion with his hand, and the small man pulls a long blade from his belt and slinks toward Hannah. The blade hovers over her as if deciding which part of her to pierce.

"Careful," Sarin says.

The knife drops and Hannah nearly cries out. But no pain comes, only a tug as he saws through the rope that binds her wrists, her ankles. She opens and closes her hands, flexing some blood back into them. The small man waves to her impatiently. Hannah stands on uncertain legs.

A hound growls when she starts forward. She stumbles over one of the skeletons. The bones clatter with the sound of an autumn forest. She sees the obsidian blade beside it and snatches it up and holds it before her, swinging it one way, then the other, though no one approaches her. They simply watch. The masks move aside, allowing her passage, but one narrow enough that their robes lick her.

Sarin nods to her when she comes near. "You okay?"

"I don't know if that's the right word for it."

"Now," the red priest says, and extends his hands. His gloves spark with electricity. "The skull."

Something bites Hannah's neck. The point of the knife held by the small man. His mouth arranges itself into what must be a smile, showing off corn kernel teeth. She's surprised by the feeling that overtakes her. Not fear. But the want to drive the obsidian dagger into his face.

"The skull," the red priest says.

Sarin bobs the hand holding the grenade. "You hurt her, we all get hurt."

"You let go of the skull and we let go of the girl. It's as simple as that."

"Back up," Sarin says. "Give me room."

The red priest does as she says, and Sarin keeps her eyes on him when she crouches and deposits the skull on the floor. It thunks the stone heavily like something five times the size. Then she says to the small man, "There's no need for that anymore."

The knife point eases from Hannah's neck, and the small man retreats from her.

Sarin nods toward the doorway and says to Hannah, "Keep going."

"Where?"

"Away from here. Fast as you can."

"But what about you?"

"I'll be right behind you. Just go."

It should be an easy decision, but something wars inside her. The scared kid wants to run home, lock the door, leap into bed, pull the covers over her head. But another part of her knows she will never feel safe again. No home awaits her. Nothing awaits her. She belongs here, beside Sarin, squaring her shoulders for a fight.

"Go!" Sarin says, this time with enough force to seemingly shake the air and shove Hannah from the chamber, into an unlit tunnel, trading one darkness for another.

✣

Hannah doesn't see the red priest carry the skull to the pentagram and lovingly deposit it there. She doesn't see the screens on the wall flare with red light. She doesn't see the masked legion close around Sarin like a knot and wrest the grenade from her hand and the pistols from her holsters. Nor does she hear the red priest say, "Let's finish what we started so long ago."

Sarin tries to fight, but there are too many of them, their hands on her, dragging her along like a current of black water. Her wrists are bound. Her body is dropped at the center of the pentagram. Her dynamite vest is torn from her chest and tossed aside. The room pulses red with the light hazing from the screens.

"Why fight?" the priest says. "You must have come here knowing the fate that awaited you. It was either you or the girl after all. We need a worthy sacrifice for a night such as this."

They waste no time. The small man raises his knife, and the red priest raises his hands in benediction. "With this sundering, I, Alastor, call on the dark. With this blood, I hallow this space. With this sacrifice, I open up the door. And so commences our first day, the Zero Day."

At that moment every flame in the room dampens. And the air stirs, as if gathering into a wind. There comes a fluttering sound.

The hounds growl in response. The masked figures turn and mutter and seem not to know where to look. Then, from the doorway, a steady stream of crows appears. Dozens of them. A hundred, maybe more. All *kak-kak-kak*ing and beating their wings and scratching their claws. They are not alone. The floor darkens and surges as if with their shadows. Rats. A tide of rats flowing forward, scrambling up legs, scratching, and biting. The threat is above and the threat is below.

The red priest ducks down. The small man drops the ceremonial knife and it clatters to the ground, and he stumbles back into the desk and knocks a candle to the floor. A crow roosts on the antler of a mask and *clack*s its beak into the hollow of an eye. A man races by with a skirt of rats clinging to him.

Through all of this, a black hooded figure pushes toward Sarin. His wart-dappled hands grip her by the shoulders. "Are you all right?" Lump says in a froggy voice, and she says, "Neither of us will be if you don't hurry." Beneath his hood she sees his face is a cauliflower mass of growths. He fumbles out a knife and works at her restraints.

But before he can sever them, a hound bounds toward them. Sarin cries out, and he turns and tosses the knife into its breast. It contorts its body in the air, gives a yelp, and falls in a heap with its legs still kicking. Seconds later it is gone from sight, the rats clambering onto it, squealing and feeding.

But Lump never gets a chance to return to her. The red priest backhands him, his glove sizzling with electricity, and Lump falls dazed to the floor.

"Run, Lump!" she says. "Just run. There's not enough time."

Sarin tries to worm away, but the red priest is already on top of her, pinning her. With one hand he grips her neck and with the other the ceremonial knife. "You're absolutely right." With that the blade arcs downward, nocking her between her ribs, entering her. "Your time has run out."

A hot ache spreads from the wound. Blood gushes, as if sucked, drawn greedily from her. It puddles and then follows the channels chalked on the floor, rippling toward the five skeletons. A red light sparks inside the socket of one. The same skull Sarin carried here. She cannot help but smile.

The red priest stands and regards her. "What's so funny?"

She can barely draw a breath to speak when she says, "Alastor."

He follows her gaze to the skull. The red light blinks now, faster.

The red priest swings his gaze between her and the skull. The red light inside of it blinks faster and faster, counting its way down to detonation. Every hollow of it is packed with C-4. She activated the detonation timer just before entering the chamber. "No." The red priest doesn't seem to know where to go, stepping on a rat, dodging a crow, chasing away from her, the pentagram.

"With your blood," she says, interrupted by a wet cough, "I consecrate this space in the name of the Father, the Son, and the Holy motherfucking Spirit."

The priest is backlit by the wall of televisions. The giant eye projected there is red-rimmed. It rolls around in its socket in fury or panic or excitement. The priest's helmet and gloves zap and string with electricity. "You're too late! It's already started," he screams. "It's already begun!"

CHAPTER 22

USED TO BE, to open a door, you rolled aside a stone. Centuries later, you lifted a latch. Then you fitted a key, turned a knob. Now you can open a door with a phone or a fingerprint or a voice command. Times change. The ways of entry change. But you still have to open the door. On this October 31—Samhain, All Saints' Eve, All Hallows' Eve, Halloween, the fall climax, when the division between this world and the other frails—they open the door.

For the past few years, Undertown has been busy harvesting information. Eighty million accounts from Anthem and seventy million from Target. Fifty-six million from Home Depot. Seventy-six million from JP Morgan Chase. Ashley Madison, AOL, British Airways, Living Social, Adobe. UPS and eBay and Blizzard and Domino's. And more. So many more. Amassing information for a cyberwar. Every time news broke about a data hack, people panicked, worrying over their credit cards and bank accounts especially. But when nothing happened—when no mysterious charges appeared, when no one applied for a credit card or a loan in their name—they forgot.

They only worried about money, as though money were the only thing worth stealing. But Undertown wanted usernames and passcodes, the more subtle but severely damaging information. Because that is the way in; the ciphered connection between your fingertips and keyboard jimmies open the lock between the physical and digital. This is what everyone should be worried about. Not their accounts, but their identity. Snowden leaks the NSA files. Hackers leak the Sony emails. Facebook and Google track your browsing habits, your buying habits, your location, your race, gender, religion, age, orientation, and custom-fit their ads accordingly. DNA has been replaced by streams of data integrated into databases. And it has become dangerously clear how your digital footprint can come back to haunt you, with so much of your life online. Just like that—you can be erased, possessed.

For now Portland is the target. Portland is the focus group. Portland is the door.

A trucker named Theo Ayala keys the ignition to his semi and pulls away from the loading zone at a bar. He thumbs open Google Maps to call up the directions for his next delivery. His trailer is full of Budweiser that will never be drunk. The screen of his phone streams with red code that finds a reflection in his eyes. He drops the phone, and its screen spiderwebs with fissures. His right hand falls to his custom-made, silver-skulled gearshift. He cranks the truck from second to third and then fourth gear as he swings the wrong way onto an entry ramp and merges onto I-5. At first the oncoming traffic zippers out of his way, wailing their horns, swinging onto the shoulder, crashing into the meridian, but then the cars come thick enough that they cannot escape him. His grille cleaves a Prius in two. A Harley gets eaten up beneath his tires. And then comes a fast, steel-screeching, glass-shattering series of impacts, sedans and station wagons and trucks and SUVs knocked aside. Tires pop. Horns honk. Hoods crumple. Sparks light up the night. Their screaming faces are lit by the wash of his headlights.

In the living room of their seventh-floor apartment, Stephen Vos and Jackie Eastman kick back on the couch and call up Netflix on their tablet. They're getting married in a few months—a New Year's wedding—and the coffee table is littered with seating charts, a DJ playlist, catering requests. They're sick of arguing over where to seat pervy Uncle Milton and whether they should order flower centerpieces for every table, so they take a break. A bottle of red, a scary movie on Netflix, and then—maybe, probably, since they can't seem to get enough of each other these days—they'll peel off each other's clothes. But something happens when Stephen logs in. The screen streams red. At first they believe it's some glitch—some pixelated version of the Netflix home screen—and then their mouths go slack, and they stand from the couch and walk into the kitchen and slide steak knives from the drawer and methodically work their way from apartment to apartment. Everyone opens their door with a bowl of candy and a smile that doesn't last.

At the Portland International Airport, people cluster before the monitors for arrivals, departures, baggage claim, all of the screens streaming red. A backpack sags to the floor. Then a purse. A satchel. Nothing matters anymore—not their pills or their money or their passports—because who they are has been flouted, hacked, raped. A Starbucks barista hurls scalding water into the face of a customer waiting for an Americano. A girl with pigtails bites the neck of a man snoozing on a bench. A Port Authority policeman unholsters his pistol and opens fire on a group of passengers lined up to board their flight. While out on the tarmac, a jet rolls suddenly off course and picks up speed as it bullets toward the airport. The atrium is like a glass cathedral, high-ceilinged and busy with potted plants and padded chairs. People flip through novels and gulp bottled water and poke at their phones. They don't see the jet coming, but when it noses through the vast window, they all stand suddenly. The fuselage sends up a wave of sparks and the tile buckles. Thousands of shards of glass sparkle the air and skitter the floor and jaggedly pierce skin. One man looks like a plate-backed dinosaur from the glass stabbing his spine. Another is blinded with two icicle-sized slivers jutting from his eyes. "Help," people cry. "Help!" But no one answers. There is only more screaming, a different threat in every direction.

There are no stars over Portland. There never are. The light pollution is too severe, thrown by the millions of streetlamps, headlights, stadium lights, porch lights, storefronts that glow even when closed. No one ever looks up anymore and feels awed and dwarfed by the infinite, aware only of the globe of light they are trapped in, where the only star is the red star of the Texaco station.

The moths are out, battering the overhead fluorescents at the gas island. A man with a black goatee and a pitchfork tattoo on his forearm moves among the pumps, filling tanks with unleaded, super unleaded, diesel, running credit cards, handing back receipts, saying, "Have a good one, have a good one."

Halloween, he deals with a lot of drunks, like this white Jeep

Grand Cherokee that pulls up, the windows down, the stereo blasting hip-hop. Four white boys, late teens, early twenties, with gelled hair, polo shirts with the collars popped, their faces painted to look like skeletons. Probably from Lake Oswego, downtown to hit the bars. The driver—a pouty-faced kid with a cigarette dangling from the corner of his mouth—kills the engine and the stereo dies.

"Fill it?" the attendant asks, and the driver says, "Yeah, with super." Smoke and beer in his breath. He fumbles with his wallet, hands over a black AmEx.

The attendant doesn't see many of these, and he taps it in his palm a moment before running the card, twisting off the cap, nosing the nozzle into the tank. The line shudders with fuel, and the numbers start to twirl.

Then the stereo starts up again, blasting so loudly, it hurts. His marrow shudders. His ears feel ready to burst and bleed. There are two other cars getting fueled up, and a few people walking in and out of the store. All of them are staring with annoyance at the white Jeep.

"You mind turning that down?" the attendant says, and the skeleton says, "Actually, I do." He blows a cloud of smoke and cranks the knob higher. The attendant shakes his head and walks away to check on another vehicle, and the driver and his friends laugh, give each other knuckles, nod along to the thumping bass.

"Check out this guy," one of the skeletons says, nodding at the figure lurching down the sidewalk, toward the station. About a block away, he appears in the pool of a streetlamp, then disappears in shadow, then flashes into existence again, getting closer, closer. He has a tromping gait, stooping forward, his arms dangling at his sides. He's a heavy guy, his big body crushed into a rabbit costume splashed with what looks like blood. "What do you think? Psycho Killer Easter Bunny?"

The man seems intent on his destination, staring straight ahead and driving his floppy feet down forcefully—until the driver leans out the window and calls out to him. "Hey, fattie—I'm pretty sure I know where you hid all the chocolate eggs!"

The man in the rabbit costume stops and slowly swivels his head toward them. The ears make his shadow appear horned. He starts toward them, and the skeletons in the Jeep giggle nervously. "Oh shit, this guy is messed up," they say. "Roll up the windows, Todd."

Todd, the driver, fumbles with the keys, and they clatter to the floor. He doesn't bother going after them, because the man in the rabbit costume is already here, only a few feet away from his open window, studying him with a dead expression. His eyes appear red-laced. What must be fake blood mats his costume and speckles his blank face.

"What the hell happened to you, bro? Get off on the wrong holiday?" Todd smiles, sucks hard on his cigarette, flicks the ash, blows some smoke that swirls around the man in the rabbit costume before ghosting away. "You kill Santa Claus or what?"

More giggles from the backseat. The music thumps like an angry heartbeat between them.

At that moment the gas tank fills and the pump *chunks* off and the man in the rabbit costume's attention turns away from Todd. He walks to the rear of the Jeep, reaching for the nozzle.

"Put up the windows, Todd—put up the windows!"

Todd ducks down for the keys, fumbling around, hooking the ring with his finger. He tries mashing them into the ignition, but it's too late. The man in the rabbit costume rips the nozzle from the tank and clicks the trigger and restarts the pump. Gas splatters the ground, then the rear of the vehicle. He holds out his arm as if firing a pistol, splashing their faces. They shield their eyes with their hands and sputter, "Oh shit, shit, shit!"

Then the man in the rabbit costume trains the hose on the front seat, at Todd's face, at the red tip of his cigarette. The gas ignites with the *thump* of a dropped crate, of misplaced air. It goes blue first, like pooling water, and then brightens to a blinding orange. The boys are screaming, their skin melting off them.

Their screams and the music give way to an earsplitting boom as the Jeep explodes, leaping up and forward to crunch its grille into the pavement. And then the pumps explode, one after the other, hurling sheets of metal. And then the underground tanks erupt, the pavement buckling and crackling to make room for the volcanic spurt of flame that will shatter windows and melt the Texaco star from its sign.

The man in the rabbit costume has been knocked twenty yards by the blast, his skin scorched and his fur smoldering, but he doesn't seem to notice. He sits up, and then stands unsteadily, before marching away.

All throughout Portland, the wind blows and the trees seethe, their leaves torched with color. Pumpkins shudder with candlelight. And screens glow with streaming red code. People look at their phones and then tear off their masks to reveal something scarier beneath. People checking scores, stocks, the weather, email, text messages, social media. Who to hook up with, who to meet up with, where to go for drinks, how to get there. Everyone minutes away from watching something, checking something, their devices like a part of their mind that needs constant access, a prosthetic cerebrum. "Hold on a sec," they say, "let me take a photo of this." "Hold on a sec," they say, "I want to show you this funny video." "Hold on a sec," they say, "I gotta send this text." And when they look up again, their eyes burn as if pocketed with embers.

A club surges with bodies until someone opens Tinder and swipes right and five minutes later people are shoving their way out the exits, screaming and painted with blood. Trick-or-treaters roam the streets hungry for more than suckers and candy bars. A window shatters, a body flung from it. A car smashes through a fence and into a backyard party lit with strings of jack-o'-lantern lights. The digital veins of the city course with the contagion.

Around midnight a private jet drops from the sky and circles the city as if to survey it before landing at the Portland airport. It does not hail control. No ground crew comes to meet it. A fire burns in the terminal, and the flames shimmer across the fuselage. The tarmac is empty when its wheels screech and it rolls slowly to a stop. The door opens and a man appears in it. A man named Cloven, who takes a deep breath of the smoke-scented air as if it were purifying.

The fall climax is a time of reaping harvest, of accounting. The sun and the night end their tug of war as the long death of winter emerges the victor. Tonight, darkness wins.

CHAPTER 23

Hannah is used to the dark, so she manages this labyrinth of tunnels better than most. Blindness feels familiar, even comforting, since she knows it is all-encompassing, shielding her from sight. One hand traces the wall; the other carries the obsidian blade. It is as long as her forearm, scalloped from the antler that punched the stone, shaped and sharpened it. The handle is wrapped in an ancient leather binding. She takes tall steps so as not to trip on anything. She is not afraid of what is ahead of her, only behind.

Maybe an hour, maybe a half hour ago, soon after she ran from the chamber, an explosion sounded. The ground shook. Her ears popped. Several bricks untoothed from the ceiling and walls. This was followed by a wall of wind that knocked her forward a step and carried grit in it.

She doesn't know which way to go or how far. She doesn't know how long she has been walking or how far. Down here time seems to pass more slowly and distances to stretch twice as long. Down here every noise is exaggerated. The scuttling of something underfoot, the fluttering of something overhead, all pronounced by the same acoustics that make her every breath and skidded heel sound thunderous. She takes care to slink along as quickly and quietly as she can and not cry out when cobwebs net her face or when a centipede scuttles across her probing hand or when bats swoop and make kissing sounds overhead.

For a few years, she played in a beep baseball league. It was a version of the game adapted for sight-impaired players. Some could see only a few feet, some couldn't see at all, so they wore eye masks to make things fair. The ball was oversize and housed a speaker that beeped. The batter swung for the sound. There were only two bases, foam pillars that emitted a screeching alarm the runner hustled toward with arms wide open. If the runner touched the base before the fielders touched the ball, they were safe. She was always fast. She was always unafraid of hurrying perilously through the dark. She was almost always safe. That's what the umpire would cry—"Safe!"—and she hopes for the same now. To be safe.

She crosses a short steel bridge over a canal. Pipes—as big around as a man—drop from the ceiling and jut from the walls. Whenever she walks past them, she hurries, as if something might reach out and drag her in. She stops every now and then, saying, "What was that?" and "Did you hear that?" her voice echoing away. No one answers. She is alone.

Until she isn't. The sound is unmistakable. A sound with gravity to it, a weighted presence: the scrape and thud of footsteps. And panting. A clicking. A hound. She stands at the junction of two tunnels and for one bewildering moment cannot distinguish the sound's direction. It seems to come from one way, then the other, behind her, before her, then all ways at once, as if she is surrounded. She spins in circles, losing track now of which way she came. The panting is louder, coming in gusts.

She's not fast enough to run. So she tightens her grip around the obsidian dagger, holding it two-handed, as if it were a bat and the hound the beep ball hurtling toward her. She tries not to cry, tries not to scream, tries not to think. Her senses narrow. Just like beep baseball, she imagines her ears growing larger, like big pouches to catch noise, every nerve in her body rooted there. She cocks her head, and the hound's approach and the tunnel system take shape in her mind. She hears air currents huffing and whistling. She hears water dripping. She hears a sniff and claws *click-click*ing against stone. She faces the tunnel from which the noise comes. Now she's certain. The hound is no more than twenty feet away, rounding a corner.

There. The deep-chested growl that signals its approach. She can feel it as well as hear it, as if her bones are being scraped over. It is a sound and she is a smell. They are both blind. She is used to being blind. She knows how to survive being blind. The hound does not creep hesitantly forward, but springs toward her, excited by her nearness. She tries to gauge its size—almost as tall as her on all fours—and crouches down with the dagger angled upward in defense.

The full weight of the hound slams into the point. There is an almost human scream in response. She falls back with the animal on top of her. She does not know where it is wounded—its breast or neck—but the dagger has buried itself deeply. She holds tight to it. Blood warms her hands. Jaws snap, nicking the air near her face. Claws scrape at her sides. But still she holds fast, arching her back and forcing all her strength upward. With a damp pop and a surge of blood, something gives. And the hound goes still a moment later.

She rolls away and scoots to the edge of the tunnel and vomits. Then she hugs her legs to her chest and shivers her way through the next few minutes. Her whole body seems to pulse along with her overworked heart. She spits away the stringency lingering in her mouth. She hears a seething, like sand run through fingers, and when she reaches out, discovers the hound gone, only ashes in its place.

Her relief doesn't last. Slowly she turns her head to the left. More footsteps sound. The clomping of shoes, hurrying in this direction. Not a hound, but a man. She feels like she can't endure any more, not one more thing. "I can't even," she says, but she can. She does. She stands, wobbling in place. She considers searching for the dagger but decides against it. "I can't do that again. Don't make me do that again." Hide. That's what she needs to do. Hide right now or she's going to die. Hannah crumples her face as though to cry, but a scuffing sound startles her back to reality and she swallows down the feeling. She edges away, hurrying along the wall until her hand fumbles into something, the metal lip of one of the giant pipes. Inside it there is room enough to crawl, huddle in a ball.

A long minute passes. The footsteps draw near. She can see the air outside barely brightening, like the breath before dawn. What must be a flashlight.

Finally she sees the source—bobbing into view—the hand and then the body and then the face of a man. The man in the black torn clothes. The man with the cauliflower skin. He peers into the pipe. A crow roosts on his shoulders. It squawks a greeting. "There you are," he says. "Let's get you out of this terrible dark place." He holds out a lumped hand. "And into the light."

She only hesitates a second. Then takes his hand and lets him help her scoot from the pipe. He smiles at her and she smiles back. "You're safe," he says, "for the moment." And she feels it. She stands a little straighter than before. She has run and she has fought and she has hidden, every test survived. She is used to feeling weak, and that's fading. Maybe strong isn't the right word, but she feels different. Resilient, ready for the next affliction.

"Sarin?" she says.

The man shakes his head *no*. "But there's you. You're here."

She's alive, he means, but more than that. She's like Sarin. That means she has a role in the story still unscrolling. Not as a victim. No longer blind and maybe no longer a child. There's something she can do. Fight back. Fight the dark. "What now?" she asks.

He smiles in response. He likes the question. She does too. The agency of it. He puts a hand to her shoulder and leads her down the tunnel, and it isn't long before she hears a distant car horn, and they follow the sound and soon feel a puff of wind and the air lightens. A ladder reaches up to a vent. "This way," he says, as her fingers curl around the rungs and she begins to climb.

CHAPTER 24

It's after midnight when Lela and Hannah sit in the dining room of The Weary Traveler. Below the table, curled in a horseshoe shape, lies Hemingway. The coffee doesn't taste good but Lela drinks it anyway. Hannah picks at a package of M&M's. Outside, sirens cry, car alarms blare, voices shout. But they hardly notice. They might be done crying—for Cheryl, for now anyway—but their minds remain deaf with grief.

Maybe fifteen minutes have gone by without either of them saying a word, when Lela speaks. "We're going to have to take care of each other."

It's a startling thing to admit, but it feels right. Lela often claimed that she never truly understood something until she wrote about it. Saying out loud that she will watch over Hannah feels similarly clarifying. It is true that Lela can barely get her clothes folded and her dishes put away. She might not take good care of herself, but she will take care of this girl. She will. She has to.

She isn't sure if the threat has passed, just as she isn't sure if this place is safer than any other. Earlier, from his bed, Juniper told her to lock every door and window and to collect every tablet and computer and phone and smash it to the floor and crunch the plastic guts beneath her heel. "Don't check your email. Don't answer the phone. Don't answer the door," he said. "Paranoia is a requirement if you want to survive this."

Not just *this,* she thought, but the world they live in. Despite legal and medical advances that make this seem like the safest time in history, there are so many more ways to get hurt, so many of them online. She did as she was told. Almost. She couldn't bring herself to destroy her own laptop. She held it over her head. But then her arms trembled. It belonged to *The Oregonian* and she hadn't backed up her work in what felt like a century, and damaging the device was a little like sledgehammering her skull. It was her, an extension of her. That was the sad truth. So she let her arms drop. And slipped the computer back into the oversize purse that rests beside her now.

At this Cheryl would have shaken her head. Typical Lela. Chronically unable to sever herself from work, to think of others first. Her sister is gone and yet still here, in Lela's head and across the table, as Hannah looks like a tinier version of her. The same brown hair. The pursed mouth. The doofy homemade sweater and secondhand jeans. But there's always been something different about the girl. She's stronger and more poised than her mother ever could be. Even now, despite everything that has happened, Hannah does not come across as afraid or broken. Just the opposite. Possessed by a straight-backed, firm-jawed resolve.

Hannah has always acted older than her years, but now she seems older even than Lela. The Mirage is scratched across one lens. Her hair is matted and tangled. Her clothes are smeared with dirt and blood. She's a survivor. A fighter. Lela remembers what Juniper said—the girl was special—and what Sarin said—the girl was like her. She knows they're right without fully understanding what they mean.

"We need a plan," Hannah says. "We can't just sit here like a couple of morons, wait and see what happens."

That sounds like something Lela would say. Hannah's right. She's absolutely right. But this is one of the few times in her life Lela doesn't know what to say or do. She folds a napkin in half and in half again. Wipes away some crumbs. Then reaches across the table. "Hold still a sec. You've got something." Lela uses her fingers as a comb, picking some dead flies and dirt clumps from Hannah's hair. "That's better." Then picks up her coffee but doesn't drink from it. "You're sure he's dead?" Lela says. "The red priest? Tusk?"

Hannah plucks two M&M's from the package and crunches them down to a wet rainbow. "That wasn't his name."

"Cheston."

"That wasn't his name either," Hannah says. "Lump said he called himself Alastor."

"Whoever he is, he's dead? That means we stopped them? It's over?"

"I guess before Alastor died, he said it was too late. He said it had already begun."

"What's *it?* What's already begun?"

Hannah hoists her shoulders in a shrug. "Something bad. Something they've been planning for a long time. Something called Zero Day."

"Zero Day? When is—" Her voice drops away when another siren wails past the shelter and a kaleidoscope of red-and-blue color momentarily lights up the room. Lela cocks her head and listens for a moment. Then slips her computer out of her purse and splits it open to check the police and fire scanner. A few weeks ago, she had someone set up her laptop so she could tune in live to the dispatch system. The screen slowly brightens to show her inbox. There is a tall pile of new messages, all from different senders, all with attachments.

"What are you doing?" Hannah says.

"I need to know what's going on out there."

But first she opens a message marked IMPORTANT from her editor. She never takes a day off, never goes off the clock, which makes it impossible to resist dipping into the office conversation now, just for a moment. No matter what Brandon wants, she'll say no, but she needs to make clear to him that she's out for days, weeks, however long it might take her to sort out the mess she's in. The computer chugs and bleeps. The screen goes dark and she thumps it with her knuckles. "Stupid thing. What's wrong with you?"

Just then the red code begins to map its way across the monitor. But Lela gets no more than a glimpse. Hannah lurches across the table and grabs hold of the laptop. "No!" Lela says, reaching for it, but the girl is too fast—hurling it against the wall. The screen snaps off and skids away. Black keys litter the ground. A green chipboard sticks out of the cracked base like a bulging organ. There is a spritz of electricity, and the fan gives a dying gasp.

A part of Lela wants to scream, slap the girl. How dare she? Lela should throw *her* against the wall. That's what she should do. Over and over again until her brains dash out her ear. She grinds her teeth and lets out an animal cry and slams a hand flat against the table.

And then she sees Hannah. Really sees her. The girl is backing away fearfully, shivering where she stands. "Don't," Hannah says, holding up her hands. "Don't. I'm sorry. I was just trying to protect you."

Lela shakes her head. Blinks. Looks blankly at her hands, which are clenched into fists so tightly that her nails bite her palms. She loosens her grip. Shudders out a breath. Whatever possessed her —ever so briefly, like the bee-buzz that bothers her brain when she stands up after hours at the keyboard—it's gone now.

"It's not safe," Hannah says. "They're in there."

"On the Dark Net?" Lela says, and remembers what Josh told her. "Digital hell."

"Yes. It's like an—I don't know—incubator for evil."

Some dampness bothers Lela's upper lip. When she wipes at it, her hand comes away bloody. She bunches up a napkin to staunch the flow. She drops herself back into her seat. "Jesus," she says. "I'm sorry, Hannah. I don't know what's wrong with me."

"It wasn't you."

"I'm so goddamn sorry. About everything."

"I need you to help me."

"I know. I will. I'm here for you."

"No, Aunt Lela. I mean, thank you. I'm glad. But I don't mean that. What I mean is, I think I know what to do. I need to get on the Dark Net, and for that to happen, I need your help."

Lela says nothing. Outside, more and more sirens rise from different corners of the city, like wolves calling to each other. "What are you talking about?"

Hannah explains what happened when the cable fitted into the Mirage port, when the red eye trained its gaze on her. The sense of simultaneously filling up on and falling through a channel of darkness. "That's where they are. That's their—I don't know the right word—womb. Well. Foundation. Factory. Battery. Source. Whatever. When they come for us, that's where they're coming from. What you saw on your laptop just now, I saw in that chamber. It's a virus. An infection. It gets inside our devices," she says, "and our devices are us."

"Possession," Lela whispers, as though afraid to say it out loud. She writes stories that consist of facts. If she makes a claim, she backs it up with data from a census or case study, quotes from expert sources. That's why she has never been able to take any religion seriously; the lack of evidence. Now she has proof, and she doesn't know what to do with it, how to process what she has for so long been in denial of, the extra-normal. It's all a matter of perspective, she supposes. One person's blue might be another person's orange. Time slows down or speeds up according to gravity, so that seconds tick along faster in space than on Everest than in Death Valley than at the bottom of the Mariana Trench. The peanut butter that makes one mouth water can make another throat close. Someone might see a ghost or a god where others see a shadow. Everyone is making sense of the unknown world with what limited, contradictory sensory equipment we have at our disposal. We're all, to different degrees, blind.

Hannah can see now. Lela still can't seem to process it all, but she's trying. She's never had trouble with confidence. She's said on more than one occasion that she has no regrets. That's because she never looks back, always forward, always in pursuit. Chasing the next story, certain she'll conquer it. But now she doesn't know what lies ahead. She doesn't know the next story and how it will end. She doesn't know anything anymore, it seems.

"Why?" Lela swallows down a gulp of coffee. "Why do you want to go there? And why would I ever *let* you go there?"

"Because I think that's the only way to stop them."

"Who says you need to stop them?"

"Lump."

"Lump? The crazy homeless guy?"

"He's not crazy. He's part of this. He's—whatever you want to call it—on the spectrum. He *saved* me."

"I'm the one who's trying to protect you here, Hannah. Let me do that. It doesn't matter how bad you begged, I wouldn't take you to a meth lab, a strip club, a dogfight in a junkyard. This is worse than the same thing."

Hannah sweeps her hand and knocks the M&M's off the table. They clatter to the floor, and Hemingway grumbles awake and crawls out from under the table to slurp them up. "I know this sounds weird," Hannah says, her voice too calm, "but I just know. Okay? I can just feel it. It's like what Juniper said before. About me being different. Having some antenna that tunes me in to another frequency." She readjusts the Mirage and tucks her hair behind her ears. "I can see the darkness. I know where it's coming from. I just know, Aunt Lela."

At that moment Lela's phone begins buzzing in her pocket. She pulls it out, still staring confusedly at Hannah. Before she can answer, the girl's hand falls over it. "Wait," she says.

Hannah takes the cell and turns it over in her hands, as if testing its weight. Then flips it open cautiously. The finish is worn off the frame, the numbers rubbed off the keypad. "Okay," Hannah says, and returns it to her. "I think analog is safe."

The caller ID reads 503—Portland—but it's not a number Lela recognizes. She thumbs the button and accepts the call and slowly brings the phone to her ear. "Who is this?"

"Thank god you're a Luddite." It's Josh, the intern, speaking in a panicked blur, each word crashing into the next. "Thank god you have that stupid Flintstone phone."

"I tried you earlier. Where are you?"

"I can't use my cell. I'm afraid to use it. I'm calling on a landline. Whatever you do, don't get online right now. There's a virus that—"

"We know."

"Whatever you think you know, you don't. You don't know how bad it really is. Now listen to me very carefully. This whole story just broke wide open."

CHAPTER 25

THE AVERAGE PERSON checks their phone eighty-five times a day. Given that we're asleep for probably half of that time, the math works out to eight times an hour. And that's just phones. How often does a face turn toward a television, a tablet, a laptop, a screen? It's night, so fewer people should be online, but it's Halloween night, so more than usual. How many are infected, whether hundreds or thousands or tens of thousands, Josh doesn't know. Nor does he know exactly how the contagion works. But he tries to explain it as best he can.

Not long ago scientists figured out a way to create mathematical constructs of patients' hearts. They can do things to these digital hearts, safely experiment, make guesses. Subtract something here, add something there, rearrange, rip, gouge, patch, stint. And based on this model—this complicated equation—they can figure out, perfectly, what will happen to the actual organ during a planned procedure. These scientists now hope to map out bodies, individual bodies, in the same way. So that you would be coded. Meaning a doctor could find or resolve—or even worsen—a problem in you by shifting some numbers around. That's essentially what's happening now, Josh says. A code is worsening us.

Everyone is code. Everything is code. You dial a number on your phone. That is code. You scratch down a grocery list. That is code. You play a folk song that makes someone mellow and happy. Or write a memo that gets someone fired. You put on a business suit because you want authority, and you put on a negligee because you want to be unwrapped. Those are code too. This is code, this conversation between Josh and Lela. A collection of sounds and signals that serves a function—to educate, to warn, to incite action.

If you eat something, your body will absorb the food, break it down into particles that will nourish or infect you. You will be altered, even if only in a small way. You might become ill. Information is the same. Opening your eye is like opening your mouth. Calling it a Twitter *feed* feels so apt. People are being fed intelligence now. Spoonfuls of ones and zeroes that are dissolving into them this very second, sparking neurons, creating a fresh pink wrinkle in their brains.

People fuss so much about what they eat. BPA this, GMO that. Trans fat. Simple sugars. Dyes, additives. But they don't worry as much about what they consume online. The people who are infected, their hard drives and their minds are now hosting something invisible, unwanted. Their bodies are presently processing it. You can think of this as a virus or as a spell, an incantation, a collection of ciphers, a protest song that brings about change.

"A possession," Lela says to him, this time with more confidence.

"A possession," Josh says. "Exactly. They're possessed. This city is possessed."

He describes what he has seen firsthand and what he has gleaned from the scanner. The bodies, the fires, the bullets, the knives. "Don't go outside. Don't go online."

"This isn't just going away."

"No, it's not," he says. "This is the battle that starts the war."

"We need to do something."

"We're working on it."

"We? Who's *we*?"

"Just lie low, like I said. You keep your phone charged and I'll keep you updated, and if we're lucky, you can write a story about this one day."

"You don't tell me what to do, intern," Lela says. "I tell *you* what to do."

To this he has no response.

"You wouldn't know fuck all if not for me," she says. "I'm the one who clued you in to what's going on."

A voice sounds in the background, and he muffles the receiver and says something in response. Then he returns to her. "I've got to go. We're busy."

"I know who you're with," she says. "I know who *we* is. It's that friend you mentioned before, isn't it? The one who told you all that stuff about the Dark Net? The hacker? The computer nerd?"

There is a long silence. A pop of static. His voice is muffled as though he just crushed his face into the pillow. "Geek," Josh says. "He prefers geek."

"I need to talk to him."

His sigh has a squeak running through it. "He's not going to talk to you."

"Just ask him."

"He hates reporters. He threatened to unfriend me on Facebook for interning at the paper."

"Let me talk to him. I can be very convincing."

"I'm telling you, he won't. He's super paranoid. All cloak-and-dagger."

"He needs to make an exception."

"He won't."

She doesn't know whether she should regret what she says next: "He will when he hears about my niece."

"Your what? Niece? What about her?"

"She's been on the Dark Net."

"She and a half million others."

"No. You don't understand. I don't even understand. But she's *been* there. There's no simple way to explain this over the phone except to say she can navigate it like nobody else. But she needs your help to get there safely. Now. She knows where to find these guys. She can stop them." Lela almost says, "Or so she claims," but doesn't.

Lela has been circling the dining room as she speaks, with Hannah trailing a few feet behind her. Now her niece nods eagerly and bunches her hands below her chin and rises onto her tiptoes hopefully, still a kid after all. Lela remembers what her sister once said to her. Once you become a parent, your sense of self is compromised. Because the child is you, an extension of you, like a third hand, an extra spleen. But you don't control it—it won't listen—even when you try to keep it from harm's way. Every time your kid approaches a cliffside, a busy intersection, a strange dog, you feel a gut-twisting anxiety, a projective sensation the childless can only distantly understand. Her sister said that a lot. "You wouldn't understand, since you don't have a kid."

Maybe she was right. Until now. Is she an aunt or a mother? Either way, Hannah is her blood. Suggesting the girl go on the Dark Net feels like shoving her fork-first into a light socket. "She can help," Lela says, her throat dry. "Now tell us where you are. We're coming."

✣

The address is only four blocks away, but they have Juniper. It takes five minutes to rouse him from his narcotic sleep, and another twenty to get him out of bed and explain what's happened. The donor bags are empty; he's flush with blood. They unhook the needles, bandage the vein pricks. His pulse is strong and his skin warm, but he moves slowly. Grated teeth. Sharp intakes of breath. When they help him into his jeans, a button-down flannel, he pops a few stitches, but tells them not to worry. "It hurts like a son of a bitch," he says. "But I'll live."

He shakes out six ibuprofen and downs them with a quarter-empty bottle of Dewar's kept on the bureau. Then he directs Lela to retrieve the .45 in the closet, tucked beneath his sweaters. She holds it in the air between them. "Is this for me or you?"

He leans on the bureau, holding himself up. "You ever fire a gun before?"

"Once. For an assignment. I went to the gun range where the Bloods and the 503 Boys practice and—"

"Then it's for me."

✣

Outside, they pause to rest every few paces. Lela isn't much help—Juniper is too damn big—so he leans against walls and street signs and newspaper kiosks. The streets and sidewalks are empty. The sky is the color of a bruise. Hemingway walks ahead of them, his ears perked, his tail tucked, confused by the alarms and sirens wailing from every direction. "It sounds like the end of the world," Lela says, and Juniper says, "Maybe it is."

It takes two blocks before they happen upon the first body. An older man in a flannel shirt and jeans, face-up on the sidewalk. A butcher knife sticks out of his sternum like an exclamation mark. Juniper says his name, "Mitch," and hovers over him.

Lela shields Hannah from the sight. "Don't look, okay?"

Then she says to Juniper, "You knew him?"

Juniper shakes his head indeterminately—yes, no—and says, "I can't seem to protect anyone. I can't seem to do what I'm supposed to do."

Lela tells him they don't have time for pity or reflection or anything except movement. "Just move. Just keep walking." She asks Hannah to hold her hand and stare straight ahead and try to ignore the bodies. But soon that becomes impossible. There are too many of them. A woman lies in the road, her stomach a saddle shape from the car that ran her over. A man hangs from a tree, swaying by a rope. And others, dozens of others.

A building burns in the distance, a pillar of flame. Smoke in the air, blood on the asphalt, but no movement. Not until they spot the sign in the distance, GEEK. Its letters glow red but the windows are dark. A computer supply store owned by Josh's friend. "Almost there," Lela says—to the others, to herself.

Stepping off the sidewalk is the worst. The walled-in canyons of the streets feel somewhat protected, but there is such hollowness to every intersection. As though the blackness of the asphalt were a void they might fall into. Halfway across the road, she hears it, the rumble of an engine. And then the headlights snap on and seize them midstep.

A squad car. Forty yards away. Lela feels a momentary relief, until the engine roars and the vehicle leaps forward and eats up the asphalt between them. There's nowhere to go, not with Juniper using her as a crutch. But he already has the .45 in his hand. "Wait," she says, a part of her still wanting to believe the world isn't upside down. If they just call out for help, wave the cop down, then he'll hit the brakes, roll down a window, ask how he might be of service.

Juniper's arm wobbles, but his aim is true enough to knock four fist-sized holes in the windshield. The driver slumps against the wheel, and at the last second the squad car veers to the right and jumps the curb and smashes through the plate-glass window of a tea shop. There is a clatter of tables knocked aside and then the steel punch of the grille striking the far wall. The siren gives a brief chirp. Plates and mugs continue to explode against the floor. Even from here, Lela can see a red glow throbbing from the car's interior, the coded stream of the swivel-mounted laptop.

"It's like I said before." Juniper doesn't holster the weapon, but keeps it by his side when he hooks an arm around her neck. Sulfur burns her nostrils. "Paranoia. It's a requirement if you want to survive."

They hump forward, reaching the far sidewalk. Twenty more paces and they arrive at the doorstep of GEEK. Lela presses up against the door. The aisles carry coils of Ethernet cables, blister packs of thumb drives, dead-screened monitors and tablets. Like everything else in the Pearl District, the store appears mismatched, a sleek electronics hub crushed between a sex shop and psychic reader.

They bang on the door—the sign there reads CLOSED—and shiver where they stand. Rain falls, dotting the glass and chilling their skin. Lela puts an arm around Hannah, draws her close. Hemingway yawns beside them, his jaws closing with a *clack*. The sirens and alarms continue to throb, and she beats the door again, needing to get away from noise, muffle it.

"There they are," Juniper says.

From the back of the shop come two figures. One of them is Josh, all sharp angles and acne and uncombed hair. The other is short but cheats a few inches with his clunky Doc Martens. He is balding, the gleaming scalp offset by forearms patched with thick wiry hair. He wears khakis and a polo shirt wrinkled at the belly from being tucked in earlier. He stares at them through the glass, then twists the deadbolt and opens the door. He studies them each in turn, finally settling his gaze on Lela. "Just so you know, if not for my man Josh, we wouldn't be having this conversation right now. Getting past him is like getting past Kerberos."

"Thank you," Lela says. "Thanks for meeting with us."

"Don't thank me for anything, honey girl. Not yet. You might have gotten past Josh, but you still have to get past me. How do I know I can trust you?"

"Can we talk inside? It's not safe out here."

He leans against the doorway, crosses his arms, no rush. "Tell me how I know I can trust you."

Josh swats his shoulder. "Come on, Derek. They're going to get killed out there."

Derek makes a dismissive notion with his hand as if to knock the complaint from the air.

Lela wears a hoodie to fight the cold, but she pulls it back from her face now so that they can look at each other plainly. "Why would I mess with you?"

"You're a reporter. You know this address, you know my face. Maybe this is all some ruse you've set up so that you can write an article."

"It's not," Josh says. "This is real. Stop being a d-bag."

Lela puts out an arm, silencing Josh. "It's okay." Her hair is damp now, and she combs the sodden mess of it back from her face. "I'll be the first to admit, I am normally a vulture who acts in complete self-interest and will do anything for a story. But this is not one of those times." Her voice thickens with emotion she isn't used to managing. "My sister is dead." She looks down at Hannah. Her face is inscrutable behind the Mirage. "Her mother is dead. People are dying all around us. And we're going to join them if you don't help us. Please help us."

Derek dodges his eyes back and forth among them, settling now on Hannah. He appears to be chewing gum though he is not. "She's the one, huh? The little girl in the weird sunglasses who says she can bring down the Dark Net and yet needs our humble help to get inside."

"Little?" Hannah says. "We're the same height."

Derek defensively straightens his posture. He appears ready to fire off a response, but instead juts his chin at Juniper. "What about the big guy? Why so quiet?"

Juniper leans against the doorway, his face mooshed against the frame. Sweat drips from him though the night is cold. "Right now I just want to lie down, but I will say that I have some experience in these matters."

"These matters?"

He holds up his pistol and then slowly tucks it back in its holster. "I'm not going to demand, and I'm not going to beg, but I will say please. Maybe we can help each other."

"Please," Hannah says.

"Please," Lela says. "Okay? We're all saying it. Fucking *please*."

"Words," Derek says. "Words are just words. They don't reassure me."

"Then what do you want?"

He's the kind of person who can't smile without smirking. "Social security numbers. Credit card PINs. And all account usernames and passwords. You write them down, I'll authenticate. Then we're in business."

"So you can ruin me if I write about you? At a time like this, that's your main concern?"

"Yep." Derek pops his lips with the *p*.

"How do I know you won't ruin me anyway?"

"You don't. But I won't. I promise. I'll keep the intel in a safe. Little insurance policy."

Lela looks up and down the street, a shadowy corridor blurred by the now steady rain. Getting inside seems more important than ever, but she won't let him walk all over her. "How do I know *I* can trust *you?*"

"Because we're the good guys."

She wants to grab Juniper's pistol, shove Derek aside, push her way into the store, demand whatever help he can offer. But she's had her share of difficult interviews and knows the only way to get what she wants. Listen and play off ego. "Fine," she says. "You're in charge. You can have whatever you want. Just let us in."

Derek considers them another minute, then steps aside, holds open the door.

✣

Past the display cases, past the neatly stocked aisles, through the cluttered storeroom, there is a doorway. It opens to a staircase that drops into the basement. Two dehumidifiers groan. Fans whir. The air is warm and smells faintly of burned sugar from all the computer terminals set up here, their screens glowing and hard drives humming. The walls are red-bricked and carry a framed poster of Orwell's *1984*, another of *The Matrix*. A Guy Fawkes mask hangs from a hook.

There's not enough space for them all, but Juniper pushes his way into the adjacent bedroom. Onto the bed he promptly collapses. Joined a moment later by a tired Hemingway, who curls up on the floor with a *humph*.

Josh and Hannah sit on an IKEA futon. They watch as Lela writes down all the requested information on a notepad. Derek plops into an ergonomic swivel chair with a netted back. "Thank you," he says, and takes the notepad and pushes off with his feet and rolls across the floor to face a thirty-inch monitor. His keyboard is split down the middle and angled in such a way that it appears almost winged. His fingers strike the keys with a strange aggression, as if he were at war with the machine. He calls up a browser called Opera and works through several websites, plugging in her information at each. Her bank account reveals several overdraft charges and a savings of $904. "Wow, you're broke."

"Writer," she says with a shrug.

Derek logs out, tears away the sheet, tucks it in his pocket. Then he swivels around to face them. "Okay. Now what?"

"You say you're the good guys." Lela tries to make her voice as encouraging as possible. "Tell me about how good you are."

A half-full bottle of Mountain Dew sits on the desk. He reaches for it, wrenches off the cap, takes a swallow. "Do you remember, last year, when the Wells Fargo website crashed for twenty-four hours?"

"Sounds familiar."

He taps his chest. "That was us. Took five minutes to bring it down."

"You'd think breaking into a bank's website would be as hard as breaking into a bank."

"You'd think, right? But no. You put up a fence in your yard, somebody can climb over it and dig under it. You put locks on your doors, but if somebody wants to get inside, they only need to put a rock through the window. Security is an illusion. We're all willfully blind to the threats that surround us. Nowhere is safe. No one is safe." She can tell this is a speech he's given before. He holds out his arms, as if gesturing the world around. "As tonight has proven. I've spent the last four hours trying to crack this thing—whatever it is—but so far I'm getting nowhere. The virus isn't like anything I've seen before."

"Why aren't you infected?"

"Are you kidding me? I've got so many security filters on this thing, I could run radioactive waste through it and it would come out purer than spring water."

"Why'd you break into the bank's website?"

Another swig. His words are hopped up on caffeine, spilling out of him: "The same reason we posted the names and addresses of those seventeen-year-old football players who raped that cheerleader. The same reason we hacked the computer of the archbishop and leaked his kiddie porn to the cops. The same reason we took over the Tacoma PD's website and posted pictures of killer clowns after they shot that unarmed black kid. Because *we're* the good guys."

"You keep saying *we*. You're part of a collective."

He tucks the bottle into his groin and swivels back and forth in his chair. "Actually it's just me. But I represent a greater good. That's what I mean by *we*."

"Do you have, like, a name?"

The smirk again. "You mean besides Derek?"

"Yes, I mean besides Derek."

"Still working on that. I've got a few avatars. What do you think about The God Virus? That's kind of awesome, right?"

The question never gets answered. Their attention turns to Hannah. She rises from the futon and crosses the basement and stands beside Derek. He feels uncomfortable enough to scoot a few inches away from her. He waits for her to say something, and when she doesn't, his hands rise and fall to slap the armrests of his chair. "What, kid?"

"We're wasting time. I need you to take me into the Dark Net."

Derek cocks his head, studies her a moment. "Why?"

"You said you're one of the good guys."

"Yeah?"

"I need to go after the bad guys."

"And who are they?"

Lela answers: "A group known as Undertown, Inc."

"Who is this kid?" he says to Lela, and doesn't wait for an answer. "Look. Listen. Let me explain something to you. The NSA knows your movement from site to site, can track your GPS, can track your credit card purchases, can hack the camera on your phone or computer and spy over your shoulder. They can follow every email you've ever sent, including edits, deletions, whether you were picking your nose or drinking a root beer when you wrote it. They know everything about you, and if you make a wrong move, they throw you in a cell and pipe Britney Spears through the loudspeakers all night and rip out your toenails until you confess to what they already know. If that's what the good guys are capable of, imagine the bad. The bad guys are on the Dark Net. The bad guys are causing all of this. You don't want to mess with them." He finishes off the bottle of Mountain Dew, stifles a burp. "Besides, you're just a kid."

Lela says, "She's not just a kid."

"I don't know what that even means."

"She's special."

"So am I."

"This is different. She's—I don't know the word—*touched*."

"By whom?"

It isn't easy for Lela to say, "I don't know. God?"

Derek rolls his eyes. "Know your audience, lady."

"Twenty-four hours ago, I felt exactly the same."

"You guys are a joke. A bunch of freak-show zealots. I can't believe you're wasting my time."

Lela tries to explain herself—stumbling through a half-assed description of *the spectrum*—and who knows how long the argument would spiral on if not for Hannah slapping Derek across the face. This silences him, makes his eyes go wide. He brings a hand to the cheek where the imprint of her hand rises red.

"Plug me in," Hannah says.

Lela blinks once and sees Hannah as a twelve-year-old girl, blinks twice and sees her ten times the size. Derek hunches down in his chair as she looms menacingly over him. "Do you understand?" the girl says again, and still Derek does not respond. Her voice sounds as though another voice threads together with it, an adult voice that amplifies her words, giving them reverb. "You're going to help me get inside the Dark Net." Her hands shoot forward and take hold of his head. Maybe it's just a trick of the light, but it appears that a whiteness hazes from her mouth, her visor, her nose and ears, as if she swallowed the moon. The ceiling seems to lift and the walls to bend and the floor to drop, every atom nudged aside to make room for something outsized.

Hemingway comes out of the bedroom and wags his tail and perks his ears and begins to bark and won't stop even when Lela shushes him. Finally she clamps his snout and says, "Stop it. Be quiet, you dumb dog." She holds him and pets him furiously and tries not to feel terrified of her own niece.

"Let me go," Derek says. "Please!"

At last Hannah releases him, and he rolls his chair away and trembles as if run through with electricity.

A long silence follows. Josh breaks it. "What the hell is going on?"

"Are you familiar with the term *jeremiad*?" Juniper says, his voice carrying from the other room. He does not wait for an answer and he does not rise from the bed, but explains that it comes from the book of Jeremiah. It is a list of woes, a lamentation that denounces society and prophesizes moral downfall. "It's a form of storytelling. Preachers use it, politicians use it. Spirit clashes with flesh. And in the end, one triumphs over the other. Sometimes the good, sometimes the bad. We're caught up in a kind of jeremiad now. Flesh and spirit, light and dark, physical and digital. A clash of opposites. Right now I'd put my money on Hannah as our only chance of winning. Do you understand?"

Derek's nose is bleeding, a thread of red that traces his upper lip and smears down his chin, but he doesn't seem to notice. His eyes are on Hannah. "All right. Sure. Let's do this."

CHAPTER 26

THE MIRAGE RUNS through the lightning port behind Hannah's ear, wiring stimuli into her brain. She unplugs the feed now and slips off the prosthesis. The sudden darkness is familiar, comforting, a pressure relieved. She senses Derek beside her, holding the cable that runs from his desktop.

"It's not going to work," he says.

"It's going to work."

"I'm telling you. It's not going to work."

But it will. The Internet is code, and so is everything around them. When you're a child, you struggle to read what later becomes second nature. A red light makes your foot depress a brake. A skull and crossbones alerts us to poison. None are direct representations, but signs and symbols that serve as vehicles of meaning and experience. The Internet is no different, made up of ones and zeroes akin to the tiny atoms that build up into the appearance of swords and books and coffee mugs. By plugging in, Hannah will simply need to learn not just a new way of seeing, but a new way of feeling, of living. Because even though the Internet might seem like an unguessable expanse, those ones and zeroes are charged with energy and so they must have mass, a physicality she can negotiate. She knows this, but the knowledge comes from elsewhere, as though voices were whispering in her ear, hands urging her forward. She feels part of a company greater than even those in this room.

Derek reaches behind her ear, fits the cord into place. The computer makes a sound like knocked door, indicating its detection of new hardware, requesting approval. She hears Derek drop into his chair and roll across the floor. The mouse clicks. The keyboard patters. His voice announces, "Okay, let's give this a try."

For now all programs are shut off, the Internet connection severed. He has only one file open. That's where they'll start, he tells her. Baby steps.

She remembers the word Juniper used on her the other day. *Aperture.* She feels one opening inside her now and bends every nerve in its direction. It is as if she were floating in some porous borderlands. She is dimly aware of everyone watching her in the chair, while also blurring into another world. A world streaming with code.

Slowly the one begins to overtake the other. How much time passes, she isn't sure, but for a long while her mind feels frayed and spastic, like so many centipedes twisting into a ball. She has no vision, only a haywire perceptual antenna. She has been here before, the sensation akin to when she first tried on the Mirage. The doctor told her she needed to be patient, needed to remain calm, and he was right. Everything eventually settled into place. She tries the same now. She tries to be calm.

But it's difficult. Because at first it feels like she's spiraling along a drain rainbowed with color or maybe funneling through a tornado that carries millions of LEGO blocks in its wind. There is no up or down or left or right, no depth or design, only a whirring sense of pieces that don't fit together.

"Where am I?" she says. "What am I looking at? Tell me how to see."

Derek's voice sounds far away. "It's just a photo I took. That's all. A JPEG of the storm front that blew through on Friday night."

She remembers the way the air pressure shifted so suddenly her ears popped, the way the wind hushed and then the raindrops spattered the windows. She had watched the weather from the living room. Watched with her new eyes, the Mirage, as the lightning forked and the clouds churned and the city blacked out. That was when this all began, it seems. As if the storm blew it in.

She calls up the memory now to fit together with the data channeling into her brain. And then—not all at once, but piece by piece—the panic wipes away and her perception clarifies. She was trying to look at something, as you would look at a screen. But she is not looking at the storm. She is a part of the storm. She can ride the lightning, brush against the stony underside of a cloud, taste the raindrops frozen in flight. Here are skyscrapers to climb, the reflections in their windows burning pleasantly. It's all there, a tiny infinity.

Derek says, "What can you see? Can you see it?"

"Yes," she says. "No."

"Which is it?"

"I can navigate it."

He doesn't respond for a long time, but when he does, his voice is touched with an almost childish curiosity. "I don't know if this makes sense, but could you—can you touch the storm? Can you change it somehow?"

"I'll try," she says.

She tries to center herself, find a place of vague untraceable calm before attempting anything. She cannot touch with her hands, so she must discover other muscles, invisible muscles that might respond to her commands. He wants her to change the photo. The possibility makes her feel like a small god who might on a whim knock over buildings, set trees on fire, blacken the world. She cycles through the data. The lightning is white-hot. The windows are orange-lit and warped with reflections. Everything is otherwise so dark. Overwhelmingly dark. It cloaks what could otherwise be seen. She recognizes the dark by its name. A string of identifiers that determine color. If she rearranges the string, changes the code, everything will lighten. She tries.

The coefficients. The bitstream. The parameters. The multiple compressions. She perceives the storm, but she also interprets its component parts. In this way she feels afflicted with a kind of double vision, like the child who experiences wonder at a fairy tale while also feeling safely tucked into a chair or who studies the sky and recognizes a cloud while also willing it into the shape of a dragon or bunny or moth.

"Holy shit," Derek's voice says. "She's doing it. You're doing it, Hannah."

✣

Lela stands behind Derek and studies the monitor. The photo gradually lightens, the pixels crystallize, and then she blinks and the city appears suddenly unrobed of shadow. As if the screen, once smudged with soot, has been wiped clean.

Hannah grips the armrests so tightly, the ligaments stand out on her forearms. Sweat gleams on her skin. Her head leans back and her teeth grit and her eyes stare at nothing, the pupils so dilated they appear bored through, gateways to something cavernous.

For the next hour or so, Derek trains her. At first they play around with more pictures. Compressing and recompressing, cropping and rotating and downsampling and block splitting. From there they move on to word processing, music files, games, websites. She gets faster, figures things out without him having to coach her. Maybe because her blindness inclines her toward the extrasensory.

Juniper is asleep on the bed and Josh is asleep on the futon, his arm thrown around Hemingway. All of them snore softly. Lela wishes she could join them. She digs around in her purse for more Adderall but the bottle is empty. She shakes it anyway. A gesture of stupid hope that captures the spirit of the room.

Her exhaustion gives her a bruised feeling behind her eyes that courses through her body and extends to the tips of her fingers. She has been standing so long, so still that when she changes her posture, the blood hurts when it floods into the crimped-off spaces. She tries to pay attention, but Derek only makes so much sense as he talks to Hannah about firewalls, VPNs, how she'll be vulnerable to attack, but he'll monitor everything, checking for viruses, worms, pirates. "I'm your wingman." If someone tries to hack them, he'll block the IP, shield her.

"But what if the IP is our target?"

"Goes both ways. There will be a wall between us."

"Then don't."

The mouse is wireless and Derek spins it in circles, while turning the idea over in his head. "The system could get overridden. You could conceivably get overridden as well."

"Possessed you mean."

"I guess. Yeah."

"Don't block the IP unless I say so."

"This is my equipment."

"Don't," Hannah says in a voice that shakes the air.

✣

Lela feels like *now* is when she should come to her senses. Now is when she should muffle her ears against whatever possesses Hannah and commands the room. Lela must see her for what she is—a girl, just a little girl—without a mother and in need of protection.

Cheryl always lectured Lela on her irresponsibility, her recklessness and selfishness and solipsism. She was trying to be good. She was trying to do what was right, but it felt wrong. Cheryl would never have allowed any of this, but Cheryl was gone. Every thought conflicts and dead-ends, and she doesn't know what else to say except "I think we need to slow down and rethink—"

Hannah's hand seizes her wrist. And Lela has a vision then. Of the great expanse of years that lie before them. Hannah is not alive. Lela is not alive. No one is alive because the world is a vast plain of fire through which figures stride, some with beaks and claws and tails and horns and scales, and some with beetles and spiders and flies spilling out of their floppy mouths.

"Don't," Hannah says again, and Lela pulls back her hand as if burned.

Derek holds up his hands in submission, then drops them to the keyboard once more. He does not look to Lela for approval but moves his fingers rapid-fire, enabling the VPN, calling up a TOR browser, and tapping into the network. There are no standard addresses on the Dark Net, everything hidden, known only by a seemingly random stream of characters that end with .onion. This makes searching difficult. So do the passwords protecting so many of them or the requirement that you belong to an approved friends list. He says he isn't sure what they're looking for, and Hannah says she is. An entity, Undertown, and a name, Cloven. They'll start by searching the wikis and directories and link dumps, maybe get into some chatrooms, see what they can turn up.

Some sites fail to load; some sites are slow to load. They scroll through political websites, some libertarian, some anarchistic, all choked with conspiracy theories. Here are jihadists from ISIS requesting funds and volunteers, and here is an Idaho militia offering up a $100,000 reward for any who might assassinate the Antichrist president. Here are music and movies and TV dumps, where anything you've ever wanted to plug into your ears or eyes is available for free. Here is a supposed assassin who will kill anyone for a fee. Here is an NYC hooker who will fuck you for Namecoins or bitcoins. Here is a digital Silk Road offering up weed, crank, oxy, roids, H, E, iPhones, iPads, pistols, pythons, whatever, everything delivered to your doorstep.

All this time Hannah's eyes remain open, twitching, tracking things unseen to Lela. Her lips move like a child's when reading.

Then Derek clicks on a link with 666 in the address chain. It loads with a slow, shuttering blackness that overtakes the screen.

Derek shakes the mouse, smacks the keyboard with his index finger several times, before giving up. "What do you see, Hannah?"

No response. Her face marbleized.

Derek twists in his chair to examine her. His face sheened with sweat. "Hannah?"

"Hannah?" Lela says, and takes her by the shoulders, gives her a gentle shake.

It is then that the girl's eyes roll back white and her mouth unhinges and she begins to scream.

"Hannah!" Lela says. "Hannah, can you hear me?"

Lela can't hear her own voice over the screaming, which continues longer than it ought to, carried by more breath than a set of lungs could bottle. Lela gives up on shaking Hannah and covers her ears and turns in a hopeless circle and tells Derek they need to unplug her.

He leans back in his chair, so repelled by the screaming that it might as well have claws that scratch, fangs that bite. "She said not to! Not unless she said to." The clarity of the monitors behind him fizzles in and out, and in a panic Derek turns his attention to the computer terminal. Something pops. Sputters. Flares. The fans pick up speed and expel the reek of smoke. "Oh no," he says. "Oh shit."

Hannah's body begins to seize. Shivering and hitching. White flecks of spit fly from her mouth. One of the arms breaks off of her chair. Lela goes to her and gets knocked to the floor by a flailing arm.

Hemingway barks and Josh tries to settle him down. Juniper stands in the doorway to the bedroom, a hand pressed painfully to his side. No one is doing anything. No one knows what to do. Hannah—absurdly—was in charge until a moment ago.

Then the girl goes silent, out of breath, though her mouth remains wide open. She continues to convulse in the chair. Her skin brightens red—and then, just as suddenly, blackens. Smoke rises from her hair before it catches flame.

Lela throws herself at Hannah once more. She misses the cord the first time—then swipes again, grabbing for it, making a fist around it. It's hot. So currented with electricity that her muscles harden, and for a moment she can't move. Jolted. Electrocuted. Then Lela falls back and yanks the cord with her weight. And at last it gives, popping cleanly from the lightning port.

Juniper is beside her now, and he kicks the cord from her hand. She breathes hard from the floor, not wanting to get up but forcing herself to. Hannah's skin has split, blackened with angry red lines running through it. Smoke curls off her. Lela doesn't know what she expects. Maybe for Hannah to rub her eyes and clear her throat, to thank her or yell at her, to tell them all what to do next. Instead she slumps from the chair to the floor, her body so limp it appears deboned, the posture of the dead.

CHAPTER 27

THE ROADS AREN'T SAFE, but Juniper drives them anyway. He has no choice. This is their only chance. The Buick LeSabre he brought to Portland so many years ago has been replaced by a Dodge truck with a grille like a clenched fist. It has a brush guard and tires treaded so thickly, he could climb the side of a cliff. A 6.4-liter HEMI V8 engine with a growl you can feel a block away. If you hoist up the bench seat in the club cab, you'll find weapons tucked into the smuggler's space: a pump shotgun, two pistols, boxes of ammo that rattle on a rutted road. The gearshift—with a twist and a yank—becomes a knife spiked by a thin six-inch blade. The topper is windowless and lined with iron, and two heavy-duty bolts lock its door in place. The color, as if there were any question, is black.

The only vehicles on the road are crashed. An upside-down SUV. A bus on its side. A five-car pileup. A sedan with its hood crumpled like an accordion. A semi that appears to have plowed through oncoming traffic. At times the way is blocked altogether, a gridlocked section of road, all of the cars with their doors open as if the drivers will be back at any second. He turns back to try another route or slowly noses through the wreckage with a rocking screech or takes the truck into the grassy meridian or onto a muddy hillside shoulder. He keeps his eyes on the side mirrors as much as the road before him, and for some time and many miles there is only darkness and his headlights reflecting off shattered glass, rent metal, and the puddles rippled by wind. He doesn't know if everybody is sleeping or hiding or simply dead.

Every now and then he checks in with Josh. The Motorola walkie-talkies have a fifty-mile range, and their voices come across with only a few hiccups of static. Juniper says, "How are you doing?" and Josh says, "Almost there."

"Same. Keep me posted."

Besides Paradise Wireless, there are four other major providers in Portland. Juniper is headed first to a data center in Tigard, a suburb of strip malls and multiplex theaters and tightly packed housing developments. This data center, like all data centers, is not advertised online and cannot be found in the phone book. The buildings are not physically marked with signage. You might drive past one every day. You might live or work nearby and not know any better. Except for the utility vans and trucks—often decaled with the company's name—that park in the lots, these are buildings that hope for anonymity.

Because they are critical arteries of digital information. People tend to think about the Internet in a blindly amorphous, almost religious way. There is an all-knowing repository known as the cloud that everyone and everything is a part of, but no one can tell you where it is. Some invisible communication is going on all around us, part of the ether. Towers are erected, steepled on hillsides, where voices are funneled like prayers and hymns.

In fact, the Internet would not exist if not for the fiber cables that vein the ground beneath our streets, through our sewers. There are around eighty major network junctions—known as IXPs, for Internet exchange points—throughout the country. These are the freeways that feed the domestic traffic as well as the international data that comes from undersea cables. They are nakedly unprotected. As are the fiber cables that branch off them and come together—at pinch points, spaghetti junctions—within the data centers. The term *wireless* couldn't be more misleading.

Every now and then, there will be a data outage due to a fiber cut. During which time you cannot text, cannot email, cannot call your sister in Omaha to wish her a happy birthday or even your local 911 dispatcher to report an emergency, cannot use a credit card or ATM, cannot watch Netflix or ask Google a question or turn on your security system or access hospital records or any of the other hundreds of conveniences we take for granted, that make us safe and happy, that make society hum.

All it takes is an earthquake—the slight shifting of stone—or a construction project—the metal bite of a payloader's scoop—and the cables are clipped and everything goes dark. Or someone could simply hoist a manhole cover, climb below the street, and use a knife or a pair of wire cutters to slow or cease all local Internet traffic. The security at the data centers is minimal—sometimes a single guard in the lobby, sometimes no one at all—but even if they hired out a small army, the cables that reach beyond it would remain completely unguarded. We worry about guns and we worry about bombs, but one of the greatest threats of this time is a mere knife jab to the physical cabling that is the circulatory system of the country.

At the entrance to the Tigard data center, there is a rolling gate—woven with chain-link—that Juniper does not slow down for. The Ram lives up to its name, crashing through with a splash of sparks and a grating screech as it carries the gate with it. He comes to a rocking stop after twenty yards, and the gate releases from the grille and keeps going another five.

The building before him couldn't be more nondescript: one-story, brick, maybe four thousand square feet, with two windows bordering the entrance. You'd think they'd be bigger, but even as traffic increases, the need for circuit-and-node real estate grows smaller. Technology shrinks even as it opens up new worlds. To serve the entire state of Oregon only requires around two hundred thousand gigs of data a day. In the building the lights are off, but in the parking lot a vapor lamp burns, casting its glow on three utility vans parked there.

He kills the engine, climbs out, and hoists from the cab the cardboard box packed with C-4 demolition charges. The puttied bricks give off the smell of motor oil and Band-Aids. It hurts to move. To turn the steering wheel, to depress the gas and brake, to open and close the door, to carry the box, which weighs over fifty pounds. He walks as carefully as he can, no sudden movements, but still he can feel the stitches straining, tearing.

He's not worried about dropping the box or fumbling the bricks—he does both as he moves around the perimeter of the building, setting them in place—because C-4 is stable and resilient enough that it will only blow when exposed to extreme heat and shock wave. This will come from the detonators he's inserted in each of them. He and Sarin had cooked and molded the C-4 themselves to take down a neo-Nazi militia compound—way up in the Cascades—headed by a demon who was readying a series of attacks on mosques and synagogues throughout the Northwest, hoping to start a holy war. Juniper kept the leftovers in case they came in handy.

In each block he stabs a blasting cap, and from this he runs a detonating cord capped at each end with a booster. There might have been a time when detonating a building would jag his heart with excitement, fill him with some boyish anticipation. No longer. There was too much lost already, and he goes about his business with a joyless determination.

He hides behind his truck for the detonation. The air pulses yellow, orange, red, and back again. The sound is thunderous, a forceful wind that pops his ears and gives way to a mosquito whine that lingers. Bricks rain down and clunk the truck and scatter across the parking lot. When he stands, with some difficulty, he sees the fiery, cratered remains of the building. Black smoke roils from it.

He unclips the walkie-talkie. "One down," he says, and Josh says, "Make that two."

Josh was in Beaverton, at another data center. Juniper wasn't sure he should send the kid off on his own, but in the interest of time, they didn't have any choice. Lela had even risen from her daze to say that Josh might look like a loser—with his pleated khakis and his pimple-rashed cheeks—but the intern was all right. And now Josh has pulled through. Neither of them has run into any trouble, so maybe things will turn out all right after all.

It is then—when Juniper says, "Nice work," and limps toward the driver's door of the Ram—that he spots the hound. It wanders out of the night, the hard pads of its paws clopping on the wet pavement like hooves. It pauses only for a moment, beneath the vapor lamp in the parking lot, which finds a reflection in the milky cast of its eyes.

He holsters the walkie-talkie. He reaches into his pocket and fumbles for his key. He cringes when he runs—as best as he can manage, more of a loping hobble—to the door and yanks it open and climbs inside and cranks the key. By this time the hound has started after him. It lowers its head and tucks its tail. Its body tightens and unclenches when it speeds forward, whippet-fast. It hurls itself against the door powerfully enough to rock the vehicle. Against the window its claws scrabble and its jaws leave a rime of saliva.

Juniper jerks the truck into gear and spins the wheel hard and plows forward and watches the hound bound after him in the red wash of the taillights. Soon it is lost from sight. He blows out a sigh and thumbs on the walkie-talkie. "Ran into a little trouble, but I'm okay now. What's your status? Over." He waits for a response, too long. There is nothing but the hush of static. He repeats himself. Still nothing. "Josh?" he says. "Josh, give me something. I'm getting worried here."

Then—in stops and starts, like when you're spinning the dial, hunting for radio stations—comes a fitful screaming. Of someone who has given up all control. Of pure, consuming pain. There is a woolly silence, and then another voice sounds. Deep-throated. Burned. And familiar. "Didn't I already kill you?" it says. "Didn't I tell you to stop with your hopeless causes?"

"Who are you?" Juniper says, but he already knows. The *thing*. The man who used to follow him from church to church, haunting him. The man who stood at the base of his bed in the hotel room. Pale-faced. Black-clothed. Whose joints moved like creaking ropes, whose voice sounded like the bottom of a well. They say you can't remember pain, but he does now: a heated knot twisting his guts, a marrow-deep fear.

"You mean we weren't properly introduced before?" the voice says, so deep it is palpable. "You can call me Cloven."

When the signal fuzzes out again, it never comes back.

He wipes a hand across his face. Checks the side mirrors. Whispers "Fuck, fuck, fuck." Raises his hand as if to strike the steering wheel, but then pauses. Because the side mirrors flash with light. There is a car behind him, closing in fast.

More than an hour ago, when Juniper loaded up the Ram and readied to depart, he got underneath the hood and beneath the dash, disconnecting radio, Bluetooth, roadside assistance, the GPS, the alarm, the warning and airbag systems, the wireless transmitter, the fuel efficiency and emissions detector, automatic locks, even the cleaning fluid and air conditioning and heating. Almost all of this was housed in the brain of the vehicle—the engine control unit, a computer attached to the side of the motor—and several were paid services he didn't subscribe to, but he erred on the side of paranoia and unplugged everything, everywhere, that still allowed him to drive. Because most cars are now riddled with one hundred million lines of code, more than a smartphone, more than all of Facebook, more than a nuclear power plant. This makes cars better, safer—with their low-emission sensors and forward-collision warnings and automatic emergency braking—but it also makes them as vulnerable to cyber-threats as any computer.

Which is why Juniper isn't as surprised as he ought to be when the Jetta that thuds his rear bumper, that roars its accelerator and pulls up alongside him, turns out to be driverless. If he chainsawed through the dash, he knows the guts of the vehicle would stream with red code. The virus is in laptops, in phones, in tablets, in cars, in people. It is like terrible birdsong heard by someone that is then whistled and then sung by another and then becomes a marching tune for the military or a rural song fiddled around a campfire or a lullaby hummed by a mother. The infection is spreading, mutating, and will continue to, unless he stops it.

The car swings into him—two light taps, then a scraping shove—meant to force him off the road. Juniper experiments with braking and gas-gunning acceleration. He can't outpace the Jetta, but the Ram is nearly three times the size. So long as Juniper muscles the wheel, he can hold a steady course.

They approach a four-way stop. It is heaped and puzzled with cars that have crashed into each other. All around it the asphalt is made even blacker with ribboning skid marks. Juniper waits until the last second and then jerks the wheel left, bashing the Jetta with enough force that it momentarily hoists onto two tires. It recovers, but not soon enough to avoid the snarl of cars impeding the intersection. Its brakes shriek. Then comes the sickening crunch of metal crashing into metal.

Juniper dives down side streets and mazes his way through a residential area, guessing the way, missing his GPS and worrying about his sense of direction. He cuts across lawns and even a park, never stopping, rarely slowing, feathering the accelerator, hunting for a clear passage. He tries not to look at the bodies. They slump on park benches and sprawl across sidewalks and hang out of windows. There are people alive out there, too, he reminds himself. People who need him.

In the near distance, a spotlighted billboard advertises a retirement community. A middle-aged man rests his hand on the shoulder of his bent-backed, silver-haired father. "Roles change," the billboard reads. Roles changed when Juniper claimed to have visited heaven and he became a sudden celebrity and everyone needed him: his parents for money, the congregations for his false assurances. And roles changed when the cancer overtook him and he drove north to Oregon, handing out cash, intent on dying well. And when instead he lived, roles changed again, as he became a kind of servant—to the city, to Sarin. Now he can once more feel roles changing, everything changing. And maybe this time, if he dies, he'll stay that way.

He can't remember how old he was—maybe twelve or maybe ten—when the tornado hit Tarn's Brook, Oklahoma. A category-five funnel sucked up trailer parks and flattened farms. FEMA flew over the disaster area and ordered 150 body bags. But as it turned out, only three people died. Juniper remembers—after he came to town for a prayer service—seeing all those body bags lined up in the Safeway parking lot, like black pupae ready to be claimed. Everyone who saw them imagined their own body fitting into a bag, had they not gotten to the basement in time, had a stray brick flung through their window listed a few inches to the left, had a meeting they thought about canceling not taken them to the other side of town. They had met death, but death had spared them. For now. The body bags wouldn't lie unclaimed forever. Theirs were waiting. His was waiting. Unzipped, gaping like a rotten mouth. Maybe tonight it will finally claim him.

His eyes jog constantly to his side mirrors, knowing it is only a matter of time before headlights brighten them again. By the time he finds a thoroughfare with signs leading to I-5, he is being pursued—

by two, then three, then six vehicles as he barrels up the on-ramp and hopes like hell the freeway is passable.

He winds his way through the cars and semis, some abandoned, most ruined. He guns it to seventy, eighty, ninety, bombing through Multnomah, through Hillsdale, to the Terwilliger curves, a six-lane section of freeway that has long been the most dangerous in the state. He skids along its perilous corners, foot off the brake, leaning into the turns, feeling all the blood in his body pulled in the opposite direction. Two of the cars catch up with him and bash him until he knocks against the safety railing, which carves into the Ram and throws up showers of sparks. He jerks the steering hard enough to run over the hood of a BMW Roadster. The truck's tires lift on the left side, and just when he wonders if he will tip, gravity brings him crashing down again. When he regains control and checks the mirrors, he sees the BMW upended and skidding on its side, the broken axle spearing from its undercarriage.

Up ahead, a logging truck has overturned and spilled its trailer, and the road is dirty with bark and messed with twenty-foot sections of pine that scatter in every direction. One of the cars meets its end here, striking a fat log with such force that it burrows beneath its tonnage, half-flattened as if by a rolling pin. Another bursts a tire when it runs over a shorn logging chain. It tries to continue on for a hundred yards or so, the tire flapping like an old black sock, the rim throwing up intermittent fans of sparks, before giving up.

Near downtown, the traffic gathers thickly, and he barely makes it onto the Ross Island Bridge, headed for another data center in Milwaukie. One of the cars loses traction on the exit ramp and hits a concrete stanchion with a punch of flame. Then there is only one left—a ghost-white Mercedes—as he rumbles across the bridge, over the Willamette River. The water is chevroned with whitecaps. A lit-up apartment building on the farther shore looks like a stack of digital bytes. The Mercedes appears in one mirror, then the other, a phantom. It tries to nose past him, but he blocks it each time with a nudge of the wheel.

At the last moment, he sees the abandoned motorcycle. He cuts right and slams the brakes and skids at a violent diagonal. The tires wail as they burn away their rubber. The Mercedes uses this opportunity to zip past him, unaware of the bike until it is too late. They collide with a screech. The motorcycle goes pinwheeling in one direction, the Mercedes in the other, striking the guardrail, spiraling off the bridge, plummeting through the air and into the river below.

✣

Crows gather on top of Big Pink, the U.S. Bancorp building. Dozens of them, flapping their wings and spiraling in the air. A man stands among them, the axis around which they spin. Lump is dressed in clothes as black and ragged as their wings. They land delicately on his shoulders, and he whispers to them before hoisting an arm to send them fluttering off in every direction.

He knows that Josh is dead. He knows that without help Juniper will soon join him. Crows take to the air, cawing while down below headlights flash on and engines rumble to life and inject themselves into the streets to pursue the black Ram.

One crow and then another and then another—and then still more—come bombing out of the night, striking windshields hard enough to crack the glass, clogging up the grilles, and slicking the tires with their guts and feathers. They are joined by rats and possums and then a doe and even a black bear. They clamber out of storm drains and from beneath porches and Dumpsters. They pour out of Oaks Bottom Wildlife Refuge and the Reed College campus and Westmoreland Park and Eastmoreland Golf Course. Some of the cars try to dodge the animals, but this spins them off the road, so the rest plow through and their windshields fissure and their tires pop. Owls and bats and swallows. Raccoons and squirrels, cats and dogs, a herd of thirty deer, their eyes candled by the headlights and taillights, charging toward the brigade of vehicles.

Sensors go wild. Airbags go off. Emergency brakes scream. Tires pop. One car careens into a McDonald's, and another smashes into a parked van. A street sign bends and clangs and skids the undercarriage of one car, and another sideswipes a fire hydrant that geysers a white stream. And through all of this—the pursuant current of cars and animals—Juniper passes unmolested. He doesn't know whether the plan will work, but he remembers too well the last words he spoke to Sarin, "Or die trying."

CHAPTER 28

HOURS AGO, they all gathered around Hannah's body. Her skin was crisped to ash. Her eyes had boiled in their sockets. Wisps of smoke rose from her mouth. Lela scooped the girl into her lap and rocked back and forth and made a high, keening sound. No one spoke. Hemingway whined and Josh closed his eyes and Derek covered his mouth and Juniper clenched his fists so tightly his arms shook. The basement air was cold. A pipe clanked. The computers fizzled and oozed white where Derek had blasted them with a fire extinguisher.

"There are ways," Juniper said, though he hardly sounded convinced. "There are ways of coming back."

"Shut up," Lela told him.

She said this in a dead voice. All of the abstract emotions—grief, guilt, anger—hadn't had a chance to take form. Lela was owned by the purely physical. She had her arms around her niece, and it felt as though they were falling together, through the concrete floor, the brick tunnels beneath, the tangle of sewer pipes and power cables, the black dirt, the clay as red as wine, farther and farther still, beyond the miles of bedrock, all the way to the molten core of the earth, where they would burn up and Lela would feel grateful because then she wouldn't have to feel or think anything more.

She wouldn't have to remember Hannah—earlier, at the shelter, when Lela promised to take care of her—saying, "If we're all going to die, I hope I die first, because then I won't have to miss you."

"Don't say that," Lela had said. "I'm here for you. You're here for me. And we're going to look after each other for a long, long time."

It felt true when she said it. It felt true even now. As if she could will her niece back to life.

A chime sounded in Lela's pocket. A text alert. One, then another, then another, then another, like a tolling. She would have ignored it except the sound kept on. She pulled out the phone with the intent of hurling it against the floor. But the lighted screen paused her hand, and she read aloud what she saw there. "I'm still here," Lela said, her voice unbelieving. "And I know how to stop it." Followed by a string of characters Derek told her must be an IP address. "XO Hannah."

✣

Her body was still in the basement, but Hannah was elsewhere.

When she first plugged in, her vision enlarged, as if she had grown another set of eyes separate from her body. She didn't know what the right word was—transcendence maybe. She had surpassed her body's limitations. Become suddenly and expansively mobile. A kind of astral traveler.

When she first learned Braille, when she complained it was too hard, when she said it felt like a bunch of random dots, her teacher talked to her about symbols. A young woman weeps with pleasure when a gold band is slipped around her finger, and many decades later weeps again before her husband's gravestone, in both cases moved by the symbol, something representing something else. "They're not just dots. They're representations of letters. And the letters add up to words. And the words add up to sentences, paragraphs, chapters, stories. Through your fingertip, you're ascending so many levels of meaning. You can't think literally and live in this world. Humans excel at seeing something more than what's there. Nobody's born fluent of course. It takes time. We spend our whole life learning what all these symbols around us mean. You've learned physical codes, numeric codes, alphabetical codes. You're learning another code now. A tactile symbology. Be patient with it. Before long it will be as easy as breathing." And it was. She read until the Braille frayed beneath her fingers.

And the same lesson applied to the Mirage. When the doctor fitted her, he had warned about sensory dissonance. Her mind would see one thing; her body would feel another, resulting in a confusion over her awareness of space. Virtual reality sickness, he called it. Spatial poisoning. It was like taking off a blindfold and learning you were balanced on the tip of a skyscraper. A second before your footing felt sure, and then you became a wobbling mess. The first few hours she wore the Mirage, she hit a neuro wall. Being blind felt easier. There was too much to take in, and none of it made sense. But then, as the hours passed, she calmed. The dizziness ceased. Her mind and body felt aligned.

And now she struggled similarly in cyberscape, slowly overcoming sensory dissonance, escaping the bonds of physicality and literality. She would see more than what was actually there. She was accustomed to projecting the world onto the black theater of her mind. The blizzard of ones and zeroes, the metrics, hexadecimals, source lines and function points, pound signs and ampersands, the competing languages of Perl, PHP, Python, Node, Visual Basic, and ADA—they all solidified into a holograph she could stand in, run her fingers across, navigate, manipulate.

And the way she saw it, the Dark Net was a vast haunted house. There were long hallways that startled her with unexpected cobwebs. Creaky floors that threatened to give her away. Locked doors behind which stood another locked door behind which stood another locked door, each lock more complicated than the previous. Shifting staircases. A kitchen full of cleavers. A fireplace in which dried corpses were heaped to burn. A pool table with clawed feet and lacquered hearts for balls. Pipes that spit black water. Basements that had no bottom and attics crammed with bats. Torture chambers hung with rusted tools. A solarium tangled with dead plants. A walled-in garden ornamented with topiaries shaped like beasts. A room mounded with thousands of television sets that played movies she had to turn away from. Ghosts hid in closets. Monsters roamed freely. And everywhere—sprayed on a mirror and stitched into the curtains and splattered across the floor and messily stamped onto the keys of a grand piano—she found the markings of a red right hand.

Every few weeks, her mother would drop her off to spend the night at Lela's. She and her aunt would stuff their faces with pizza and ice cream, crank up Taylor Swift too loud, and dance until they felt like they were going to puke. And sometimes her aunt would tell her scary stories. Stories her mother thought were wildly inappropriate. Such as this one. Once there were two college roommates. One was a straight A student and the other was a party girl. On the night before midterms, Party Girl—of course—goes out to slam Jell-O shots at a frat bash. When Party Girl stumbles home around 3 a.m., she finds the lights off and her straight A roommate face-down at her desk. In the darkness Party Girl digs around for her books, pops a few caffeine pills, and takes off for the library, spending the last few hours before dawn cramming for her exams. Maybe she actually does okay. Or maybe not. She's too tired to know and still mildly drunk when she gets back to the dorm. Here she finds her roommate still face-down at her desk. "Hey, you," Party Girl says, and nudges her shoulder—and screams. Because her roommate's body slumps over. Her face has been clawed apart. Her chest is an open cavity from which her heart has been ripped. And on the desk is a note, inked in blood: "Aren't you glad you left the lights off?"

That story had kept Hannah up all night. She felt like Party Girl now. Observed as she roamed stupidly through the dark. A portrait on the wall followed her with its eyes, one moment appearing like an old woman, the next a gray-haired devil. Whispers seem to come from a crackling fireplace, from the leather-bound books stacked in a library, from an antique candlestick phone cocooned in cobwebs. There was a phone in every room. Sometimes perched on a desk and sometimes mounted on a wall. A number was printed on its base, what she understood to be an IP address.

Sarin said they were the same. But though Hannah might be part of some larger tradition, though she might join so many others on the spectrum, she knows she stands apart. The Mirage port has given her access to another world, one absent of light altogether. The old wars were fought purely in the physical world, but a new fight has come to this digital pit. Before, Hannah had wondered if she was old like Sarin, if she had lived other lives, but she feels certain now that isn't the case. She's new. Necessarily new, as though fated for this next level of warfare.

She came to a door behind which she heard children crying. The wood was splintery and wetted with the shapes of red right hands.

She didn't want to open it, but she had to. She had to look everywhere to find what she was hunting for—the source of the infection, the factory of nightmares.

Just as when she first wore the Mirage in the real world, every time she entered a new space here, it took her mind a minute to catch up, as if she were stuck temporarily between channels. She pushed through the door and waited for her brain to make sense of what she found. Everything she experienced in this coded otherworld was filtered and contextualized within her mind, and this was a room that reminded her of something she'd seen long ago in a movie or picture book. A Victorian orphanage, similar to the one from *Oliver Twist*. Everything solidified in this context. The beds in the room reached off forever. In them children writhed in torment. They did things children were not meant to do. They cried, but over the top of their cries came snarling voices that threatened to hurt them, to maim or even kill them if they shared a word of this with anyone.

Hannah tried to wave a girl toward her, but she would not come. She tried to cover a boy with a blanket, but he kicked it off. She tried to grab them, pick them up, lead them away, but they would not budge. She looked at them again, this time from another angle, peeling through the programming constructs that comprised them. These were not children, she came to understand, but representations of them, shadows of them, shared on the Dark Net for pornographic distribution. This was not the reason she plugged in, but she could not move on without erasing them. Only light would wash away the children, and in this case the light would take the form of a disbanding equation.

How long she had been in the Dark Net, she had no idea. Thirty seconds or thirty days or thirty years. Corporeal and temporal limits were no longer relevant. It had taken practice, but in this otherworld she was learning how to break locks, open cabinets, climb stairs, tromp across a floor, up a wall, across a ceiling. There was impermanence to everything. Code could be shoved around, erased, made to signify something else or nothing altogether. Her literacy was ever-expanding. With time she thought she could probably breathe fire or blow a hurricane-force wind. She could probably grow as big as a tree or as small as a mouse, like something out of *Alice's Adventures in Wonderland*. She could probably fly. Cyberspace was a whirling codex, a living infinite.

Now she wanted to make light, so she taught herself to burn. A dust-clotted lamp elbowed from a brass anchor on the wall. She grabbed hold of it and yanked. The fixture tore from its casing, and the wall's plaster crumbled to make way for the cords beneath. A foul-smelling dust came off the wall when she ripped at it, pulling out a few yards of cord, enough to twist and mangle and tear apart. Electricity spit from it like a fuse. She applied the shorn wire to the floor and to the blankets and to the tossed-aside nightgowns. Tiny flames sprung up and spread greedily and soon the room was ablaze. The children dimmed and their crying muted, and only then did Hannah turn to go.

In the hallway she heard a noise. Like many doors being slammed. Or many feet pounding toward her at once. She was no longer an anonymous guest. With the fire she had announced herself as an invader, a terrorist. And she was being pursued because of it. She began to run. Back the way she came. Spiders skittered out from beneath rugs, paintings, the seams of the hardwood floor, a black mass of them pursuing her, biting her. She stomped at them. And she swiped at the bats that swung down to scratch her face. A trapdoor opened before her, and she leaped over it. An enormous grandfather clock tipped over, and she dodged out of its way as it crashed to the floor with a metallic *doom*. Her feet grew faster and faster, blurring through the house, outrunning them all.

She ran through a vast ballroom lit with blood-red chandeliers in which skeletons waltzed. She ran through a nursery full of dolls—with black eyes and cracked porcelain skin—that turned their heads to watch her go. She ran through a chamber of meat hooks dangling from chains that rattled in her passing. And then she turned a corner and came to a skidding stop.

There was a worm. Black-skinned and pulsing with muscle. As big around as a man and as long as a garden hose. The wrinkled seams of its skin contracted and expanded with its movement, as it wound and surged itself across the room, and she saw within it a light. A red light. This same light slimed off the worm and stuck to the floor, marking its passage. This detritus squiggled with its own life, as though egged and hatching. A code. The code. Here was the contagion. One source of it anyway. She knew she should run. She could hear the spiders and the skeletons and the bats clattering and scuttling and hissing toward her. But this was what she had come for.

The worm paid her no attention. When it moved, it made a sound like a hand dragged across a blown balloon. An open window awaited it. It wanted to leave, to portal itself from the house, where it would feed. She yelled for it to stop, and it turned its blind black face toward her, before continuing to slough and heave forward. She knew from the fire she set that she could war with her surroundings. She looked around for a weapon and found it in an armored display. A knight stood on a short platform, a sword in its hands. When she seized it by the hilt, the knight tugged back, the armor rustily coming to life. She shoved it, and it toppled and split apart with a crash. Dozens of bald rats raced screeching from its hollows.

The worm was nearly to the window when she brought down the sword. Its blade cleaved the worm through the middle. There was a mewling sound. The two sections of it rippled and twisted and bled a stream of digitized red code that soon blackened and ashed away.

She didn't have more than a moment before the room filled with those who pursued her. The spiders bit and filled her with poison that iced her skin. The bats tangled in her hair. The skeletons reached for her with their gray fingers. She screamed and thrashed and swung the sword and ran stumbling through the swirling mess of it all until she was free.

Far in the distance, down a hallway that seemed to reach on for a mile, she could see the front door. It was slowly closing. On the other side of it, she could see everyone—Lela and Juniper and Hemingway and Josh and Derek—begging her to wake up, to come back. Maybe—maybe—she could run fast enough to make it through the crack before it closed.

But right then another worm squirmed into view, pushing itself along the floor. She stutter-stepped, trying to decide whether to run or linger. She gave the front door one long, lingering glance before turning away from it. She hunted down the worm and pierced it through the middle. And then followed its slime trail. The fading stream of code led her to a room full of doors that opened the walls, floor, and ceiling. One of them was painted red, the edges of it glowing with a light of the same color.

She found a candlestick phone mounted to the wall and ripped the receiver off its cradle and dialed her aunt Lela's cell. She needed help, but she couldn't leave now. She was almost there.

✣

Derek took the cell from Lela. He turned the palm-sized scarred-up phone over in his hand, saying, "I didn't know these things still existed." As though this was the greater marvel. Then he flipped it open, and his face lit up with the green glow of its screen. His eyes dodged back and forth between the body on the floor and the message that seemingly came from it.

Juniper carried a sheet from the bedroom and laid it over Hannah's body. Lela stared at the shroud until he rested a hand on her shoulder, and then she folded into him and let him wrap her into a tight hug.

Derek tapped the phone against his chin. Then he went to a shelf and pulled a laptop off it and booted it up. He opened a TOR browser and accessed the Dark Net and tried to recall their previous path. "The trouble is, these websites are all named by a scramble of letters and numbers. It's difficult to remember the way."

He worked his way through several websites before tapping 666 into the opening of the URL and saying, "I think this is it, but . . ." He swiveled the screen for them all to see. It was black except for a blinking white cursor in the top left corner, as though the script was waiting to be written.

"We're cut off," he told them. "If she's in there, she's in there alone. I can't do anything from here."

"From *here,*" Lela said. "But there's another way?"

Derek shrugged and Josh said, "The IP address. If that's what it actually is."

Derek's fingers punched the keyboard, swiped the touchpad. Another few minutes of digging and he confirmed the IP was local. "And I'm pretty certain I know the source. There are only two Dark Net hosts in Portland, and one of them went offline Halloween night."

"That was Babs," Juniper said. "A local crime boss. He was hosting servers out of his club, The Oubliette, that got knocked out when . . ." Here his eyes dropped to the shrouded figure on the floor. "So where can we find the other?"

A few blocks away, Derek said. In the Pearl. At the high-rise apartment of one of his frequent customers, Cheston. "Which means Hannah's hiding somewhere in the forest of his blade system."

This would be their plan then. Lela would go to Cheston's apartment and retrieve her niece, while Josh and Juniper shut down the databases all across the metro. "Or?" Lela said.

"*Or?*" Derek said. "*Or* we die. *Or* Portland falls into a permanent darkness. Forget *or.* There is no *or.*"

CHAPTER 29

THE DOOR TO THE APARTMENT building is shattered, and Lela's shoes crunch through the glass. Two bodies lie in the lobby, their arms around each other. Here is an overturned ficus tree, a messy pile of mail. Lela hears a *ding,* followed by the rattling shudder of elevator doors. She almost runs back into the street but instead dives behind the doorman's desk. She holds her breath and tightens the grip around the pistol. She waits for the sound of footsteps that never comes. Another *ding* sounds, and the doors once again shudder in their tracks. A minute passes before she investigates. She turns the corner to find a third body lying with one leg outstretched and the jaws of the elevator closing repeatedly around it.

She takes the stairs. Her footsteps make a spiraling echo. She pauses at every landing, waiting for the noise to die down so that she can confirm she is alone. On the top floor, she finds the hallway empty. A TV blares behind one door. A stain seeps from beneath another, and she steps around the damp half-circle. And then she arrives at his apartment—1408—the door already open a crack, a red light leaking from it. She supposes she should rush inside, in case anyone lies in wait. That is her standard. To rush. Her sister often called her out on it, saying she hurried everywhere, like a kid in the cereal aisle. But right now she seems capable only of slowness. Hesitation. One inch at a time, one foot in front of the other. Any sudden movement makes her feel like she's untethered from her body and waiting for it to catch up. So she gives the door a push and reforms her two-handed grip on the pistol and waits for something to come charging toward her.

The door swings and softly thuds the wall. The living room and kitchen are visible from here. The walls swim with a rippling light that emanates from another open doorway—an office or bedroom. The light is the color of blood. The color of an emergency. The color of a stop sign. A color that tells her to turn back.

She steps inside. Her pistol follows her eyes. She thinks about hitting the light switch, but the floor-to-ceiling windows already make her feel too exposed. There is a leather couch and a coffee table with a tablet and a laptop on it. On the wall is a mounted big screen surrounded by game consoles and speakers big enough to compete with a concert hall. It's tidy. Empty of any decoration. Functional but devoid of personality.

She moves toward the light and finds what she is looking for, an office dominated by a multi-screened computer terminal. It is blindingly red, streaming code. The beating source of it all. Even out of the corner of her eye, she feels sickened, dizzy.

✣

There are hundreds of cell towers in Oregon, many of them in Portland, all with fiber cables trenched between them and the data centers. Each has three faces—alpha, beta, and gamma—that can handle around eight hundred transmissions. Too many people try to make a call, too many people try to stream a YouTube video, then everything slugs to a crawl. Or you get booted off, at which time your phone will relay to another tower, maybe with a rival company. If you've ever glanced at your phone at a concert or a football game, and wondered why—in the middle of a city—your signal is spotty, it's because the towers can only accommodate so many.

When Derek sent Juniper and Josh off to bomb the data centers, he didn't want them to bring down Internet access. He wanted to knock out every data center but one. In doing so they would push every signal-seeking device onto the same conduit—the biggest in the area, the only one with enough bandwidth to handle the overflow—Paradise Wireless.

Its towers bristle from hilltops and its fiber cables tentacle the ground, and every screen, every wireless and cable transmission will shuttle through its port. So long as what Hannah says is true, so long as she can stop this, then they need only tap her into the master cabinet at the Paradise data center, and she'll be able to stream into any connected device.

"How the fuck do we do that?" Lela said.

"We'll have to go on-site. Their firewall is unbreachable." Even now he couldn't stop his mouth from cocking into a smile. "I've tried."

"That doesn't sound easy."

"It won't be."

"Given what's happening outside, that sounds like the hardest thing in world history. We don't even have Hannah."

"We'll need to go on-site to retrieve her as well. At Cheston's apartment."

Lela said, "How did you even come up with this plan?"

His superior tone would be horribly obnoxious in any other circumstance, but what they needed now was confidence and he was soaked in it.

An embattled race had been taking place on the digital frontier for some time, and the United States, China, and Russia were the main players. Engaged in secret stealing. Sabotage. Derek knew digital warfare would break out at some point; he was surprised now only by the supernatural powers of the aggressor. "The next world war began a long time ago," he said. "Welcome to the front lines."

✣

Derek told Lela what to look for. The metal chassis carrying seven blade servers. She stands before them dumbly, the technology alien to her. The fan system gives off a breathy heat. She runs her finger across the servers, as though she might be able to guess which one hosts Hannah.

She digs the thumb drive out of her pocket, what Derek called a dongle. She closes her eyes until she can see only through her lashes. And approaches the computer terminal. When Derek realized how ignorant and allergic to technology she was, he made her practice on his own system. He knew that Cheston would have several computers running and the servers would be managed through one of them. She needed to track the wires to the right hub and then insert the dongle into the port. Derek's beacon program would siphon the data they needed. That's how he referred to Hannah. As data. Code. An anti-virus program. Human software.

Of course Lela cares about helping others, preventing the virus from spreading further, but the goal feels abstract. Hannah is what she's here for. She promised to take care of the girl, and this is the only way she can redeem her failure to do exactly that. The dongle scrapes its way into the port. A light blinks on the butt of it. There is a sound—like an engine chugging to life—as the beacon software goes to work.

Derek told her to wait five minutes, what feels like an interminable amount of time, before retrieving the dongle and unplugging and destroying the system. "Don't throw it out a window or toss it in the bathtub and think you're in the clear," he said. "I need you to smash everything you see to pieces. Get a hammer, find some scissors, a screwdriver. Whatever it takes. I expect your hands to be bleeding and your shoes to be shredded from the effort." If people can scour dumps in Nigeria and dig out a dirt-clumped hard drive from a computer owned fifteen years ago by a guy from Pittsburgh and steal his credit card and social security information off it, then she needed to do more than yank a power cord. Total and immediate erasure. That wasn't going to take back what had already occurred, but it would prevent its further dispersal. One step, then another—slow progress—just like the way she entered the apartment. Just like the way she leaves the office now, returning to the living room.

She can't abide the red code. She remembers catching a glimpse of it on her laptop. That was all it took to sharpen her temper, flood her with the urge to hurt. Lose her sense of self. She had nearly struck Hannah when the girl slammed shut the laptop, hurled it against the wall in a splintering mess. Lela doesn't trust herself. She worries that a part of the virus still chugs away inside her, waiting to load completely.

A telescope is stationed by the windows. Her foot accidentally thuds its stand, and the telescope swings in a wide arc as if to take in the span of the city, and she pauses to study Portland. She has always considered the skyline beautiful. Maybe now more than ever. Buildings rise all around her, weirdly bright with electricity and firelight. It is an odd but striking contrast, the manmade and the elemental. Black smoke rises into the murky red sky that soaks up the reflection of the city burning beneath it.

When she was down in the street, she could never see much, walled in by buildings. Trapped in what felt like a prison with all its cages rattling. But from this high vantage, she can see the city as a whole and even imagine what lies beyond it. The Cascade Range rising from the wilderness like broken teeth. The cars streaming toward roadblocks on the many arteries leading away from Portland. The National Guard units establishing a perimeter. People wanting to get in and others desperate to get out. Emergency shutdowns of all data systems and power grids. A press conference. Crowds of reporters speaking into cameras. She feels strangely naked when she thinks of them, as if every camera and microphone and notepad has swung toward her expectantly. She is the one they want, the source at the center of it all, the actor in and—maybe?—one-day chronicler of the story unfolding. But that flash of excitement lasts only a second as her gaze travels farther, and farther still, beyond the Cascades, beyond Oregon and the Pacific Northwest, beyond the borders of this country, to the world, and the shadows and the signs of war are everywhere. Portland is today's tragedy. Torment and peril await everyone, everywhere. The Dark Net knows no borders; it is the trapdoor beneath all our feet. Immeasurably deadly. And with such a broad view of the terror that awaits, she feels small and adrift, and it is too much to hope that she can make any difference.

Something erupts in the near distance—maybe a gas line—a floral bloom of flame. The force of the explosion arrives a moment later. The window wobbles. The glasses in the kitchen cupboard chime. Because of this she doesn't hear the footsteps behind her, but she sees a glint reflected in the window. She tries to turn, too late. Someone shoves her. Her body pitches forward—her face slamming the glass—and then the arms belt around her chest and belly. Her body hurls over the couch and onto the coffee table. Its wood jars her spine. One of its legs snaps beneath her weight, and she rolls off it and onto the floor. She has lost all sense of up or down when she scrabbles to right herself. The pistol has fallen from her hand and she reaches wildly for it, and then gives up.

Because the man is moving toward her. His arms are out, lashing the air, reaching for her. His face is masked in blood, making him appear all the more inhuman in the half-dark.

She backs toward the entry door, the hallway, but can't leave despite every nerve in her body crying at her to go, *go*. At the last second, she darts into the kitchen. The man follows. She dives over the counter and into the dinette, circling back into the living room. And still the man follows. She dodges one way, then the other to grab the neck of the telescope. She wrenches it off its stand and takes a batter's stance. The man reaches for her and she swings. The telescope clangs the side of his head, and only then—in the stunned silence that follows—does she recognize him.

Doughy-cheeked. Wild-haired. Ink-stained fingers. He wears a cardigan and corduroys and wingtips. "Daniel," she says.

He has lost his glasses. His eyes are capillaried with the infection. His face matches their color—reddened with blood—his own or someone else's. He opens his mouth, but not to stammer out a *hello*. His intention is to bite. When he creeps toward her, she says, "Don't," but he doesn't slow, so she swings again, and then again, striking him across the belly, the shoulder, the wrist. She hears the glass inside the telescope tinkle, and something damply crack inside his body, but not even that stops him, so she puts her whole body into a swing to the temple.

He falls to the floor in a heap. She waits for a moment, trying to decide whether to check for a pulse, when she sees his chest expand with breath. She retrieves the pistol from the floor and tucks it in her belt. Even if he stands up and lurches toward her, even if he means to kill her, she won't use it. She tells him that she's sorry, that she hopes she can make this right.

✣

In the room of doors, Hannah creeps toward the red one. The floor is tacky and fluorescent with the many worm trails leading from it. A sound comes from the other side, a squelching and popping, like tongues moving in mouths. There is no knob to turn, no lock to pick. She pushes at it and it won't give. Tries to pry it open with the blade, with her fingers. Nothing. So she waits. Knowing it will be only so long before they find her again. The fanged and winged guardians of this place.

At last the door coughs open and a worm pushes through, nosing the air, blindly creeping forward. She hacks at it and steps over the spasming remains and enters the room before the door can close.

The space opens up into a high rocky chamber with a vast red lake at its center. The surface bubbles and steams, appearing volcanic. From it breach the worms. They slime onto the shore and glop and twist their way toward any of the hundreds of exits. The light makes her squint. The sulfuric reek makes her gag.

A worm rolls toward her and she slashes at it. And then another. And then another. Trying to hem her in, to tangle her legs, bring her down. She slices and stabs her way toward the lake. Before her the worms bleed out and crumble, the digitized code of them scattering like kicked LEGOs. And the more she swings, the longer and sharper and faster and hotter the sword seems to grow in her hands. A white light comes off it, and within that light—in the very grain of the sword—exists the code, honed to deadliness, weaponized to counter the virus.

But there is no end to the worms. She can track hundreds of them, and every second another breeds its way from the muck. She could swing the blade until her arms fell off and not make enough of a nick.

Her whole life she had felt powerless, because of her age, her gender, her dead eyes, and her broken family. She isn't a kid anymore. She's no longer a girl. She doesn't wear secondhand clothes or stumble around with a cane and pretend not to hear people whispering about her. Her father didn't run away and her mother didn't die. She isn't even human. She has no limitations. This world is hers to own.

So she tightens her grip. Turns in a half-circle. Swings. And releases. The sword spins through the air in a flashing arc. Headed toward the womb of the thing, the core of it all. When the point plunges into the lake, white lines zigzag outward from it, as if she has tossed a stone onto ice. There is a sizzling sound. The white streams continue to zigzag and cross and expand, gradually lighting up the lake, the walls, the ceiling with a multiplying force.

In this chamber, the worms slump and crumble, while elsewhere spiders curl up, bats fall, skeletons collapse, fleshy curtains blow off their rods, clocks chime midnight, and shadows limp to the corners and die. The Dark Net is suddenly and completely aflame with light.

But Portland remains infected. To cure the real world, Hannah must escape the digital. So she follows Derek's beacon program onto the thumb drive.

And when her aunt Lela steps again into Cheston's apartment office, she finds the computer terminal aglow—no longer red, but white—and the thumb drive so hot the sun might be trapped in it.

CHAPTER 30

THEY WALK DOWN the middle of the street, through the Pearl District, a familiar place reduced to ruin. Lela, Juniper, and Derek, with Hemingway trotting beside and before and behind them, perking his ears and sniffing at the rubble, the crashed cars, the occasional body. The wind pushes trash around, cartwheels the Metro section of *The Oregonian,* which Lela stomps in her passing. Dawn is coming. A pink light rashes steadily across the lane of sky above them. If not for the growing brightness, they would not be able to see the crows that follow—hundreds of them—silent except for the beating of their wings. Feathers pinwheel down like black snow. The birds are a boiling confusion. To look at them causes motion sickness.

They remind Juniper of the threat they face. The milling, roiling uncertainty of the virus as it channels through the digital landscape, hunting for someplace to roost. It's difficult to fight and comprehend in that way. He remembers a verse from Proverbs: The locusts have no king, yet all of them go out in bands.

At first that might seem the case—that the virus is a kingless horde—but would the Nazis have risen to power without Hitler, would the heroin trade have flourished without Pablo Escobar or Al Qaeda without Osama bin Laden or the Red Skeletons without Sam Creel? A monstrous face anchors every evil, makes it feel singular and conquerable. Even a hurricane has an eye.

And Juniper knows the eye of this storm is the one who goes by Cloven. Every time Juniper pulls the trigger—shooting more than sixty people who come racing out of doorways and alleys, their eyes giving off a faint red light—he hears that subterranean voice, he sees that pale, bent face.

Juniper tries not to kill, aiming for the knee, the thigh, the shoulder. There has to be hope for them yet, some sort of salvation, even if they appear doomed by the infection. In the five blocks they travel, he leaves behind a wake of brass cartridges that smoke and glint and litter the street. Lela hands him fresh magazines to slam into place.

Something is burning nearby. The smoke gives the air the quality of an erased chalkboard. The data center looks like any other building—squat and brick, the sort of place you'd expect to house a small-town DMV or post office. They only know they're in the right place because of the Paradise service vans parked in the lot. When Derek named the address earlier, Juniper noted it was directly above The Oubliette. That's why Babs stationed his club there, and that's why Cheston wished to take control of it—to tap into the digital artery overhead.

As they start for the building, a voice sounds behind Juniper, deeper than any human register, the voice he has been waiting for. "Timothy Milton," it says.

They turn to see the thing that speaks. A man. He wears a black suit with a narrow red tie. His hair is slicked back into an inky ponytail. His face is obscured by a set of VR goggles that emit a red quavering light. He is flanked by two hounds, their snouts bristling with teeth. "Or would you prefer Timmy? Tim Tim?"

He, Cloven, looks different than he did twenty years ago. Not older. But updated. Yet even from here—twenty yards away—Juniper can hear the tendons that creak like old ropes when he lifts an arm and curls his fingers in a wave.

"I go by Mike these days," Juniper says.

The air trembles with his words. "You think that makes you a new man? You think that beard or that muscle makes you any different? I see the same lying selfish weakling as before."

A deep-bellied growl rolls off Hemingway. Lela tries to grab his collar, but it's too late. He springs toward Cloven, and the hounds leap to meet him midway. Hemingway rises up on his haunches and captures one of them in a snarling embrace. They drop almost immediately when Hemingway clamps his jaws around its neck and shakes. The other hound scratches and snaps at his hindquarters until Juniper knocks its flat with a bullet to the ribs.

Hemingway readjusts his grip, drawing the neck deeper into his mouth, when Cloven takes two steps forward and kicks the dog in the belly. Hemingway yips and flops through the air and comes to a rolling stop. Lela calls out to him, and he struggles to stand and then limps back to her with his ears flattened and his tail tucked.

The hounds begin to dry out and crack and sink, and when a wind rushes through the buildings, a few flakes of their skin peel away.

"You're supposed to be dead, Timothy."

"Decided to stick around."

"I always knew you were a threat. That's why I wanted to end you. But I never would have dreamed you'd grow into such a ridiculous do-gooder, a toxic pain in my ass."

Juniper realizes he is slumping, as if ready to curl in on himself, and makes an effort to square his shoulders. "We're going to stop you."

"Me?" Cloven crouches and punches through the shell of one of the hounds and scoops out the ash to filter through his fingers. The air flecks black, like a staticky screen. "Don't you remember what I told you before? I'm one of many. And we're all around you."

Lela clutches Hemingway. The dog trembles in her arms. "Who is he?" she says to Juniper. "Why is he calling you Timothy?"

Juniper can't answer. The man is smiling at him, and he feels reduced by his red gaze. Brackish water bubbles in his mouth, lily pads and frogs and mud choke his throat. He feels like he is shrinking, like he is becoming that boy in the lake again, as if the body and the life he has built for himself are all merely a costume, easily removed. "Go," he says to his friends. "Run."

Derek starts immediately for the data center, but Lela hesitates and Juniper says, "You've got to go. Hurry. I'll hold him off as long as I can."

✣

The inside of the building is as plain and anonymous as the outside. There is a reception desk with a phone and a mug of pens and a dish of mints and a *Far Side* day calendar. Its chair lies on its side. The tiled foyer opens up into a carpeted office area segmented into cubicles. She takes one last look at the street—where the two men remain footed in place—before following Derek, dragging Hemingway along by the collar.

Among the cubicles, they find two bodies, one of them the security guard. Derek kneels beside him. At first she thinks he is retrieving the gun, but he is not. It's a keycard bound to a spiral cord. He holds it up with a smile. "Phew."

She asks why he is relieved, and he says that without the card, they'd never get into the vault, not without a jackhammer. The database is protected by a two-challenge system. The keycard and a key code that swings open the steel door. "I was betting on us being able to find one. We got lucky."

They will need to be luckier. Once they get through the vault door, they will need a twenty-two digit password to access the system. For this, he has a password generator program—that should take five minutes or less. "Should?" Lela had said earlier, and Derek firmed his chin and said, "Will."

The program is stored on the same thumb drive as Hannah. Or Hannah's consciousness. Lela isn't sure how to refer to her niece anymore. Even before she vanished into some trapdoor of the Internet, she seemed to have exceeded her body. Lela keeps the dongle in her pocket and every now and then touches it to reassure herself it's still there.

They head down a hall, past a water cooler, a potted fern, the restrooms, to a windowless door with a scanner and a keypad housed on the wall beside it. "Let's see if we get lucky again." Derek explains that every keypad—on elevators, routers, gated communities, even ATMs—comes with the same factory default setting—0911—which most administrators are too lazy to change. "Given the lackadaisical security of this place, I'm hoping we're in business."

Derek slides the card and then blows on his hand as if it held a set of dice. He punches the four-digit passcode and says, "Come on, baby." The light blinks red three times. He tries the door and it clunks, locked in its frame. He pinches the bridge of his nose. "We might be here for a very long time." He wears a backpack and swings it off now to remove his laptop.

Lela peers at the keypad and he says, "Don't touch that. Leave this to the experts."

The security card lies on the floor, and she snatches it up and runs it through the slot and punches in four digits, and Derek says, "What are you doing, you idiot? You only get three tries on these things before they lock down for—"

But he never finishes the sentence because the light blinks red twice before turning over to green. The lock thunks open, and she twists the handle and yanks open the door and makes an underhanded motion with her arm as if to say *voilà*.

Hemingway trots inside the room and she follows him, and Derek lingers in the doorway. The storage center is about the size of a low-ceilinged basketball court. Before her is a cross connect that reminds her of an old operator's booth, with different colored wires yarning into different ports. And then there are the cabinets—taller than her, winking with lights, a mess of inputs, jacks, cords, USB connectors. Each cabinet is labeled odd or even. Alleys run between them. Fans whir.

Derek remains in the doorway as if he can't quite believe they've made it inside. "But how?" he says, and she says, "An old Luddite hack. You just check to see which keys are smudged from repeated use. I got lucky on the order."

Derek gives her an appraising smile and wags a finger. "After this is all over, you and me are doing some kamikaze shots. You are my lucky charm!"

It is then his smile fails and his body shudders as if run through by a current. A wheezing sound comes from his mouth, where a moment later a bubble of blood swells and pops. When he falls to his knees, she sees the reason. Behind him stands the small man with the old face. His clothes are singed and the skin along his right side chewed up like hamburger. In his hand he grips the ceremonial knife used during the bomb-blasted Sabbath.

By now she should be attuned to danger. She remembers what

Juniper told her—"Paranoia is a requirement"—and knows she should have expected this. Something will always go wrong. A threat will always be lying in wait. With that kind of defensive mindset, you're always ready to slam on the brakes, strap on a Kevlar vest. She thinks of herself as vigilant, but she has been pushed too far. To an emotional brink. Death is starting to feel less like something to fight than accept. Because then all the pain and anxiety would simply vanish.

A very real part of her wants to push back her hair, reveal her neck to his blade. But then Hemingway gets in between them and bunches his shoulders and growls so deeply, she can feel it in her teeth. By putting himself in danger, he forces her to care. She still has someone to look after.

Hemingway hunches low to the ground, his whole body coiled, when he tests his way forward. The small man slashes the blade as a warning. Lela remembers her pistol then, and pulls it from her holster and empties every last bullet into the small man. He jumps and spins and tremors, and when he collapses, there is less of his body than when he was standing a few moments before. Her finger keeps snapping the trigger after the magazine empties.

It takes a while for her hearing to come back, and when it does, a voice burbles out of the tinny whine, and she realizes she is talking to herself. "What do I do?" That's what she keeps saying. "What am I supposed to do now?" To stand alone in a room such as this. Surrounded by equipment whose function eludes her. She turns in a slow circle, taking in the many cabinets. The vault reaches no more than a thousand square feet, but she couldn't feel more lost if dropped blindfolded in the Mount Hood wilderness.

Derek lies in the open doorway, and Hemingway stands over his body. The dog whines. She calls for him, but he ignores her, dipping his head to nuzzle Derek, lick his cheek. She assumed him dead, but he stirs in response. Lifting a hand and dropping it as if in protest. "Derek," she says, repeating his name as she rushes to him. His skin is ghost-white. Offset by his blood-painted lips. His eyes flutter open and closed, and she slaps him across the cheek. "You need to stay here. Stay with me. Tell me what to do."

His eyes focus and slide from her to a nearby cabinet. "That's the one. That's it."

"The master cabinet?"

"Just like we talked about. Insert the thumb drive." He swallows. "And pray for a miracle."

She shoves a hand into her pocket and closes it around the thumb drive, around Hannah. *We're going to take care of each other,* she thinks. The master cabinet is a metal tower stacked with black metal boxes, some of them knobbed and slotted, and others crazed with yellow wire. Red lights flash their warning. It makes a chittering noise as if geared by a thousand insect mandibles. She points at various USB ports until Derek nods his head weakly, *Yes, that one.*

If they unleashed Hannah into this system, then supposedly she could stream into every home, every phone, every tablet and television and device connected to it, as human software, the anti-virus, a digital rite of exorcism. It seems the stuff of miracles, impossible.

Pray? That's what Derek wants her to do? She pauses her hand as all the nerves in her flare at once. "It's not going to work," she says. How can it? She wasn't even a teenager when people started referring to her as cynical, biting, sarcastic. She has always seen the world through a darker veil. There must have been a time when she looked at an ornamented Christmas tree with wonder, when she heard a concert and felt overwhelmed by the sound. But she has since lost her ability to hope and her capacity for awe. The death of her parents secured this, and every year since has whittled away whatever faith and reverence she retained until she feels there is nothing left but her black, rotten, pessimistic core. Nature is the closest she gets to astonishment anymore. When she wanders the tide pools beneath Haystack Rock or splashes through the headwaters of the Metolius River or takes in the banded color of the Painted Hills. But every day on the job, she creeps further away from that feeling as she visits the morgue, a crime scene, the site of a seven-car pileup on the freeway. She knows too well the awfulness of the world. Indifference or outright hostility feels like the safest response. Why would she bother voting? Or use less water or recycle or eat organic, humanely raised livestock? People like her sister and Juniper always strike her as blindly hopeful, unable to recognize that people are hell-bent on killing themselves and ruining the planet. So this is hard for Lela. Making a leap. Extending her whole body in a kind of prayer. Even on a good day, it would be hard. But now, surrounded by so much despair, how can she believe she might make a difference? How can this thumb drive in her hand hold any promise?

"It's not going to work," she says again.

From where he lies on the floor, Derek says, "It's going to work. Take a leap of faith."

The thumb drive is hot in her hand. Hemingway licks her knuckles as if encouraging her.

"Believe," Derek says, choking on his own blood. "Just believe."

She guides the thumb drive toward the USB port and closes her eyes and takes a steadying breath and clicks it into place.

✣

Juniper has fifty pounds on Cloven, but he shrinks before him like a child who fears his father's fist. He isn't sure how many rounds remain in his pistols, and he never gets the chance to find out. When he raises his arms, Cloven strikes them down with enough force to send the guns clattering away. A fist bruises Juniper's stomach. An elbow jars his throat. A knee batters his face. Fingers twist his hair. Teeth gnash his ear. He is too big to be thrown, but his body is somehow soaring through the air, striking the pavement, rolling several yards until he comes to a stop.

He keeps trying to fight back, and Cloven keeps striking him down. He has to hope Lela and Derek stand some chance inside the data center, but right now they feel far away. Portland feels far away. The life he has built there feels far away. The only thing that feels near is water. It puddles around his feet, splashes past his knees, his waist, his chest, siphoning into his open mouth and gurgling his screams. He tries to kick his way up, but two bony hands hold him down. Above the rippling surface of the water, a face stares down at him. Grinning. Red-eyed. Bubbles escape Juniper's mouth until there is no air left in him. And the water comes flooding in to fill every chamber of him with thick green algae-stinking water. A fish pecks at his eye and a water beetle claws its way into his nose and a frog slides down his throat. He was supposed to die. He is going to die. He is dying.

And then somehow he is not. He is curled in a fetal position in the middle of the street. Gulping air. Shuddering with a chill. As though the city walling him in is a reservoir suddenly emptied.

He hears a screaming that seems to come from many men, but its only source is Cloven. His ponytail has come undone. Strands of long inky hair fall across his face. He staggers back, clawing at the virtual reality goggles. Instead of red, they now glow white. The illumination soon seeps from his nose and mouth and ears, the tips of his fingers, cracking through his skin, consuming him, making his body, and then the street, and then the city indistinguishable from light itself.

EPILOGUE

THE LINE ISN'T LONG at Customs. No one wants to come to this country. Especially now. It isn't safe. Always on the news for another kidnapping, another beheading, another suicide bombing. She flew from New York to Berlin to Dubai to here, and on the last leg wore a hijab that has soured with her breath.

The floor is made of broken tiles and the walls are dirt-colored. A light fuzzes on and off. Four soldiers with assault rifles stand nearby, watching the line with stony expressions. A stand-up fan with a rusty blade blows nearby, but makes no difference, the air hot and dry, baking her throat. When it is her turn, the agent waves her forward. He has a thick black mustache and wears a blue collared shirt with a black tie. Sweat rolls down his forehead, and he dabs at it with a handkerchief. When he sees her passport, he says, "Let me guess. Aid worker? Or reporter?"

"I'm a journalist," she says, and shares the authenticating letter from her editor at *Harper's*.

He takes it, gives it a cursory read, and then begins to fold it into smaller and smaller squares. "You're here to tell the world all about our troubles."

"I'm afraid so."

"We are not entertainment."

"I didn't say you were."

"Yet you're here to write your little stories."

"Maybe my little stories can make a difference," she says. "Maybe I can help."

And now he has folded the letter so many times that it can be bent no further, a tight white square pinched between his fingers. His tosses it to her and she pockets it quickly.

"What about the dog?"

She looks down at Hemingway, who wears a blue vest with a fluorescent yellow border. "He's a service animal. I have epilepsy." She pulls out another paper, but he waves it away and stamps her passport and makes a note on her Customs card. His eyes are already on the next person in line when he says, "I would take care when you're here, Ms. Falcon."

And then the man behind her—a big man with a jutting forehead, dressed in preacher blacks—steps forward. And the Customs agent says, "Let me guess: a missionary? Here to save the heathens of this backward country? How wonderful."

Lela doesn't turn to look, but she listens to his familiar baritone and smiles beneath her hijab when Juniper says, "I'm just here to shine a little light on the dark."

✣

The magazine set her up with a trusted fixer—a man named Abed who wears a prayer cap and an overlong shirt embroidered at the breast. He meets her in baggage claim. He takes her suitcase and smiles at her dog. As they walk outside—into the furnace-blasted air—he tells her how much he admired her work in *The New Yorker, Mother Jones,* the *New Republic,* the *New York Times Magazine,* especially "The Red Zone," the Ellie Award–winning, 10,000-word feature she wrote about what happened in Portland. "You are fearless," he says, and she says, "Hardly."

"And yet here you are." He holds out his arms as if to acknowledge the airport, the city, the country as a whole. A few men with wiry beards pause to look at them.

She readjusts her hijab and lowers her voice. "That doesn't mean I'm not afraid."

Sometimes it all feels like a dream, but that's true of everything in life. Every moment—stored in the unreliable hard-wiring of your mind—is suspect, a foggy replication, a prejudiced illusion. She rereads her article every now and then just to prove to herself it happened. She trusts in the writing. That it won't shape-shift on her like everything else in this impermanent, virtual world. And that she might make some incendiary difference with it.

Juniper walks by then, but she doesn't acknowledge him except with a stare. He carries a heavy duffel to a taxi waiting in the roundabout. It's an old Subaru with white doors and a yellow hood and trunk, the paint peeled off in long scratches. When he tells the driver the name of his hotel and settles his body into the rear seat, the shocks give a squeak and the taxi lowers noticeably with his weight.

She watches the taxi pull into the dusty stream of traffic before telling Abed, "Let's go."

✣

She's staying a few blocks away from the U.S. Embassy—in a safe house with seven other reporters and three aid workers. One of them—an Irish writer working for the *Guardian*—pours hot water over tea leaves in the kitchen. The others she can hear snoring or typing or listening to music in their rooms. "What story are you here for?" the Irish reporter asks, and she says, "You'll hear about it soon enough."

"Ah, come on. Just tell me." He's smiling but she can sense the twitchy eagerness behind it. Journalists aren't colleagues but starved dogs chasing the same bone.

"I'd tell you," she says, "but then I'd have to kill you."

He laughs, not knowing she means it.

Abed will pick her up tomorrow for the first of her interviews. In the meantime she needs to prep and get some sleep and reset her clock.

Her room is the size of a closet. The desk and the single mattress take up so much of the floor that she can't lay her suitcase down. Hemingway whines before entering and then turns three circles on the bed before settling into the nest of blankets. She's going to join him soon, but first she plugs the SIM card into her phone and powers it up.

While she waits for the screen to brighten, she hears the call to prayer as it purls and echoes through the city. It's a sound she feels inside and outside her, like a waterfall's shushing boom or a wolf's plaintive howl. She goes to the window and pulls aside the blackout curtain to look out at the city, at the streets crammed with motorcycles and bicycles and cars, at the stacks of mud-colored buildings. Across the way, she watches a man lay down his Kalashnikov rifle and unroll a prayer mat. He is guarding a French restaurant whose windows are barricaded with piles of sandbags.

Her phone startles her with a chime. She lets the curtain fall back into place and ignores the text messages and voicemails and inbox alerts. Instead she brings the phone to her mouth and says, "I missed you, Hannah."

"Don't get all gross and sentimental," the voice says. "I'm right here."

✣

The next morning Abed takes her around the city. She and Hemingway sit in the backseat of his Nissan. The windshield is so dust-stained and wind-scoured that she can barely see out of it. This makes her feel safer, shielded. They pass an open-topped Jeep filled with men whose arms bristle with rifles, and then they get stopped at a checkpoint by soldiers who stare at her while talking to Abed in their rough, musical voices.

She has three interviews set up that day. The first is at a women's shelter. A table is pulled aside and a rug lifted off the floor and a trapdoor hoisted to allow her down the stairs, into a hidden basement full of women who have been raped, women who have run away from their marriages, all of them with husbands or brothers or even fathers who have threatened to kill them for their offenses. The women —some only teenagers—coo over Hemingway, who falls onto his back and lolls his tongue and presents his belly for them to rub. Abed translates for her as she scratches notes in her Moleskine and holds out her phone to capture their voices. "I don't think you hit record," Abed says, and she says, "It's fine. Don't worry."

Their next stop is a house owned by a white-bearded man in a brown vest who arranges safe passage from the country for these women. He offers Lela a steaming cup of chai and a cold chickpea salad. While they sit in the living room—with the television on but muted—the man falls asleep twice while talking to her. Each time he spills his tea, which rouses him and he begins speaking again as though without interruption. He refuses a photo, but she can feel the slight shudder of the phone as it secures several images of him and the room—not to publish but merely for recollection and editorial verification.

And then it is time for her third and final interview of the day. This takes place at the edge of the city, past the checkpoints, in a walled-in compound with a square-shaped two-story concrete building inside it. A guard with a beard running halfway down his chest stands at the gate. They climb out of the Nissan to speak with him.

The sun is sinking and the air has taken on a hazy, purplish tincture. While Abed and the guard speak, she surveys the surrounding area. Half a block away there is a market with a few tables out front. Juniper sits there, drinking a chai and pretending to read a newspaper.

Abed says, "Lela? They want to know why you have the dog."

She returns her attention to them. "Just say I have diabetes."

He does and the guard spits and says to her directly in broken English, "What does dog and diabetes mean? Not sense."

She tries to look as meek as possible. "He's a service dog. He helps me."

Hemingway sniffs the tire of the Nissan and raises his leg to piss on it, and the doofy look on his face seems to relieve the guard. He digs through her satchel, tossing everything onto the ground for her to gather. When he pulls out a bottle of water, he uncaps it, sniffs it, spits in it, and hands it back to her. Then he pats her down, and when he does, his hands linger in the wrong places. He says something and laughs harshly, and Abed does not translate. He only says, "Be safe. I'll wait here."

The guard busies himself with his phone, tapping the screen to unlatch the gate. While he is distracted, she leans in to Abed and says, "You need to leave. Okay? Right now."

Abed has a look of panic on his face. "But—"

She hands him an envelope wadded with cash and puts a finger to her lips. "Trust me. Go."

The guard waves for her to follow, and she notices then the insignia printed on his back. That of a red right hand.

She enters the compound, and the gate clangs into place behind her. The system beeps and the lock sleeves into place. Off in the distance, from atop a minaret, she hears—again—the muezzin singing the call to prayer. She pauses so that the guard might drop to his knees and bow toward the east. But he doesn't. He keeps going. He's deaf to prayer.

The courtyard is obscenely green compared to the rest of the dun-colored city. A lush lawn. A fountain. Pomegranate trees. Benches set along white gravel trails. In the middle of it all is a severed head on a pike. She spots one, two, three more guards stationed around the compound. All of them watching her. All of them carrying the mark of the red right hand. Crows circle high above them, like early slivers of night searching for a place in the sky.

The front door is also secured by an auto-lock system. The guard taps his phone and pushes open the door, and she steps into the dimly lit foyer. She smells tobacco and cooked lamb. On the first floor, she spots a kitchen and a living room packed with mismatched furniture and another room in which at least twenty men work busily at computer terminals. From the wall oozes a giant bloody rendering of the hand. The staircase is barricaded with gated doorways, one on each landing, each boxed with a keypad and wired with an alarm.

On the landing, on her way up to the second floor, she peeks through a doorway. A man sits in a dark room. A man she at first believes to be sleeping upright, his head nodded to the side. He is smiling at whatever dream possesses him. But she realizes he only appears to be smiling because he has no lips. He is tied to the chair and the skin has been flayed from his face and tossed on the floor. In between their footsteps, she can hear the flies buzzing.

On the third floor, the guard escorts her down a hallway and knocks gently on a door and waits for the voice that beckons them inside. At a desk sits a man in desert cammies. A former Marine who one day, without warning, walked away from his unit and over the past two years became the reigning warlord of the insurgency. His name used to be John Slater but now he goes by Wisam. His neck and face appear slim, but his belly bulges so hugely that the bottom three buttons of his shirt are undone, as though something gestates within him. He is balding but he keeps his hair long. The wooden desk is carved with ciphers that she distantly recognizes. The floor and walls and ceiling are busy with painted versions of the same. The room is otherwise crowded with filing cabinets atop which rest several blade servers. In the corner sits a minibar festooned with cut-glass tumblers and bottles of single malt. Beside it is a dead body, bloated with rot. Hemingway perks his ears and whines.

Wisam looks at her for a long minute. "What's with the dog?"

"He's a service animal."

"What's that supposed to mean?"

"He helps me. I have asthma."

Wisam gives up on English to ask a question of the guard and then addresses her once more, "He said you said you have diabetes."

She shrugs. "Translation issues."

Again he and the guard speak—their eyes on her—and when they finish, her phone chirps to life and Hannah's voice translates their conversation: "She is a lying whore. What part of her should I cut off first?" and "Maybe we should keep her? She might be an interesting toy as well as a tool."

The men's faces flatten. A fly lands on her hand and she shakes it off. The guard starts toward her with his rifle, butt raised, ready to strike—but Wisam calls him off. "Leave us," he says with a soft chuckle.

The guard protests, but Wisam cuts him off. "You think I can't protect myself from a girl?" He waves him away with a flap of his hand. "Go, go." Then he motions to a chair across the desk from him.

She sits and Hemingway settles in beside her. She breathes through her mouth to avoid the smell of rot. His lamp is poled with stacked vertebrae, and his clock is a skull with a timepiece housed in an empty socket.

"Didn't anyone tell you this was a bad idea?" Wisam says, and combs back the long strands of hair from his forehead. "Meeting with me?"

"No one believes you exist. They say you're a myth. Like the boogeyman."

"Yet here I am." One of his eyes is brightly bloodshot. "You can take it off. The hijab."

She doesn't hesitate, pulling it off, bunching it into her satchel. With her fingers she tidies her hair, now short, cut just below her ears. She still hasn't gotten used to the feeling of air on the back of her neck.

He smiles so widely, she can see he's missing a few molars. "Not bad," he says, and then offers her a bowl of nuts, and when she refuses, he scoops a handful to pop in his mouth. For a time there is only the sound of his jaw crunching them down to swallow. "Why do you think I met with you?" There is a squeak and a grunt at the edges of his voice, as if there were other voices hiding inside it and waiting to get out.

"So that you could be heard," she says. "So you get the grand profile you deserve."

"I like flattery. I do. But let's get this out of the way: the moment you came through that gate, you lost control of this story. I only agreed to this interview so that I could kill you."

She digs out a pen and her Moleskine notebook. "I see you have Laphroaig 18. You like Islay whisky? Have you ever tried Lagavulin?"

"What?" He can't seem to comprehend her calm. Then he glances at the minibar. "Oh, yes. The peatier, the better. I like the taste of smoke."

"You would."

"Excuse me?"

"I like the taste too," she says. "Like a candied ashtray. Like a charcoaled sheepdog. Like a burned Band-Aid."

His eyes narrow, assessing her. He reaches for another handful of nuts. "You've got a devil's way with words."

"You're suspected for leading the hack that took down Merrill Lynch."

He says, between bites, "Is that a question?"

"As well as the blackouts in Paris and New York, the braking system software malfunction with Ford, the mid-flight failures of a dozen Delta Airbuses, the nude photo leak that—"

"You like Islay. Let's have a drink. Would you like a drink?"

"Oh, only if it's not too much trouble. I'd love a taste."

He hoists himself from his chair and follows his belly to the bar, where he pours two fingers of Scotch. He sets a tumbler before her and raises his in a toast. "Death to the enemy," he says.

She unscrews her water bottle, adds a splash to her whisky.

"What are you doing?" he says, fogging his glass with his breath.

"Adding a little water. Especially with the cask-strength, it reduces the burn, opens up the flavors more. You want a drop?" She tries to make her voice as nonchalant as possible. "I wouldn't have it any other way."

He shrugs, *fine,* and she leans forward to plop a dollop of water in his glass.

She tucks away the bottle and takes an appreciative sip of the whisky. "Boy, that's great. Mmm. Thanks." Then poises her pen over the notebook. "So what's motivating you? What's your purpose? What do you want? It's obviously not about money."

He takes a long sniff of the whisky. "I want to listen to the world scream." He tips back the tumbler for a sip. Runs his tongue across his lips. His eyes, closed a moment before, bug open. He drops the glass and it shatters on the floor. His face goes red. He gags. His hand goes to his throat and steam leaks from his open mouth. His tongue, when it bulges from his mouth, is blistered, swollen.

She says, "How's the holy water taste, you son of bitch?"

He doesn't answer except with a strangled cry. He fumbles for a desk drawer but never gets it open. Hemingway is already there, snapping his teeth around the man's arm and shaking him from side to side until he slips from his chair and onto the floor. Here the dog finishes him.

Lela finishes her whisky before standing and wiping her mouth.

She goes to the desk and yanks open the drawer and removes from it a pistol that she then tucks into her belt. She locates two thumb drives and pockets them. Unplugs the blade servers and drops them on the floor and stomps on them until they shatter beneath her heel.

She hears crows shrieking outside. Then the shout of gunfire. A single shot followed by the rattle of assault rifles. "Hannah?" she says. "Are we good?"

Her phone immediately responds. "All good. I've disabled the alarm system, frozen their accounts, and uploaded all data into the cloud."

"I should be able to file the article by tonight." She pulls Hemingway off the body and shushes his growls and tells him he's a good boy. Then she holds out the phone to snap a photo of Wisam's corpse. "I don't want to get scooped, so let's wait until then to contact the embassy."

"FYI," Hannah says, "North Korea just test-fired another missile into the Pacific and the internal chatter at the Pentagon seems to confirm that Jong-un had everyone at Work Camp #22 executed. Should I confirm tomorrow's flight to Seoul?"

"Please."

A crow lands on the windowsill then. It cocks its head to regard her with a black eye. Its beak taps the glass—once, as if in salutation—before it flaps away.

By the time she works her way outside, the sky is black and Juniper is waiting for her in the courtyard. He wears his preacher blacks. Two pistols hot in his hands. Gun smoke drifts like a fog taking form. Crows caw from the walls and garden.

She walks up to him and tugs on his beard playfully. Both of them smile, and she remembers that moment, two years ago, when her hand plugged the thumb drive into the USB port and the blade servers hummed and their red lights blinked white and it became suddenly possible to believe that though winter was upon them, the ice and the cloud-clotted skies and the confused screaming winds and the seemingly endless dark would eventually give way to the determined sunlight and warmth and music of spring, a world swung back into balance.

Juniper says, "You get everything you need for the story?"

"Enough for a happy ending."

"Where to next?" he says.

She readjusts the strap of her satchel and heads for the gate. "Follow me."

ACKNOWLEDGMENTS

Thanks to Helen Atsma—my longtime editor and fellow displaced Oregonian—for bringing me with her to Houghton Mifflin Harcourt and for bullying yet another one of my manuscripts into shape. I'm excited to be part of the HMH stable, and I'm grateful to the team there for making me feel welcome and helping launch this digital nightmare into the world.

Thanks to Katherine Fausset, a good pal, a great agent. Thanks to Holly Frederick at Curtis Brown, and Noah Rosen and Britton Rizzio at Writ Large, for muscling Hollywood on my behalf.

Thanks to Tina Grazo, not only for building my website, but for serving as a tech adviser on this book. This is a supernatural story, but I tried to ground it in reality as best I could, and she helped tremendously. So did Geoff Sauer and Mike Edwards, who coached me on the mysteries of the Dark Net and cybersecurity. I also owe Steve Edwards—and his intentionally unacknowledged friend and wireless mole, T.A.—for helping me better understand cellular networks and their vulnerabilities.

I read many articles when researching this novel, but I want to give special credit to Lev Grossman's "The Secret Web: Where Drugs, Porn and Murder Live Online," which appeared in the November 11, 2013, issue of *Time*. That's when I became keenly interested in the subject of the Deep Web and spiraled down the research rabbit hole.

Thanks to Thomas Maltman for biblical counsel. Thanks to Debra Gwartney for haunting and inspiring me with an image (a vampire cemetery in Sozopol) that became centrally important to this novel. Thanks to Paul Weitz and Stacie Toal for many gallons of bourbon and hours of companionship. Thanks to Peter Geye and Dean Bakopoulos for friendship and council.

And of course thanks to Lisa Percy for her continued love, patience, and support.

ABOUT THE AUTHOR

Benjamin Percy is the author of four novels—*The Dark Net, The Dead Lands, Red Moon,* and *The Wilding*—as well as two short story collections, *Refresh, Refresh* and *The Language of Elk,* and a book of essays titled *Thrill Me.* His fiction and nonfiction have been published by *Esquire* (where he is a contributing editor), *GQ, Time,* the *Wall Street Journal,* the *Paris Review,* and *Tin House,* among many others. His honors include an NEA fellowship, a Whiting Award, two Pushcart Prizes, and inclusion in *The Best American Short Stories.* He writes the *Green Arrow* and *Teen Titans* series for DC Comics. He was raised in Oregon but now lives in Minnesota with his wife and children.